# THE RACE

WRITTEN BY
PARADOX DELILAH

Print ISBN: 978-1-9992716-0-2
E-book ISBN: 978-1-9992716-1-9

Edited by Ellen Michelle

Front cover image by Alan Chen

Book interior design by Michael Niemi

www.paradoxdelilah.com

For Grandpa Delilah,

Whose gleeful cackle is the best sound in the universe.

From your Granddaughter,

Who *is* nuttier than a fruitcake.

# CHAPTER ONE

RACER IKK47, Ikka, was not expecting to cross paths with other racers this evening, but her navigation screen is suggesting four other X-Runners are heading her way. She doesn't relish the prospect. She can't remember the last time she camped near other racers, but in her experience—she pauses at this thought, pursing her lips and leaning back from the pilot console. No experiences come to mind, only feelings of unease. She considers firing up her X-Runner's engine and driving to another sheltered location to dock for the night, but the rules for The Race are clear—no vehicle may move after dusk. If she drives in the final twenty minutes remaining before the sun exits the sky, she will only make it far enough to stop in exposed tundra with no boulders to protect from the night winds. She can't risk the delays mechanics damaged by glass sand will cause, so she must stay where she is and weather this unwanted company instead.

By the time the sun sets, the four other X-Runners are docked beside Ikka's vehicle at the base of a cliff wall. The titanous, eight-wheeled vehicles are intimidating, but they seem small and insignificant framed against the staggering height of the cliff. Smaller still are the forms of four men huddling around a campfire in the centre of the vehicles. Ikka watches them from inside her runner, swathed in darkness. Their faces look like variations of the same theme: brown hair, brown eyes, light to dark tanned skin. There is a man close to Ikka's age, early thirties, with muscles evident under his racing clothes. He talks with animation, playfully patting the shoulder of the man beside him. That man is more rotund and perhaps a decade older. Beside him is a scrawnier man of the same age, and beside him, the fourth man sits, his body language the most wary. Ikka wonders what he knows, before realizing there is a fifth figure at the fire, nestled in behind him. A child.

Ikka leans forward in her seat, her face now inches from the runner's window. Not just a child—a girl. Pale skin, burnt orange hair the same shade as the desert floor. Inside Ikka, something tightens. It is not fear, nor dread, but a knocking at the edge of her consciousness. The presence of the girl *means something*. Ikka swings herself off her pilot chair and pats her wrists and waist for reassurance her three blades are still where they belong. She pulls up the X-Runner's interior roller door before unlocking her three homemade bolts on the inside of the exterior door, opening it and stepping into the night.

All five heads pivot at the noise, and all five sets of eyes widen. The girl—Racer CHL03, Chloe—is particularly surprised to see an adult woman, although she does not know the reason why. She tells herself it is because this woman looks so different from the men. The woman has golden brown skin, accented by hazel eyes that glint with menace in the light of the fire. They are betrayed by the soft oval shape of her face, and counteracted once more by the callous restraint of her black hair at the base of her neck. Chloe can see her racer code glinting off the identification chain on her neck. She sounds the alphanumeric code as she reads it. I-K-K-4-7.

The woman's eyes snap down to hers as if aware of her gaze, and Chloe blushes at being caught staring. Ikka's eyebrows tighten for the briefest second and then relax. She offers Chloe a smile before taking a seat and redirecting her attention to the men around them. The rotund man is speaking, offering a pompous welcome to their shared fire. Chloe's father—Racer ISAA4, Isah—interjects.

He says, "I was beginning to wonder if your X-Runner was abandoned. Seemed odd someone would be sitting in it with the power dead for so long."

Ikka offers a small head incline that feels like a measured shrug.

She says, "I had thoughts to consider. I found it strange so many of you came to dock in this place tonight."

The scrawny man leans forward. He says, "Yeh know, I was thinkin' that, too. I mean, on some days I'm for thinkin' it doesn't make sense our runners are all sendin' us in different directions, when we're all racing for the same prize and destination. And then there are nights like this, and our vehicles have no interest in discretion."

"Discretion?" The rotund man inhales sharply, shallow breaths labouring his words. "It's just bloody logistics. The computers work out the best route based on your ranking, the weather, and the terrain. This race isn't a sprint, lad—it's a damned marathon, and tonight this just happened to be the best spot to dock for miles."

"Yeh I don't know about that. It don't make sense."

The rotund man inhales again, readying himself for another speech. The younger muscled man—Racer VELA4—speaks before the rotund man can steady his breaths.

He says, "Look, who cares? We're here. I don't know about you lot, but this fire is warm, the stars are shining bright tonight, and it's nice to have company for the evening. Let's just enjoy it."

"Enjoy it?" Ikka spits the words out. "Do you think those stars are your friends? This fire, something that can be tamed? We trust our entire existence to these vehicles, and you brush another's concerns aside without a second thought?"

"Well I don't really know him, do I, buddy? Or you. I'm just trying to have a pleasant evening."

"Besides"—the rotund man jumps into the conversation again, before steadying himself with another shallow breath—"the X-Runners are faultless machines. In addition to their superb racing capabilities, they protect us from desert storms, control the climate, and regulate the airflow inside while we sleep. You can't fault the bloody things."

"Can't you? I should think a clever racer would keep a tighter oversight on the workings of his X-Runner. But none of us know how to do that, do we? I would gladly give up my rankings in The Race to understand how they work."

"Well then you're a damned fool."

"Am I?" Ikka looks around the fire, her gaze ending on

Chloe. She nods in the direction of the scrawny man, slowing her voice for effect. "We should be listening to him. It don't make sense.

# CHAPTER TWO

SCORCHING morning light reflects off the desert floor and into Chloe's eyes as her small hands work on the X-Runner's exposed mechanics. It doesn't matter that at some angles the shards of light blind her. Even though she is only eleven, Chloe has done this pre-race check every day for as long as she can remember, and her hands can work without the guidance of her eyes. As she cleans the machinery, her eyes sweep over all the engine components, noting the condition of every single piece. Traces of her precise welding skills are scattered all over the vehicle's underbelly. Some are barely visible, faded with age, but Chloe's hands can remember executing each one. She pauses her inventory, searching for the reasons why the repairs were required. She can't locate them in her mind.

Her father, Isah, shouts to her from inside the X-Runner.

"Hey, Chloe, we've got to get going."

She scoots out from beneath vehicle's underbelly and

notes three other X-Runners are still docked beside them. The fifth vehicle, the runner belonging to the woman, is already gone.

Chloe bounds up the steps of their runner, closing the exterior door behind her as she enters. Her father doesn't look up from the pilot console as he scans the day's planned route.

"Looks like an all right strip today. Not much elevation change, so we should be able to cover a good distance. You ready?"

Chloe doesn't answer, but plops into the co-pilot seat beside Isah, securing herself into the chair.

She says, "Engine's good."

"Good," Isah says, as he engages the X-Runner engine.

The machinery is silent as it whirs to life, and within a matter of seconds they are moving over 70 miles per hour. The vibrations of the ground beneath reverberate through the main cabin of the runner, making the vehicle roar noisily. Chloe loves the sound and way the wind smashes its way inside her window, slamming against her face. Despite this, her mind wanders, and she thinks of IKK47 and the conversations of the night before. There is a feeling in the base of her stomach, an incessant fluttering that is filling her with unease.

More desert streams past, and she pushes these thoughts aside. They pass occasional trees—grey stilts with tragic foliage—and small boulders, unmoved even by decades of desert storms. She expands the navigation screen to study the route suggested for the day. It's not particularly complex, but a duststorm is predicted for the afternoon. Before Chloe can point this out to her father, the niggling sensation in her stomach manifests into a sharp, stabbing pain. It feels as though there are hundreds of tiny daggers scraping away at her from the inside. She gasps and her arm fumbles for her father's shoulder.

It misses, and she redirects her attention, floundering with the restraint at her waist and limply sliding off her seat. The chaotic vibrations of the vehicle ricochet up her knees as she hits the floor, and she crawls towards the runner's living compartment. By the time Isah kills the engine and sprints to her side, she is lying on the metal floor, her face void of colour, and arms clutching at her lower abdomen. There are tears pooling in the corners of her eyes as she looks up at her father, her lips quivering as she whispers to him.

"I don't know what's happening, Dad. It hurts… so much."

Isah looks as confused as she feels, concern contorting his face.

"Where does it hurt, Chloe? Everywhere?"

She holds back a sob as she shakes her head.

"Just here…"

She gestures to the space between her stomach and groin region.

"Does it go through, all the way to your back?"

Chloe shakes her head again.

"I'm going to have a feel, and you tell me where it hurts the most, okay?"

Chloe nods as her dad kneels beside her. With the utmost care, he presses his hands down under her rib cage and gently compresses the flesh beneath.

"Here?"

She shakes her head. His hands compress around her

stomach, the space to either side of it, and then below. It is the flesh at level with her hip bones that hurts the most, the aching throbbing screaming out at this point. She winces when her father touches her there, and he looks at her in alarm.

"Have you banged this part? Why didn't you mention it before?"

Chloe shakes her head and whimpers.

"I didn't, I didn't."

"I'm going to roll you onto your side, Chloe. I want to check your back."

She nods, and lets herself be turned over, waiting for more gentle prodding. It doesn't come.

"Dad?"

His voice is quiet as he says, "I'm going to get the medical kit. You've lost a lot of blood."

• • •

The blood is coming from between her legs. Not gushing, but as slow drips of thick, black goop. The pain is less intense now—it presents itself in alternate waves of dull knocking and painful excavation. Isah has wrapped Chloe's abdomen in bandages from the runner's medical kit and sent out a medical beacon. He is endeavouring to appear calm, but Chloe can tell he is as terrified as she is.

Chloe dozes in and out of alertness as Isah pilots. The sky outside is dark before Chloe is able to fully comprehend that they are driving uphill. Drowsy and befuddled, she stumbles to sit beside her father at the control panels. Their altitude is registering just over two thousand feet above sea level.

"Dad, why are we up so high? None of the systems

recommended a mountain route today."

"The computer says to go this way for medical help." He shoots her a concerned look. "Are you okay? Do you need anything?"

Chloe shakes her head, scanning through the topography on the co-pilot computer.

"Dad, I checked out this mountain this morning. There's only one route in and out of it. There's nothing up there."

Her dad frowns, tapping the screen with one hand as he drives.

"I don't know what you think you saw, Chloe, but this is where the facilitators say we should go. They're not offering any alternatives."

It is Chloe's turn to frown, the ache in her abdomen mingling with a new swarm of nerves. The sensation rises up through her chest, unease forcing its way to her throat. Her voice comes out like a squeak.

"Dad, I don't think this is right."

"It ain't right what's happening with your body, Chloe, but we're going to get you some help. We're nearly there."

She shakes her head, immersed in discomfort. Her eyes keep flicking from their tracking dot on the computer screen to the view out the forward window, wondering where she will see it first—whatever is lying in wait for them. They are nearing the top of the mountain, and still no structures or heat signals are reading on any of the maps. She doesn't want to cry, but the stress of heading into imminent danger—and she is certain that it is imminent danger—causes tears to moisten her eyes. Her dad mistakes it as a sign of her abdomen pain increasing.

"It's okay, Chloe. We'll be there soon. Everything's going to be fine."

• • •

Everything is not fine.

There is a hissing, and the danger does not present itself in the view ahead or even on the computer systems. Instead, it descends upon them in the air they breathe. The ventilation shafts in the X-Runner chamber start to secrete a noxious white gas. On instinct, Chloe coughs and the foul poison invades her lungs. It takes only a few moments for her brain to switch itself off, but before it does she processes the following three things:her father, panicking, attempting to open the X-Runner's windows, and failing; their loyal X-Runner killing all engine and generator power, plummeting them into darkness; and the dull drone of a distant engine descending, intertwining itself with her father's coughing and her last muddled thought.

*Everything is not fine.*

# CHAPTER THREE

SUNSET has long passed and darkness descended when Ikka docks for the night. She is alone, no other X-Runners present on the horizon. This is the way she prefers it, there are too many complications that arise from interactions with other racers.

As she gathers her supplies for her night outside—her swag, fire fuel, and a serving of the liquified meals the X-Runner dispenses—something catches her eye. The nav screen, which she left on for heat signal tracking when she was searching for a docking position, has latched on to the thermal pattern of another racer. Two racers in a runner moving high up on the rocky mountain to her east.

Ikka slides back into her pilot seat and tracks the monitor's mapping function out wider to survey all the potential paths up the mountain. She's sure she had ruled this out as a nonviable route earlier today. No matter which way she examines the map, there is no way that runner will be able to get off the mountain other than the exact way it is travelling up it. What can its racers be thinking? Once they hit the top, they're going to have steer themselves right back down the way they came. Idiots.

Ikka leans back in her pilot seat and decides to watch their progress on the screen as she consumes her meal. She can see very faintly, if she strains her eyes, the light of the X-Runner moving slowly near the top of the mountain. It is glimmering like a distant star reflected in water, but then…

It disappears.

Ikka blinks, searching for it again.

No more glimmer on the mountain.

She checks her X-Runner's computer system.

No heat signals present, no other racers.

No sign of any life for miles, other than her own.

She frowns, re-collects her items, and goes outside.

She's going to have to sleep on this.

• • •

Ikka is up well before the sunrise. She has spent the last few hours sitting in darkness inside her runner, staring at her heat signal tracker. There have been no more movements, no re-emergence of the disappearing X-Runner on the mountain. She drums her fingers on the runner's dashboard in the dark. Tut-tut-tut-tut. Tut-tut-tut-tut.

As she sees it, she has two options:

One, she can forget what she saw, or what she thinks she saw, and continue on with The Race. Or,

Two, she can give in to the nagging voice inside her head, the one that is always telling her *something is not right*, and make her way up the mountain to see what she can see.

Tut-tut-tut-tut.

She narrows her eyes at the fingers responsible for the drumming and snaps her hand back, placing it in her lap. It's time to invest in herself and investigate option two.

• • •

Even at 100 miles an hour, it's a two-hour drive to track back east to the mountain. In the final half hour stretch, another runner starts to blip on the radar, approaching from the south. It is near the base of the mountain when it stops moving. It remains stationary for the next twenty minutes, and is still static when Ikka reaches the mountain. The mountain is rocky, barren, and tall—so tall it blocks out the morning sun on this side. The stationary X-Runner is swamped in shade, forlorn with inactivity. It's in similar condition to Ikka's Runner, but there are modifications on it that Ikka hasn't witnessed before. There is an array of jagged wire prongs attached to its front underside. They extend forward into crooked knives, searching for victims to slice in two. Ikka examines the tip of one of them. Its peak is one inch in diameter, and has been sharpened by hand. As she traces over this detail, she becomes aware of someone standing behind her.

"Hey, I-K-K-4-7! I knew you wouldn't be able to resist me for too long. What are you doing stalking me?"

Ikka recognises the voice, but is immediately on guard. She swivels around, a twelve-inch blade extracted from her racing jacket and extended, before she completes the turn. She regards the man in front of her. He is roughly her age, possibly a year or two older. Cropped black hair, dark mischievous eyes, and muscles evident beneath his modest racing clothes. He smirks at Ikka's outstretched weapon, grinning as though this is expected behaviour. Ikka frowns, unable to place his face.

She glares at him, "How do you know my code?"

He laughs at her, "How do I… know your code? I hate to tell you, but you're coming off a little foolish."

Ikka appraises him for a moment, focusing on the flow of his voice in her head.

"We've met before, haven't we?"

"Well, yes. Two nights ago. We shared a campfire. Do you honestly not remember?"

Ikka closes her eyes and shakes her head.

"My name's Veela. I don't think you liked me that much, which is much shame to you. I'm a pretty great guy."

*Vee-la.*

Ikka opens her eyes and nods slightly.

"We've met before."

"Yes."

"Okay."

"So are you going to tell me your name this time? I-K-K-4-7 is a bit of a mouthful."

"It's the only ID I have. I can't find any others in my runner."

It's Veela's turn to nod slightly.

"Okay, we can hold that thought for a moment," he mumbles under his breath, "and all the others…" He returns to a normal speaking level, "What are you doing out here, touching my modifications? Not thinking of stealing them, are you?"

"I saw you on my sensor. It seemed strange to me that a runner would come to a stand still so early in the day. As I was heading this way, I decided to stop and check."

"But you came from a westerly direction. Why would

you be heading back this way?"

"I'm researching an inconsistency. What about you? Is your runner okay?"

"An inconsistency?"

Ikka watches Veela for a moment, weighing the pros and cons of telling him the truth. She decides to test the waters.

"I saw an X-Runner disappear on the mountain peak last night. I don't see how that's possible, so I thought I'd find out."

Veela looks at her stumped, unsure if he should believe her.

"Right. You saw a five point three ton vehicle just disappear. Poof!?"

"That is what all the facts I currently possess seem to indicate, and why I want to find out more."

"Hmm. And you're going to let yourself slip in the race rankings for that?"

"It seems prudent. Now do you need assistance with your runner or shall I continue on my way?"

"Ha! So cold, IKK47. No, my engine is burnt out. I called the facilitators and their ETA isn't till after dusk tonight. Hey, why don't I come with you? Up the mountain. I could be your second set of eyes."

"I'm not sure I'd trust your eyes."

Ikka watches Veela's reaction carefully. He is not affronted, but accepting and forthright.

"Why not? Two sets are better than one. And look, I'm not like you. I don't carry weapons around with me everywhere. You can even search me before I come aboard. It's going to be a long boring day for me waiting for the facilitators otherwise, and

I don't know when the last time was I had some real company. You either, I bet. What's the worst that could happen?"

Ikka's response is flat. "You cross a line, I have to stab you, and then I'm left searching for a suitable way to cleanse my runner of your blood."

"Yikes!" Veela purses his lips, unsure if he should burst into laughter or frown seriously. "Okay. How about I promise not to cross any lines so you don't end up burdened with cleaning up after my untimely demise?"

Ikka considers his proposition for a moment, appraising the earnest nature of his tone.

"Okay."

"Okay?"

"Okay. But we should leave immediately if you don't want me to change my mind. And I wasn't joking about stabbing you if you cross any lines."

"Oh, I don't doubt it! Come on, let's go."

Ikka nods, gesturing for Veela to walk before her so she can keep her eyes on him at all times. She is still suspicious, but she cannot deny that nagging voice inside her, the one that suggests it wouldn't be the worst to find an ally amongst the layers of deception dictating her life.

• • •

Ikka requires some time to adjust to Veela's mannerisms. On the drive up the mountain, Veela punctuates his thoughts by touching her shoulder, prodding her back, or nudging her arm. It isn't sexual, but seems devised to accentuate his every thought and physically instil it upon her. Ikka isn't used to physical affections. Any kind of bodily contact—no matter how well intentioned—makes her feel unsafe. She ignores her discomfort by focusing on the rocky ledge they are navigating.

Veela has asked several times to share the piloting duties, but he talks so much Ikka would not trust his concentration levels on such a perilous strip of terrain. Every other rock the runner passes comes loose, jumping over the mountain ledge and attempting to drag the runner down with it. All of Ikka's steering prowess is utilised to engage the wheels in a manner that counterbalances this constant upheaval.

"You know, I-K-K-4-7, I get that you're the strong and silent type but I really thought you'd open up a bit more on this ride. What's your deal?

Ikka, "I don't like the way you spell out my racer code every time you talk to me."

"No?"

"No. It feels unnecessary. When I say it in my head it's not individual letters, but a blur of sounds. Ik-ka. Don't say the four or the seven."

"Okay." Veela nods his head in amusement. "You finally have a name. I like it. Ikka. But you've just handed it to me, you know. If you ever annoy me, I'm just going to have to call you Icky."

Ikka releases her gaze from the road for the briefest second to glare at Veela. He reacts as though she's poked him with a burning rod.

"Okay, okay! No Icky. Just Ikka."

The line of her mouth curves in the slightest, but Ikka keeps her eyes focused on the road ahead.

"We should be there soon. Keep your mind open, I'm not

sure what we'll find."

•  •  •

Nothing is the short answer.

The top of the mountain is barren and empty. There isn't much girth at its peak, perhaps one hundred square yards. It is desolate and exposed. No foliage can survive the harsh winds at this height—some have tried and evidence of their struggles remain in occasional stumps snapped clean half a foot off the ground, their debris vanquished by the wind. There is no trace of the X-Runner Ikka watched disappear on her nav screen. She stands still, the wind biting her face, her eyes lost in contemplation.

Veela returns from walking the peak's circumference and sidles in close to Ikka.

"What were you expecting to find up here buddy? Cause whatever it is, I ain't seeing it."

"I saw an X-Runner drive up here last night. I was watching it on the radar and once it reached this peak, it disappeared. No electronic trace of its existence remained. I thought there'd be some kind of physical clue up here. Some indication of what happened."

"Maybe it was just a glitch?"

"No. I saw a light up here on the mountain. I'd ignore it if it were just one or the other, me or the radar, but both together... it doesn't make sense."

"No, but life doesn't make much sense. We're just here for the ride. I wouldn't waste your time worrying about this."

Veela offers her a consolatory wink. Ikka scowls.

"Are you so lazy that you're unwilling to ask for even one

second, what is going on?"

"Well…"

"You are, aren't you?" Ikka sighs, her thoughts travelling inwards, questioning herself as much as Veela. "Do you know why we're racing?"

"To win?"

"No, specifically, what are we racing for?"

"Ah. Umm."

"Do you know how many days you've been in this race? How many years?"

"Well it can't have been years."

"Why not? Do you remember anything else? Anything before The Race?"

"… No."

"No. Neither can I. To me, that seems worth questioning, instead of 'just going along for the ride.'"

Ikka strides away from him, disdain and frustration shadowing her movements. She arrives at a small boulder, kicks it in a momentary lapse of control, and then plonks down on its hard surface. Once seated, she kicks the dirt at her feet, feeding her annoyance. She watches the specks of dirt, little clusters of burnt orange soil, fly away from the impact point and leave the rocky ground beneath exposed. There are black marks on the rock. Ikka crouches onto her haunches, looking closer, and clears more dirt away with the sleeve of her racing vest.

Veela watches from a distance. He is drawn closer as Ikka pushes more dirt away, intrigued by the black markings marring the rock. They form a pattern made up of individual diamond shapes with lines weaving between them. It is unmistakable—they are tire tracks, burnt to the rock in a desperate friction. Ikka runs her fingers over the ground, and little flecks of black soot latch onto her skin. She sniffs it, and her nostrils are greeted by the subtle scent of burnt rubber.

Without raising her eyes, she says, "Definitely fresh. At the rate new soil is blown in up here, it's more than likely these tracks were made last night."

"So where's the X-Runner?"

Ikka stares at the bare mountaintop before them.

"Gone."

"No surprises there, genius."

Ikka stands to connect deeper with Veela, the golden glint in her eyes betraying her excitement. "But it was here, and it disappeared. Five point three ton vehicles don't just disappear."

Veela says, "Okay… Do you have any suggestions what happened?"

"I have no idea. Only feelings, violent dreams of unease."

"Hmm. Okay. So…" Veela trails off.

Ikka's eyes cut through his facade of coolness.

She says, "You don't believe me. That's fine. We should get going if we want to reach your X-runner before nightfall. We'll get you back to 'enjoying the ride' in no time, *buddy*."

Her mocking tone shames him, though he has no understanding of why.

He says, "And what about you?"

"Me?" Ikka's eyes flit between all the possible futures she sees before herself. "I'm not sure how, but I'm going to figure this all out. Come on."

# CHAPTER FOUR

**THE LIGHT** is so bright it feels like it's burning. Even with her
eyes closed, Chloe can see only white. That doesn't change when
she opens her eyes, but then her vision readjusts. There is glass in
front of her. Glass three feet to her left, and glass three feet to
her right. There are figures beyond the glass, but her eyes can't
yet see what they are. She tries to turn to look behind her, but
her neck feels stiff and her legs won't move. Why won't her legs
move? She is too scared to look down. She can still feel the
warmth of blood on her vaginal lips, but with complete dread she
realizes that this is not all she can feel there. There is metal.
Cold. Hard. Persistent. It is wrapped around her entire lower
torso with a series of complex tubing connecting it to the floor.
She tries to ignore her horror, her need to cry out for her father.
She focuses on more details. The floor is tiled. White tiles, white
grouting. It is cold underneath her feet, but not icy.

She closes her eyes. Breathes. She is Racer CHLO3.
This is not a part of The Race. It cannot be real. There has been

some mistake, perhaps in her brain. This is not reality. But she reaches down and her fingers touch the metal. Cold. Hard. Persistent. It is real. Her breaths get shorter, shallower. Her lungs keep failing to hold on to the air. All of the glass, the whiteness, builds into a disorientating snow, it's spinning, there's a warmth in her temples, her breaths get shorter, shallower—

"GIRL!" The voice is stern.

"Take a deep breath—a really deep one—and hold on to it. Don't let it go. Feel it fill you up until all your extremities are tingling and you're almost ready to fall asleep. Then let it go, and take another one, a giant one, and let it do the same. Each breath is yours. Don't waste them."

Chloe does as she's told.

She breathes.

Moments, minutes later, she feels calm again. It's too soon to panic. She needs to learn more about her situation, to understand it further. The voice had come from her right. It was a female voice, a woman in her early thirties. Looking through the glass wall on her right, she sees it is a room exactly like her own. Three glass walls, a tiled floor, a tiled ceiling. She still can't turn far enough to see what the back wall is. But in the centre of the room, there is a woman with metal similarly wrapped around her lower torso, connecting it to the floor. Brown hair, matted, pressed against the back of her neck. No clothing to cover her body, her breasts. Chloe's arms instinctively move to cover her own cleavage, ashamed she hadn't realized sooner how naked she is. The other woman's hazel eyes follow her movements.

"Don't be stupid. Your arms will cramp if you always try to cover yourself. What's your number?"

"C-H-L-O-3."

"Charlize Hannah Loretta Ophelia 3? They've gone a long way on that line now. I'm S-A-M-1-4. Sarah Amy Maria 14. Call me Sam, it's easier. I might call you Charlize. Now, Charlize. Your body is going to eventually stop working if you don't use your muscles. Don't just sit on the bench all day. Make sure you move, stand, walk around, do squats. You don't ever want to be unable to run if you get the chance."

A lot of the words don't sink in, but *bench* echoes in Chloe's mind. She is sitting on a bench. It's low enough that her feet can touch the floor and it's stretched across the width of the room. She wiggles her toes, wondering if she can stand on her feet. It seems daunting, with all this metal strapped around her waist and tubing running between her legs.

"How old are you, Charlize?"

"Eleven."

"Eleven. Early bloomer. Unlucky."

Chloe focuses on her feet. She presses the palms of her hands against the bench, using her arms to propel herself up. The weight of the metal burns down her legs, starting at her inner thighs. Her legs buckle under the weight of the device and she crashes to the floor. One leg gets jammed under the metal diaper. She tries to lift herself up from the ground but is unsuccessful. She lets her upper torso join the rest of her body on the ground, her head resting on the floor's cool surface.

"Unlucky?"

From her position on the floor, she can arch her neck to look out past the underside of the bench to the fourth wall of the room. It is another glass wall, and behind it is another glass room. Beyond that, another glass room and another glass room and another. Each containing a woman, each one naked except for a metal diaper with metal tubing connecting her to the floor. Chloe cannot see at what point the glass rooms end, cannot count how many chained women are in her sight.

"Where are we, Sam?"

Sam looks down at her, her hazel eyes unapologetic, her voice gruff.

"It's a birthing farm."

Chloe can't stand to look at the endless horizon of glass cells much longer. She gives up and looks directly above her at the tiled ceiling spread out atop. Her leg is beginning to ache from the weight of the tubing pressed upon it. Her eyes are growing tired, the brightness of the room enveloping her.

Before she passes out, she manages to say, "Birthing farm? That doesn't… this doesn't… but what about The Race?"

• • •

When Chloe wakes, she is on the bench. Lying on her back, the stark white ceiling bearing down upon her. She can feel her left leg pulsing with an unrelenting throb, but cannot see the extent of the damage; it has been wrapped, the bandages pristine and taut. She surveys the room about her once again. There are no doors, no windows, no hinges. How would someone have got in? Pulling herself upright, Chloe looks to Sam's cell. Sam is sleeping seated, her shoulders pressed against the glass wall. One of her legs juts off the bench, suspended in air. Her head is flopped forward, like a rag doll propped on a shelf. This rag doll has no clothes though, only a metal diaper, exposed limbs, and uncovered breasts. Chloe hadn't ever seen another's breasts before, and she has avoided looking at her own since they began to grow—except for the occasional glimpse when changing—but she knows there is something wrong with Sam's. It is not that they are large, it's that they seem engorged. She shudders to think what it must feel like to have them attached to her body.

"GIRL." The voice is not Sam's. It is not stern. It is desperate, weak. A whispered shout. "Girl, come talk to me. Let me see your face."

The voice is coming from beyond the glass wall on Chloe's left. A skinny woman. Short brown hair, sharp cheekbones. The hair is short because in some places it has been torn out, in others ripped a few inches above the roots. Her cheekbones protrude so violently from her face because there is no padding between their edges and her skin. And her skin has a blue-grey tinge that steals any light from the blue of her eyes—it disappears into the squalor of her complexion. As Chloe edges along her bench to the left wall of her cell, this frail creature awaits eagerly, her hands pressed against the glass. Her voice is welcoming and gentle.

"It's good to have a new girl here. It's not nice to pass the time without friends."

The woman smiles at Chloe as she arrives at the glass. Chloe reaches her hand up to the window and touches the outline of the woman's hand. There is a quality to this woman, despite her dilapidated appearance, that draws Chloe in. The woman's eyes search deep into Chloe's soul.

"I need to know, have they told you the secrets yet? Have they told you where they're keeping them?"

Chloe shakes her head, "I don't know what you're talking

about."

"My children. Don't you know where my children are?"

"I haven't seen your children. I haven't seen any children."

"There was a boy, and a girl, and another girl, and then a boy, and then a girl, and then another girl, and another girl, and another girl, and then a boy."

"I promise you, I haven't seen any children."

The woman's eyes stare beseechingly at Chloe through the glass. Her pupils are locked in on Chloe, but she is seeing her somewhere else.

"I know they've told you the secrets. You have to tell me. Where are my children?"

"I don't know where your children are."

The woman's lips begin to bare a little, the edges of her teeth revealed.

"Tell me where my children are."

"I'm sorry, I don't know. I don't even know where I am. I'm just as confused as you."

"LIES!"

The woman brings her fist up, and Chloe braces, pulling her own hand back as the woman's slams against the glass. There is no loud impact, only a dull thud as Chloe watches the woman's wrist bounce off the glass and hang limply at her side. The woman's eyes well up with tears.

"You have to help me. I need to find my children."

She begins to sob and follows her tubing chains back into the centre of her cell. As soon as she turns, she loses all awareness of Chloe. She starts walking circles around the tubing's anchor point on the floor, humming an indistinguishable tune. As Chloe watches her she notices a figure beyond, in the cell past the frail woman's. A young girl, perhaps only a year or two older than Chloe. She is staring impassively in Chloe's direction. Her straight black hair is not torn but sleek, and her hands rest on her belly, swollen with child. Chloe raises her hand to wave, offering a smile, but when the girl registers Chloe's gesture, she turns away. She does not look back.

• • •

It feels like years pass before Sam ceases to be a rag doll. Chloe wants to raise her from her slumber with a shout, but she is too scared to yell. Noise feels unwelcome in this place. When Sam does wake, she bolts upright, jolting with an inexplicable urgency. She jumps off the bench, swearing under her breath, and proceeds to do sit ups, her legs parted to allow for the metal tubing. A savage ferocity guides her movements. Chloe is nervous to bother her, but she cannot wait for Sam to finish before starting a conversation.

"Sam?"

Sam does not acknowledge her.

"Sam. Did you see who bandaged my leg?"

Sam continues with her crunches.

Chloe shouts, "Sam!"

Her shout is desperate. Sam pauses mid-crunch to stare her down.

"Yes, Charlize?"

"I'm sorry." She falters, embarrassed to have Sam's piercing gaze focused on her. "Do you know who bandaged my leg? I woke up and it was done. There are no doors to these rooms, Sam… I don't understand."

Sam exhales with frustration. Chloe can't tell whether or not it is directed at her, until Sam begins to talk. Her condescension makes the answer clear.

"I didn't see who bandaged your leg, Charlize. No one would've. They gassed us to knock us all out. It always hits me worse than the others. I've got to work it off. Re-oxygenate."

Sam continues with her exercises. She switches to push-ups. Chloe can see sores on her legs from where they've repeatedly rubbed against the metal diaper.

"Why did they gas us, Sam?"

"So we don't see them. They don't want to cause unnecessary stress to the facility."

"The facility?"

"This facility. Us. They don't want to cause us stress. They think it's bad for the pregnancies. It probably is. The gas probably is too, though."

"The pregnancies?"

"I told you before. This is a birthing farm. They get us pregnant. We are here to be pregnant. All of the women around you are pregnant. Or about to be."

Sam hasn't ceased her push-ups during this speech. She seems nonchalant about the entire situation.

"I'm not pregnant, Sam. I don't even know…"

"No. But you're on borrowed time. You've got until the end of your session and then you're theirs."

"Session? I don't understand."

Sam scowls. She sits still to impart her meaning with greater tenacity.

"The bleeding. It's the first part of the process, your body getting ready for fertilization. It lasts seven days in total, less if you're cursed, longer if you're lucky. Once it's over, your body will be ready for the next part in the process, where that shiny metal around your waist gets to sing."

"Sing?"

"You'll understand when it happens. For now, just enjoy your vacation."

Chloe is baffled, and watches as Sam returns to her push-ups, continuing her spiel.

"The gas affects me more 'cause I'm older than most of them in here. Thirty-three. You know how I've stuck it out this long? I exercise. I take care of my body. I stay ready for everything. You want to survive in here? You should do as I do. Get up—hold on to your bench for support this time—and get used to the weight of that thing on your body. Your muscles gotta get used to it."

Once again, Chloe does as she's told. It's comforting to follow orders, like following out instructions from her dad in The Race. It's best not to over-think the situation. She doesn't want to consider the prospect of her session ending and the next stage of the process beginning. If it lasts the full seven days, she has roughly five days remaining. Five days to regain her strength, five days to figure out the mechanics of the diaper and dismantle it with only her hands, five days to escape from this glass cage. And she will escape, even if it kills her. She has to return to The Race.

# CHAPTER FIVE

AS DUSK descends, Ikka and Veela arrive at the base of the mountain and are met with a surprising sight. Ikka is inclined to take this new turn of events in her stride—treat it as another piece in the ever-growing riddle of The Race—but Veela is intent on taking the matter personally. He leaps out of Ikka's X-Runner, cursing profusely and hitting his own legs in frustration. His runner, which Ikka can only imagine is his pride and joy based on his modifications to it, is gone.

The modifications remain.

Pronged metal teeth are strewn in a haphazard manner on the desert floor, heaped in a pile with a strange dark textile, trinkets Ikka cannot name, and bizarre old crockery. It looks like a junkyard. Ikka smiles at the simile and decides that she is indeed amused.

"Do you realize..." she stops, there is a lilt to her voice that is too mocking. She pauses, running her tongue against her teeth and continuing in a more controlled voice. "Do you realize that whoever stole your runner decided the mods were so worthless that they took the time to remove them, one by one? It's amazing, then, that you decided they were worth the time to add on, one by one."

Veela's spine stiffens, and Ikka reigns in her jovial mood.

"I wonder if The Race facilitators decided you had abandoned your X-Runner and confiscated it. It seems strange they didn't try to find you."

Veela stays silent, searching through the mess. He looks out of place, muscular and well kept, burrowing amongst a junk pile in the middle of the desert. There is no sign of life for miles, no indication that anybody had been this way today.

And no tracks.

No X-Runner tracks.

Veela's runner wasn't driven away. Wasn't dragged away. Wasn't loaded onto something else and taken away.

It was *lifted* away.

Like the racer on top of the mountain must have been.

Vanished into the air.

• • •

Ikka looks upwards, even though she knows she will find no answers there. Her eyes are greeted by the billowing animosity of storm clouds rapidly approaching. Even in the dusk air she can spy their red hue; a dust storm come to destroy all those in its path—Ikka has found racer bodies mutilated from dust storms before. The particles of sand on the desert floor are as sharp as broken glass, and just as potent in two hundred mile an hour winds.

Veela is still pottering amongst the rubble, and has not yet noticed the approaching storm.

"Veela. We have to get back to my runner, now."

Veela looks back to Ikka and follows her gaze to the onslaught of red clouds. His eyes boggle, and he quickly bends to start collecting items off the ground.

"Help me gather this up."

Ikka strides over to Veela and touches him on the shoulder; the first contact between them of her own intention, and clenches down on it. Her voice is stern and authoritative.

"We don't have time to collect this junk. The storm will be here in a few minutes. We have to get inside my runner, now. Do you understand?"

Veela nods, so Ikka releases her grip. He immediately presses a few pieces of the rubble into her hands; some small tubes and an obscure looking box.

"Take at least one small load back in with you okay? I'll be right after you. There's just a couple more things I need."

Ikka's jaw clenches.

"If you're not back in the runner when the storm hits, I will be closing the door. I can't risk damaging any of the internal mechanics."

Veela nods.

And Ikka sprints back to her X-Runner.

• • •

Boom. Boom. Boom.

The approaching winds have already started pounding against the bow of Ikka's runner. She stands in the doorway, goggles on to protect her eyes, giving her silhouette an inhuman appearance.

Boom. Boom. Boom.

A strong gust blows in. Little shards of dust, sand, and rocks scratch past Ikka's face. She won't be able to keep the door open much longer.

Boom. Boom. Boom.

"Hey catch this, will ya!"

Two metal prongs fly through the dust towards Ikka's face. She only just intercepts their trajectory before they can crush her nose. She palms them off into the runner behind her and glares back into the gloom in front of her.

Boom. Boom. Boom.

"Hurry up."

"Yeah, yeah, yeah." Veela's voice is far too casual for her liking, "I'll be in in... just, one, second."

And he is.

Leaping up the two steps into the runner, arms full of the strange prongs and some of the dark textile wrapped around his neck. Ikka slams the runner door shut behind him, locking it in three places, pulling an internal roller door down over the door, and locking it shut as well. She turns to see Veela watching her with a smug look on his face.

"Really don't want me to leave, do you?"

She bares her teeth at him for the briefest second, shakes her head and walks to the other end of the runner.

"Don't. Even. Start."

And then the storm winds become so loud that he can't.

Boom. Boom. Boom.

• • •

For the first half of the night, Ikka sleeps sitting upright in her pilot's chair. Her feet are hooked up, resting on the runner's dashboard. The turbulent dancing of the dust storm outside casts a myriad of shadows that slash against her face and into the interior of the X-Runner, whipping and cascading against the walls like violent ocean waves.

Around three in the morning, Ikka wakes up and tries to clench her right hand. She cannot—the muscles are already taut around a knife handle. It is always this way. Ikka never sleeps unguarded, especially in the rare event of sleeping inside the X-Runner. Ikka looks into the depth of the runner and her eyes trace Veela's outline in her swag on the ground. He had suggested they share it, which she had declined. He is amusing, but she doesn't yet trust him. Even if she did trust him, that is too close for her liking to any other human.

Veela is odd. There is a charming openness about his manner, yet his incessant talking is annoying. He also doesn't have reasonable priorities, salvaging all that junk when faced with the impending destruction of a dust storm. The items are scattered next to him on the runner floor. He managed to salvage eight of the pronged knives, the textile, some random pieces of crockery, and a small box. The box is the least conspicuous of the items—it has no discernible markings—but as soon as her eyes rest on it Ikka feels fraught with suspicion.

Ikka's eyes flick in Veela's direction again. There is no movement, only the deep breaths of intense dreams. Ikka moves without noise, swinging off her chair and padding over to the box. She reaches out to touch it, but her fingers recoil as if they have been burned. It is a trick of the mind. She pushes past her hesitation and holds it up. It is heavy for its small size, but well balanced. Ten inches wide, four inches long and deep, it has been neglected for so long that there is no shine to its surface, and dust covers its long forgotten colour.

Her fingers trace around the lid, searching for the opening latch. There is no obvious demarkation between the lid and the body of the box, let alone a catch or keyhole. The smooth wood shaping the box seems continuous—perhaps decades of dust accumulation have filled in the joints and hinges. Ikka checks on Veela, who is still a stagnant lump on the runner floor.

Ikka carries the box with her to the X-Runner's small bathroom. She closes the door behind her with unprecedented silence and places the box in the compact sink. She pours decontaminant salve on it, the kind she uses to purify wounds or gashes. A sharp, acrid smell envelopes the room, and the dust lining the box begins to froth with small bubbles. They rise into a small mountain, and Ikka uses a gloved hand to rub them in further. She adds some water to the mix and the bubbles subside. The water streams off the box a fluffy grey, and then dirty brown, before turning clear. Ikka turns off the tap and then uses a small hand towel to dry the box, swathing it in the folds of the cloth. She sits on the closed toilet seat and unwraps the cloth, poised to observe all that she can about the newly clean box. This is how Veela finds her, several hours later, when he finally wakes.

# CHAPTER SIX

STARING, but not seeing, Ikka is seated atop the toilet, the box resting in her hands. Veela crouches in front of her, waving his hand in front of her eyes. There is no response, not even the slightest flicker. Veela grabs her face, angling it so she is looking directly into his eyes.

"Ikka?"

There is a minuscule movement in her pupils. They refocus a little.

"Ikka, you're scaring me a little here, buddy."

Buddy.

That word does it.

Ikka's eyebrows furrow and her eyes focus on Veela with contempt.

Those little daggers, ready to stab him.

He smiles a wide, smug grin and removes his hands from her face.

"Hey, you're back."

She looks tempted to spit into his face, but instead snaps her head back and jumps to her feet. She shoves the box into his chest and leaves the bathroom.

Running straight out of the X-Runner.

Outside, into the dust storm.

Veela manages to catch on to Ikka's arm before she can unlatch the outer door and plunge into the chaos of the storm. He pulls her back into the X-Runner, slamming the door shut and holding onto both her shoulders, pinning her against the runner door and searching into her eyes.

"Ikka, what on Earth is going on?"

Her face is neutral. Always so damn neutral. And her voice… Too neutral.

She says, "Let go of me, Veela. It's not going to work out well for you if you don't."

"Work out well for me? Are you… threatening me? I'm twice your size. Don't be so damn petulant."

Her face doesn't move, but the expression in Ikka's eyes makes Veela feel as though she is raising an eyebrow at him.

"Petulant?"

In a flourish, Ikka brings her left hand up to grip onto Veela's right tricep, and with the same momentum brings her right arm up onto the left side of his face. Before these movements are even over, she twists his body around and connects it against the wall of the runner. For good measure, in the small moment where he is a little winded, she hooks her left ankle under his right leg and drops him to the floor.

Her face is still neutral, but she offers a small head incline as way of sighing.

"I suppose that was a little petulant, but you shouldn't be such a cocky... suck, Veela. I just meant it wasn't going to work out for you because I'm almost certain I'm going to—yeah..."

She stops to cough, drop to her knees, and vomit.

• • •

When Ikka is done vomiting, she sleeps. Her body is exhausted, her mind unwilling to function at full capacity. Hours pass before she wakes, and the sun has risen high into the afternoon sky. When she rouses, the X-Runner is in motion, Veela is in the pilot seat, and the faded scent of vomit in the air. Ikka's throat is burning. She crawls slowly to the kitchenette area—a system of two pipes in the wall, one that dispenses water and the other the liquified meal solution. She uses the small bench to pull herself up, and then fills a canister with water. She drops back to her knees, letting her head bang slightly against the wall beneath the pipes and sits still, slowly sipping the water.

Veela talks to her over his shoulder while he drives.

"Hey, you're up. Want to tell me what that was all about? The sitting and the staring and the vomiting? Not to mention decking me?"

Ikka doesn't bother talking through the burn. She shakes her head. She knows he's watching her in the rear-facing mirror.

"Hmm. Don't want to take responsibility for your actions. That's fine. Take a little while to think it over. I want some answers when we camp for the night though. All right?"

Ikka inclines her head a little, then rests it back against the wall while massaging her neck with her hands. She tries to make sense of the last thirty-six hours. She cannot. And now? Now she is full of dread. Heavy hands are wrapped around her intestines, her heart, and her lungs, squeezing down on them and making her feel uncomfortable in her own skin. None of her limbs or extremities feel like they belong to her. They are foreign objects attached to her being. Even the abstract idea of her being doesn't feel like it belongs to her. She feels violated, and she cannot name the reason why.

She tries to whisper.

"Veela."

It comes out as loud as a tiny twig scratching on the ground.

She clears her throat. Coughs.

"Veela."

The hoarse whisper is still not loud enough to breach the noise level of the X-Runner's engine.

She hits herself in the sternum in order to jump-start her control of this body.

"Veela!"

Her voice reaches his ears, as well as the several coughs that immediately follow.

His eyes flick over to check on her in the mirror.

"You all right, Ikka?"

She coughs in response, hitting herself in the chest until the hacking stops. Her voice is barely above a whisper level now, but he can understand what she says.

"You have to stop the runner. I can't stay in here any longer."

• • •

As soon as Veela kills the engine, Ikka is unlatching the cabin doors and jumping out of the X-Runner into the open desert air. Her body is still weak from the retching. Her legs give way as soon as she hits the ground, and she stumbles on her hands and knees away from the runner. This doesn't stilt her progress—she crawls as fast as she can. She's crossed twelve feet of desert before Veela reaches her.

He kneels down beside her, putting his hand on her shoulders to settle her.

He says, "Hey. What's going on, buddy? Why the panic?"

She looks up at him, her face the opposite of neutral. Pooling tears nestle in her eyes, refusing to fall but stinging as she holds them in. Her jaw is clenched, not with rage, but uncertainty. And in her eyes; in those stoic, hazel pupils, the only emotion present is fear.

She opens her mouth to speak, and the words come out quivering, almost lost on the wind.

"It's not safe, Veela."

"What's not safe?"

"It." Ikka inclines her head back to the X-Runner, and searches Veela's eyes as he contemplates what she is saying. "It's not safe in there. It tells them everything. They monitor everything."

"What are you talking about, Ikka? Who?"

"The facilitators."

"I don't understand what you're saying. Of course they're monitoring us, to help us with break downs and to keep track of who's in the lead."

Ikka shakes her head, biting her lower lip. She tries again. Her voice has a fraction more control this time.

"It's not like that, Veela. The facilitators aren't trying to help us. They're harvesting us."

# CHAPTER SEVEN

CHLOE can tell her body's session is getting lighter. She's running out of time. With Sam's guidance, she's training her body to stand under the weight of the metal diaper and its tubing. She can do a few squats now, and is endeavouring to stretch all her muscles several times a day. She can tell when the days start and end because the lights in the facility completely shut down at a certain point, and then, just as abruptly, switch back on. It's possible they're not synchronised with the sun, but if Chloe sleeps for the duration of the darkness, she has enough energy to endure the astounding brightness of the lit hours. She never naps—she needs to maximize her time.

These three days, she's only had contact with Sam and the frail woman in the cell to her left. Sam tells her the woman's name is Hannah (Hannah Betty Maria 12). Hannah has been in the facility for roughly twelve years, and Sam estimates she's twenty-five years old. Like most of the women in here, she arrived at the age of twelve and gave birth to her first child at the age of thirteen. Sam doesn't talk much about her own experiences, but she will deliver long monologues about the mental states and histories of the other women. The nature of the cells is that each woman can communicate to those next to her, and sometimes overhear loud noises from the cell directly past that, but no more. Over time, a broken-whispers style of communication has spread information throughout the facility.

Sam doesn't expect Hannah will last much longer. Hannah's physical appearance has been deteriorating rapidly since she last gave birth and her mental state has chosen to accompany her body on its journey. This new pregnancy is draining her further. Sam said if Hannah's body survives the labour, she will be surprised. Chloe can't stand to engage much with Hannah. It is hard to be drawn in by her gentle voice and crave the companionship it offers, when at any moment her voice will lose all grasp of reason and her eyes will beg for impossible assistance. Each interaction Chloe has with Hannah leaves her feeling drained, so she attempts to spend as much time to the right of her cell as possible. She even avoids looking to the left of her cell for hours on end, for fear of accidental eye contact. This in turn causes her to feel guilty, abandoning Hannah to face the bright nothingness alone, but she tries not to focus on those feelings.

"And what about the young girl in the cell past Hannah?"

"She doesn't speak much. Not surprising, really, with that nutter Hannah as her first point of call. She got here around two years ago, maybe. I reckon she's very near the end of her second pregnancy and now she just stands in silence all day. She watches, too. She watches everyone but says nothing. Sometimes I can make her out staring at Hannah, watching her do her walks around her cell. Hannah will even talk directly to her and she'll just watch silently, and when she gets bored she'll turn away. I don't know how long she'll last, but hopefully not too long. We need someone who talks in that cell. I need to know what's going on further that way. It's no good having this silence. Hannah needs to go, too. The information she passes on is getting more and more unreliable. But that doesn't mean you shouldn't try to get some, find out what she can see past the girl."

Chloe nods, but makes no moves to venture to the left of her cell. She focuses her attention down, her gaze penetrating the metal diaper fixed around her torso. She has stared at it many times these past three days, attempting to understand its design. She runs her fingers over it again, tracing the edges where it meets her limbs. She can fit the tip of her index finger under its edge at the top circumference of each leg, and at the point where it meets the top of her pubic line on her skin. She can spy her hairs waving from under its ridge, and remember her abhorrence when they first grew. Sam says the metal stops at this point so that when her belly becomes tumid with pregnancy the metal won't cut too deep into her body. It will probably still cut though. Many of the women, Sam included, have scars at this point from years of the metal rubbing against their skin.

There are four smaller pipes, each with a diameter of two inches, and a larger fifth pipe, which is five inches in diameter, all sprouting from the base of the diaper. (It is easiest to call it this, Chloe cannot think of another name for it and Sam's use of the term *thing* gives it a power she is not comfortable with.) The pipes are all made from the same unyielding metal, and are quite thick based on their weight. It would be near impossible for her to make a dent in them without any tools—the tubes have been welded expertly where they connect to the base of the diaper.

When Chloe goes to the bathroom, the machinery of the diaper will start whirring. One of the four smaller tubes acts as a suction tunnel, vacuuming the diaper of any urine or faecal matter. A pulsing can then be felt vibrating through another tube, before a flush of water washes through the diaper and Chloe's genitals. The water is then also suctioned away. A pulse of warm air dries everything before all the hums and whirring cease and the metal diaper returns to inactivity. Even in this state, Chloe knows it can't be trusted.

"Hey, girl."

Chloe is stirred from her reflections by Hannah's voice. It sounds even more melodic today. Hannah is kneeling at the glass wall, her face low, her waning eyes fixed on Chloe.

"It's not going to work. Whatever you try. These things don't break."

"I'm not trying to break it. I'm trying to understand it."

Hannah seems more lucid than usual, as though she's grabbed hold of a string inside her mind and is holding on to it, climbing her way to the top to actually grasp what's outside her eyes.

"It's not worth understanding. And it's not worth trying to break. It won't work and even if it does, they'll just fix it. They'll gas everyone near and fix it and when you wake up it'll be the same again. It's no use, this training Sam's got you doing. You can't run or fight back when you're knocked out, when you're chained to the ground. It's about as useless as trying to scream for help. I know, she had me training for a while and I've screamed my fair share. It achieves nothing."

Chloe edges towards the wall. She keeps her voice low, not wanting Sam to hear.

"How do you know all this? Have you seen them?"

"Them?" Hannah sits on the word a moment, and the thought pushes her a little back down her string.

"The people who run the facility. Sam won't tell me about them. She says I'm not ready."

"You're probably not."

"But I'm here aren't I? It doesn't matter if I'm *ready*, I need to know what's going on so I can get out of here."

The urgency in Chloe's voice triggers something inside Hannah. She rappels further down her rope, retreats further down her well.

"You don't want to see them, girl. But if you do, find out for me. Find out where my children are. I need to know. You have to help me."

The gears in Hannah's mind have returned back to autopilot, and the woman Chloe briefly glimpsed now safely returned to the darkness below. Chloe knows there's no use trying to engage with her like this. If she could shake her, she would—shake her until that woman inside re-emerges, but no actions can be taken with the glass wall between them. So she turns away, averts her gaze from those faded blue eyes, and tunes out the voice reciting behind her.

"I have to find my children."

• • •

Chloe wakes with a jolt, but is immediately met with a need to stay still and silent. It is dark, the regulated night not yet over. The silence in her cell is usually oppressive when the lights are out, but tonight Chloe can hear whispers echoing from the cell to her right. From Sam's cell. It does not sound like Sam's voice, but it is. Gentle, tender even, it sings a muted lullaby. Straining her eyes in the dark, Chloe can distinguish Sam's form, lying on her side, left hand rubbing her belly. Since Chloe's arrival at the facility, Sam has not once acknowledged her own pregnancy. She has made comments about pregnancies in the facility as an overall whole, but not stated her own condition nor invited any questions. There is a coldness to Sam's disposition that does not allow for such openness.

The minute curve in Sam's stomach suggests she is probably just three months pregnant, yet the tone of her voice implies a deep love for the life inside. Sam is roughly thirty-three years old. If she came to the facility at thirteen like she states, she has been a captive here for nearly twenty years. Twenty years facing impregnation, nine months gestation, and childbirth, rewarded only by having her offspring stolen and then herself impregnated again. In all likelihood, this is her nineteenth pregnancy.

As Chloe allows herself to drift back to sleep, Sam's whispered lullaby continues to seep into her cell. It is soothing, the melody caressing the air, which is normally so stagnant. As it wraps around her, escorting her to reverie, Chloe realizes why it had originally woken her with a jolt—it is the same tune that Hannah sometimes hums. Chloe wonders if she will remember this in the morning.

• • •

Chloe does remember, but doesn't know how to address it. Instead, she spends many hours staring at the nothingness past the front wall of her cell. She can see nothing beyond it—only a black void. Yet it is so bright in here, and it seems to be lit from the outside. There are no traceable light bulbs, like those inside an X-Runner's operating or living chambers. She can see cells as far as her eyes can discern past the left and right walls of her own cell, and as far as she can tell behind her cell as well. There are so many cells behind her that she cannot count them; not without her eyes becoming sore from the strain. Chloe has tried learning the names of some of the women in the cells behind her, but it is harder to hear through those walls. There must be a gap, an invisible darkness, between each of their bright glass walls.

This doesn't explain the front wall. A logical answer is that they are in the first row of this facility, but it is an answer that brings many new questions to mind. To begin with, why can't they see anything there? Sam has no suggestions, and Hannah doesn't understand the question.

"There's no more cells there."

"I know, Hannah, but what is there? Shouldn't something be there?"

"No. It's just the end." Hannah pauses her pacing for a moment, to shoot an inquisitive glance into the darkness. "Do you think my children are there?"

"I don't know, Hannah."

Hannah's eyes turn to Chloe.

"Will you find out? Will you help me find my children?"

"I don't—sure, Hannah. I'll help you find your children.

It's just going to take a little bit of time. But you can wait, can't you? I mean, that's all we do in here. We just wait. Wait for noth—"

"GIRL."

It is Sam. She is standing next to the glass between their cells, her arms crossed, her face set with disapproval.

"Come over here."

Chloe obeys, Hannah's interest lost before she even turns.

"Don't mess with Hannah. You'll break her, and you don't want that weighing on your conscience." Sam's hazel eyes are fixed on Chloe while she proffers her advice, "There's no escaping your conscience in these glass boxes, stuck with your thoughts all day long."

"Is that why you're sad?"

"I'm not sad."

"I heard you last night. You were singing that lullaby, the one Hannah's always warbling."

"I taught it to her. Years ago. When she was normal."

"And when she stopped being normal. Was that your fault?"

"How could it be my fault, Charlize? We're all in this together. But separately, separated by glass walls, by strengths— and by weaknesses. Hannah is weak. I can't be held accountable for her weakness."

Chloe says, "I can see it in Hannah's eyes sometimes, she's still there. She's just hiding somewhere out the back. Why is she hiding?"

"You're too fresh, Charlize. You're not gonna get it till

you've been through it. There's no point my trying to explain it till you have. You should've nearly finished bleeding by now, yeah? Well, it'll start happening soon, and then you'll understand. Then we'll talk. In the meantime, get some rest. You're gonna need it."

Sam speaks with such a finality that Chloe doesn't pursue it further. As Sam turns to continue with more exercises in her cell, Chloe returns to her bench. She needs to think this through some more—and to rest.

# CHAPTER EIGHT

IKKA can't count how many days it's been since she and Veela abandoned her X-Runner. Definitely over a week, perhaps nearly two. She knows for sure their bottles of the X-Runner's dispensable liquid meals ran out around day six, and that even with strict rationing their water store was completely depleted yesterday. There is only so much that two people can carry, and Veela was adamant he bring along much of the useless junk he salvaged from his runner. It has been a source of conflict between them, but in the last seventeen hours, neither of them have had the energy to argue, or even speak at all. They only know that they must find water and, until they do, everything else is irrelevant.

The landscape they have crossed has not varied much. Burnt desert, sparse grey trees, and sporadic boulders. The boulders create good wind coverage for sleeping, but the exposed skin on their faces and hands are lashed with windburn and sunburn from long days walking, searching for any kind of reservoir or real shelter. The outlook for their short-term survival is bleak, yet Ikka is certain leaving the X-Runner was the right choice. Even in her current, heat-induced delirium, she is aware that the small weight she felt cinching her innards her entire life (or what she thought was her entire life) is now gone. Or at least, its grip is relaxed. She still feels unbalanced inside.

As they trudge in silence, Ikka surveys the horizon and her peripheries take stock of Veela's body language. She's not sure how much longer he'll last. He may be stronger than she is, but the lack of food resources has depleted his energy stores faster. His footsteps are faltering more and more often, and he is refusing any assistance. She suspects he may have given her more water in the final rationing doses. Idiot. Now instead of being on equal footing, there is a chance Ikka will have to leave him behind.

Ikka's eyes catch sight of something in the distance. Little bumps of grey scattered across the horizon, covered in smatterings of green. She strains her eyes through the desert haze. The lumps take on a more defined shape—hills. They are small, but definitive. Hosting trees with green foliage; it is the most green she has seen in one place for as long as she can remember. The tree line is approximately four miles away; Ikka knows if they can make it there, she'll be able to leech water from the trees. At the pace she and Veela are walking, they won't make it there until well in the afternoon, meaning they'll have to continue through the heat of the midday sun which is approaching its peak above them. She wonders if their bodies can risk losing the fluids they'll sweat out in the coming hours. There is no choice in the matter though, they either try, or they sit down and wait to die.

Minutes pass, hours expire. Ikka has not looked in Veela's direction for over an hour, but she measures his pace by gauging the toiling of his shadow beside her. She is concerned by how much his steps have lagged since she first spotted the horizon. There is perhaps only one mile left, but his feet are now barely lifting off the ground, and she hardly has the strength to move her own. Carrying him is out of the question, but it seems she may soon have to try. Ikka gulps. The desert dust is doing its best to work its way down her nostrils, and she has to snort to keep it out. It deflects on the air spouts into her eyes, lining her lashes, causing her eyes to blink multiple times and fill with water. She raises a fingertip to wipe the droplets away, but catches herself, instead drawing them to her lips. They are salty, and as they dissolve onto her tongue she is transported elsewhere. Away from the hot sand, burning her feet through the base of her boots.

No, she isn't in the desert anymore. She's in a climate controlled room. Cool, stagnant air caresses her skin—all of her skin. She's completely exposed, chained by her lower torso to the ground of a bright, stark cell. And she's crying.

• • •

Thirteen year old Ikka is terrified.

It's so bright her eyes can hardly focus on the space around her. She knows where she is, though. She has been trapped inside this space for so long that she can see all of its details with her eyes closed. It's her prison cell, a white box with glass walls. Through the walls she can see other women. They are all sad—distressed, catatonic, depressed. They never smile. Ikka also never smiles. Instead, she sobs, tears always staining her cheeks.

Through the tears she can feel aching; the dull aching of her head, the vacant aching of her heart, the painful aching of her legs. There is a space inside her that screams in constant pain. She cannot see it, cannot touch it with her hands. There is metal—cold, hard, persistent—acting as a barrier between her and this place. Every day beneath this wall her body is attacked, brutalised by an unseen villain. Ikka cannot stop it. None of the women have been able to stop it.

Today is different. The device doesn't launch its assault. Ikka sits on the floor of her jail, quivering in fear, waiting for the attack to come. She hears a strange hissing from the other women's cells. Ikka watches in confusion as their heads all start to droop, and as all of the bright lights fade to black. In the darkness she is blind, and she is terrified, scared of what is to come.

• • •

A gust of wind smashes sand against Ikka's eyes, awakening her from her reverie. She has had moments like these—awake and functioning, yet dreaming—many times since the incident in her X-Runner. Each time they feel more real, but she can't reconcile with them as reality. Yet, despite her apprehension, there is a nagging, deep in the darkness inside her, like hands wrapped viciously around her stomach. It knows.

"Heeeeeeey, buddy." Veela's voice croaks through the static air. "I have this hunch, that, yeah, I think it's best if you maybe go on without me."

Ikka turns her head in time to see Veela's knees impact

with the ground, and his pack topple him face forward into the ground. She is concerned for him, but a wry smile crosses her lips. She mutters under her breath,

"I bet you regret bringing all that useless crap now, hey, buddy."

She steps over to him and gently kicks his side with her left foot.

"Veela, rest time's over. We've got to get going."

He doesn't respond, so she kicks him a little harder.

"Veela, come on."

His body lies there in incompetent silence. Ikka grits her teeth and slides to her knees, reaching over and turning him onto his back. She pries his left eye open, then his right, but neither offer any reaction. She frowns and leans her face in close to his. Her left ear hovers over his mouth, so intimate that his scrappy facial hairs scratch her cheek. She holds her own breath for a moment, straining her ears to their limits. And then she hears it, a faint whistle over cracked lips. She sits up, resting her hand on his chest to monitor his breaths as she thinks. If her wary participation in The Race has prepared her for anything, it is relying on no one other than herself.

She empties the contents of both their packs, ruthlessly dividing out anything other than the bare minimum required for survival. She condenses the remaining items into one pack, and ties the empty water canisters to hang on its outside. She is about to navigate shouldering the bag when her eyes pause on Veela's trinkets. Most of them she has no issue discarding, but the small box catches her eye. She would love to remove its existence from her life, but she knows that there are answers inside it she can't risk abandoning.

Ikka shoulders the pack and, knees bent, lifts Veela's ineffectual body up so his face hangs in front of hers. She scoops under his legs with her right arm, and supports his shoulders with her left. It is an excruciating strain, but she reminds herself there is no alternative option. One mile left. She takes the first step. Then the second. She estimates there are roughly two thousand to go. Maybe it'll help if she counts them down.

• • •

The sun blisters down on the rocky desert floor as Ikka limps along, shouldering her own and Veela's weight. Her voice carries like a gentle whisper rasping on the wind as her feet plod forward.

"One hundred and thirty five. One hundred and thirty four."

A section of her hair has escaped its holdings in her bun, and flays at the side of her face.

"One hundred and thirty three."

The renegade hairs move like independent appendages, seeking entry to her eyes, her nostrils, her mouth.

Ikka can feel herself being pulled down, hundreds of malicious vines dragging her to the ground.

Ikka stumbles, nearly tumbling Veela out of her arms. A pang sings out from the hidden place inside her, an echo of forgotten pain. She tries to shake it out of her mind, but it remains a physical presence in her body. Wind lashes sand against her skin and the pain sears stronger, dropping her and Veela's bodies to the ground.

She screams, but the women in the other cells don't hear

her.

On the desert floor, Ikka coughs and sputters. She can see the tree line, offering them salvation, maybe two hundred and fifty feet away. She wills herself to stand, but at this point even her will is not strong. The leaden weight of her limbs refuses to become upright again. She tries to shake Veela awake, if only he could rise to carry them this final distance. He does not, and Ikka's neck becomes heavy, forgetting how to hold her own head.

She cannot fight back. They are too strong. She has no hope.

Sweat stings Ikka's eyes, and she can no longer hold them open. Her lip curls at the injustice of her final moments; confused, bleeding from an unremembered wound, cradling the chest of a fool such as Veela. She would never have believed that this would be her end.

She should have met her end a long time ago.

# CHAPTER NINE

CHLOE is sitting on her bench, eyes closed, trying to visualise the outside world—imagining herself experiencing the joys of The Race. She can feel sunlight on her skin, and hot wind streaming past her face as the X-Runner hurdles across the desert. She can hear rocks and logs pass underneath the tires, and the low rumble of the X-Runner engine humming to life. Except it's not the X-Runner engine. The rumble is not part of her visualisation. It's the metal diaper.

Chloe's eyes snap open. The diaper has never resonated at this frequency before. It's not the water or air suction pipes vibrating this time. It's the larger one, the heaviest of the pipes with the diameter of five inches. It's vibrating in pulses of three seconds with two second intervals, and it sounds as though it's warming up for something. Two smaller pipes, those with which Chloe is yet to identify tasks, also start to hum. The combined vibrations of the pipes begin to shake her entire body as she sits on the bench. It becomes too uncomfortable to sit, so she stands.

As she stands, she can hear a shrill, high-pitched whistle. It is followed by a sharp stabbing sensation on one of the outer lips of her vagina. Whatever stabbed her retreats as quickly as it surfaced, but a tingling sensation remains where it pierced her skin. The tingling spreads as the vibrations continue to intensify. It takes Chloe a few moments to realize the intention of the jab—it's a local anaesthetic. It seems counter productive. The tingling and resulting bizarre numbness are making her more aware of all the sensations taking place. And more paranoid, too.

The diaper appears to be expanding where it meets each of her inner thighs, pushing her legs farther apart. It stops after a couple of inches—enough to make standing difficult and closing her legs impossible.

And then there is a single, solitary splash.

A thick residue, warmer than water, drips off her lips and vaginal opening.

A grating sound of metal on metal echoes out, and then, Chloe can feel it.

Cold. Hard. Persistent.

Forcing its way inside.

A place where she's never felt space before is being filled; slowly, tediously, it inches its way inside. With each inch it hurts more, and Chloe's face feels more flushed. The pit of her stomach feels ill. The vibrations are shaking her whole body now, their pressure too much for her legs to bear. She begins to fall, reaching out for the bench, for the wall. Her hands miss both; she lands on the floor with a metallic twang. It can hardly be heard over the machinery.

Then it stops. The metal thing inside her. It stops

moving.

And then a new sound starts.

From one of the smaller pipes, there is a hissing of hydraulics.

The metal thing inside her moves. The anaesthetic is useless this deep inside; she can feel everything. The metal thing contracts like a syringe, injecting her with a fluid. This part is not painful, but unnerving.

A moment of silence follows. Chloe can hear only her breaths.

And then it pulls out, faster than is comfortable. The unknown space is empty again, but it no longer feels unknown. Chloe can hear the machinery folding itself away, back into the pipes, and then the familiar water flush resonates, followed by the pulse of warm air.

And then the diaper is silent again. Inanimate. But not harmless.

• • •

It takes some time for Chloe to realize that she is crying. The flesh surrounding her eyes is so swollen that it hurts to close them, so she can't even shut out the oppressive brightness of this prison. And it is a prison, barbaric in its unflinching disregard. She hasn't moved since the machine withdrew. Lying on the cold ground of the cell, her body is rigid. She has no willpower to move; wherever she moves the device will follow. But if she lies still enough, maybe she can pretend it's no longer there. Maybe it will dissolve into the air, chasing after the last traces of her joy.

Her left arm is aching, presumably strained in the fall. She does not look at it, does not try to move it. The space inside her, the one she's never felt before, is refusing be silenced. Being aware of this point, now that it's been so clinically invaded, makes her entire body feel out of balance. She has been robbed of her centre of gravity. It is definitely best to stay still. The local anaesthetic is beginning to wear off. She can feel, at the opening, a throbbing ache. It feels like the time she fell and grazed her knee, the skin torn from her flesh. And it is only starting to intensify. Stinging pain is singing out, she can tell that it is going to become operatic.

As she lies still, focusing on her breathing—in, out, in, out, slowly—she becomes aware of the cells beside her. Sam is at the far side of her room, doing push-ups, eyes cast into the ground. Hannah is also at the far side of her room, peering into a corner, head turned away from Chloe's cell. Are they allowing her privacy or are they just blocking out her shame? Chloe does not know what she could have expected from them, but she feels abandoned by them both. And then she sees the young girl, in the cell past Hannah's, peering at her with pity. The girl doesn't look away this time when she feels Chloe's gaze. She holds it, silent in solidarity. A small gesture, no promises or empty words attached, but it is comforting. They hold this connection, until Chloe's body gives up functioning and passes out.

• • •

Chloe is not sure if it is the same day when she regains consciousness. She returns to the bench and notices that her left arm is now wrapped tight. Peering into the cells beside her, Chloe can see that both Hannah and Sam are awake. It does not take long for Sam to register her eye movement and try to engage with her. Chloe doesn't take heed of what she's saying,

has no interest in deciphering the muted tones invading through
the glass walls. She closes her eyes and waits. Sleep will have to
come again soon.

• • •

Once the next day definitely arrives, Chloe still has no
inclination to move from her post on the bench. Her arm is
throbbing beneath the wrapping and her opening still feels raw.
Sam very quickly observes her consciousness and moves to the
connecting wall to talk to her. Chloe doesn't acknowledge her,
but this time she lets the words form meanings in her brain.

"Charlize. You're going to have to get up soon or you'll
get too stiff and it'll hurt next time you try. Hurt more, I mean."

Chloe doesn't respond.

"You're gonna need to eat soon. Why don't you at least
walk over to your feeder, eat something, and then you can rest
again. You don't have to talk to me. Just eat something. I'm not
gonna leave you alone 'til you do."

Despite the concern conveyed in the message, Sam's
voice is still gruff. Chloe wonders is she knows what tenderness
is. Wonders if she would even accept it from this woman, the one
who looked away. But Sam is right, Chloe needs to eat. She can't
tell at what point her insides stop feeling weak from being
violated and start feeling weak due to hunger. She sits upright
and descends from her bench. Shifting her weight onto her feet
sends a burst of pain up to her arm. She ignores it and walks
resolutely to the feeder. Sam continues to talk and Chloe
continues to refuse her audience.

She wraps her mouth around the feeder. It is a
disgusting consistency of mushed greens that finds its way into

her throat, but the flavour is not dissimilar to that of the liquid meals distributed in The Race. She manages a few gulps before she has to stop, coughing and spluttering. Even a day without food has conditioned her body to be wary of its consumption. She tries again, taking a few more mouthfuls before it happens.

The hum. The machine in the diaper. It begins again.

• • •

Chloe cannot believe it is happening again, and so soon. But the vibrations, and the shaking they elicit from her limbs, cannot be ignored. She whips her neck around, stares with anger at Sam.

"How is this happening again?"

Sam is unperturbed. She says, "It's a part of the process, Charlize. It's going to happen every day until they're certain you've been impregnated. You have to stay calm, learn how to deal with it, and help it pass easily. Don't make it harder than it has to be."

*Don't make it harder than it has to be.*

The words send a flush of rage burning across Chloe's forehead. She wants to smash through the glass wall and throttle Sam's neck, extinguish all the life from those stoic hazel eyes. And she wants to cover Hannah's mouth, silence the warbled non-melody that is mocking her in this moment through the walls, and cover her nose, prevent noise from ever coming out of her shelled being again. But the vibrations of the diaper rip her from her thoughts. She falls to the ground almost immediately. There is no strength in her to stand while the mechanism is at its work. She crouches helpless, listening to its machinations.

High pitched whistle.

Sharp stab.

Tingling.

Expansion.

Splash.

Metal against metal.

Cold inside, pushing.

Pushing.

Pushing.

Silence.

Hydraulics.

Contraction.

Exit.

Water flush.

Air dry.

Silence.

She spends the entire process with her back against the wall, her eyes staring up at Sam. She tries to find an anchor in Sam's gaze, a lifeline to hold onto, but there is none present. Her mind returns to the murderous thoughts, to the beautiful dream of violence, but it is not entirely sustainable. She is in no position, as a gangly child of eleven with a metal diaper violating her so completely, to inflict any kind of damage on anyone.

As quickly as it started, the device shuts down and the violation ceases. The rage abandons Chloe, and she instead feels embarrassed, gazing up at Sam. It is humiliating, in the presence of such a controlled woman, to be so weak. She begins to cry, and it is at this point that Sam finally turns away from her.

• • •

Sam turns away from her, but after a moment's pause she

turns back around. For the first time, her voice almost sounds gentle.

"Stand up, Charlize. Can you try?"

Chloe nods, as tears sting her cheeks. She uses her right arm to push against the wall behind her, as a propellant to help her knees bend and take her weight, as well as the diaper's. She manages to bend-stand, her upper torso hunched forward, and take a step. On her second step, her left foot catches on the tubing and the motion tosses her face first, back to the floor. As she lifts her face towards Sam, she can feel swelling on the left side of her jaw.

The left side of her body feels forsaken. Left leg, twisted in tubing, a bruise forming on the knee even underneath its bandage. Left arm, torn inside its wrapping. Left jawbone grazed and enflamed with swelling. Her right limbs by nature are attached to these failures and unable to stand free, her breasts taking too much weight as they are pressed into the floor. The coldness burns her nipples, forming yet another burden for her to bear. And her eyes, red from the salt of her tears, want to retreat—like they have seen Hannah's do. To go back inside her mind, down the back, away from the realities of this present.

Sam sees all this. She kneels down next to the glass wall and talks in more soothing tones.

"It's okay. Just try untwisting your leg from the tubing. You can do it. Okay, now use your right arm to pull yourself this way—try pushing with your feet to help. You can do it, Charlize. Okay. Now try sitting up, use the wall to rest your back. There you go. Let's just sit like this for a while, shall we?"

Sam turns herself around to rest with her back against

the wall as well, not so they are back to back, but next to each other, heads able to turn and look at each other if they choose.

"I'll sit here with you as long as you need, Charlize. I'll stay quiet if you want, but I won't leave you."

"No."

Through the salt water and the puffed up flesh, Chloe can see hardly anything in front of her other than the whiteness of her cell. She needs Sam's voice to hold on to.

"No. Please talk."

"Okay. Well, we're going to have to get you training again soon. Not right this minute, but soon. We need to stop you getting injured all the time. It's going to be an issue for you if you get the chance to escape, if you have broken limbs and torn muscles."

"Is that actually going to happen?"

"What?"

"A chance to escape. Have you ever had one before?"

Sam is silent for a beat too long—Chloe lets the heavy folds of her eyelids close in resignation of the word to come.

"No."

A tear pushes its way out from under Chloe's lashes, finding slow passage down her cheek.

"But I've heard of a woman, in the cells to our far left. She almost made it out once. She was five across, two back. When I was in my fourth year here, just after my third pregnancy. She was an *H*. Hannah Betty Maria 04. I guess that's why I expected so much of Hannah, pushed her so hard with her training. I thought if they came from the same line, the same Hannah Betty Maria, then they must have the same genes, and she might be able to do the same as H-B-M-0-4, maybe better. But she didn't."

"The same line?"

"Your number, how do you think it was assigned?"

"I don't know. The race facilitators just assigned it to me when my dad and I enrolled."

"Can you remember that?"

"What?"

"The day you signed up? Can you remember signing up to The Race, can you remember The Race beginning?"

"Yes... Well, no. All the days are kind of blurred into one. There was so much going on every day and the days were so long, by the time it was evening I'd forget what I'd been doing in the morning."

"Yes, because you were being drugged. You've been in The Race your whole life, Charlize, ever since you were assigned to your father as a child. Is your race number, very different to his?"

"I guess. He's I-S-S-0-4."

"And if you had started The Race at the same time—together—don't you think you would have been assigned similar numbers? You were racing together after all, as a team. Why do you think they were so different?"

"I don't... I never thought about it."

"No, because you were being drugged. Long-term memory loss. Our numbers have nothing to do with The Race, other than the fact that the organisers of The Race are the same as the facilitators of this farm. Our numbers are codes to track our genetic histories. My number is S-A-M-1-4. So I am the

14th child of Maria who was the child of Amy who was the child of Sarah. Which means that Hannah, our Hannah, and the woman who almost escaped, were both daughters of the Maria who was the daughter of Betty who was the daughter of Hannah, but eight births apart. Do you understand?"

"They're sisters?"

"That's why I thought Hannah might have a good chance of escaping too, if they shared the same genes."

Sam goes silent for another moment, mourning a buried wound. Chloe tries to grapple with the premise that she has spent her whole life in The Race. It is unfathomable, even in light of her recent entrapment.

"How could I not know?"

"Have you been listening, Charlize? I keep telling you. You've been drugged your whole life. Similar to the gas they use when they want to put us to sleep, I think, except excreted in your racing vehicle to wipe your long-term memory. Since birth. Since you were taken from here. It's unlikely she's still alive, but your mother, she would have been here, in a cell like ours, somewhere else in the facility. You would have been born here, and then taken, and at some point paired with your father in The Race. Just like at some point he was born here, then taken, then paired with a different father in The Race. I don't know if there's a time, between birth and The Race, or if the babies are immediately put into it after birth. I can't remember from my own experience, and neither can any of the women I communicate with in the channels. We just remember racing, maybe a month of racing, and then we were moved here, and suddenly we can remember every day in too much excruciating detail, one day after the next after the next. I don't know why they don't wipe our memories here. It wouldn't be the worst thing, to not know how long you've been here, to not remember the feeling when they take your newborns away."

Sam pauses for a moment, her eyes glazed over with sadness.

Chloe whispers, "Have you had many babies?"

Sam sighs, running a hand through her matted, brown hair.

"You don't want to know how many I have had. Too many to name, except in here—" Her index finger points to her temple. "What's sad is even though I know they're going to get taken, I always get attached. I crave for those moments, between birth and theft, when I get to hold my child. To stare into their beautiful eyes is the most wonderful feeling. And then they get taken, ripped out of my life. These last few births, I've gotten stronger, able to hold on to them even as the facilitators try to pry them from my arms. So my last birth, they wouldn't even let me look into my child's eyes. I don't even know if I had a boy or a girl. I just know there was a life, a precious, glorious life I'd been nurturing inside me, and they came into existence, and I didn't even get to look at them before they were gone. Can you even imagine how that feels? I loved them from the moment I felt them inside me, and then they were gone. Like they all are. Gone to The Race. It's... I'm sorry." Sam's voice begins to trail off, following her thoughts. "This isn't what you need to be hearing right now."

"No," Chloe sniffs, wiping her nose with the back of her hand. "Tell me about Hannah, the other Hannah. How did she almost escape?"

Sam wipes her own nose, her posture stiffening as she returns to her strong woman defence.

"It's hard to know exactly, the way information is passed through the cells. There are always things lost in the translation from one cell to the next. What I've gathered is that H-B-M-0-4 was very strong. She found a way to destroy the machine and tunnel out of her cage. But an alarm was set off and the facilitators descended, shutting the whole thing down. She was stunned badly and afterwards, when everything had calmed down and she'd woken up, she couldn't remember any of it. She never attempted escape again. That was years ago now. I've tried so many times to find flaws in that thing, with no success. I can't work out how she did it."

"Then why are you still training?"

"Just in case. I don't want to miss the chance if one arises."

"But how long have you been here, Sam? You've been training for so long already. What can you possibly be hoping will happen that hasn't already?"

"I just… I have to always be ready. And the fitter I am, the stronger I am, the easier my pregnancies are. I'm sure it's better for my children, too, when I'm stronger."

"Better for your children?"

"Yes, Charlize, my children. I have to give them the best chance at surviving. I have to be my best for them, so they can be as healthy and strong as possible."

"So they can live through this life?" Chloe pauses to consider the thought, consider her current physical predicament.

She has long since stopped crying, but the flesh around her eyes is sore from the effort, the flesh along her jaw is throbbing from her fall, and she is doing her best to ignore the screaming of raw flesh in her now known place.

"Do you really think a life of suffering through this is better than no life at all? It's not... It's not better for your children Sam. It's not better for any of us."

• • •

It takes a few days, but the swelling around Chloe's jaw and knee begins to dissipate, and she is able to start training again. She manages to surpass the strength resistance level she was at before the first attack, and Sam watches on proudly, eliciting tips and demonstrations wherever she can. There have been three more events since then, five total. They occur once daily, but never at the same point in the days.

Chloe has learnt to lie on the cell floor the moment the machinery whirs to life to avoid further falls and tumbles. Her now-known place has been rubbed so raw from the repeated violations that it is continuously stinging, and the external physicality of the attacks is no longer registering with the nerves in that area. She is training now, not to be like Sam—not in the spirit of being prepared for a virtually nonexistent chance, or of being healthier and fitter to help whatever creature the machinery brings into genesis within her. No, she is training so she will be able to create her own chance, to orchestrate her own escape. She may be only eleven, but she is determined.

This will not be her life.

# CHAPTER TEN

IN THE DARKNESS, Ikka can feel the creatures chasing her down. No matter which way she turns, their limbs shoot forward, pulling her back to the ground. They pin her in place, pawing at her skull, binding her torso, pulling her feet behind her even as she struggles to her knees. She doesn't understand what they want, but she knows they have no interest in keeping her alive. And then a roughness, bristled and slimy all at once, forces its way inside her mouth, travelling down her throat, choking her.

Ikka coughs. She is so dehydrated that her larynx cannot complete the action. She splutters, the air scratching her vocal nodules, and a hand brings a small bowl of water to her mouth. It is not her hand, nor Veela's. It is pale, like it has spent its lifetime unacquainted with the sun, and it belongs to a man named Delu. Ikka knows this, because he has been talking to her as she has dozed in and out of consciousness. His voice has been inviting her to a safe place, even as the far reaches of her mind have been pulling her inwards to a dark gloom. He smiles as he registers her alert state, a kind curve that moves like a gentle ripple across his face. He looks younger than her and Veela, though there is a sadness in his light brown eyes that ages his energy. He has two long braids of sandy brown hair cascading behind his head, and trinkets of old stones and cables adorning his wrists and neck. Beside him is another man, one or two decades older, with a larger stature and gruff bemusement on his face. He is also pale, but wiry hairs cover all his skin, darkening his complexion a little. He has a scar across his left eye, preventing it from seeing. He is the first one to speak.

"Yer awake now, eh? We're been wondering how long it would take yer. I'm Gaarwine, this is Delu. We're been looking after yer."

Delu says, "Your companion is also fine. He woke some time ago, but he is sleeping again now."

Ikka tilts her head to acknowledge their words, her eyes scanning about for Veela. They are in a thicket amongst trees, slender boughs of brown swooping over them, protecting them from the sun. The ground is thick with branches, moss, and fallen leaves. Gentle whispers of wind blow at their limbs, reminding Ikka's nerves that her skin is burnt from her desert sojourn. She winces, and Delu reaches forward to help her into an upright position.

He says, "Your body is still healing. Your companion's as well. See, he is here."

Ikka tilts her head again, and her eyes appraise Veela's body on the ground behind her. Like her, he is resting on a bed of leaves and a thin blanket, grey and distressed with age. She recognises the faded markings on its edging. It's from an X-

Runner.

"So, yer going to tell us yer name or what?"

Gaarwine speaks roughly but there is a grin on his face.

Ikka tilts her head again, considering her words. "My name is Ikka. My companion, Veela. I—you must understand, I'm a bit disorientated. This is a lot to take in."

"Mus' we?"

"Come now, Gaarwine, play nice." Delu smiles at Ikka, another ripple of kindness dancing across his face. "You needn't be so wary, Ikka. We only wished to save your lives, and now our natural curiosity has taken over. It is so very rare to see people abstaining from The Race. Would you indulge us a little, while we wait for your companion to wake? We would very much like to hear your story."

Ikka is saved from indulging them by the arrival of a third man. He is whistling as he enters the thicket, a satchel brimming with flora upon his shoulders. He is in his early twenties, with curly dark brown hair swinging in short stalks above his shoulders as he walks. His body comes to a standstill when he sees Ikka awake and watching him. His face is nervous, twitching as she assesses him. Delu fills the silence.

"Chiyo, this is Ikka. Ikka, Chiyo."

Ikka offers a stiff nod, Chiyo a timid smile. He looks to Delu and Gaarwine for some kind of rescue, but none is forthcoming. Chiyo is forced to fill the silence himself, rummaging through his knapsack, casting sideways glances at Ikka as he speaks to Delu and Gaarwine.

"I've found everything on the list. Should be enough to keep the Settlement going for at least a few more months. The

Elders weren't clear on how long it would be until they approved another excursion, so I kind of overcompensated with some of the medicinal items. Better prepared than dead, right?"

Chiyo offers a cheeky grin at this point, which Delu and Gaarwine accept but do not return. They begin asking the younger man for details on what was procured, and where; he obliges by showing the contents of the overbrimming satchel. Inside there are all different species of roots, nuts, and plant cuttings, which he handles with great care. As the three men discuss whether or not any of the provisions should be increased, Ikka pries inside her racer jacket for the longest of her blades— the twelve-incher. With swift movements, she reaches forward, placing the blade at Chiyo's throat with nonchalance.

Her voice is steady as she demands of Delu and Gaarwine, "Tell me who you are."

Delu stops Gaarwine from springing forward with the raise of a hand, and locks his eyes onto Ikka's.

"We have told you, Ikka, I am Delu, this is Gaarwine, and the man you currently threaten is Chiyo. There's no need for violence. Please, ask us what you wish to know and we will answer all."

"Why aren't you in The Race?"

"We chose long ago to leave The Race. We haven't participated in it for many, many years," Delu says.

"Years?" Ikka presses the blade a little tighter against Chiyo's neck, her eyes searching Delu and Gaarwine for any glimmer of falsehood. "The Race hasn't been running for that long."

"It has!" The voice of Chiyo squeaks at her from within

her grasp. "Please put your knife down. We're not going to hurt you."

Chiyo's fear resonates with Ikka's consciousness, speaking to her long suppressed fears. Her blade hand drops, and she collapses on the ground behind her. She looks up at the three wary men before her.

"Please, tell me everything."

Delu says, "We came upon you two by chance only. We are on a harvesting mission for our home Settlement, where we do not have access to plant life such as these. On our lunch rest yesterday, we spied you in the distance—when you collapsed, we decided to intervene. Yes, you have been sleeping since yesterday. Your bodies were very weary from your journey."

"Why intervene?"

Gaarwine chuckles, "Why intervene? Ye'd be dead if we hadn't!"

Ikka says, "It would have been far less inconvenient to you than carrying us here, and seeing to our recovery. What are we to you?"

Gaarwine shakes his head in amazement. "I think she would've rather we left 'em to die!"

"So it would seem." Delu appeals to Ikka in solemn tones. "Gaarwine and I do not believe in letting others die needlessly. I can see it is not in you to trust others, Ikka, but please, trust in this. We know what it is you are going through— we have been through it ourselves. All three of us were once in The Race, and understand your need to be free from it. That is what our home is—a sanctuary from The Race, and seeing you yesterday, we knew it was sanctuary you were seeking."

"Sanctuary from what?"

Delu says, "That is what I am most curious to learn from you, Ikka. What drove you to your exile?"

Ikka's eyes do not look away from Delu, but a wall behind them closes.

"You said years, before."

"Yes. Thirty for Gaarwine and myself. Twelve for Chiyo."

Ikka's eyes flick over to the other two men, staring them both in the eye to find any tells of untruth. She sees none, but before she can respond, Veela's voice croaks into the fray.

"Twenty years? Buddy, I hate to break it to you, but I'd say you're not very good at counting then! There's no way The Race has been going on that long."

Veela sits upright behind Ikka's left shoulder. She casts a sideways glance at him as Delu speaks.

"I am afraid it is not. Tell me, can you remember anywhere you ever called home, a location before The Race?"

Veela shakes his head, and Ikka frowns as her mind travels back inside itself.

Delu continues, "And have you, either of you, ever had a memory that extends past your immediate present? Something other than the daily facts presented to you in The Race?"

Veela narrows his eyes, trying to grasp a memory. He opens his mouth to speak, then closes it, turning to ponder Ikka for a moment. He says, "Now that you mention it, no... I can remember the past few weeks travelling with this one in full clarity, but before that all I can really remember is driving. Flashes of desert. Hills. Boulders. Campfires with changing faces.

But nothing—"

"Tangible." Ikka finishes the sentence for him. "Nothing solid to latch on to. Just fragments."

"She even forgot me."

"You claim I forgot you."

"You did."

"Maybe." Ikka shrugs. "Maybe you weren't worth remembering."

"Hey!" Veela feigns outrage, swatting at Ikka's shoulder; an action she deflects, before using her blade-free hand to shove him to the side. This exchange relaxes the group. Even Chiyo grins at the charade, comforted by the break in Ikka's countenance. But his grin does not last for long—a new threat descends down upon them.

Thwack—thwack—thwack—thwack—thwack.

Where once there was only the sound of wind passing through trees, an engine far louder than that of an X-Runner descends down upon them. Delu, Gaarwine, and Chiyo scramble for their belongings, packing everything they can reach as fast as possible into their packs. Ikka takes their cue, lacing up her racing boots and preparing to run. Veela sits, stupefied, unable to comprehend what is happening. Ikka lifts him up by his shoulders.

She shouts, "Don't you dare make me carry you again."

Veela nods, his eyes searching the canopy above them for the source of the noise. He shouts to Delu, "What is it?"

Delu and Gaarwine exchange words they cannot hear, but then Gaarwine grabs Veela by the shoulders.

"Ye'r with me! We don't 'ave much time before they get

closer. We 'ave to get to the Settlement."

Veela looks back to Ikka, but she is already gone, running at speed with Delu and Chiyo down a different trail.

• • •

They sprint through the forest, their strides urgent and powerful. The pursuant sound stalks them even as the ground passing beneath their feet changes colour, density, and orientation. The trees become tighter, blocking out more and more of the sun, and the air becomes stickier, like a layer of cobwebs wrapping around their skin. They are not running aimlessly—Ikka can see Delu is keeping score of their path, following signposts hidden to her eyes—but they are running urgently, desperate to survive.

The drone of the engine advances on them, ever closer to their heels. It is a thunderous, discordant roar, dispersed with deep swooshing as their mechanical assailant siphons in large chunks of air. This they not only hear, but also feel. The air pulls at their skin, hair, and clothes, attempting to lift them off their feet. Chiyo is wrought with panic, his boyish face visibly paled, his eyes shooting apprehensive looks to the sky above their heads. Delu remains focused, even as the ends of his braids raise above his ears. Ikka forces herself to stay calm, unflinching in this bizarre situation. But then Delu leads them right into the middle of a clearing, a clearing where they are completely exposed. It is here that Ikka has her first sighting of the airships.

There are two of them, each larger than two X-Runners combined. They are blinding, silver ovals of destruction. The air immediately below the ships takes on a hazy quality, like a layer of fog beginning to vibrate, and a new tone emits from the ships.

It is lower than 60 hertz, and as soon as it is heard, Delu, Chiyo, and Ikka's bodies begin to slow down. Their limbs feel weighed down by rocks, the blood in their veins replaced with cement. Delu calls something back to Chiyo and Ikka, an urging, Ikka thinks, to reach the other side of clearing. It is as if her mind is moving at quarter speed, and her body even slower.

The deep tone grows louder, and the haze of air descends lower. It has now expanded so much that its bottom edge is nearing the top of Ikka's head. She does not want to know what will happen once it reaches her skull. Delu makes it to the far trees, wrapping one arm around a tree trunk, another searching the nearby ground. He lets go of the tree, dropping to his knees and crawling into the bush. Ikka wonders if she is imagining this, her brain feels so heavy that it may be backfiring. She is near the end of the clearing now, eight more feet to go. And then she hears Chiyo shout.

Just three feet behind her, his feet are beginning to lift off the ground. The haze from the ship has a hold of him, pulling him from his nose up. His short stalks of hair are all standing on their ends, and the skin above his eyes is being sucked upwards, so the folds of flesh above and below his eye sockets are being drawn up an inch higher than where they normally sit. Ikka shouts to Delu, and then runs back to Chiyo.

She grabs him around his waist, dragging him earthwards. She can feel her long brown hair floating up above her ears, its roots wishing to disengage from her skull. She fights through the pain, pushing Chiyo's body against the force of the haze and across the clearing. Delu is watching them, a rope poised in his hands. He tosses it out to them, and the end slaps against Ikka's wrist. She lunges for it, looping it around Chiyo's mid-section, pushing him as Delu pulls. As they reach the limit of the haze's grasp, the extreme bass of the drone clings on to them, sending waves of nausea down their spines. Delu gives a forceful yank, and they manage to break through the haze, falling to the ground. They crawl forward, the threatening vibrations of the haze still present above their heads. And then they fall.

• • •

The fall is abrupt. Where once there was ground, there is vacancy, and then the harsh slap of air exiting their lungs as they slam against a new layer of earth. There is no time to absorb their surroundings, only the sharp jabbing of rocks into their hands and knees to indicate the rough and raw nature of the earth beneath them. They crawl forward in the dark, the menacing drone of the airships stalking them from above, their guts and minds free from the menacing grip of the haze.

With time, the sound of the airships fade into the distance, and their eyes begin to adjust to their new surroundings. They are crawling forward in a tunnel burrowed with hands and shovels, not tall enough for a human to stand. Delu and Chiyo are at home in this space, moving through familiar ground, but Ikka is cautious, expecting danger or deceit around each bend. As minutes fade into hours, no new threat appears, only weariness. And then, the prattering tones of Veela's voice come to greet them in the gloom.

He is quite relaxed, talking with Gaarwine in a small chamber where four tunnels intersect. When he sees Delu, Chiyo, and Ikka approach, he grins wide, his teeth and gums exposed as he shows his relief.

"Well there you all are. You sure took your time."

Gaarwine and Delu chuckle at Veela's mirth, but Chiyo is indifferent and Ikka's eyes scowl even though her face remains flat. A few more words are exchanged, before the small troop moves forward down the smallest of the tunnels, inching deeper into the earth. At the end of this tunnel they are greeted by two men who share whispered words with Gaarwine, and then nod, allowing the group of five to continue down tunnels that are tall enough to walk in. The tunnels are a dark blur, a maze of openings and closings and small chambers filled with intersections. This walking tour of silhouetted passages ends with Delu opening a door to a small room, indicating for Ikka and Veela to enter.

He says, "Rest here tonight. We will be back to fetch you in the morning, and then you can meet the others in the Settlement."

Veela scoffs, "Morning? How can you even be sure it's night right now?"

"Well, Veela," Gaarwine says, "It's just something yer body gets used to. Try not to annoy Ikka too much tonight, I'd hate to see yer pretty face all sliced up in the morning."

Gaarwine chuckles as he closes the wooden door to the chamber. Veela turns to Ikka in the darkness.

"Why is it nobody's concerned about my being shut in a room with a knife-wielding maniac?"

Ikka squints her eyes at him. "It's because I'm not a maniac, Veela, and even if I was, you take too many liberties."

"And they haven't? Some giant flying attack vessels were hunting us today and then they lead us to some kind of underground maze and shut us in a dark room acting like we should be able to get to sleep no problems, this is all part of a normal day?! This is *not* a normal day. This is *nothing* like a normal day."

When Veela finishes speaking he exhales with a huff, and Ikka has to fight back a smile.

"I've been debating similar thoughts. Tell me, are you prepared for the morning?"

"Prepared?"

"Will you be ready to fight, if we need to? As presumptuous and annoying as you act—don't protest, I said *act*—it would be tedious to face an entire Settlement alone."

Veela says, "Well, I've followed you this far, haven't I? I'm not sure I have another choice at this point."

Ikka says, "You always have a choice, Veela. We all do. I don't mean to force anything on you—"

Veela interrupts, "That's not what I meant, buddy. I just... something about that internal compass of yours makes me trust you, one hundred per cent. That's all I'm saying."

Ikka raises her eyebrows in the darkness. She removes her boots and lies down on one of the sleeping mats on the floor, her face staring at the dark ceiling above. Veela takes his cue from her, removing his boots and lying down on the mat next to hers.

"You're not going to respond to that, are you?"

"No." Ikka rolls onto her side, her back towards him. "Some things don't need to be said."

Veela sighs and turns onto his side as well, their backs facing each other in the darkness.

Ikka says, "Veela."

"Yes."

"I'm not sure at what point I stop finding you irritating and at what point I begin to trust you, but I'm glad I'm not alone in this."

It is Veela's turn to incline his head in thought. They lie in silence, with honest acceptance of these facts and each other drifting around them. They fall into quiet reverie, and Veela has his first peaceful sleep in many weeks, and Ikka her first peaceful sleep in many years.

# CHAPTER ELEVEN

IT HAS been seven days since the bleeding ended and the attacks began. Seven days of brutal shame, as the part of her body with which Chloe had never identified is singled out for persecution again and again. Lying in the dark, her naked back against the cold surface of the cell's bench, Chloe is ready. She runs over the plan she has formulated in her head. It is haphazard at best, but worthy of an attempt. Anything is in this situation.

Chloe starts tinkering with the diaper from morning to night. She tests it for stress points, studying each length of tubing for any sign of weakness. She examines the way the tubes move, what directions they are predisposed to coil in, and how strong the welding joining them to the diaper is. She also casts a calculative eye over the other objects in the cell: her body, the bench, and the feeder. The bench is going nowhere fast, and her body is a useless flesh sack. But the feeder—with its dualing pipes hanging down from the ceiling, disappearing into the roof—the feeder has potential. She grabs hold of one mouthpiece, pulling it farther away from the wall. It bends, and bends. She might actually have a chance.

When no one is looking, Chloe slides off her bench and feels the cold metal of the diaper's pipes beneath her finger tips. She follows them, the ridges of the piping's grooves pushing forward like never ending waves beneath her fingertips. She has never seen an ocean before, but as she travels to the tubing's anchor point, it feels as though she is surfing along the water's surface. When she reaches the base, she gropes to feel the meeting point between the pipes and the floor's surface. It feels secure, but she hovers her hand over it for a moment and is duly rewarded.

A breeze.

Faint, but a breeze nonetheless. Below the surface is a way out.

She twists the tubing's ends a little, feeling the tension build and a little more breeze trickle out. She nods her head, to no one but herself, and then slowly crawls back to her bench. She is going to be ready tonight.

• • •

That night, once the others are sleeping, the pads of Chloe's feet descend onto the cool floor of the cell. She tiptoes to the feeder, her feet moving from memory until her eyes adjust. She pauses before it, her ears straining for noise from the other cells—or from somewhere else. The tiny hairs on the back of her neck stand in anticipation, and an impish smile at the prospect of freedom crosses her face. Chloe reaches forward, grabbing hold of the water-delivering mouth tube. She pulls it towards herself, as far as it will come. And then she pushes upwards, bringing it parallel to the ceiling. It protests, small metallic groans emerging from its base. She pushes onwards, her two arms pushing the mouthpiece up high above her head. Small droplets of water trickle down her hands and arms, trying to loosen her grip, but she soldiers on. Finally, she sees it. Small droplets begin to pool at the base of the tube, where it exits the cylinder. Her spirit rallies and she begins swaying the mouth tube back and forth, weakening the connection.

The groaning of the joint grows louder, and Chloe is aware of small movements from the cells beside her. Sam and Hannah have begun watching. It probably won't be long before the facilitators start watching, too. Chloe moves with more force now, jumping up to her full height, and then dropping down into a crouch, her hands yanking the tube with all her body weight. After a few jumps, she is rewarded; the joint snaps. Chloe lunges to the ground, spreading her legs spread wide to allow full access to the diaper. She sits splayed, her left hand holding the metal tubing out from the diaper base at a ninety degree angle, her right hand slamming the sharp, broken edge of the water feeder into the welding connections on the diaper. She bashes it, again and again, working on the smallest of the outside pipes. The water feeder leaves scratches on the surface of the diaper, but there are no dents. Yet.

Chloe keeps working, ignoring the eyes of the women around her. She begins to make progress, small dents forming on the edge of the tubing, but not fast enough. An alarm sounds out—chaotic but quiet—accompanied by the swooshing sound as gas begins to flood her cell and the cells around her.

Chloe whimpers as she keeps punching into the base of the diaper. "No! Not yet!" but before she makes any more progress her lungs are flooded with the invading poison and her body collapses to the ground.

• • •

The next day, Chloe's head is groggy from the gas, her mind barely registering the shining glint of the new feeder, or the eyes considering her from Sam's cell. Yet Sam's voice calls to her.

"That was a good attempt you made, Charlize. I didn't know you had it in you. I don't know what you thought you were going to achieve, but it was a solid effort."

Chloe shoots an injured look in Sam's direction, "I was so close."

"Not really. Did you leave any marks on the diaper?"

Chloe shakes her head, "Only tiny ones."

"Hmm." Sam is doing stretches, stretching out her neck and arms. "I tried something like that once, you know. Breaking the tubes from the diaper. I can't remember what I did—they knocked me out pretty hard after that attempt—but I have vague memories of trying to fall on the ground at an angle that would knock the tubing back against itself. I think I only ended up breaking my leg." Sam's back stiffens, pushing aside the memory of her failure. "We just don't have the right tools in here. But still, maybe one day the facilitators will make a mistake. I'll be ready then."

Warm up stretching now complete, Sam launches into her exercises. Chloe doesn't join her, her eyes focusing on the diaper. She knows she was close, that if she had had more time, eventually enough pressure would have been applied. But she couldn't build momentum, not in such a short space of time. She frowns at her conundrum, and then the diaper hums to life. Its vibrations shake her where she sits, and another idea comes to mind.

# CHAPTER TWELVE

WHEN THE MORNING arrives, it is heralded by sunlight.
Limited in its scope, it illuminates the shabby, straw-lined wall in
front of Ikka's face. It originates from a collection of three shafts,
jutting out of the wall near the ceiling. The thin streams of
sunlight bounce off the pale straw, providing the faintest illusion
of warmth.

Ikka is shivering underneath the thin blanket covering
her. It is one of the fire safety blankets stored as a standard
precaution in X-Runners. They are made out of a durable but
thin fabric, their design purpose not to warm a sleeping human,
but to suffocate any accidental flames. Ikka places the blanket
aside and laces her boots back on. She has to pound them
roughly to break off the dried mud caking them. She wonders
how many weeks she has worn her clothes unwashed, and is
grateful she is too used to her own scent to register the stench
perfuming the cavern around her. She taps Veela on the shoulder.

"Whaaaat? What's going on?"

"It's time to wake up, *buddy*."

"Buddy, heh. Hey, I'm rubbing off on you."

"Unlikely." Ikka reaches down to Veela's discarded boots. "I'm going to look around this place without our hosts limiting our views. You coming?"

She gently tosses the boots to land on Veela's chest and stands to inspect the wooden door. As she listens through the wood Veela laces up his boots, and comes to stand next to her.

"Do you have a plan of attack?"

She offers him a wry smile. "Observation." She opens the door and steps into the cavern. "Come on."

● ● ●

The first room they enter is void of tenants. Over three times the size of the room they slept in, yet it feels like more of a glorified passageway than room. It is lined with doors, all leading to more chambers, all deserted. Each are lit by the same method—a collection of shafts delivering feeble light into the rooms. The main room is lit in an analogous manner, but with many more shafts; below each of these, wooden shelves are holding up rows of root plants and herbs to bask in the light. There is a small table in the middle of the room made from a metal hacked together with old screws and a resin Ikka hasn't seen before. The table feels inordinate amidst the room, it is not long before Ikka realizes why.

"It's made from the outer panels of an X-Runner."

"Hmmf?"

Veela has his head buried in one of the shelves of plants, fossicking for something to eat. He comes up with a pale orange finger, six inches long, one inch thick at the base, tapering to a point at its other end. He slings one over to Ikka as he crunches down hard on the root, his eyes taking in the table.

"Oh, yeah."

Ikka shakes her head at him, but accepts the food, tucking it away into one of her jacket pockets. She motions for him to follow her down the small passageway exiting to the left. It maintains the room's height, but is only three feet wide, and, rather than straw-lined walls, it is sparsely laid with wooden beams to reinforce the mud. It has only one light shaft in its centre. The next room they enter is a crossways; there are three dark tunnels leading out from it. Ikka pauses to listen carefully under the arch of each one. She strains her ears and inhales as deeply as she can, her mind searching for distinguishing scents and sounds in the distance. There are no differing scents between them—only the same mix of damp earth and scant vegetation emitting from each one—so she focuses more keenly on the resonances travelling from the tunnel ends. The air moves in wispy breaths, the heart of the earth pulsing rhythmically in her ears. It is down the third tunnel—the one on the right—that she hears a higher frequency, the faint murmuring of human voices.

With silent steps, she and Veela make their way down it. The tunnel is longer than the previous one, and darker with no light shaft in its centre. After some time, they start to hear the voices with more clarity and steady their steps to a close. They stand in the gloom, listening as a round voice echoes out.

"You say there were two attack vessels?"

"Yer."

Gaarwine's voice. It is uncharacteristically stoic.

"About say, fifty yards from the network's fringe tunnels."

A sharper voice cuts in, "Fifty yards? And you led them to straight to us?"

"Led? Nah, we fled. But they gave up fairly quick, once we were down below. I was a bit worried we were gonna lose one of our visitors in the process though."

The round voice rejoins the fray. On second hearing, it sounds a bit wobbly, belonging to a man in his fifties or sixties, with a fair bit of fat on his jowls.

"And these visitors, how do we know we can trust them? It's all very well bringing them into our settlement to protect them from the airships, but what's to protect us from them? How do you know they're not working with them?"

"Because they are humans." This time it is Delu's quiet voice ringing out. "They came from The Race, like all of us here did originally. They are seeking sanctuary from the same horrors from which we hide. And it is not humans from which we hide."

"Speculation, Delu. Unfounded speculation."

Delu's voice remains steady.

"Even if you still cling to an archaic ignorance of our situation, you cannot deny that these two have the right to seek our protection."

"The right?" The wobbly voice's quivering is exacerbated by this word. "Don't speak so foolishly. It is not up to you to decide who has the right for what."

"Perhaps not, but according to Settlement law the decision does not belong to you either. It belongs to The Mother."

"We should not disturb her for so trivial a matter."

"I disagree. These are exactly the incidences in which her

guidance is required the most."

"He's right, Ocnus." The sharp voice again, "It must be The Mother's decision. It is her right."

"Thank you, Azzam."

"Don't thank me, Delu. I do not speak for your benefit, only for that of the Settlement. The Mother has never led us astray. Isn't that so, Ocnus?"

The wobbly voice answers, having difficulty concealing the reproachful edge to its response, "Very true, Azzam. You bring brevity to our proceedings as always."

"Well if yer three are finished with yer squabbling, I think our guests are standing by, waiting to introduce themselves to yer. Though ye'll have to pardon their appearance. Delu and I are yet to show them to our bathin' facilities, so I reckon they'll be smelling mighty fine right about now... Come on yer two, quit hiding in the shadows."

The room erupts into discordant chatter as the Settlement citizens express surprise at being watched by unknown strangers. It sounds like there are maybe twenty, thirty men in the cavern. Veela shrugs at Ikka as if to say, *What have we got to lose?* and Ikka's narrowed eyes shoot back, *Quite a lot, buddy.* But she starts walking forward, her body language was restrained and unreadable. Veela follows with his casual lope, and is the first to speak when they reach the bright opening, peering past Ikka's right shoulder to address the room of men staring at them.

"What's cracking, fellas? Whoa, there sure are a lot of men in here. I've never seen so many in the one place before!"

His voice echoes out across the room. It is a large cavern,

twelve feet high, twenty feet long, and fourteen feet deep. There are light shafts scattered densely across its ceiling, and a raised stage section on the far right on which three men are seated. The one in the centre, with scraggly brown hair and loose fat hanging off his jowls, is the owner of the wobbly voice, Ocnus. To his right is a leaner man, possibly a little older, with a thinner face and cropped white hair. His brown eyes are so sharp—as is the cut of his beard—that Ikka is sure he must be Azzam. The third man, a short blond haired lad with slanted eyes, sits poised with a quill in his hand, the dumbfounded expression on his face making it clear he has stopped writing mid-sentence to stare at the newcomers.

But it is not just him. All of the men in the room are staring at Ikka in shock. She has not yet noticed, her stealthy eyes consumed with noting all the physical elements that make up the room. In addition to the stage and surprising lack of root vegetation in this chamber, there are five rows of seats, six seats across. Each seat has been uprooted from the racing compartment of an X-Runner—they are the pilot and co-pilot seats from the racing vehicles. From mere glancing, Ikka cannot determine how they have been fixed to the floor, but she notes that all of the bodies upon them are adorned in refashioned racing clothes. She looks to their faces and registers their eyes boring into her.

"Is there a problem?"

Her voice, in its flat uninhibited glory, manages to break a spell of sorts. The room is once more overtaken by chattering, lead by the jowlish man, Ocnus, who shouts straight to Delu.

"You did not mention one of your visitors was a female!"

Delu, who is standing in the second row of the room, looks innocently to him.

"I did not think gender was important when relaying the facts of the situation to this meeting."

"Not important? Well I never… such disrespect…"

"Disrespect?" Ikka cuts in. "Ocnus, is it? Disrespect is not addressing my companion and me as though we are standing here in the room with you, which we are now. This is Veela"— Veela waves happily at the room—"and I am Ikka. I apologise for listening to your proceedings from the shadows, but we wanted to ascertain if we would be safe amongst your company. Now that we have been met with such a lousy reception, I am not entirely sure we are. If you would like to point us to the nearest exit, we will gladly be on our way."

Many members of the room appear petrified by the time Ikka finishes speaking. Ocnus jumps to his feet, waving his stumpy arms back and forth.

"No, no. That will not be necessary. If you permit us, we will take you to The Mother and she may talk with you, and tell you of our home. You will be safe here. Tell me, did Delu and Gaarwine treat you well on your journey?"

Ikka raises her brows at Ocnus, baiting him with silence. He stammers to cover the gap. "Since you already know them, perhaps it would please you if it is they who accompany you to her?"

Ikka stares at Ocnus for a few more moments, before slowly nodding her head in assent. His face is relieved, and he motions for Delu and Gaarwine to escort the two strangers away with haste. As they exit through a tunnel to the back of the room, his voice carries on after them.

"Oh, and Delu, once you have shown our guests to their destination, please come to my chambers. Azzam and I should have a word with you in private, I think…"

• • •

"Well, that was all a bit weird."

Ikka and Veela are sitting on a small bench in the hall outside the chambers that belong to The Mother. Gaarwine is standing a few feet away from them, and Delu has gone inside. Veela leans conspiratorial in to Ikka, continuing his train of thought.

"You've still got your knife, don't you?"

She nods slightly, directing his eyes with hers to her legs, where her fingers are indicating the number three. His eyes bulge.

"Three?!"

She kicks him in the leg to shut up as Gaarwine turns to watch him.

"Ah, I see ye've learnt to count Veela. Yer, there are three of us in here." He chuckles and shakes his head at the two of them. "I don't know why yer both look so glum. Sure the old ones are a bit slow—it happens when yer spend too much time down here without visiting the surface—but they're all good people. Ye'll be safe here, and if Delu is right, ye'll probably shake things up enough that we might not have to stay down here much longer."

Ikka says, "Shake things up enough?"

"Well… yer see, that's not for me to be explaining, but maybe he'll tell yer once ye've spoken to The Mother…"

"There's something I don't get, though…" Veela cuts in. "Whose mother is she exactly? Doesn't she have a name? She can't be everyone's mother…"

"No."

Delu's quiet voice cuts through the air, and they turn to look at him in the doorway.

"All the answers will await you inside. When you enter, you will see a small room to your left, please wash yourselves in the facilities inside. There are clean clothes waiting for you both. When you are done, please return to the main chamber and seat yourselves on the floor. The Mother will see to you when she is ready. Gaarwine will be waiting for you out here."

Gaarwine nods. "Aye."

Veela stands, but Ikka remains seated, debating whether or not to stand. She queries Delu, "And you?"

"I will confer with Ocnus and Azzam, as per their request."

Ikka nods slightly, but doesn't move. She watches Delu walk past them and disappear down the tunnel connecting The Mother's wing to the rest of the Settlement. Veela looks at her, perplexed.

"Are you coming or what? The man mentioned bathing and clean clothes. Even if the talk is gobbledygook, at least we can get clean!"

Ikka's eyes smile and her lip twitches a little. She stands and joins Veela in the doorway before they both walk through.

• • •

After showering and changing into fresh, repurposed racing clothes, Ikka and Veela meet in the small corridor. They stop to survey each other for a moment. It is the first time in weeks they have seen each other without dirt caking their faces and sand and twigs in their hair. Ikka looks as if she is about to say something to Veela, but thinks the better of it. She stands and moves across the room, preparing to enter the room beyond. She pauses at the doorway, and it is only when Veela catches up with her and places a hand on her shoulder that she forces herself to move forward.

He says, "It's going to be okay, buddy."

"I highly doubt it," she says, and then opens the door.

Seated in the middle of the room on a floor cushion, her legs crossed and arms resting daintily on her lap, is The Mother. She is in her early fifties, silver circlets of hair framing her face, her skin pale as moonlight. She looks up at them as they enter, and, without speaking, invites them to sit on two floor cushions positioned in front of her. As they comply, she pours a herbal tonic into short wood-carved cups and hands one to them each.

She offers them a warm smile, and Ikka realizes this is the second female she has ever met. She can't remember the first one in detail; the memory is a sliver of orange in her mind. She doesn't know how to express her wonder at witnessing this woman before her, and clearly neither does Veela, who sits dead still. After a few moments pause, the woman offers a gay laugh and raises her glass to a toast.

"Welcome Ikka, welcome Veela, to the Settlement. They call me The Mother here, but you may call me Nnamdi. Please, let me tell you my story."

# CHAPTER THIRTEEN

"MY LIFE began at the age of twenty-four.

"My existence had obviously been in effect for many a year prior to this moment, but as I have no clear memory of that time, only insignificant, minute images that do not amount to much, I believe that I maintain the right to mark my life as starting at this time.

"I woke up and it was a Tuesday. I know that it was a Tuesday in the sense that the computer system of my X-Runner informed me that it was a Tuesday, and on some instinct I trusted this computer system—and the X-Runner itself—unequivocally. It told me what day of the week it was, the best possible route for me to travel, where I should camp at night, how many hours I should sleep, and I knew that all of these facts would hold true. But then the most peculiar event happened, that Tuesday when I woke up and my life began. As I lay there staring at my runner's ceiling, wondering if today would be the day I won The Race, I heard a small cooing from something on my chest. I looked down, and there against my breasts was a small baby.

"I did not know what to do. How had this creature come to arrive at this juncture, so neatly wrapped in a blanket and placed in my arms? There was no sign of intrusion or break-in during the night. The navigation system informed me that no external heat signals had been detected within a thirty-mile radius of my vehicle in the past twelve hours. Yet here I was, with an infant that looked nearly fourteen months old tenderly tucked against my bosom as I slept; and I was certain I had never seen it before in my life. I would remember if this were my child. I would remember if I had ever had a child. I was certain I had not. There was no voice inside me that yearned to nurture and care for this being. I felt no connection to it, no more, or perhaps even less, than I did to the vehicle in which I raced. At the least the vehicle I knew, this tiny vat of life was a total anomaly in my world.

"I tried to place it on the runner floor, peel it away from my body so I could clear my head and think. But as I removed it, it cried. The most irritable, disturbed yelping I have ever heard. It penetrated through my ears and went straight through like claws raking into my brain. I tried to shake the sounds loose, to imprint into the child's mind the need to stop screaming, but the demented outbursts would only cease if I held it close to me. I became a prisoner to its cries. I did not have the heart to simply dump the creature outside my runner and drive on; I knew the desert heat would kill it within a matter of hours. So I decided to continue on—the child in tow, clutching to my body like a parasitic entity, refusing to let me go—until I could find someone to help me, to free me from my dilemma.

"I raced for days with this hope, the infant wrapped in sheets across my front as I piloted the X-Runner. When I eventually crossed paths with other racers, it was the evening of the fourth night since the child had been with me, and I was nearing my wit's end. There was a small campfire attended by three different racers, all men. They had rough faces, worn by The Race, but I didn't mind so long as they could help me.

"I stumbled out of my X-Runner, child strapped to me, and took long, desperate strides towards them. 'Please!' I shouted to them. 'You have to help me!'

"One leapt to his feet immediately, and rushed over to me, steadying me by my arm. 'What's the matter?' he said, his face rife with concern.

"'This baby,' I said, my eyes nodding over my chin to the bundle on my chest, my voice quivering with apprehension, 'I don't know where it came from. You have to help me find its parents.'

"His hand relaxed its grip, and he took a step back from me, his eyes transformed into pits of disdain. He grunted back to the others. 'We've got a crazy one here.' They chuckled where they sat by the fire.

"'No, please.' I looked back and forth between them all. 'Before four days ago, I'd never seen it in my life. Does it look like it's four days old to you?'

"The man's crinkled face peered down at the infant. He said, 'No.'

"'Someone put it in my runner when I was sleeping,' I said. 'I don't know why, but it won't stop crying, the only thing that stops it is when I tie it to me like this, and it's so hard to race like this. I don't what to do. I don't know how to find its parents. You're the first people I've seen since it happened.'

"'Won't stop crying, ay?' he said, sneering at me. 'Don't untie it then.' Then he turned his back on me, and the three of them wouldn't look in my direction again.

"Over the next few weeks, it happened like that a great many times. No one would listen to me when I tried to tell them the child wasn't mine. They would turn their backs, mumble that I was crazy. Quite a few thought I was trying to trick them, to steer them foul in The Race with a divergence. I gave up talking to them, resigned to the fate of being scorned. I told myself it wouldn't be too long now—couldn't be too long left—and then The Race would be over, and I could find the child's parents. The facilitators would help.

"There were times though, when particularly low, I would try again if I saw a racer on the road. When they responded the same as all the rest, that I must be crazy or in denial, I would begin to wonder if I was. I couldn't remember any specificities of my life before that Tuesday, and even though I had felt so sure I didn't know the infant, had never set eyes on it before in my life, it clung to me so tightly, so scared of a moment without me. What if I did know it, what if I had birthed it, and I simply couldn't remember? The thought tortured me for so many hours, for so many days. What if I were simply a bad mother? A hateful mother so inept at loving that she had wiped her own child from her memory? It filled my stomach with lead to consider it, my throat with bile to force those doubts back down. I couldn't be that person. I was so sure the child wasn't mine. I had to believe I would find someone who could make sense of this for me.

"But as the weeks turned into months, I became more suspicious, suspicious that The Race would never end. I thought I was passing certain strips of terrain over and over again—but with the pacing of two or three months in-between. As the infant grew, its cries continuing, its body learning how to take steps but screaming if I were ever not directly by its side, I began to realize that more than just this child not being my own, something else, even more incredible, was wrong.

"The more I thought about it, the more I thought really hard, there was so much I couldn't remember, so many details I didn't know about my life. I was in The Race. We were all in The Race. Our vehicles were our houses, our source of food, we only saw each other on the rare occasions our navigation systems allowed us to camp together, and even then we never saw the same people more than once—or we couldn't remember if we did. And our navigation systems, it was these systems of the X-Runners that told us everything we knew about The Race. If we didn't have them, we'd be blind and useless, traipsing across the desert like fools.

"I still continued on with the ruse I considered The Race to be, as I knew no alternative. I couldn't comprehend a possible alternative, and these days my mind still blurred in the mornings until I would see the child and remember the confusion since it had arrived in my life. Then one day, a slightly overcast day with a static humidity on the horizon that might zap your skin, I saw a young man, no older than seventeen, shouting at his runner. He was shaking his fists about with an animosity so futile, it could only be directed at an inanimate object. He was cursing so loud I was sure he was going to wake the infant, so I rather impishly hurled a small stone at him and gestured for him to be quiet as I approached. He turned and looked at me, and the shock that registered on his face surprised me.

"You cannot be real," he said.

"I asked him why and he replied, "There are no adult women in The Race."

"And then, with one last rude gesture towards his vehicle, he walked over to me and we had a long talk.

"He had grown up with his father, he said, in The Race. It was all he had ever known, from the moment he had started remembering, and yet his father had never remembered more than four days of it. There were times when his father might remember a little more, and worse than that there were conversations from the day prior he would have no knowledge of participating in. He had thought maybe his father was ill, even though he didn't look that old, and even though he had been like this since the young man was very young. And then that morning, with no explanation, the young man had woken up in a different X-Runner. His father was not inside. No information of his existence on the X-Runner's mainframe. Only that of the young man. As if he had been participating in The Race from day dot alone.

"I could not believe it at first when I heard it. I did not want my suspicions confirmed—not in this way. Yet here it was in front of me, so clearly explaining the blurred haze of my past. I told him of this, confided of my entrapment with the infant. And he believed me. When he told me, I felt a million tons of pressure evaporate from my temples, felt my brain exhale all the minutes, all the days, all the weeks and months of doubting my own sanity. Finally someone else was in this nightmare with me, and it no longer seemed quite so terrifying.

"But it was still terrifying."

• • •

"The young man—Azzam—and I drove in convoy for many days. We were searching for his father, searching for the parents of the nearly two-year-old child who still clung so ardently to my side, and searching for anyone else who would listen to us, who had had a similar experience to ours.

"As we travelled, I found the first words Azzam ever spoke to me rang true—there were no adult women in The Race. I was the exception to the rule; the only other females we encountered were pre-pubescent girls travelling with their fathers. There was no shortage of adult men. Most scorned us, believing us to be attempting to derail their attempts to win The Race. None would take heed of our warnings. Azzam took interest in my blurred memories each morning, and how they became clearer as the hours passed each day. He put forth the theory that something in my X-Runner was causing my memory lapses—was manipulating my brain and the brain of every person participating in The Race. He was unsure why he was immune, but we decided to put his theory to the test. We stopped racing. We set up camp thirty yards from our vehicles for three nights. We abstained from the X-Runner's liquified meals, instead foraging from the desert floor and sustaining ourselves on weeds and strange crisped fruits hidden amongst the scarce shrubbery. Each morning, I woke with more clarity, with less-to-no moments of confusion as to where I was. It was as though I was detoxing from the X-Runner's hold on my mind. We began to realize that we would be able to free the minds of others if we did this to them also, if we could convince them to stop racing long enough to detox.

"It was an idea that worked in theory, but in reality, it was brutal. Everyone we met had it so thoroughly set in their minds that they had to race. No one would stop during the day to talk. We would try signalling racers that passed us to stop and they would charge forward without heed. We could only meet them when they camped, but the navigation systems of the X-Runners rarely guided them where they might camp near other humans for the night. And talking did not reach the resolution we desired.

"Azzam and I decided to utilize a more aggressive tactic. We started searching out night camps occupied by solitary racers. We would wait until their eyes started to nod, in the moments before they would normally retire to their vehicles, and then we would attack. We would lasso them with ropes, dragging them many yards away from their vehicles, and tie them to trees or boulders, whatever anchor was available. As they would detox from the memory eraser, swearing and threatening us, we would keep them fed, and feed them the truth of all our situations. It wasn't always a success. Many were violent, desperate in their bid to return to The Race. Upon release, one nearly killed me, bludgeoning me with a rock. But sometimes it worked. We had a success rate of one in three, of those who would take heed and boycott The Race.

"After three months or so, we had grown our numbers to

be a small collective of nine. We set ourselves up a base camp many yards off the clear racing route, eating only what the earth provided us. We would send one or two people off in X-Runners at a time to find more solitary racers to join us, and we started breaking down our remaining X-Runners, scouring them for more clues to our situation, and the purpose and reasoning behind our entrapment. We also started stripping them of elements to make our campsite more comfortable. We found no clear answers, and the comfort we sourced was short lived. Instead, we managed to bring about a new threat. In hindsight, we should have known that what we were doing would not go unnoticed, but hindsight is not a tool available for those who are desperate.

"It was when the child was perhaps twenty-eight months old. I had resigned myself to act as its guardian for the foreseeable future. I was still not entirely comfortable with it—it represented to me everything that was my stolen identity, the manipulation so present in all of my existence. But I made its daily survival my burden, along with my own. I was teaching it to forage for root vegetables—we had discovered these to be the most readily available food in this environment—when we first heard the drone. Thump. Thump. Thump. As though the air was being pushed down all around us. There was a loud sucking sound, like an amplified version of the air vents in the X-Runners working in overdrive. And then a bang. Thunderous. As though lightning had struck in the middle of our camp. And screams.

"I ran back to the camp as fast as I could, the child clinging tightly to my arms. Our group of seven was scattered, divided on different sides of the camp by a crater in its midst. One man was screaming at its edge, a stump where his left leg used to be. Before I could reach him, the sun's heat left my neck and a shadow larger than an X-Runner covered the ground between the man and I. A great whirring sound shrieked across the air, and then the man's remaining form, the earth surrounding it, the campfire to its right, and two other members of our camp cowering on the sand behind him, all exploded. They were decimated, obliterated by an ancestor of the flying ships you encountered yesterday.

"We escaped, the child and I, by the most tenuous of chances. I was so close to the outer radius of this new explosion that I was propelled back through the air, down the pre-existing crater. I—we—tumbled down a fissure in its base, and there we remained as more explosions rattled the earth and screams penetrated our ears. Finally, there was silence.

"I do not know how much time passed—how long the infant cried clinging to my chest—until we heard the dull engine roar of an X-Runner approaching in the distance. Azzam's X-Runner. We came crawling up the fissure, shouting at Azzam to collect us from the crater in the ground. When he pulled us to the surface, our camp was no more. Instead, scattered ashes remained where our friends had last stood, and all of the X-Runners had disappeared, no wheel tracks marking their journey. We were back to our core group of three—Azzam, the child, and I—plus a twelve-year-old boy, the man you know as Gaarwine.

"It became clear to the four of us that we needed to develop a new strategy. Whoever The Race facilitators were, they would not sit idly by and let us withdraw from The Race. As long as we remained connected to the X-Runners, we remained connected to them. We travelled farther off the beaten track, travelling only by foot, carrying and dragging what our bodies would allow. And then we burrowed, creating the beginnings of the settlement you now see around you. It took many years, fraught with fear of discovery, heightened whenever Azzam and Gaarwine would travel to the surface to free others from the grip of The Race. Each time they would also pillage their X-Runners, tearing from them what we could use here. We have grown our numbers exponentially over the past three decades, as well as the space we have occupied here below the surface.

"We know they are searching for us. Whenever any of us emerge to forage for food—we stopped searching to free other racers some time ago—their airships are quick to appear, hunting us until we manage to disappear from their tracking devices, which seems to happen once we are underground. We are very careful now to limit our surface excursions, for as long as we remain underground we are safe. We are a peaceful settlement, with few disputes, and Azzam and Ocnus, another of our oldest occupants, run our community meetings. They defer to me on any matters they cannot reach a consensus on, and despite my lifelong claim that I am not anyone's mother, I have become *The* Mother of this Settlement."

# CHAPTER FOURTEEN

IN THE LIT hours, Chloe continues with her training. Her body goes through the motions—squats, one, two, three, four, five; lunges, one, two, three, four, five—but her mind is focused on the diaper. She is not filled with trepidation, but anticipation. As she completes her exercises, she skims over all of the mechanical information she has stored in her mind; what she understands to be the weaknesses in the machinery's construction. There is no device impervious to the right amount of pressure and force. The diaper cannot be the exception to this rule.

Chloe is doing sit ups—one, two, three, four, five—when the machinery hums to life. The vibrations are loud, ricocheting off the tiled floor. She takes a deep breath, and then springs to her feet. She has approximately 30 seconds to get her plan in motion, or her window of opportunity will diminish and she will have to wait for tomorrow to try again. Once on her feet, she begins spinning. She moves in a flurry, her tiny frame twirling on the spot, legs leaping over the tubes as she turns. Even in her disconnected state in the cell to the left, Hannah can understand that something peculiar is going on. She watches, transfixed, as this tiny girl with her rag of orange hair spins, her body defying the violent vibrations of the mechanical diaper strapped to her waist. With each twirl, a section of the tubing begins to twist. As Chloe continues, more of the piping curls on itself, becoming stiffer and unable to move.

Two thirds of the tubing has twisted when the hydraulics began hissing and the local anaesthetic is injected. Chloe grimaces at this already-old enemy, focusing on the task at hand. She keeps spinning, racing to twist the pipes all the way up to the base of diaper. She succeeds—just in time.

The diaper starts its temporary expansion.

Chloe doesn't even take a moment to steel herself for the next portion of her plan. She throws her body with careful but fierce calculation against the cell bench. The impact is precise, and effective. The base of the diaper slams on the edge of the bench, the weight of the mechanical vibrations pushing it deeper forward. The piping wants to uncoil, but Chloe has thrown herself so that the motion has propelled the piping further in the wrong direction.

It snaps.

So beautifully, so simply, the piping snaps.

Two at first, hidden pop rivets ejecting from the casing, pranging off the cell's glass walls. And then others, built up pressure causing them to burst outwards. Only the smallest of the pipes remains, determined to see out its next action.

The single, solitary, splash.

Chloe is waiting for it. And as she feels it gear up, feels the air pressure in the pipe build as it brings the fluid forward, she impacts once more against the bench. Without the other pipes there to buffer it, it concaves almost instantly, but without the other pipes there, Chloe's legs are exposed. The rough edge of the pipe's lip cuts a deep gash down Chloe's right thigh as it snaps away. Pain erupts down her thigh in harmony with the spill of the pipe's contents, the oily water-based lubricant. The resulting mixture is a bizarre bloody oil trail down her leg, echoing the trail of her first session, the only glimpse of it she's seen. But there is nothing Chloe can do about it for the moment.

Instead, she rushes to the base of the pipes, the anchor point in the corner of the cell. She grabs the pile of tubes, beginning to twist them hard around themselves, and applies pressure to the point where they rub against the floor. It takes more strength then she should have, but her desperation steers her forward, commanding her arms and her core muscles to keep moving, to keep pushing, to use the pipes to tear an open hole in the floor.

And she does.

A sharp gust of wind pushes past her hands, forcing its way into the air pressure controlled cell. It rips through the atmospheric balance and causes a vacuum of outer air into the cell. This works to Chloe's advantage. The air pushes at the floor tiles around the opening at the same time as she tugs at them, causing more to crack under the pressure and the hole to widen. It is now wide enough that she should be able to fit through. Chloe pushes the piping aside and scoots her legs inside. The air is still trying to push into the cell, and her hair slaps against her eyes as she lowers her torso in the hole as well. Her eyes water from the impact, and as she wipes the liquid away she glimpses back around the cell that has been her prison for the past thirteen days. The tubing that has been her chain is now cast limply on the floor, and the bench that has been her bed is missing chunks from its melee with the diaper.

She sees Sam, cheering her on with stoic appraisal—that is, standing with arms crossed, hazel eyes watching the drama unfold, face impassive. But then she sees Hannah. Broken. Sitting in the centre of her cell, arms clinging around her legs. The person inside holding onto her rope, standing right at the edge of her eyes, almost ready to engage. But unable, forever unable. And the young girl in the cell past Hannah's, as neutral as Sam, but eyes seeking Chloe's out. When she has them, holds them, she looks as though she is about to smile. But then she shouts, so loud Chloe can hear it echoing through Hannah's cell and into her own, even though when it reaches her ears it sounds like a muffled whisper.

"Hurry up—They're coming—"

Chloe doesn't give it a second thought, doesn't pause to see where they might be coming from. She drops her head under the hole and plunges into the darkness.

• • •

Once Chloe breaches the darkness below her cell, the air vacuum ceases to slap past her face. It becomes more settled, though there is still a definitive breeze in the space. The darkness is not as synthetic as those encountered in the cell's nights. Instead, her eyes can wrap around it, make out silhouettes of the world around her. Three feet high, the space is endless in width.

Every six feet there is a stalk of tubing hanging from the ceiling and tethered to the ground below, where it meets a stream of piping canvassing the entire floor's surface. It could be that the space is actually six feet high, but the mountains of piping along its surface have rendered the free space in which she is crawling shorter.

The breeze is originating ahead of Chloe's current position, angled to the left. She makes for it, crawling as fast as she can in the sea of piping. Her hands and knees keep slipping down their contoured sides, becoming lost between smaller pipes and bigger pipes. The gash on her thigh is still bleeding, and each fumble causes the wound to bleed deeper. In this sterile space, the smell of her blood mixes strangely with the iron of the tubing beneath her. It feels like eons that she is crawling. She moves forward, desperate. She must escape.

She doesn't.

There is a loud alarm blaring from the spaces below and above her, and then an eruption. The flooring beneath her disappears, and she falls.

• • •

She falls only a short distance—four or five feet—and then something catches her. Not a human, not an object. A creature Chloe has never seen before. A creature Chloe would never have imagined possible.

A giant, floating sack of a dark liquid, shadows where she might believe a more normal creature to have eyes. It has tentacles, hundreds of them, wrapped around her waist and back, cradling her neck with a gentle force. They feel at once prickly and wet. She feels both unclean and irrelevant under their grip.

The shadow eyes watch her closely, as her own eyes bulge and she realizes she is in a room full of these creatures, all floating over eight feet off the ground. They are all watching her—and they are all giant.

There is a gurgling sound, harmonic and guttural, that disorientates Chloe further—even as she realizes it is the creatures communicating to each other, even as the one holding her plunges a needle into her neck.

And then everything goes black.

# CHAPTER FIFTEEN

AS SOON as her speech is over, The Mother ejects Ikka and Veela from her chambers. They are left pondering in the hall outside, waiting to be collected by Gaarwine. They are both at a loss, but Veela fills the silence first.

"She was rude, right? This is my story—now get out of my personal space. She was a bit weird, too, right? I felt like she was trying to hypnotise us with all that prolonged eye contact."

Ikka offers a small nod. "Something was a little… off. I've been searching for proof that I'm not crazy for so long, and here she is. A woman who has carried that same feeling with her, as me. But as she speaks, everything is in the past. As though she believes it's all over, now that they have this underground home. They are no longer witness to it, so it doesn't exist. So it isn't a problem. Do you think they're all like this, minds addled from decades underground, and selfishness binding them to inaction?"

"Well," Veela attempts diplomacy, "That's a little damning. Might just be they've had some bad leadership…"

"Aye." Gaarwine's voice greets them from the shadows to their left, where this hallway connects to the tunnels. "But wer all hoping that'll be changing soon, thanks to yer arrival. Delu'll explain it later, I'm sure."

Ikka says, "When?"

Gaarwine is unfazed, "When 'e comes back from talking to the elders, I guess. Fer now, yer must be fairly starving, and they'll be expecting yer to contribute to the daily chores, as well."

The three of them trudge down the hallway, and Gaarwine explains more ways of the Settlement to them. Everyone has a role here, a duty to fulfil each day in order to keep the mechanisms of the Settlement liveable. Some are in charge of the hanging gardens, others food preparation—most of which involves ensuring none of the plants go to waste, there is not much cooking involved—some routinely clear the light shaft and air vents, others monitor the integrity of the Settlement construction, and so on. As newcomers, Ikka and Veela will still be expected to perform a role to earn their keep, which will commence once they have eaten. The meal is simple, a mix of root vegetables, grasses, and herbs. The vegetable pieces have been softened—soaked in water—but all the food is uncooked.

Gaarwine explains, "It's healthier this way. Less people get sick, eating it the way it's earthed."

It is difficult at first for Ikka to chew the vegetables, and she wonders if this is the first time her teeth have ever had to work, after an apparent lifetime of liquid meals provided by her X-Runner. She grows used to the motion, but it takes a long time for both her and Veela to consume their meals.

When the business of eating is over, they follow

Gaarwine down more winding corridors lit by occasional beams of light. It is shining brighter than they have seen it before, indicating the sun is at its highest point for the day. The stronger light allows them to take in more details. While the tunnels are very basic—sparse amounts of wooden beams at intervals and suspended plant baskets wherever the light shafts have been meticulously carved—there is an efficient numbering system attached to them. Each passageway has a stone embedded in its floor on the left where it connects to other passageways, and different letters and numbers are inscribed on the stones. So when travelling down the L1 tunnel, one will come to a juncture of the L1, J1, and K1 tunnels, and from previous knowledge know which way to continue. The tunnel they exited the lunchroom from was H1. Since then they have passed down H2, J2, K3 and L3. It is from L3 they reach their new destination, a dank little room that is maybe seven foot by ten. Inside it, the young short blond haired lad from the meeting hall is waiting.

His name is Aldric. He tells them so as soon as they enter and then ushers Gaarwine away—"It's much nicer without these oldies watching us, don't you think?"—immediately setting about the business of instructing them in their chores. The room they are in is the Clothing Fortification Room. Here they are in charge of repairing torn clothing, darning socks, stitching patches into worn jacket elbows and pant knees, and foraging fabric from the irreparable garments. Aldric advises them to get comfortable on a pile of the clothes, as they'll get washed in the Clothing Cleansing room next anyway and the floor gets cold when you're hand stitching for hours on end.

It is hard not to like Aldric's manic energy. He seems a

stark contrast to the young man who'd stared mouth agape at them in the meeting room.

"I wasn't expecting to see you, is all. Not you"—he nods cheerfully at Veela—"but a woman. We'd begun to suspect, or rather it's been general consensus in this place for at least two decades now, that there aren't any more adult females out there. The facilitators"—his mouth quivers a little at this word—"must be using them all for something. So you've somehow got through the cracks of their system and ended up here. Is that news to you? Or no, it's not. You just thought you were the only one that noticed. They wised up to things a long time ago, this lot, it's just they decided to stop wising up to things once they reached a certain point. You know they still consider me to be the newbie? I've been here for nine years."

"Nine years?" Veela is incredulous. He waves his stitching—which is neat and firm—in the air for emphasis. "You've been down here for nine whole years? Don't you get bored?"

Ikka says, "Don't you listen? The Mother and Azzam started this colony over thirty years ago."

"Settlement," Aldric says the word with a curt nod before continuing. "They're very adamant of that detail. Yes. I get bored. I find it best to talk through the silences, keep things active. You wouldn't be used to entertaining yourselves, after having the thrill of The Race and your few day memories keeping the world full of constant new delights for you. Oh, I remember those days. Well, I don't really, other than the final few. But it was nice, having a purpose that wasn't just darning socks. Not that I regret coming here, but it's all rather frustrating living down here now that I have a memory and true concept of time, knowing that there's no end game to this whole situation. The elders all seem perfectly content living out their days as cavern dwellers, but it's a prospect that gets me down on the quieter days."

Aldric pauses, his attention turning back to his stitching. After a few moments, Ikka interjects his reverie.

"How many people would you say are down here, Aldric? I glimpsed at least thirty at the meeting this morning."

Aldric continues stitching as he talks, "Well, yes, there would've been about thirty-eight at the council meeting, plus you two, The Mother, three at the water station at all times, another eight across the outer posts, and the morning shift of tunnellers makes sixty-five. Yep. That sounds about right when you two are added into the mix."

"The morning tunnellers?"

"Mmhmm. There's always an outpost of workers expanding our tunnel networks. The longer we spend down here, the more space we seem to crave from each other. And you never know what new resource you might find in the tunnel walls. We haven't had a big discovery for a couple of years, not since they found a new type of moss growing amongst the rocks. So far it's only in the P2–T2 wings, but it has wonderful medicinal properties."

Veela asks, "Medicinal properties?"

"Yep, they found out quite by accident. One of the tunnellers on that excavation managed to slice his arm on a sharp rock, and as he recoiled his arm back, the open wound was exposed to the moss and it acted as an adhesive, sealing it shut.

By the time the arm was back by his side, he had a long green scar up his arm with splashes of blood either side of it. They thought for sure it would become infected, but it never did. Since then, they've tried it out on several minor gashes and it's done the same thing each time. So partially they tunnel to give us all more space, and partially in case there is something else new worth discovering."

"Maybe something to help fight back against the facilitators?"

Aldric shakes his head at Ikka, and looks both her and Veela in the eyes very seriously.

"I wouldn't going around saying or suggesting things like that. I know you're new, so I'll explain this as best I can... They don't like that kind of talk around here."

Veela scoffs. "What do you mean, they don't like that kind of talk. Which they?"

"The Settlement elders. They think it creates unrest. They say it's unproductive and stops people from being grateful for what we have down here."

Ikka puts down her stitching, the jacket elbow now fully patched over.

"And what exactly is that?"

Aldric meets her gaze evenly.

"Safety."

• • •

There is a dinner that night to celebrate Ikka and Veela's arrival. It is held in a large hall, twice the size of the council room, lined with low table benches. Everyone except for the very old sit on the stone ground. The space is not lit with fires, but by

small mirrors erected under the light shafts to amplify the pale
sheen of the moonlight. It is cold, despite the mass of bodies, and
each time someone speaks a fog of air emits from their mouths.

Ikka and Veela are seated by Gaarwine, a few places
away from Azzam at the council elders' table. A sea of male faces
stream past them in the pale blue, all paying respect to The
Mother and nodding curiously at the new arrivals before they
take their seats. Delu is absent in the crowd. As the flow of faces
begins to slow down, Veela starts eyeing off the meal placed
before him—more root vegetables, more herbs, and a strange
rock shaped item the colour of wilted trees. He picks it up
curiously to sniff before Gaarwine slaps him across the back of
his head, causing him to drop it back to the table.

"Hey, what was that for?"

"Where's yer manners? No one eats till The Mother
eats."

"You could have just said that."

"That wouldn't have been half as much fun."

Ikka strangles a laugh into her water glass. Veela misses
this, but Gaarwine chuckles conspiritorally with her. The rotund
rhythm of his laughter is caught by the beady eyes of Ocnus. He
glances their way and Ikka is sure one of his many jowls ripples
with disdain. Gaarwine pays him no heed, and before Ocnus can
show his disapproval further, The Mother places a hand lightly
on his shoulder. He nods politely to her and stands.

He rings no bell, makes no noise whatsoever as he rises,
but by the time he is erect the entire hall is silent. He clears his
throat, and when he speaks, it is a calm conversational tone that
rings out across the hall.

"Thank you for your silence, friends. As many of you are aware, our peaceful Settlement has encountered some... excitement the past night and day, as two new arrivals have entered our home. They have met with The Mother and she has officially sanctioned their status as new members of our community. Please join with me in welcoming Ikka and Veela to the Settlement."

Here, Ocnus raises his water cup, and fifty-three hands throughout the hall mimic his action. "Welcome, Ikka and Veela."

Fifty-three voices echo the utterance, the drone of male voices harmonising at a deep and unnerving frequency that transports Ikka's mind to another place. She is no longer ensconced a dark cavern filled with men, but harvested in a brightly lit chamber, within an over populated field of women. Ikka blinks, startled, looking with suspicion at her cup, wondering what is in the water.

Veela catches her look and remarks, "Tastes like they threw a pinch of dirt in for good measure, hey."

Ikka doesn't respond, surveying the medley of pale blue faces in front of her, and the stern figures of Ocnus, The Mother, and Azzam overseeing the crowd. Ikka clenches her teeth and talks out of the side of her mouth to Veela.

"I don't think it's the water, Veela. It's this place. We've traded one form of prison for another, and I'm not sure The Race was even the first prison I've been in."

Veela says. "We shouldn't have this conversation here."

"No, but I think we need to find Delu. And then we need to leave."

• • •

Once the dinner is over, Gaarwine returns Ikka and Veela to their sleeping quarters. There has been no sight of Delu since the morning, but he does not mention it. At one of the passageway intersections a man Ikka and Veela hadn't noticed before steps out of the shadows to whisper something in Gaarwine's ear. His hair is black, nearly as thick as Ikka's, but his eyes are the shade of overcast grey skies, glinting out behind crescent moon shaped eyelids. He barely glances at Ikka and Veela, and is gone before Gaarwine can respond to his words. Gaarwine refuses to relay the purpose of the secretive meeting, but his shoulders slump, relaxed by what he has heard.

Once they reach Ikka and Veela's chamber, he leaves them with cheery but resigned words.

"Come on, get some rest. I'll come fetch yer in the morning. Try not to cause trouble before then, yer only been here one day and yer don't want to outstay yer welcome too soon."

Ikka inclines her head at this, but Veela chuckles as Gaarwine closes the door on them and they are plunged into darkness.

# CHAPTER SIXTEEN

THE MEETING chamber is stark and brightly lit, similar in its bright oppression to the whiteness of the birthing farm, but here there are no chains. There are no women, no glass walls, and no b'leies—b'leie is the Gu'ten word for the mechanical diapers that sanitize and impregnate the human breeders.

The congregation taking place in the meeting chamber is the usual corporate nonsense. The higher-ups want production yields to increase, and wastage and costs to decrease, a concept K'vinna would find laughable if the underlying consequences were not so dire. Lowering production costs and speeding up timelines will lead to a more fallible product, and when dealing with the survival of one's own species, fallibility is not an option. However, K'vinna does not want to be the one to voice this observation to the upper echelons. K'vinna is not upper management or even upper middle management—K'vinna is the head of the research division, and over nir short thirty years ne has never developed the skills required for navigating business politics. As a scientist, ne deals in facts, and is all too aware that the facts behind these new targets are not in their favour.

At present, U'mulig is holding the floor. A few years younger than K'vinna, U'mulig has recently skyrocketed in the esteem of The Facility. The breeding division, for which U'mulig is responsible, is continuously finding small corners to cut, new ways to shorten the humans' gestation periods, even if just by a day or two. These minuscule victories always cast the research division in bad light, despite the ludicrous nature of comparing the very different work of the two divisions. It is not hard to improve upon an already existing system, but it *is* hard to create an entirely new and—in K'vinna's view—implausible one.

The current victory that U'mulig is touting is a greater ratio of female to male infant births. It has always been a rigged percentage, but apparently the birthing division has decreed it paramount to rig it further. Charts illustrating the effects of the new ratio over the coming years are being projected for all the meeting members to view. K'vinna's mind flits between the different facts as they all absorb through the neural channels of the consciousness. An internal sigh echoes in K'vinna's being. It is obvious where the breeding division's new development will lead—to more work for the research division.

*Is there something you want to add, K'vinna?*

K'lappstol, the chair of The Facility, focuses everybody's attention in the consciousness to K'vinna's indiscretion. K'vinna decides it best to answer out loud, and nir vocal chamber echoes to life. An assortment of deep, harmonic notes sound out, sending little vibrations across the room. They mix together, not as a symphony, but as a gurgle of textured sounds, reminiscent of items suctioned down in mud, bubbling up to the surface.

"Pardon me, Chair, for my intrusion into the breeding division's briefing. I saw a matter of concern with the information we were being presented, and at my young age I am not yet skilled in restraining my thoughts that arise in shock. I do apologise."

*And what of this concern? Disseminate.*

"Perhaps it is best I not voice them yet, lest the close of the breeding division's briefing addresses the issue."

*The consciousness does not suffer impudence. Speak now.*

"Very well. Whilst I acknowledge the achievement of the breeding division to narrow the number of male births, I fear this accomplishment might cause a new problem. Female infants may be more desirable byproducts due to their ability to generate future product, but we must take care not to overlook the role of the male infants in that process, too. Evaluating these forecasted figures, in a few years time, there would be a very limited male infants."

*Correct.*

"The gene-pool is already becoming muddled. It may become too incestuous if these ratios come to fruition, and the product may become sullied further."

Silence—In the consciousness as well. K'vinna takes a small breath, hoping ne is not making a mistake in continuing on.

"Should we not be concerned that by narrowing the gene-pool further, the product will be weakened?"

*No. The research division is meant to be circumventing such a liability.*

"Ah, but in the eventuality that such a breakthrough is not immediate, it may be unwise to limit the product yield so soon…"

*The research division will have to work harder to meet their assigned targets then.*

"Chair, with the utmost respect, the research division is already under immense pressure to yield a more definitive cure from the product we are currently being given."

*We will give you more staff then. How many do you require?*

"It's not a matter of staff members, Chair—"

K'vinna is silenced by the consciousness—travelling into nir neural pathways, denying nir ability to continue.

*We will not discuss this further, K'vinna of the researchers. Your division will make progress by the close of two trimesters, and it will be significant. There is no other option for our species.*

• • •

K'vinna returns to nir section of the building with haste—ne does not feel comfortable spending much time in the corporate areas of The Facility. The research division is in the third basement level of the building. It used to be higher up, but as the number of breeders increased, the research division was relocated lower and lower in The Facility to make room for the continual expansion of the breeding division.

As K'vinna travels down the levels, ne gazes through the void opposite the commuting chutes. The pride of the breeding division—and indeed the entire facility—is on display for all those passing to see. Rows upon rows of pressurized glass cages, each containing a human female in the process of gestation. There are ten thousand of these tanks per level, seven levels high.

They are so brightly lit it is like staring into the sun, but a sun covered in little black lice. Their ages span 11–30, although those 25–30 are in a stark minority. The breeding division terminates the breeders after two failed pregnancies or more than one menstrual cycle between conceptions after the age of 25, and many die of stress before even reaching that point. Their deaths are considered irrelevant. The number of breeders is so high that new females are introduced into the system at a rate of 50.18 per day. A working lifespan of 19 years is perfectly acceptable, yielding 16 births on average.

Upon reaching the research division, K'vinna is assaulted by a multitude of scents. Chemicals, cleaning compounds, and the acrid stench of human bodies, both alive and dead, absorb into K'vinna's consciousness. It is the live human bodies, the rank odour of sweat, that ne finds the most offensive. Ne can smell the fear in the sweat. It is more pungent than diseased skin or rotting bodies. This is the one aspect of the research division that K'vinna does not enjoy—excluding the unrealistic targets placed upon them. Every other division in the facility is free of this scent. Even U'mulig and the breeding division workers are not exposed to this revulsion on a regular basis, as the pressurized cages also work as scent vacuums.

Before K'vinna can slip into nir office unnoticed, nir key research adviser, T'vil, jostles up behind nem. Ne connects K'vinna into the consciousness almost immediately so that none of the other researchers can hear nem talk.

*K'vinna, I've been sent a staff acquisition form. Why have I been sent a staff acquisition form? Have more of our team fallen ill?*

K'vinna waits until they are inside nir office, and the

outside noise and stench has been shut out. Ne hastily withdraws from the consciousness.

"No."

Ne scans nir desk, the corners of the room. Ne turns back to T'vil.

"K'lappstol has imposed a new deadline upon us."

"How soon?"

"Two trimesters."

T'vil looks notably alarmed.

"Two trimesters? Human or Gu'ten?"

"Human. That's how they measure time now. By the worth of the humans."

"That's not enough time."

"No."

"They want a more effective product *and* a way to yield it without the use of the human males, by the close of *two human trimesters*?"

T'vil slumps onto a resting stool opposite K'vinna's desk. K'vinna watches nem silently, waiting for nir key research adviser to advise. T'vil looks absolutely hopeless. At last, ne manages, "Well, we will need a lot more staff then. How soon can we get them? Can we poach some from the breeding division?"

"So they can teach us how to cut corners? No matter what deadlines they impose upon us, we cannot forget, our division is in charge of research. Not compromising."

T'vil nods and departs from the room. K'vinna watches after nem, and knows they are both wondering the same thing. How on S'vekke will they accomplish what the past three generations of the research division have failed to achieve? If the past 78 years of research are indicative of anything, it is that the Gu'ten are not meant to be saved.

• • •

This thought it still haunting K'vinna when ne is trapped in nir second meeting of the day—the research division progress meeting. It is tedious, but a necessity. As per K'vinna's orders, the consciousness is used in this meeting exclusively for uploading information—all other communication is verbal. Currently G'nist, one of the oldest Gu'ten in the division, is addressing the room. G'nist was born on S'vekke and transferred to this facility as soon as ne came of age. It has been forty-three years since then, and G'nist's entire life has been dedicated to finding a cure for the be'lysning. As has K'vinna's, and every other Gu'ten in the room.

K'vinna wonders how much longer G'nist will be able to defy the be'lysning nemself. At forty-five, ne has dodged the disease for ten years longer than most Gu'ten of nir generation and the two before them. Perhaps G'nist is immune to the disease. Should they actually be performing their tests upon nem, and not the humans? K'vinna smirks and dismisses the thought. It is more likely that the old crone has been smuggling nemself extra rations of the fo'ster-vi'kle over the years in a preventative effort.

G'nist is now requesting five more staff to join nir team.

"How about ten?"

G'nist—and the other researchers in the room excluding T'vil—are all surprised by this offer.

"Five is plenty, thank you, K'vinna."

"Nonsense, G'nist. Maybe even another twenty would

serve you better than ten. You need the capability to delegate more, G'nist, so you can cover more ground faster. I suppose now is as appropriate time as any to inform you all"—here K'vinna pauses to look meaningfully at all of the researchers, a management tactic ne learnt years ago from nir mentor—"the Chair has given us a new deadline. Two human trimesters. The conditions on S'vekke are becoming critical. Whatever you need to make more progress, tell me now."

The researchers' reply with shocked silence.

"In fact, if any of you research assistants think you are also bright sparks, now is the time to come forth with your ideas. I am willing to hear out any idea. Do not let any hierarchy stop you from speaking. You will not be penalized by your superiors, under my orders."

The shock does not leave their visages. They remain in silence, so K'vinna continues.

"Now is not the time to be humble. Our previous methods do not seem to be working. If any of you have an idea that could save us, we need to hear it."

K'nurre, the lead researcher of the secondary research team, clears nir vocal chambers softly. Ne has a gentle manner, studious in a very quiet, observational way.

"More staff are welcome, but what we really need are fresher subjects. We cannot keep waiting for the breeding division to use them first. We need access to the humans before they have been sullied by U'mulig's methods. The food ne feeds them is corrupting their natural state. I suspect it might be gearing our results to the negative."

K'vinna nods.

"T'vil, log that down. What else?"

A young confident voice gurgles out.

"I have an idea."

It belongs to U'ngdom. At four, ne is one of the youngest research assistants on G'nist's team.

"Go ahead."

U'ngdom looks furtively around the room.

"I would prefer to explain it to you through the consciousness. It will be easier for you to understand. But you, alone."

K'vinna observes the condescension withering G'nist's visage as ne contemplates nir young assistant. G'nist seems concerned, and nir concern alone is enough to convince K'vinna that it is worth entering the consciousness to hear U'ngdom out.

• • •

All the Gu'ten in the chamber perch nervously as U'ngdom approaches K'vinna. It is inappropriate for a researcher so young to request private council with the division head, let alone the audacity of doing so in a room filled with nir superiors. Yet, U'ngdom does not seem nervous. Perhaps it is the false confidence of youth with which ne saunters, but when ne extends forth the invitation to shared consciousness, there is no self-doubt in nir demeanour. When ne and K'vinna are connected, U'ngdom's every thought is available for K'vinna to download. This is not reciprocal—K'vinna makes sure to keep nir mind silent in the consciousness.

As K'vinna tours U'ngdom's mind, different thoughts flash past nem at speed. Late nights doing secret research when the laboratory is empty. Cell manipulations in the dark. G'nist choosing to pursue lines of inquiry ne finds useless—U'ngdom shifts nir weight with unease when ne feels K'vinna access this thought. More late night research. U'ngdom forcing nemself to reproduce. Infecting nir undeveloped offspring with the be'lysning, cell manipulations that do not involve fo'ster-vi'kle. Improvements in the infant's condition. Then death.

K'vinna stares hard at the young researcher in the consciousness. To the others in the room, nir facade remains impartial.

*You killed your offspring.*
*The be'lysning killed my offspring, K'vinna.*
*You infected your offspring with the be'lysning intentionally.*
*Yes.*
*That is the same as murder.*
*It was an experiment.*
*I could have you executed for this.*
*Yes, but you won't.*
*And why is that?*
*Because the only reason the be'lysning killed nem was because I lost my access to certain supplies. I could have cured it completely, but G'nist—*

Sirens erupt throughout the meeting chamber. Their screaming is amplified through the consciousness, the perilous result of two minds linked. K'vinna ejects nemself from the connection immediately, seeking both solace and answers from the noise. This particular siren has not been heard in the research division in over two decades.

• • •

A human female has escaped her cage. She is crawling—

thumping—in the crawl space between the cell floor and the research division's ceiling. If she had been contained on one of the higher levels, she would be in the crawl space between two levels of the breeding division, but as she was on the lowest level, she is currently causing a ruckus on K'vinna's roof. Contemptuous creatures.

T'vil coordinates some of the research division's workers to set upon the roofing panels. They wait for the maladroit bashing to be directly above them before they rip the panels free, dropping the human to the ground. They are going to let the breeder connect to the ground at full speed—none think to break its fall.

At the last possibly second, K'vinna whips forward and softens the impact by the slightest margin—enough to prevent the breeder's spine from crushing, at least. K'vinna is not sure why ne does it. Perhaps to preserve the human's single worth, the creation of the fo'ster-vi'kle, but ne is unsure. As ne holds the human, and T'vil, the workers, and other members of the research division watch on in surprise at the commotion, ne accidentally enters the consciousness with it.

• • •

Chloe is paralysed with fear. She is not sure what is holding her. Hundreds of thin tentacles are wrapped around her waist and back, cradling her neck with a gentle force. They feel at once both prickly and wet. And strong. Their colouring is inconsistent. Some black, some grey, some clear. And the face peering down at her.

She is not sure that it can be called a face.

A rotund, nearly translucent bulb larger than her entire

torso with dark pits for eyes and no discernible pupils.

But somehow she knows.

It is watching her with as much confusion as her own.

And does it have a mouth? She can't see one. She hopes it won't eat her.

*Eat it? What a notion.*

Chloe gasps, how did it hear her thoughts?

And the creature. The creature barely moves its bulbous head, but gives the appearance of frowning.

*Can you hear me?*

Chloe tries to clear her throat, to—

*Do not answer out loud, whatever you do. Think it.*

Chloe nods. *Yes.*

The creature appears to frown again, and suddenly a warmth Chloe hadn't noticed in her head disappears. Before she can wonder what it was, she realizes that it is hard to breath. The air feels as though it is choking her, and with each haggard breath her throat seems to asphyxiate. Her eyesight begins to fog over, but as she loses focus, she is aware of flurry of motion. A collection of the tentacles release their grip on her right shoulder in order to receive an object from another creature to the side, and then come down with force upon on her neck.

There is pain, and then there is darkness.

# CHAPTER SEVENTEEN

VEELA DISAPPEARS into sleep before Ikka even has her boots off. She sits, her back against the straw-lined wall, legs stretched out in front of her, as Veela's chest rises and falls in a steady rhythm. He seems so at peace, face serene in slumber. As she watches him, Ikka realizes her fingers are tapping again, this time on her right thigh.

Tap-tap-tap-tap-tap.

Tap-tap-tap-tap-tap.

She wills them to stop, wrangling her body back to stillness. She keeps her eyes trained on them so they can't start up again, seeing them but looking past them, dissolving into the feeling of her hand on her leg. She doesn't often take the time to feel her own body, to remember what it's like to be inside it. It feels... constrained. As though she is trapped inside a tainted shell, a prison of past horrors. Her hands are her own, these fingers she's staring at connected to her brain, but she knows they've failed her before. Her entire body is a sensation of betrayed inaction.

She's beginning to remember more. The flashes of nightmares teetering at the edge of her consciousness. They're becoming clearer, consistent in their horrific content. Rows and rows of brightly lit chambers, her body a useless cage chained to the ground. She can feel the hard metal biting into her thighs, the thick pipes bouncing against her shins. And being hurt time and time again from the inside out. But then there's that other section of these memories, the one that makes no sense. Thick grey worms, writhing amongst her limbs. Weighing her down so she can't move, eyeless faceless stalks performing experiments upon her form.

Tap-tap-tap-tap-tap.

Her eyes refocus on her fingers. They are unmoved.

Tap-tap-tap-tap-tap.

The soft repetitions come from the door.

She says, "Who's there?"

Three syllables echo back, perplexing her enough to her inch open the door.

"An ally."

Through the crack she sees his eyes, slanted crescents with grey-blue peeking out from within. It was the man from the passageway shadows who had spoken to Gaarwine. His face is lacking the serious nature it held before. It is now mischievous in composition, making him look younger, kinder.

"I'm Daracha. I'm going to free Delu. Care to join?"

• • •

Once again, Ikka and Veela find themselves traversing

dark passageways, trusting the navigation of a stranger. Ikka tries to keep track of the tunnel identifications they pass as best she can, but after the ninth intersection they become a jumble of letters and numbers in her mind. Veela grows restless by her side. To him, Daracha is a confusing mix of black hair, blue eyes, and unexplained ease in a secretive situation. Veela gives Ikka a look to suggest they should ditch Daracha, slip down a different tunnel at a crossroads and not look back. Ikka ignores him.

The farther they walk, the colder the tunnels become. The air drops steadily in temperature and fog escapes their nostrils with each exhale. The tunnels grow narrower and less finessed. There are no hanging plants, fewer support beams, and no stones lining the ground. Any trace of a breeze has dissipated, and the air is steadily becoming more stagnant. A lack of air vents causes the space to darken with each step, until Daracha pulls a small glass lantern from within his coat and lights the candle inside it with a flint. The intersections become scarcer, and then Daracha introduces them to a new figure hiding in the shadows.

This man is very slim, narrow from his toes to his face, his gaunt cheeks accentuated by a tight topknot of thin brown hair resting above his head, making his head look both narrower and longer. He has a quiet presence, not in aid of being secretive, but from a lifetime of introversion. Daracha greets him with a hearty slap on the shoulder and wide smile.

"Ikka, Veela—this is Callyr. He'll show you to the others, I'll be with you shortly."

Callyr nods at them, polite but not interested in further exchanges. Veela is amused by him, but Ikka looks to Daracha.

"And Delu?"

"I'll fetch him. See you soon!"

• • •

Callyr leads them to a cavern three times the size of the one they sleep in, filled with plants—and seven other members of the Settlement, all under forty, sitting in the shadows between the plants. Gaarwine is the only exception to this age bracket, and he starts when he sees Ikka and Veela in the door.

"I thought I told yer two to stay out of trouble tonight. This counts as trouble!"

He throws a menacing grimace in their direction which Callyr stares down.

"Daracha summoned them."

Gaarwine says, "Aye, I'm sure he did."

Callyr gestures at Ikka and Veela to settle themselves on the ground, and moves away to sit by himself in another section of the chamber. The room waits in silence, until Delu and Daracha arrive.

"Sorry we left yer there all day. Thought it was for the best."

Delu's eyes twinkle. "It was. Convening like this during working hours is not possible, so you saved me my strength from the day's chores. I've had time to think."

Delu and Daracha sit on the ground next to a plant with small red fruits hanging from pale orange leaves. All faces in the room are turned towards the two of them, and Daracha begins to speak.

"This morning, Ocnus and Azzam, and their secondary trio of council elders, banished Delu to the S4-Q9 tunnel end.

They disposed of him there, in the hopes that if he were out of sight he would be out of mind, and we would forget what they consider to be his crazy theories. I know you're all aware of the truth, but we need to find a way to get through to more members of the Settlement. We need to fight back. And we need to do it now."

There are nods from the other men.

Delu says, "Not fight—we need to talk to them. We need Ikka to talk to them. They will listen to her."

Ikka's mind attempts several responses. It settles for the most basic.

"What?"

"You are the second, Ikka, the second ever female any of us have seen. Most of us thought The Mother was the last, that the female line ended with her. But here you are. Your existence proves that there's hope, that we don't just have to roll over as a species and give up until our time is done."

The muscles on Ikka's face don't move, but her aura projects intense skepticism.

Delu says, "Don't look at me so. You told me yourself, you left The Race by choice. Even without your memories intact you knew it was wrong. You knew your only hope was in abandoning it. And I know now you've seen our Settlement you must understand this isn't the right option either, hiding underground for the rest of your days. Whatever hurt you, we need to fight it. We need to stop it from hurting anyone else. And you are so unique down here, so singular in your existence, that they will listen. They will hear your words."

"My words?"

"You merely need to tell them what happened. Why you left The Race."

"Why I left The Race?" Ikka gazes around the room, eyeing off the men crouched in the darkness beside her. They are all watching her, acceptance of her importance firm in their minds. Delu, Gaarwine, Daracha, Chiyo. Even Veela. Veela is looking at her like he knows, too. Knows that she's important— has always known that she's important. She says, "I'm not anyone's salvation. I'm a racer with an X-Runner phobia."

Delu says, "That's not true."

"Yes, it is. I wouldn't even sleep in my vehicle I was so scared. I'd lie on the desert ground next to the dying embers of a fire, knife always in my hand, I was that terrified of being taken. So all right, yes, the vehicles aren't to be trusted, I've always known that. But that doesn't mean I know why, not any more than The Mother or the other leaders of your Settlement already do. I'll help you with whatever you try, but I can't be the one you pin your hopes on." As she finishes this speech, Ikka realizes that many of the men in the room are averting their eyes—Gaarwine included—to leave this as a conversation between herself and Delu. She inclines her head at their downcast eyes. "So you're the leader of this resistance?"

He smiles. "Resistance. I hope that's what we will become. Please, Ikka, we need you."

"No, you need my memories, and even I don't have them. Not here"—she gestures with her fingers to her skull—"But just below the surface, somewhere. They're not quite ready for extraction. I'm sorry."

Delu nods in understanding, his eyes sympathetic. They

sit in silence and after a time the other men all raise their eyes. No one is sure what to say, and the quiet stretches out like a noose intent on strangling them all. It is diverted by the loud crunch of Veela biting into a cream coloured, oblong shaped vegetable. All the heads in the room snap to the noise source, and a wry smile is brought to both Ikka and Gaarwine's lips. Veela is oblivious to the fact he's interrupted a rather morose moment.

He says, "Hey, what about my box?"

"What are yer going on about now?"

"You and the guru one"—he nods towards Delu—"must have that pack of ours somewhere. There was a box in it. Last time Ikka had an episode, I found her with it in her hands."

He has everyone's attention now—Ikka's included.

"I found it—actually I'm not sure when I found it. But I knew there was something special about it, so I kept it. When Ikka and I hooked up, it did something strange to her."

Delu says, "Is this true?"

Ikka nods. "He's right. There's something… wrong with it. It brings out something wrong inside me."

Delu exchanges a look with Gaarwine who nods, rises, and leaves the room.

• • •

As they wait for Gaarwine, a chap with soft brown hair and large dimples fossicks through his pockets before handing some small nuts around the room. He ends on Veela and Ikka, offering some nuts with his right hand and miming eating some with his left.

Veela chuckles. "Yeah. Got it."

Ikka smiles. "Thank you."

His dimples deepen and he bows his head, scurrying back to his seat across the room. Delu and Daracha are holding counsel, Veela is occupied sampling each new bounty the various plants have to offer, and no one else is brave enough to talk to Ikka. It suits her fine, and she allows herself time to scan further through her broken memories. She is not sure if she is ready to discover whatever lies in the depths of her mind, but one day in this place has shown her that inaction is intolerable. It doesn't matter how tight the darkness wraps around her heart, attempting to pull her brain down her throat to drown it in her stomach, ignorance will never be her choice.

She hisses over to Veela, "Come here for a second."

He complies, passing her a small freckled green fruit as he scoots in beside her. "Make a hole in the skin with your teeth, and then suck out the insides. They're incredibly sweet and delicious."

Ikka's unimpressed. "I doubt the purpose of this room is to be your own personal buffet."

He shrugs. "Well no one's asked me to stop yet. Try it."

She scowls, but follows his instructions. He is right, the soft pink flesh is sweet and juicy.

"Happy?" She doesn't pause for his reply. "Do you honestly not remember where you found it?"

Veela's face slips into seriousness. He leans in closer, his head resting against the wall beside her so he can whisper.

"No. I've had it for a long time though, I think. Every time I considered doing a cull of the bits I've collected, I'd hold on to it. I thought it was important. I guess I was right."

Ikka can hear the smile in his whisper. She turns the

empty fruit skin over in her hands. She says, "Have you always collected things?"

"I think so. You wouldn't even believe how much I've collected this past day, it's a habit."

"What do you mean?"

"Just that I like taking things… I don't have them on me, since we came here straight from bed, but if you were to look over our room, you'd find a few things that probably aren't meant to be there."

"What kind of things?"

"Well, your knife for one, though that doesn't count as you gave it to me—"

"Lent! For safeguarding. You should have it on you now, nitwit. What else have you got?"

"Let me see, in order of our day, there's the cup I drank from in The Mother's chamber, the wee plate our lunch was on, the shirt I stitched up in the afternoon, one of the tunnel naming demarkations, a flask of that nettle-blossom drink from dinner, not to mention all the foods I've sampled throughout the—"

"An entire flask?"

"I saw an opportunity and I took it."

Ikka shakes her head, some strands of her thick brown hair brushing against the whiskers on Veela's face.

"You have a problem."

He remains positive. "Oh, I don't know. I find everything always comes in handy at some point or another. Think about now, thanks to my supposedly problematic habit, you've been able to try a wonderful new fruit. Also this whole box thing. Seems like everyone in this room's going to be thankful for my proclivity very soon."

Ikka peers at Veela out of the corners of her eyes. She says, "Do you think it's going to work?"

"If you let it."

"That's very non-committal."

"So's asking me a question only you have the answer to."

Ikka narrows her eyes at him. She says, "I don't like it when you adapt my speech patterns."

Veela grins. "Annoying, aren't they? Look, I know it's not much comfort, but when I found you last time, no matter what you've told me, I know you remembered something, and it scared you, hard. But this time it's not going to be a nasty shock. You'll be ready for it. And I'll be right here, supporting you. They all will, too."

Ikka begins to respond, but is interrupted by Gaarwine's return to the room, his silhouette blocking almost all the light drifting in from the entrance tunnel. As he steps in, his shape grows more definition, and Ikka can see a hessian cloth wrapped around a rectangle object in his hands. Her stomach tightens at the sight.

Daracha speaks. "Any trouble?"

Gaarwine shakes his head. "Nah. No one's up an' about in those sections."

Gaarwine kneels down, placing the hessian cloth in the middle of the room. He looks to Delu for confirmation, and then lifts the cloth aside to reveal Veela's box.

There it sits, in its brown simplicity. Its smooth edges catch the moonlight, rolling down its sides in a continuation of shape. There isn't a hard line in it. Everyone in the room is silent, forming their own impressions, waiting for either Ikka or Delu to do something. Delu starts talking to Veela across the room.

"Is there anything of note you can tell us about this device?"

Veela smiles apologetically. "Sorry, buddy, I really wish I could, but it's just something I collected over time. It didn't even look like this when I found it. It was a lot... grimier when I had it."

"Grimier?"

"Blacker. It was in a layer of dirt. Ikka cleaned it with the high-grade disinfectant the X-Runner's are stocked with."

The lad with the dimples leans in to whisper something in Delu's ear. Delu nods and looks to Ikka.

"Do you think it could have been the fumes that triggered your memory?"

Ikka is insulted by the suggestion, but keeps her tone even. "Perhaps, but it had a delayed effect if it was."

"And so what happened, when you opened it?"

"Oh, I didn't open it. There's a little hook on the underside, but I couldn't pry it open. Cleaning it was as far as I got, and then I—"

*Seized up.*

"—And then I fell into some kind of trance, till Veela broke it in the morning."

Delu nods again. Ikka is growing tired of his nodding. Her right fingers start tapping aggressively on her thumb. She says, "Why don't one of you try opening it? Stop waiting for me to have a meltdown and do something proactive about this."

"Ouch!" Veela intones under his breath.

Delu looks steadily into her eyes. "Is something bothering you, Ikka?"

Her face radiates a heat that suggests if she weren't holding her body so rigid, she'd like to tear everyone's faces off. She can feel her nails indenting on her thumb. But her voice stays even. "Just open the damn box."

• • •

Of course, it isn't that easy.

Dimple man and another with short, sandy coloured hair and hazel eyes are the first to attempt prying the box open. Its exterior is so smooth that the edge between the lid and the body of the box is invisible in its surface, forcing them to simply imagine it's really there. There is no obvious place for them to insert a knife and wedge it open. They fiddle with the hook on its underside, endeavouring to push it down and force a reaction. Instead, one of their hands manages to ricochet back and slap them in the face. The man with the sandy coloured hair, Madoc, is swearing under his breath. Gaarwine gives him a gentle slap against his head and suggests he calm down. The exchange belies a history on Madoc's behalf of being quick to temper. The lad with the dimples—Hurste—cheerfully passes the box over to Daracha to attempt opening. He doesn't feel like trying again.

Daracha is careful, tracing his fingers over the entire surface of the box, searching for irregularities. He pulls out his knife and stabs it into the compacted dirt floor. He digs into it, upheaving some of the earth, and then places it on the box. He rubs it in, roughly covering the entire surface in dirt, his hands becoming filthy in the process. When he's done, he lifts it to his face and gently blows the loose dirt off the box. As he blows, most of the box returns to its clean form, but tiny lines of dirt remain, embedded into microscopic grooves in the box's surface. He allows himself a small smile before holding the box up for the others to see.

The grooves trace along the bottom of the box, travelling up its sides in intricate spirals, free flowing across the horizontal panels in a wave-like pattern. They culminate in a sphere of speckled dots, resting upon the box's lid. There is a murmur of appreciation from the men in the room. Ikka remains silent, a weight plunging into the pit of her stomach. None notice. Daracha runs his finger over the sphere of dots, peculiarly positioned off centre to the left end of the lid. He traces down the tails of the waves, which dissolve into two single strands that wrap under the box's base and around the little hook. He endeavours to push the hook, first in, then across. It doesn't budge. He looks to Delu for guidance, but Delu's eyes are trained on Ikka. Her body is more rigid than the wooden posts reinforcing the mud walls. Her pupils are wide, entranced with fear. Her breathing has slowed to the edge of usefulness.

"Ikka…"

Delu's voice is soft, barely knocking at the edge of her consciousness. Ikka does not notice; her eyes are trained on the box as though it is an enemy preparing to pounce. She inches towards it, her fingers reaching out to touch its surface. They hover above it, like magnets unable to connect.

"Ikka? You okay, buddy?"

Again, her brain doesn't register the words. Her lips begin quivering and tears bite at the edge of her eyes. She is unaware of them, her pupils scanning the dots in frantic desperation. Her fingers press against the invisible barrier, pushing onto the box's cool surface. The moment they connect, she gasps, years of pain rushing to the surface of her mind.

They are tentacles; the worms, the vines, the objects that have been stalking her dreams. They belong to giant creatures that hover above her, their army of appendages inflicting unbelievable pain.

Ikka yelps, and then recoils, throwing her body away from the box and the centre of the room. She crawls to the wall, hiding underneath the leaves of a plant, her mind not present in the reality of the room.

Veela moves towards her, and she flinches, whimpering as he touches her hand.

"Hey, Ikka, it's okay, buddy. You're okay here."

Ikka doesn't see him, her eyes are lost in that other location, her body frozen in pain.

She whispers, "*I* am not okay. *This* is not okay. I told you they were harvesting us. I didn't know for what, or why. But now I know who they are now. They're them—" Ikka nods in the direction of the box, tears glazing her eyes. "They're not human, Veela. They're monsters. And this whole race thing is a sick front for some kind of birthing farm."

"Okay." Veela nods and wipes some of Ikka's tears away with his thumb. "I believe you. And if you don't want to talk at their meeting tomorrow, I won't let them make you. I'll fight every last one of them to keep you safe."

Ikka chuckles, despite herself, the mirth reaching her eyes. She gently pats Veela's hand away from her face, and looks to Delu and the other men in the room, who have been listening to her and Veela's exchange attentively.

She says, "I'm sorry, I can't be here right now. I'll talk to your Settlement in the morning, but for now I need some time to myself. I need to…"

She trails off, unsure of what she needs. But then she stands, the movement distressed, and stumbles from the room. Veela follows her, and another—perhaps it is Madoc, or Callyr—to guide her where she needs to go. When she reaches her sleeping chambers, she collapses. Her body is overcome with sadness. Every limb, every digit, every muscle, and every inch of flesh wants to recoil off her bones, to cower and cry at the horror. Yet she doesn't cry. She doesn't know how to release it, isn't sure if she'll ever be able to stop once she starts.

She lies in the darkness, spine rigid, every muscle clenched to hold in the tension. She can hear Veela standing in the doorway, unsure of what to do. He closes the door, takes off his boots, and lies down next to her. He takes her right hand in both of his and pries open her curled fingers, holding onto them gently. They begin to relax, and it sets off a chain reaction across her body. As her muscles release tension, it feels as though old wounds burn to the surface. Her forehead is on fire, her throat swollen with needles. She lies still, the pain forcing its way out of her eye ducts in icy, biting tears. She doesn't heave loudly, her chest doesn't rock with the expulsions. Instead, she squeezes Veela's hand, so tight she feels as though his fingers will break under the pressure. And through that grip, and through the flames in her mind and the stinging of her tears, she lets the horrors leave her. One wave at a time.

# CHAPTER EIGHTEEN

K'VINNA has the division's assistants contain the human in a pressurized chamber when U'mulig and other members of the breeding division arrive and demand to speak to nem. U'mulig latches on to K'vinna with one of nir black consciousness tentacles.

*Where is the breeder, K'vinna?*

K'vinna refuses to use the consciousness with U'mulig. Ne disengages.

"We have the contained the human, U'mulig. You are not needed here."

U'mulig is less versed at speaking out loud. Ne is uncomfortable doing so in front of all these witnesses.

"K'vinna, the *breeder* is property of the *breeding* division."

Nir emphasis is stressed with unease.

"The human ceased to be property of the breeding division when the breeding division ceased to adequately contain it. We do not have the time to clean up after your poor management, U'mulig. We are already doing so in so many other ways."

K'vinna can feel T'vil's anxiousness behind nem. Perhaps ne is crossing a line. K'vinna forces nir voice to sound more pleasant.

"Either way, U'mulig. We will be obtaining a younger spread of humans from your division in due course, unworn ones, as this one seems to be. It is a necessity in order to improve the fo'ster-vi'kle. Why go to all the effort to take this one back up with you, wipe its memory, and reintegrate it without disturbing the others, when you will just be ordered to return it down here in a day's time. This is not a battle you should fight, U'mulig. It is not worth either of our time. You might as well leave it here. We do not mind what it knows."

U'mulig is affronted, but has no case to argue. After a pause, ne nods curtly and exits the division, nir workers in tow. As K'vinna watches nem leave, T'vil floats up behind nem, discreetly engaging the consciousness.

*What was that about? The human?*

*No. It was time U'mulig was taught a lesson. We are not here to serve the breeding division.*

T'vil is quiet for a few moments, and K'vinna can feel nir heightened concern when ne says, *Are you sure that is wise?*

K'vinna doesn't reply, disconnecting and leaving T'vil confused behind nem. K'vinna nemself is haunted by a singular, much more pressing concern. How on S'vekke did that human hear nir thoughts?

• • •

The research staff have all finished working for the day.

As K'vinna drifts in a repetitive loop around nir office, ne can tell there are no Gu'ten left on the floor. K'vinna is still confounded by the day's events. How could the consciousness be engaged—without nir choosing—by a creature as lowly as a human?

None of the Gu'ten's research has shown that humans have the neural capacity to facilitate such an event. Their intellectual development is at minimum several millennia behind the Gu'ten. It is possible that this breeder is an anomaly in the system, but even this is not an acceptable explanation. The human species is too young for such anomalies to occur. This one is most likely not special. Ne should not have fought U'mulig to retain it. K'vinna sighs. A trickle of motion travels down nir tentacles to reflect the internal signal.

Ne knows it was unwise to berate U'mulig in front of nir staff. U'mulig will not let it slide, and ne has too many problems in need of addressing without adding animosity from other divisions to the list. Ne stops looping to catalogue them in nir mind.

1] Find definitive cure for the be'lysning by the close of two trimesters (highly unlikely),

2] Find method of human reproduction that doesn't utilise the inseminators—human males (possible, but accompanied by genetic complications that will create more work).

3] Prevent the breeding division from cutting more corners that will demand more of the research division (possible, but more difficult now that ne has addressed U'mulig with public hostility).

4] Address the issue of the breeder who read nir

thoughts. Ne cannot have a member of the division (or worse, another division) scan its mind and register K'vinna's connection with the creature through the consciousness. An enquiry will undoubtedly be launched, and K'vinna would be publicly shamed. (Easy. Ne can kill it in the cell and claim the pressure levels were accidentally changed overnight. Ne can do this without delay. One problem off the list. Excellent).

5] Deal with—

Oh, dear. U'ngdom.

• • •

K'vinna absorbs nemself back into the consciousness, reconnecting with the memories U'ngdom shared. As K'vinna scrolls through them, ne experiences them how U'ngdom did— in the first person. K'vinna can see U'ngdom's offspring E'neste in nir tentacles. So small, barely one-eighth the size of an adult Gu'ten, E'neste cannot be more than a few weeks old. Too young to initiate the consciousness, but K'vinna can tell that that's what E'neste wants. To connect. Like every new Gu'ten, before even knowing what the consciousness is, E'neste wants to feel the connection; to access the knowledge of hundreds of millennia passed down through the neural pathways of one Gu'ten to the next. But there is something else. The way E'neste's tiny tentacles are moving—attempting to cling to nirs (but failing, they have no gripping fibres yet, no muscular strength)—K'vinna can feel something else. Not the consciousness, but in the way E'neste clings to nem, K'vinna can feel the trust. The unconditional love. And in this moment, as K'vinna feels the younger Gu'ten's yearning for a connection, ne reaches with a splatter of nir labour tentacles and injects E'neste with a large does of the be'lysning.

It doesn't resonate immediately, either with K'vinna or the young Gu'ten in the memory, what has just transpired. Then, like a rock thrown into a pond, there is a tidal wave in E'neste's small bl'omsterlok (the seemingly translucent sack that contains a Gu'ten's neural pathways and vital organs). The tidal wave is small at first, an inconspicuous pinprick of white that after a second begins contaminating the lake around it. The murky white fluid ripples across the f'et (the insulating layer that protects the bl'omsterlok's content). By the close of four seconds, it has covered two thirds of the f'et, like a cloud of dust and gas. E'neste's kinetic reaction follows immediately after that. Nir young tentacles seize up, then droop helplessly. It is only K'vinna's grip that prevents E'neste from sliding to the floor like a pile of sludge. And then, the young Gu'ten cries. A wail so pitiful, it transports K'vinna deeper into nir own consciousness, back to a time when—

*No.*

K'vinna closes that memory. Ne returns to U'ngdom's pain in poisoning nir offspring with the be'lysning. It hurts, but it is for the greater good. U'ngdom knows this. K'vinna sighs, closing the consciousness. Ne knows it, too.

• • •

K'vinna glides down the length of the research division, passing the empty work chambers of the different research teams. First is K'nurre's chamber, an immaculate, organized space. The only element of K'nurre's research not tidied away overnight is the centrepiece. A breeder in the process of gestation floats in a translucent sack in the middle of the chamber. Its flesh has been sliced down the middle, peeled back to provide access to the exposed organs and growing foetus beneath.

The breeder, a human female reaching thirty years, stirs into half-consciousness, eyes struggling to open through the pain—it is mildly sedated so the pain does not shock it to death, but anaesthetics are not administered so as to not corrupt the research findings. When the breeder opens its eyes, K'vinna is unmoved by the dull terror present in them. The fact that they have been stained red by burst blood vessels is not important, nor is the involuntary salivation dripping out its mouth anything other than repulsive. The bodily functions of humans have always felt particularly rudimentary and garish to K'vinna.

Ne turns nir back on it and continues travelling past the other research chambers. G'nist's research chamber is a lot busier—K'vinna can tell G'nist worked nir team until the last possible moment, and that they will pick up exactly where they stopped in the morning. There are human foetus specimens preserved in jars lining the bench space closest to the entranceway. Little trophies, harking back to when G'nist first made a significant contribution to the Gu'ten's research against the be'lysning. At the beginning of nir career, G'nist managed to extend the effectiveness of the fo'ster-vi'kle—ne developed it from a mere painkiller to something that might stave off the terminal effects of the Be'lysning by a year or two by changing how the fo'ster-vi'kle was pried from the human offspring. It was before K'vinna was born, and G'nist is yet to make any other contributions of note. The foetus jars, once a source of pride, now seem to K'vinna like a cruel mockery, a reminder of the Gu'ten's failure to preserve their own species.

Ne continues, more research chambers, office chambers,

and storage pockets flit by. Everything is clinical and smells unnaturally sterile, until it doesn't. K'vinna can feel the rancid perspirations of the caged humans wrap around nir body before ne can see them. There are rows of them in cages barely the width of their bodies, deep enough only for them to stand, lining the walls of this section. The tanks are made of a reinforced glass that is engineered to prevent the outside air pressure from rupturing the lungs of the human test subjects inside—in order to float and breathe, the Gu'ten require a mix of two complex gasses in the atmosphere, which are not naturally occurring on this planet, or hospitable to human lungs. Some of caged humans are awake, weary eyes watching K'vinna drift past them. Others are sleeping, their heads pressed against the glass walls, their knees and elbows jutting against the walls to keep themselves upright in their slumber. Others still are less fortunate, their bodies a huddled mess of limbs and torso compacted in the bottom of their tanks. These ones in particular are covered in sores and callouses, their skin rubbed raw from continual contact with the glass. Their flesh is a patchwork of bruises and sallow skin.

Unlike the humans in the breeding division, these ones are not fitted with the b'leie—the mechanical diapers—so they can be removed from the tanks for experiments at any time with ease. Instead, the humans' urine and faecal matter is allowed to fall down their legs and amass on their tank floor until the weekly tank flush—which happens whilst the humans are still inside, doubling as their sole source of cleaning. Prolonged exposure to standing in their own waste has caused the humans to develop a condition on their feet whereby the skin turns blue or red, swells, and then blisters until many layers of flesh peel back and the offending feet need to be amputated. When this happens, the humans are then returned to their tanks and quite often the process repeats itself on their remaining stumps or knees—as long as their reproductive organs are not affected by these events, the Gu'ten are unconcerned.

K'vinna might be inclined to pity the human test subjects this one aspect of their confinement, if it were not for their odour's ability to violate the air beyond the glass walls, especially after the rot has set in. K'vinna increases nir pace, eager to leave these scents behind. Ne knows the breeder that escaped this morning is at the very end of this section. It will be easy, as easy as dialling back the atmospheric gauge on its tank, to cease the breeder's existence and solve nir problem. It will be attributed to a mechanical error, and listed as an acceptable loss in the system.

Yet, when K'vinna arrives at the breeder's tank, ne eyes it with curiosity. How could a creature so base connect to the consciousness? It is narrow, like most of the specimens bred within the facility, but paler than the standard complexion. Over the past seventy plus years of breeding, each new yield of humans loses their distinct characteristics, turning several breeds of humans into a more uniform, singular race. An earthy brown complexion, brown hair, brown eyes, is the norm. But this human—the ID tag around its neck declares it to be C-H-L-O-3—has paler skin than most, a shock of orange hair, and green eyes. It is peculiar to gaze upon.

The green eyes watch K'vinna with concern, and for a second K'vinna remembers seeing nir own face—that is the human word for it, inadequate as it may be—from the human's eyes. How strange ne looks, a floating sack of liquid with shadows for eyes. K'vinna smirks at the description as ne shakes off the memory, and wonders what the human is thinking now. It is inconceivable, but this particular breeder appears more unique than repulsive to K'vinna. Ne wants to know what else is inside, what, if anything, is happening within its brain.

So K'vinna decides to throw all caution to the wind. Ne's going to open its tank.

• • •

The glass dissolves like thousands of water droplets evaporating into the air. There is no splashing, no shattering, only a giant whoosh as the air around Chloe's head is torn away into the outside space and the momentum throws her body forward. Her ears begin to pop and her body makes headway towards the floor. A cluster of tentacles intervene, catching her moments before impact. She breathes a sigh of relief, and the last of the tank air evacuates her lungs. They are invaded by the general building air. Her lungs feel as though they are going to explode—she can't breathe this new air, can't exist with it inside her.

She tries to cough it up—her ears and sinuses are shouting with pain now—but it is only replaced with a new batch of poisonous air. Her vision begins to blacken a little, little pinpricks of darkness massing between her brain and what is in front of her. Her coughing and spluttering begins to slow down, the movements laboured, but she becomes aware that the tentacles have carried her to a shelf. She is spasming on it, sharp pains shooting through her body, and then something metallic is slammed into her mouth. Her nose is pinched shut. With nowhere to go, the poisoned air inside her expands, pushing her lungs to their limits, and then dissipates. A natural breath follows, accompanied by the cold, bitter taste of iron. At least it doesn't hurt. The screaming in her ears pops away with a single gulp, and her vision begins to clear.

The creature is staring at her. She can tell it is the one that caught her earlier. It moves in a different way to the ones who placed her in the tank, and the others she's spied drifting in the corridor. This one is more contained. Its tentacles don't spread so far as it drifts, and its water-sack-head-thing seems to have specific shadows for its eyes, or at least she thinks they're eyes. They always seem trained in her direction. She doesn't trust this being—she doesn't have any idea if its shadow eyes see her as friend or foe, but she feels as though she should thank it. She raises her hand and gestures at the metal contraption in her mouth, and tries to smile around it. It's a foolish move. The outside air sneaks its way inside, attacking her windpipe with a force as she tries to cough it out.

A single black tentacle disengages from the creature's retracted mass, and wraps itself around her right arm. The moment it settles, her body is flooded with a warmth and a strong voice enters her mind.

*It is unwise to open your face-sucker. It will prevent the o'rdne from working correctly.*

Chloe nods, unsurprised this time to hear its voice inside her head.

*You're not, are you?*

She shakes her head, unsure how else to respond.

*You just have to think it. Whilst the consciousness is engaged, I will know everything that you think. I will think it, too. Your thoughts will be my thoughts, your mind will be my mind.*

*Will your thoughts be mine?*

*No. My thoughts will remain my own. We will not be having a repeat of this morning. But I will advise you of anything I deem necessary.*

*What happened this morning? Where am I?*

*Why is it you assume I am here to answer your questions?*

*I...*

Chloe gulps. She does not know how to present herself to this creature. She is completely exposed. A naked eleven year old. Hair matted, legs and feet stained with the day's urination. Dumped on a bench, nothing to cover her body or her fear. And this creature. This alien. A floating mass of tentacles, one wrapped around her wrist, present inside her mind. She cannot imagine what it would want from her, or what she has to fear.

*You have nothing to fear, at present. I want to know why you are different.*

*I'm not.*

*Not in an overly significant way, but you are different to the other breeders I have witnessed. Would you not concur that you are different?*

Chloe is confused.

*I have... red hair? I haven't seen another racer with red hair before?*

*No. I am not talking about the surface level.*

The creature extracts more tentacles from its fold. A collection of the grey coloured ones reach up and wrap around her skull, plying their way underneath her hair. They don't feel wet, but prickly. It gives her skin goosebumps to feel their touch.

*I am referring to what is in here. Is it not different?*

*... I don't know. I don't think so. I don't know how I would know.*

*No. I suppose not. Even if you are different to the others, it is unlikely you would be that advanced.*

*Would you know? If you were different to the others of your kind?*

Chloe suddenly feels cold. Not externally cold, rather the warmth has evacuated her mind—and it makes her feel empty, more vulnerable than when it was inside her. The creature is as silent as it has ever been, shadow eyes watching her, grey tentacles still gripping her skull. She tries to hold its gaze. Stares deep into those shadow pits. She speaks out loud, the first time since her failed escape, her voice unsure and weak. It is muffled by the presence of the o'rdne in her mouth.

"Please don't leave me."

The creature tilts its head, and she realizes it cannot understand her.

She reaches with her left hand, clings onto the black tentacle wrapped around her right.

"Please."

The bulb's tilt increases another degree or so. And then—

The warmth returns.

*Please don't leave me.*

Silence.

She can feel it thinking, feel the indecision, but not the

thoughts. She wants them back. It's not justifiable, this need. She doesn't know if she can trust this creature—she doesn't even know what this creature is. But even after this brief, ambiguous interaction, she knows that its company is preferable to the silence, to being alone in a glass tank without any indication of her fate.

*I cannot change that, C-H-L-O-3. Sharing the consciousness will not prevent your existence from returning to your holding tank.*

*But it will delay it.*

Chloe's thoughts sound needy. Her cheeks flush, embarrassed. She knows Sam would not risk showing this much vulnerability.

*Perhaps. But here you are, in another level of The Facility, and this* Sam *is still in the breeding division after how many— nearly twenty—years. There is no need to hide the truth of your situation. It will only be an attempt, a waste of precious energy resources, which are already low in you.*

Chloe nods. Or maybe it is just that her brain thinks the silent acknowledgement that is so often portrayed by a physical bowing of one's head.

*I suspect I would also be unaware if I were different to the others of my kind. It is not something one is instructed in, yet I imagine there would be an inkling, some sense of intuition that something is different.*

Chloe nods again. This time it is a definite physical action. And then she asks, *What is your name?*

There is silence again. She can feel the alien's surprise at her question, as though she should be too self-involved to wonder about it. When its voice resonates in her head again is it careful, measured.

*K'vinna.*

*And what are you?*

*I am a Gu'ten. We are a species far more advanced than your juvenile race.*

*And where are we?*

*We are in the research division of The Facility. I am the head of the research division.*

She can feel the new sternness in the alien's voice, and in the feelings motivating its speech. It is threatened by something about her.

*Yes.*

Its voice is now as hard as the biting metal in her mouth.

*I am certain that you are an anomaly. The fact that you can read my feelings without my choosing to allow you the access is evidence enough. I should terminate you and be done with it. But—*

Chloe can feel a definite sigh resonate from the creature's warmth in her mind, followed by a mental scowl as it registers her feeling the sigh.

*I am concerned it may be a bigger folly to not study you and determine why you are different, what error has taken place, and ensure any potential catastrophe does not occur and impact the Gu'ten further. We will have to move you from this section.*

Chloe's mind perks up, the possibility of leaving her glass tank on a more permanent basis outweighs any concern or intrigue of this creature—K'vinna—considering her a threat.

*Don't be too excited. It will have to wait until the morning, and even then it will not be what you expect.*

Chloe allows herself a small smile around the mouth

breather—the o'rdne—and floods K'vinna's mind with her hope. She won't give it up.

*Perhaps. Goodbye for now, human C-H-L-O-3.*

The warmth dissipates as K'vinna disengages the consciousness and removes the singular black tentacle from Chloe's right arm. The cluster of grey tentacles wrapped around her skull stay there for a few more moments, gently tilting her head from the left to the right as the shadow eyes peer down at her. Then they, too, disengage and she is gently returned to the glass tank, the front wall materializing as swiftly as it had disappeared. And then K'vinna disappears down the corridor and Chloe is left wondering what the morning will bring.

# CHAPTER NINETEEN

THE COUNCIL meeting starts in a manner Hurste informs them is tradition. Once the hall is filled and its occupants silent, Ocnus and Azzam enter and stand beside their seats at the front of the platform. Ocnus smiles gratuitously out at the crowd, and Azzam nods once and promptly sits. Next, Ocnus says a thanks for the Settlement's safety and the guidance of The Mother that has brought them to this place. Once this is done, the whole chamber sits and the meeting is open to questions and discussions from the floor.

When they reach this point, Gaarwine stands, clearing his throat with a gusto and calling for the attention of the room.

"Excuse me, Ocnus and Azzam, I have topics on which I'd like to speak."

Azzam says, "Very well. Proceed."

"First, I want to discuss the matter of Delu Dhara being locked in the S4–Q9 tunnel end with only a small ration of water. Yer can't go treating our citizens like that, just cause yer don't like what they're saying."

Ocnus's jowls wobble. "Unfounded accusations, Gaarwine."

"Yer lying sod, founded accusations. Founded! We found him in there last night."

There is a ripple of consternation throughout the room. Ocnus rises in his seat, his chin rolls teetering under the movement and the fat on his arm vigorously shaking as he points it Gaarwine's way.

"Do not speak to your elders like that! We protect you all."

"Yer, that's the other matter I want to be talking to yer about. Some of us are starting to think all this protecting ain't doing us much good."

"How dare you, you—"

"—Sit down, Ocnus." Azzam's voice cuts through. Ocnus scowls, but complies as Azzam peers at Gaarwine. He says, "I would have thought your recent brush with the airships would have made you hold the sanctity of the Settlement in higher esteem, Gaarwine. What is this group of yours is so concerned with?"

"Inaction, Azzam."

"Inaction?"

"Yer, the fact we're"—Gaarwine pauses, and shouts to the back of the room—"I think it's better yer explain this one, Delu."

Ocnus's face becomes strained at this announcement; Azzam's merely changes from being bored to intrigued. Delu enters from the back doors of the room with a neutral expression on his face as he walks through the rows of uprooted X-Runner seats to stand before the stage. Delu looks to the elders, but his face is angled so most of the room can see it as well. He is flanked by Daracha, Madoc, and the other three men who had been in the planting room. The initial roar of shock at their arrival dies down, and Delu begins to speak.

"Thank you, Gaarwine. Elders, fellow citizens, this has gone on too long—"

"Hold on, hold on," Ocnus interjects. "You can't just barge in here and take the floor. There are protocols."

"Yes, he can." Daracha steps forward, menace in his eyes and a subtle arm movement revealing a knife stored beneath his vest. "You will face extreme levels of resistance if you don't let him take the floor."

Ocnus's eyes widen in disbelief. He sinks a little deeper into his chair.

Delu carries on as if this exchange had not occurred. "Friends, we are not protected down here, we are trapped. The Settlement founders mistrusted and abandoned The Race because they did not know what was happening, and it seemed safer to withdraw from The Race than continue to live in a state of perpetual ignorance. However, that ignorance has continued on—I have lived in this Settlement since I was two or three years old, and I am now nearing thirty-five years of age. After all this time, nothing has changed. We are as ignorant of the evils behind The Race as we were when the Settlement was first established. The only difference now is that instead of living inside a moving prison, we are contained within a stationary one. I know many of you have not seen the sun in more than two decades. Can you call this living?"

Ocnus scoffs. "Of course you can. It's living free from danger."

"And how long do you think that can continue? How long until those that operate the airships realize we have gone underground? Our technology is rustic, the temperature controlling measures we have in place are no match for whatever sensors they will use when they begin to search for us underground. We are living on borrowed time. We need to fight back before we lose our only advantage, the element of surprise."

There are some approving nods and murmurs from the crowd, yet the majority look unsure, uncomfortable with upsetting the elders. Azzam is unfazed by Delu's speech.

"You have spoken along these lines before, Delu, and we have given you the same response I will give you now. The Mother started the Settlement for our greater good, to keep us safe from the airships and the manipulations of The Race. We know that whenever we leave our underground home the airships hunt us down, and the havoc they cause is devastating. We cannot risk the safety that the concealment of the Settlement provides just because you cannot keep your mind occupied down here. Without conclusive evidence that it is dire for us to remain, it is foolish to even consider leaving the safe haven The Mother has created for us. You already put us at risk every time you sneak off on one of your surface expeditions." Azzam turns to look directly at Gaarwine at this point, his tone dry and unimpressed. "And yes, Gaarwine, on your first matter of concern, we did lock Delu Dhara at the end of the S4–Q9 tunnel yesterday, in the hope that some solitary reflections may bring calm and sense to his mind. Evidently, it was ineffectual."

Ocnus looks smug, content that Azzam has made their point, impervious to further objections. But again, Delu's voice rings through.

"We have conclusive evidence."

The smugness drops from his face, replaced by mild concern.

He says, "I highly doubt it."

Delu calls out, "I'd like to invite the newcomer Ikka to address the council."

There is a substantial shift in the room when Delu mentions Ikka's name. Everybody in the room turns their heads, searching out her position. She inclines her head ever so slightly to acknowledge them and makes her way to where Delu stands next to the stage. Veela and Hurste shadow her there. She looks up at each at Ocnus and Azzam, noting the suspicion and unease manifesting on their faces, and then she looks to the crowd. There she is greeted by curiosity, minds eager to absorb new information. She decides to aim her words at them, not the elders. When she speaks, her voice is steady.

"My name is Ikka. This may seem like a fact to you that could be taken for granted, but for me, it is not. I never said my name out loud until a few weeks ago, had never heard another say it. I have no discernible proof it is my name, either. It is merely the way I pronounce my racer ID in my head. And I still keep that around my neck"—she reaches down the neck of her top, revealing the small ID tag she has tucked next to her breast—"because I'm terrified of forgetting, of not knowing my own name.

"I grew up in The Race, like all of you. I can't remember it, but I know it must be the case, because now... now I can remember an absence from it, during which I wished I was back in it. You all know there are no adult females in The Race—know because meeting The Mother helped you realize that you'd never seen any others. There's a reason why. And no, it's not because we simply don't exist, because look—here I am! It's because when we reach a certain age we get taken. We get taken..."

Ikka's voice trails off, as she's not sure how to continue or if she can survive saying the words out loud. Veela's hand reaches in from behind her, giving her forearm a reassuring squeeze. She doesn't shake him off. Instead, she uses the sensation to steady herself, to centre the storm inside her mind. She tries again.

"I don't know how old I was when I was taken. Still quite young, but my body was transitioning to adulthood. My breasts were growing and it was the first day of my session—when a women's body discards its eggs in blood—that I was taken. I went to sleep in my X-Runner and I woke up in a brightly lit prison. I was naked, chained to the floor by a machine wrapped around my lower torso. I was kept in a small glass cell, only wide enough to walk in, in a forest of glass cells, all occupied by women, all chained to the floor with contraptions like the one around my waist. A lot of the women were pregnant, and the ones that weren't were attacked repeatedly by the machines around their waists until they became with child. Once the babies were born, they were taken—we never saw by who—and the process was repeated. Over and over again.

"For me, it never got to that point. My body was never

able to conceive. I watched the women around me go through the trauma of never holding the lives they created, becoming pregnant and living through the next nine months knowing at the end they'd never even get to look into the child's eyes. And I was attacked every single day by the machine around my waist. I don't know how long it lasted, how many days, months, or even years I was held captive in that cage, my internal spaces brutalised by its mechanics. All I know is that one day it stopped. A gas was secreted into the tanks surrounding mine, all the women inhabitants and I were knocked out. And then I woke up back in The Race. They put me back into The Race."

Ikka falters and then starts again.

"I know I should be grateful—I'm free of that glass prison now—but I'm not free. None of us are. There are creatures—inhuman ones—imprisoning all of the females you've never seen. They're using The Race to control us and track their wares. We're some kind of commodity for them to harvest at their will."

There is a smattering of voices at her words. Azzam raises a hand to silence them.

"And how exactly does this information change our situation? We already knew someone was controlling us through The Race. It makes no difference if that someone is a something." He offers a tight-lipped smile to the faces amongst the room. "We are safe here. The Settlement is a sanctuary for us all from the dangers of The Race. The Mother built it for us, led us here to safety. Naming the horrors outside of this place gives us no reason to leave it. To the contrary, the stories this young woman tells do nothing but strengthen the elders' resolve that the Settlement is not to be left."

Ocnus applauds Azzam's last sentence with a nod, gazing about the room as though he is sure there can be no objections to this logic.

"A sanctuary for you all?"

Ikka walks closer to the stage, staring Ocnus and Azzam down with a glare so harsh, it takes all of their self-control to not flinch. Her words come out stern, unrestrained, and powerful.

"What good is a sanctuary if it's housing a dying breed? I've been told there's sixty-three of you down here, sixty-five if you count Veela and me. All male other than The Mother and myself, and I suspect the reason she and I are both down here rather than in the glass prisons is because we're not going to be of any help to you re-populating the Settlement. You're all going to die down here without furthering any genetic lines. No legacy other than empty tunnels and caverns, if you even manage to escape detection by the aliens for that long."

There is a pronounced intake of breath from the men crowding the hall when Ikka mentions the word aliens. She turns her head sharply back at them, making piercing eye contact with as many of them as she can.

"Yes, aliens. The human race is being farmed by bizarre creatures with hundreds of floating limbs and your wise elders want to do nothing about it. They're content dying in an underground cavern while our female counterparts are being tortured daily and our male counterparts are being constantly drugged by eight-wheeled racing vehicles. This doesn't sound wise to me, it sounds cowardly. Not doing anything about this is as bad as being the perpetrators ourselves. We have a moral responsibility to stop this, no matter the risk."

Ocnus scoffs. "A moral responsibility?"

"Yes. To the women who birthed you. And to your brothers and sisters trapped in The Race. Don't you get it? We come from them. You may have found some sanctuary down here from The Race, but your existence is certainly not separate from it. We are all connected."

When Ikka finishes speaking, the whole chamber is silent, even the elders sit with their brows furrowed at her words. Before any of them can voice a counter argument, she adds one final note to all present in the room.

"Delu, Daracha, and Gaarwine have all tired of the elders' inaction. They're going to do something about this situation, and I'm going to help them in whatever way I can. You should, too. All of you."

Ikka gives her own curt nod to the room, retreating behind Madoc and Hurste. As she passes Delu, he softly intones, "Thank you," before moving forward to address the crowd once more.

• • •

It is painful for Ikka to listen to the discussion that follows. The majority of the meeting participants agree that something *should* be done, but the elders stand firm that they should not risk the Settlement being discovered by the airships. Ikka is not surprised, yet still disappointed by the selfish manner with which they are making their decisions. Delu and Daracha are doing their best to bring sense to the proceedings. Delu is addressing the elders directly now.

"Please, at least let us send a small search party out to

scout and understand what we are up against. Then, with more information, we can form a new plan. I've walked the trails outside of the Settlement before. There are ways to remain undetected and we can swear to not return to the Settlement if the airships are on our tails."

Azzam shakes his head.

"It is not that easy, Delu. To be of any success as a scouting party, allowing for the likelihood of losses along the journey, you would need to take at least, ten, maybe twelve or fourteen members with you, and that is not an easy number to move above the surface undetected."

Ocnus frowns at Azzam.

"You're not considering this madness are you?"

Azzam shrugs ever so slightly.

"It is our duty as Settlement elders to listen on all matters and consider all variables with equal deliberation. Ultimately, Ocnus, it is not our decision to make. Instead, we must offer our advice to The Mother. You know this."

Azzam turns to the fifty heads or so in front him.

"We shall defer to The Mother on this matter, though I believe it is clear the council deems it ill-advised."

• • •

In The Mother's chambers, an air of reverence smothers all hostility between the elders and Delu's faction. Delu's faction kneels in front of The Mother, and the elders kneel to her side. All voices are reduced to hushed tones in her presence, and each awaits their invitation to talk. Azzam has finished relaying the events of the council meeting to her, and Delu is now explaining that he and Daracha wish to take a search party out to gather more information on the alien forces.

The Mother's expression is unreadable, a casing of warmth set in a wise, loving smile that doesn't move an inch. As Delu speaks, she daintily pours each person in the room a small clay cup of warmed herb water. Once this task is complete, she drinks from her own cup, her eyes dancing behind the earthy rim. When Delu finishes speaking, she nods sympathetically, the silver curls lining her face dipping with the motion, and then she places her cup on the ground. She clasps her fingers together, resting her chin on her forefingers to speak. Her voice is gentle and pensive. It brings hope to Delu's faction.

"It is a difficult situation, that is certain. It is heartbreaking to hear tales of fellow women in captivity, and I understand your wishes to help them. However, I am still not sure it is in the best interests of the Settlement to help them. My priority is first and foremost to my children, the citizens of this sanctuary. Each time you have left this place, Delu, you have brought the airships closer. I cannot risk you exposing those under my care to danger because the newest addition to our home is suffering from nightmares."

"Hey—"

Ikka discreetly hits Veela in the side and shakes her head at him before he can continue in her defence. She steels her gaze back in the direction of the Mother, who is not acknowledging her, and still locked in on Delu with her parental gaze.

"I have cared for you nearly your entire life, Delu. Since you were an infant I have carried you on my breast, clothed you, fed you, taught you all that I know. And I have been patient as you've grown into your own person, perhaps more lenient than I should have been, on your desire to explore. Curiosity is natural, but if—as you say, as this stranger states—we are in a war, then it is more pivotal than ever for me to make all decisions based on the best interests of the Settlement. I am our general, Delu, and I say it is madness to risk drawing the airships any closer to where we are safe. You need to trust my wisdom in this matter, and respect my authority as founder of the Settlement, as all others do."

When she finishes this speech, The Mother relaxes a little where she sits, smiling even more broadly at her adopted son. He doesn't return the gesture. His face is etched with quiet sadness, and there is a trace of disappointed petulance in his eyes. He speaks carefully.

"There is no greater reverence than that which I bestow upon you, mother, but I cannot allow it to lead me down a path that I know is wrong. Inaction is the greater madness, wrought from denial of the truth. Trust in me and what I have learnt in all my years as your son. We cannot turn our backs on this. Please, listen to what Ikka has to say for yourself."

The Mother's smile does not diminish an inch, but Ikka can see a hardness register behind her eyes. Her voice maintains its lyrical warmth.

"If that is what it takes for you accept my judgement, my son. I might ask you all to wait outside my chambers, so I can speak with this young woman alone."

Veela throws Ikka a protective look, which she ignores. She keeps her eyes trained on The Mother as all the men start to vacate the room. When Azzam walks past, The Mother asks him to kneel down, and she whispers something in his ear. He nods and then follows the others out of the room, closing the chamber door behind him. The Mother's gaze then comes to rest on Ikka, and the two sit in silence for some time. Ikka waits, allowing The Mother to make the first move. When she does, her face is frozen in the expression of benevolence with which she treated all the men. Her voice matches it, even though the tone is a contradiction to her words.

"So here you are Ikka, to persuade me to abandon all reason."

Ikka raises her eyebrows a little, as if to say, Oh, really?

The Mother purses her lips for a half second and then smiles wider.

"Come, let us speak woman to woman. It seems you have made quite an impact in the council meeting. What is your end game?"

"End game?"

"Yes, Ikka, what is it that motivates you? Do you hope to overthrow me, turn the hearts of the Settlement against their own Mother?"

"Overthrow you? No. I want us to work together. I want us to protect the others, all those suffering in The Race."

The Mother lets out a short, sharp laugh. "Those suffering in The Race? They're fine as long as they stay ignorant!"

"But the women…"

"The women?" The Mother stares across at Ikka, the benevolence still caked onto her face. "My dear, foolish girl. You don't believe we can actually help them, do you? Whoever this enemy is, however normal or strange and monstrous as you have described them to be, we are no match for them. All the technology we possess is from luck or scavenged from theirs. They have designed the X-Runners, and the airships, and this prison you have memories of—and we live in a hole underground. It is our hole, and we have made it as comfortable as we dare, but we face the risk of exposure every time we leave here or another is added to our ranks. We have no hope of beating whatever is out there, of even protecting ourselves on the surface, let alone saving some strangers from their grasp. So no, Ikka, I do not believe we can save the women, and I do not believe we should attempt to remove any others from The Race. It is not in our best interests, and I would take it kindly if you were to stop filling Delu and the others' heads with the notion that it might be."

As The Mother finishes speaking, Ikka takes a moment to sip from her cup before speaking in a civil and even tone.

"What are our best interests worth when they condemn others to a lifetime of pain? You cannot truly believe hiding down here is the best course of action."

"I can and I do. It is my responsibility to make these decisions, to protect my children."

Ikka says, "You're not their mother."

The benevolence evaporates from The Mother's visage. She says, "Pardon?"

"You're no one's mother. A true mother would act in the best interests of her children. You have not."

The Mother's voice takes on a waspish tinge. "How dare you."

"How dare I?"

"How *dare* you speak to me in such a manner! I am *The* Mother! I welcomed you into our home!"

"Into your prison." Ikka holds her ground, her voice firm. "How dare you hold all these people hostage from the truth? You must have known, remembered the horror at some point in all these years. And even if you didn't, you felt it in the terror of being saddled with a child that isn't yours. In the brutality of the airships hunting down your troop, decimating the lives of those you took from The Race. You've brought so many here against their will, awakening them to partial truths, and yet you refuse to let them access further knowledge because you're scared? To prevent them from freeing their brothers and sisters, and mothers and fathers because you're a coward?"

The Mother's eyes are consumed with malice, and her spine stiffens, rising slightly as though she is preparing to strike. She spits her words out between her teeth.

"Don't test my patience, child. I am not here to suffer insolence. This is *my* Settlement, they follow *my* command, *I* know what's best for them, not you." The hostility in her expression makes her face gaunt, and the animosity ages her drastically. She shouts out, "Molan, it is time we deliver this Ikka back to her companions."

• • •

Molan is a ruff individual. Tall, arms trunk-like with muscles, possibly in his late thirties, but with scars that confuse the age lines on his face. The moment The Mother calls, he storms into the chambers from a hidden side door, roughly reaching to pull Ikka to her feet. Ikka relaxes her body and lets it move amicably under his grip as he drags her out the main chamber door to the waiting hall occupied by the elders and Delu's faction.

They are all surprised by the unceremonious motion with which Molan dumps her in front of them, his stump-like fingers still wrapped around her arms. Daracha is the first to his feet, hand reaching for a blade in his belt as he strides forward. Gaarwine intercepts, stepping his large girth between Daracha and Molan. As this exchange plays out, the elders remain seated, watching with mild interest.

"What are yer doing, Molan? That's no way to treat a guest to our Settlement."

Molan sneers. "An unwanted guest."

"Unwanted? Says who?"

"I do." The Mother's serene tones sing out as she steps in behind Molan. "She is filling your heads with nonsense, and I cannot tolerate her presence any longer. Yet, as it is too dangerous for any to surface at this time, I will not banish her, but rather send her to a holding cell until she finds clarity and ceases to be a nuisance."

Ocnus smiles. Delu pushes forward to stand next to Gaarwine.

"Mother, you cannot believe that this is the best course of action."

"I can and I do. No one will be leaving the Settlement. Am I clear?"

"Don't do this."

"Take her now, Molan."

Ocnus's smile widens as Molan begins to shift Ikka through the crowd. Gaarwine follows Delu's move and steps aside to let Molan pass, but he doesn't make it farther than that. Once he is past them, Daracha steps in behind him, so that Molan is now encircled by all of Delu's faction—the elders on the side bench pose no threat. Daracha taps Molan swiftly on the shoulder, and no sooner does Molan's head turn to establish the tapping's source than Ikka raises her right knee up and swings her foot back into his groin. His reaction is instantaneous—he howls, releases her arms, and looks forward in surprise. Daracha seizes the moment to kick him in the back of his knees, which makes him collapse to the floor, his arms clutching his genitals and his eyes resting at level with one of Ikka's three blades.

She smiles at him with quiet amusement. "Sorry about that," she says before staring down the Mother across the crowd. She talks to the others in the space. "Your Mother's been down here too long. She's scared, her judgement has clouded with the years. Now is the time to act, before she finds some cockamamy way to stop us."

The Mother stares back at her, not with indignation, but with a twinkle in her eyes. She claps her hands twice, emitting sharp, flat sounds.

She says, "Too late."

The hall becomes flooded with other inhabitants of the Settlement. They are all in their forties and charge from both ends—deeper in the hallway and from within The Mother's own chambers. They are equipped with crude weapons, broken wood posts with sharp rock fragments attached the top, and sheer numbers. Faces Ikka has never noticed before leer at them, poised to attack.

Azzam rises to his feet, standing on the bench he was

previously sitting on, so that all in the corridor can see him. He directs his speech to Ikka and Delu's faction.

"You have two choices, my friends. You can fight, risking your own lives and those of your fellow inhabitants, because your youthful arrogance makes you believe you know better than our leader. Or you can place your weapons on the ground and our men will escort you to the holding chambers until your heads have cooled and a peaceful resolution can be met."

Those in Delu's faction shift uncomfortably, waiting for Delu to choose their fate.

Daracha whispers, "We can't trust them."

Delu whispers back, "No, but I can't be responsible for so much unnecessary violence. They have us at a bottleneck. We would have to injure them all to get through."

Daracha nods his permission, relaxing his hand once more from the blade on his belt. Delu raises his voice for the benefit of all, but his eyes implore The Mother.

"We will not fight our own brethren. Our wishes are not to cause harm, but to seek knowledge that will protect us in the future and save those who cannot defend themselves. Please, don't do this."

The Mother ignores him. She nods at Azzam.

"Take them away."

She turns on her heels, the crowd parting around her as she returns to her chambers. Delu's faction is then swarmed, their weapons seized and their bodies escorted away. From his seat on the wall, Ocnus claps his hands, his jowls wobbling in delight. Azzam regards Ocnus with disdain, but waits for the hall to become vacant before dismounting the bench. He peers at the now-closed door to The Mother's chambers, regarding it for some time before turning to the darkened hallway, navigating its labyrinth of tunnels on a mission of his own.

# CHAPTER TWENTY

A CLOUD STALKS K'vinna from nir resting chambers to the research division. Yet, even its oppressive weight doesn't prepare nem for the sight of the new addition to nir office chamber. The deep maroon-curtain-covered box mocks nem and nir inability to kill the breeder. K'vinna turns on nir tentacles and exits the chambers as fast as ne arrived. Out in the communal section of the research division, K'vinna feels all of the others watching nir every move. Ne seethes and exits the entire division.

    K'vinna travels the entire length of this building level, passing the designated sleeping places and social areas for all of the research division workers. As a youth, K'vinna had found it odd that The Facility divided the rest areas of the building by division, but, as a department head, ne is now thankful ne doesn't have to navigate interdepartmental politics in nir rest time. As K'vinna continues navigating the labyrinth of corridors, their condition diminishes. The lighting is less prevalent and the walls cleaned less frequently. K'vinna knows ne is nearing nir destination when the walls have an ashy hue and the space is so sparsely lit the hallway has a sallow yellow glow. K'vinna braces nemself outside the doorway, then uses a column of nine labour tentacles to knock against the wall. The thudding sound barely registers in K'vinna's hearing receptors, but is enough to notify the occupant of the room. The door opens and K'vinna drifts inside with caution.

The chamber is small and lit even worse than its hallway entrance. The building's synthetic atmosphere has been altered in this room, so substantial in effect that it colours the space a murky blue. An insipid yellow light illuminates a central resting pod, casting its inhabitant in a squalid green. It is this inhabitant that K'vinna has come to visit, nir old mentor, T'arahn. The poor lighting disguises the extent of T'arahn's illness—if it weren't for the obvious lack of muscular control, one wouldn't know T'arahn was besieged with the be'lysning. T'arahn's bl'omsterlok is resting inside the liquidous pod, nir tentacles spilling over the edges. The majority of them do not move, and there are stumps where the black consciousness tentacles have been amputated. T'arahn's f'et is discoloured, no longer shining its translucent camouflage, but stained a murky off white. Nir two seeing pods are crystallised, unmoving. It is not until K'vinna speaks that T'arahn is able to identify who has come to visit nem.

K'vinna says, "I'm sorry it has been so long between visits."

A ripple passes through T'arahn's bl'omsterlok as the older Gu'ten attempts to speak, nir weak tones amplified by the pod containing nem.

"K'vinna. Time does not register much to me now. What

is the reason for your visit?"

K'vinna stalls in the doorway, guilty that ne has come for selfish reasons.

"Don't hover so awkwardly, K'vinna. Come inside, you'll upset the balance if the door doesn't close soon."

K'vinna complies. The chamber door closes behind nem as ne drifts closer, resting on the floor beside T'arahn's pod, careful to keep their tentacles separate.

"So?" T'arahn says.

"You are unkind," K'vinna says. "Can I not simply wish to see my old mentor?"

"You can, but we both know you are too busy to not have additional motivation."

K'vinna sighs, nir bl'omsterlok rippling.

"I met a breeder yesterday. I have taken it under my dominion."

Even in nir poisoned state T'arahn is taken off guard.

"What? Why?"

"It's… different."

"Different? I'm sure they're all different to each other. That's no reason to take one under your dominion. What does that even mean?"

"I"—K'vinna falters, having to justify nemself to nir mentor for the first time in years—"This breeder was able to enter the consciousness with me. Uninvited."

"Uninvited?" T'arahn's vocals peter off into silence, considering K'vinna's words. Ne tries again, nir voice gentle and concerned. "That is unheard of, K'vinna."

"I know. I have told no one but you. I was going to

arrange its death, to prevent others finding out."

"But you didn't. Why?"

"What if the humans have evolved? What if their species is at a turning point?"

"So what if they are? The higher ups will persecute you if you follow this line of inquiry."

"I know."

The two Gu'ten fall into silence, their minds consumed with thoughts of treason and possibility. T'arahn is the first to break the quiet.

"Do you think this will help with the fo'ster-vi'kle?"

"I do not think so. However, if the humans are becoming more intelligent, their progress needs to be monitored, so an uprising cannot be staged."

"True. Yet it is dangerous, K'vinna, taking this on yourself. How are you justifying the breeder's presence in your dominion?"

"Well, there is a young research assistant who has committed treason."

"Treason?"

"Ne has been experimenting on nir own offspring. I am also taking nem under my dominion. Ne shall continue nir research in secret, under the guise of researching a new extraction method on this human."

"This seems unwise, K'vinna."

"I know, but we are scientists, T'arahn. I cannot turn my bl'omsterlok on this."

It is T'arahn's turn to sigh, the slimy pod barely allowing nem this movement.

"Well, be careful, K'vinna. I would hate to see you terminated before my own existence ends."

"I shall do my best, T'arahn, for all our sakes."

"That is good. Now tell me, what idiocy are those loons in the birthing division up to these days?"

K'vinna chuckles—the Gu'ten version of a chuckle, which is expressed by the rapid flinching of nir clear reaching tentacles. T'arahn cannot see it, but the small hairs on nir own tentacles feel the air displaced by the motion, and ne cannot help but respond. This is an old joke shared between old friends—one neither of them may be able to enjoy again.

• • •

When Chloe wakes she is in yet another glass tank, covered on the outside by a dark cloth. In the dark gloom of the tank Chloe strains her ears, but all sounds are muffled beyond its curtained walls. She looks up to see the familiar sight of a feeder and a drinking tube attached to the tank roof. She realizes she is starving after her past day in the standing tank with no access to food. She jumps up to feed, but her leg gets caught on something in the motion. Something cold. Hard. Persistent. It is the mass of tubes that connect a mechanical diaper to the tank floor. A mechanical diaper containing her lower torso once more.

"No! No! No!"

Chloe shouts at it in distress, hitting it with her fists, tugging at the cables soldered to its base.

"Not again. I can't go through this again."

Tears stream down her face as she keeps hitting at the contraption, her nails clawing at it. She knows attacking it is futile, but she can't stop. Her lungs heave up and down as her distress amplifies and her breaths become quicker and shallower. Somewhere in the back of her mind, she can hear Sam's voice, "*Girl.* Take a deep breath and hold on to it. Each breath is yours. Don't waste them."

She re-slumps to the tank floor, her hands still slapping at the diaper, her sobs only marginally subdued. She sits like this for several moments before flaring up again and punching at the device, hurling abuse its way. Her cries grow louder and louder and she becomes so engrossed in her rage that she doesn't notice the curtain drop, or three of the four glass walls disintegrate around her. She is barely aware as grey tentacles swoop in and intercept her hands, slithering around and lifting her skull, gently hoisting her whole body so her feet are dangling just above the ground. A solitary grey tentacle places a breathing device in her mouth, and a black tentacle creeps forward, wrapping around her left arm. Chloe's eyes are cast down, and she does not raise them even when she feels the warmth of K'vinna's mind engaging with her own. *What are you doing, breeder?*

Chloe clenches her jaw, clenching also at her mind.

*Respond.*

Chloe focuses on the tears clinging to her lids, imagining them as water seeping down the side of an impenetrable brick wall. She can feel abhorrence leaking over from K'vinna's mind.

*Are you... blocking me out?*

The black tentacle tightens around her arm, and more black tentacles descend upon her body, wrapping around all of her limbs. The feeling of warmth intensifies, but Chloe stays strong. She is that brick wall. She raises her eyes to stare at the shadow bulges in Kvinna's head bulb.

*You* are *blocking me out.*

K'vinna tilts Chloe's head to each side, examining her reactions. She keeps her eyes trained on nirs. Ne tries a different tactic.

*Why were you hurting yourself?*

K'vinna lifts Chloe's hands up higher for her to see. The skin on her palms are badly grazed and already bruising. Her lip trembles a little as she sees her injured hands, her memory jogged to the painful reality around her waist.

*I can't go back to this. I can't have it attack me again.*

K'vinna looks at the device on Chloe's body.

*The b'leie? It is designed for your benefit.*

Chloe continues staring at K'vinna's soulless pits. The tone of her answering thought is acidic.

*My benefit?*

*Yes. I requested the b'leie so your waste excretions are of no disturbance.*

*My waste excretions?*

Chloe stares at K'vinna with a furious menace.

*I would rather poo down my legs and stand in my own pee than wear this thing.*

She feels K'vinna consider her words and search her memories of the birthing section and the repeated attacks by the device. K'vinna's thoughts of these memories feel very pensive to her. Ne makes no comment, but moves a flurry of grey tentacles out of her sight. The mechanical diaper drops off her body onto the floor. K'vinna's voice sounds wearily in her mind.

*Very well, then.*

The warmth of the consciousness abandons her and

K'vinna drifts backwards. The glass walls of the tank re-materialize. Chloe watches K'vinna pause in a moment of apparent indecision, and then some of nir tentacles, translucent ones she hasn't seen in action before, shoot out in rapid movements, alighting the dark cloth and slinging the tank back into darkness.

• • •

K'vinna can still feel the traces of Chloe's pain tingling through nir outer f'et layers, the trauma of the *attacks* as her mind has named them. K'vinna has never considered the process used to facilitate the breeder's fertilization. There had been no need. The breeding division had determined it to be the most effective method, and K'vinna has had no interest in delving into the functions of that division. Still, K'vinna cannot shake the fear, the pain of Chloe's violations refusing to quiet down in the recesses of nir bl'omsterlok. K'vinna felt it in her mind, as she showed nem the memories, that she would not let nem in further as long as the b'leie was on her body. K'vinna does not want to give her any power in their exchanges, yet ne understands her mind will be of no use as long as it is focused on the machine. Let the human rot in her waste excretions. It is not nir concern.

K'vinna's thoughts are interrupted by the soft thud of a column of labour tentacles rapping against nir chamber door. The vibrations of the door moving under the thuds sweep a pulse of air across the room, gently tickling the minuscule hairs covering nir tentacles, alerting nem to the sound. Over the millennia that the Gu'ten have evolved their communication through the consciousness, their aural senses have taken a back seat, only coming alert when the consciousness or vibration senses of their tentacles nudge them into action. K'vinna glides over to open the chamber door, and T'vil floats in. T'vil immediately registers the presence of the cloth-laden box in the room. Ne extends a black tentacle to K'vinna, who answers with one of nir own. They hover in the centre of the room, two effervescent masses of tentacles joined by a narrow black bridge of neural energy exchange. T'vil's mind immediately inquires after the box. K'vinna responds with an image of Chloe inside.

*The breeder? Why?*

*Research.*

*Research?*

*With U'ngdom. I am removing nem from G'nist's research team. Ne is going to continue nir research here, under my supervision.*

*What research?*

K'vinna's mind flashes an image of U'ngdom requesting to enter the consciousness to share nir idea in private. K'vinna can immediately feel T'vil's suspicion of U'ngdom's competency.

*That is my concern, T'vil. Yet, what ne was able to show me yesterday before the disturbance was enough to warrant further investigation. This breeder will be the test subject for this new approach. We will not divert resources from G'nist and K'nurre's efforts. U'ngdom will work here under my supervision, so I can ensure maximum efficiency and put a stop to the project the minute it becomes unproductive.*

T'vil nods, a motion that sends a ripple down nir bulb-shaped body all the way to the bottom of nir beige rainbow of tentacles.

*You are the head of the research division. I defer to your experience in this matter.*

*Indeed. Now, what was the purpose for your arrival?*

T'vil blinks, the long dark folds of goopy f'et behind nir eyes sliding up and down in concentration. An image appears in K'vinna's mind. It is of a summoning arriving through the building's consciousness channels for K'vinna to report to K'lappstol's chambers.

*Anything else?*

*No.*

*Very well.*

K'vinna starts to disengage from the consciousness, and as the warmth of their connection begins to dissipate, a faint echo of T'vil's voice cries out.

*Wait, K'vinna.*

K'vinna re-engages the consciousness back to its full connection.

*Please be careful. Don't let your personal feelings towards U'mulig cause strife with the chairman. We are already on perilous grounds.*

K'vinna glares at T'vil, nir animosity causing the warmth of the consciousness to intensify to a burning heat.

*Of course, T'vil. Now leave me.*

Ne can feel nir grip burning T'vil, but holds it for some moments before releasing. Once they disconnect, T'vil departs the chambers in silence, and K'vinna wonders why ne was so disgruntled by T'vil's concern.

• • •

K'vinna hovers by U'mulig's side whilst K'lappstol reviews U'mulig's memory of their confrontation.

*What is the meaning of this, K'vinna?*

K'vinna steadies nemself, preparing to recite the speech ne practiced on nir drift to the chairman's chambers. Ne can feel the Chairman's impatience and begins humbly.

*Only that I am endeavouring to deliver the results you have requested of me. In order to improve our studies, the research division requires less damaged test subjects. Yesterday, one literally fell into our chambers. I do not understand why U'mulig has chosen to waste your time on this matter. The breeder is not in gestation, so it is not of immediate value to nir division.*

From beside nem, U'mulig glowers. K'lappstol is quiet at first, considering K'vinna's words.

*You are making progress?*

K'vinna answers with caution.

*It is not misguided to suggest that with more adequate specimens, we will.*

*How many do you require?*

Before K'vinna can answer, U'mulig interrupts, nir mind looking directly to K'lappstol.

*This is absurd. Wasting fresh breeders on the research division?*

K'lappstol doesn't outwardly turn, but nir mind icily regards U'mulig.

*The research division is the reason why the breeding division exists, and it is the reason why we shall all continue to exist, or shall perish. K'vinna, how many do you require?*

K'vinna is careful in nir response.

*Six more would be sufficient for the interim, and perhaps two of the males. Their status is less important, as long as they are still functional. We may require more in the future.*

K'vinna is aware of U'mulig seething beside nem as K'lappstol considers the request. K'vinna attempts to remain neutral in composure, keeping all of nir thoughts focused on Gu'ten, not on humans, or breeders, or one breeder in particular. Ne thinks of U'mulig and when they first met. Their original encounter was when K'vinna was a young research assistant, perhaps five years of age. U'mulig had only been two then, and yet to be assigned to a particular division. The Facility decrees it important for each young Gu'ten to work a trimester in all nine divisions of The Facility, culminating in their third anniversary of existence, when they are assigned to a specific division based on their personal aptitudes. The Facility believes this is the best way to gauge where each Gu'ten will be most efficiently utilized, as well as create cross-divisional friendships.

As a promising young research assistant, K'vinna seemed the perfect worker for U'mulig to shadow. However, even then K'vinna had preferred nir own thoughts to the company of others, more interested in making progress on nir work than explaining steps to the younger Gu'ten or engaging nem in conversation. U'mulig had spent nir trimester in the research division only speaking when K'vinna's superiors had questioned nem directly, and never with any insight of nir own to offer as K'vinna had never engaged the consciousness with nem or allowed nem to partake in any tasks. At the end of nir term there, U'mulig had not bothered to thank or even farewell K'vinna, and, true to form, it was many days before K'vinna noticed ne was working without a shadow. Three trimesters later, U'mulig had been allocated a position within the breeding division, and the two didn't cross paths again for several years.

When K'vinna reached nir twelfth year, ne became a research team leader and had to begin attending operational meetings. U'mulig was present at one meeting, but K'vinna had not recognised nem until the younger Gu'ten had approached nem and introduced nemself. K'vinna was unperturbed when U'mulig had pointed out that K'vinna had not shown nem the business of research thoroughly, or even been civil, and then gloated over already becoming the assistant to the head of the breeding division at the age of nine. K'vinna remained uninterested in this revelation, the skill set required for maintaining the gestation cycle and fo'ster-vi'kle harvesting process was nominal, and not something K'vinna believed should be respected. Nir conceit had undoubtedly shown, as U'mulig had never voluntarily approached nem again. Over the years, the two Gu'ten have fostered a healthy disdain for each other. It is for this history that K'vinna is not just relieved, but also smug, when K'lappstol responds.

*Very well. Six breeders and two gleaners shall be transferred to your division—but I shall expect progress, K'vinna. You will report back to me in forty-five rotations. Do not disappoint me.*

K'vinna nods—a mental, not physical act that sends a wave of deference down the consciousness.

*As you see fit.*

Ne removes nemself from the consciousness, the connections filtering out into coldness, and glides silently from the room. Behind nem, ne can feel U'mulig seething. K'vinna will have to careful of that one.

• • •

Chloe isn't sure how much time passes before the cover

to her new prison is removed again. Enough time for her to
urinate twice, the at first innocuous scent now invading all of her
senses. She imagines she can taste ammonia in her mouth, faint
hints of it tainting the papillae on her tongue. She sits as far
away from the liquid as she can, but with time her nose deadens
towards the smell.

She remembers the aromas of The Race. The tantalizing
mix of desert air, crushed tree leaves, and the promise of fresh
water dancing in through the X-Runner's windows on the
occasions it rained and her father would let her have the
windows open. She'd have to fight for this privilege repeatedly, as
her father thought open windows made the vehicle less
aerodynamic and would slow them down. But she lived for these
moments—the mingling of the outside scents with the jejune
cleanliness of the X-Runner's interior and the smoky traces
lingering on their racing clothes from evening campfires. There
is nothing she wouldn't do to return to this symphony of
fragrances, to be at home with her father once more.

Her father. He has been far from her mind for many
days now, herself so selfishly guided. Was he also taken when
their X-Runner was intercepted? There were no men in the over-
lit birthing chambers she was first placed in. Sam had not
mentioned them, no trace of the male sex had ever crossed her
lips. Chloe will ask K'vinna, and if ne doesn't answer, she will
find a way to rip the answer from nir mind. Ne. Nir. Nem. It
surprises her how quickly these terms, the alien's version of him
or her, have assimilated themselves into her mind. Every thought
she has shared or received from the alien feel like truths she has
known since birth. It even feels strange to consider nem an *alien*,

so natural nir existence feels to nem and therefore to her. But she cannot allow this false intimacy to make her dormant, she has to find a back to The Race…

It is this thought that Chloe is torn from, her two by five foot tank ascending into brightness. It takes a few seconds for her eyes to adjust, to see K'vinna's atypically rigid mass gazing down at her. Ne emits sounds, tonal hums that are deep, resonant notes of varying durations. She cannot see their origin, but understands that K'vinna is saying something to her. Nir vacuous dinner plate sized shadow eyes blink slowly—thin stretches of flesh rising up and down behind nir version of pupils. And then ne gestures, nir plethora of tentacles mimicking a human shape standing up, pausing in the standing position, and waiting for her to comprehend. She nods slowly and stands. The instant her body is upright, K'vinna's tentacles start in a flurry of motion. There is a downpour of water in her tank, then a burst of air suctioning away all the liquid, the walls of the tank dissolving, and the cold twang of an o'rdne jamming into her mouth and jolting against her teeth. And the warmth. K'vinna's mind wrapping itself around hers.

She looks from her arm to nir face with an air of teenage rebellion

*Hello.*

She can feel K'vinna's mind chuckle in amusement.

*Hello, indeed.*

*It's not funny. I'm being civil.*

*Civil?*

*You know, polite but without the intimacy of friends. We're not friends.*

*I had never presumed so. Why are you intent on being "civil"?*

*To show you that I'm reasonable, and that we can work together. I know you want answers from me. I'm willing to help you as best I can—share my mind, like you want—if you answer some questions for me. It's only fair.*

*But we are not equals, breeder C-H-L-O-3. Our interactions do not have to be fair.*

*That doesn't mean they can't be. And please, don't call me that. My name is Chloe.*

*Chloe?*

*Yes. Like yours is K'vinna. Mine is Chloe.*

*Very well, Chloe. You can ask your questions, and I will consider answering them, if you keep your mind completely open to me. The moment I feel it close, I will tell you no more. Do you understand?*

Chloe nods. That is, she pictures herself nodding, sends the image of it running down the consciousness as her head stays still, eyes watching K'vinna's reaction. Ne blinks—a barely perceptible mucous layer streatching out across nir shadow eyes—a gesture Chloe thinks must mean ne feeling vulnerable in the consciousness, and attempting to create a mental wall. When it is down seconds later, K'vinna secretes no trace of insecurity. Instead, ne emanates confidence.

*What is your first question?*

*What happened to my father? Is he here, in this building?*

*Father?*

It is clearly a term K'vinna is unfamiliar with.

*The man I was with in The Race. He was with me when I*

*was taken.*

She can feel K'vinna flitting through the memories in her mind to find those that relate to this word. She brings one to the surface for nem, and the warm emotions of safety and comfort his presence brought.

*Thank you.*

K'vinna flits through the memories next to this one, observing the parental-child interactions.

*Father is… the human whose offspring you believe to be. Who raised you?*

*Yes.*

*Father can be male or female? The one present?*

*No. Father is the man. Mother is the woman. I never knew my mother.*

*No. You never knew your true father, either. This one was a substitute.*

Chloe doesn't like this statement. She doesn't release K'vinna's gaze, but she mimics nir slow blinking with spite before responding.

*He is my father. I want to know where he is now. Is he here, somewhere?*

*It is unlikely. Presumably, he will have been returned to The Race to continue the gleaning process. He may even have a new child assigned to him by now.*

K'vinna is unsure why ne added this last fact. Why does ne feel the need to throw this breeder off guard and gain the upper hand? Ne is clearly already in control. She is so pitiful, and fragile.

*A new child?*

Chloe struggles with this thought. Small pools of liquid collect on her lower lids. K'vinna can see her fight them back, her mind turning back to nirs with a coldness unusual for a human, rebuking K'vinna's evaluation of her as fragile.

*Can you find out for me? I'd like to know.*

*Perhaps. First, it is time for you to answer some of my questions.*

The questions K'vinna asks Chloe are more like directions—raise your hand, take two steps left, sit down, and stand up again—but nir interest never falters. Chloe can feel the focus with which ne studies her movements.

*I can feel you thinking, you know.*

*I am aware. Shift your weight onto your left body anchor, then onto your right, and back to the centre.*

Chloe does as she's told.

*I can't hear your thoughts, though. Why is that?*

*I am not choosing to disclose my thoughts. Step backwards.*

*But you're choosing to disclose your mood?*

K'vinna pauses, relaxing the grip of nir many grey tentacles wrapped around her limbs.

*No. But it is a situation I shall remedy in time. Now, back into your tank. I have other work to do.*

# CHAPTER TWENTY-ONE

THE HOLDING cell is dark. The only light sources are thin shafts of moonlight glistening down. There are no candles in the room or in the hallway outside it. Ikka sits with Veela at the back of the space, where they listen to Daracha and Delu discuss possible escape plans. They whisper to each other while they wait for a decision to be made.

"I was wondering what was up when you let that oaf carry you out of The Mother's chambers like that. I thought, no way that pile of flesh is any match for Ikka's mountain of internal rage."

Ikka smiles at him. "You do think so very highly of me."

He grins back at her. "You love it. That someone knows you for what you are."

"What I am?"

"A pool of violence, drowning a broken soul in rage."

She tilts her head at him, raising her eyebrows and smiling through distant eyes. "Perhaps. Now, what are we going to do about this lot? They don't seem to be making much progress, and I'd rather not stay in this dank space for too long. We have some tentacled monsters to overthrow."

"Indeed we do, buddy."

Veela follows her gaze to Daracha and Delu. What they are saying is inaudible, but their expressions are tense. Around them, the other members of the faction are sitting in morose or pensive silence. Gaarwine, Madoc, Hurste, Chiyo, Esej, and Callyr. Ikka listens to them for a moment. Esej is bemoaning that all of their possessions were taken from them. He is a scrawny man with short, knotted hair resting above his ears. Like all the others, it is brown. He is gesturing to the cell door, a composition of thick wooden posts arched together to create a giant grill. The locking mechanism is a thicker wooden post in a brace point two feet across the wall, fastened in place by a recycled iron casing.

Esej says, "If they'd let me keep my tool kit, I would have been able to break us out of this room."

"That's probably why they took it," says Callyr, whose brown locks are once again in a bun atop his head, pulling his face further lengthways.

They return to silence, Esej kicking the dirt floor with his foot to vent. Hurste sits the closest to him and looks embarrassed by this display. He consoles himself when he thinks no one is looking, syphoning a steady stream of nuts into his dimpled face. Veela notices and tries to signal him discreetly. When his various head nods render no results, he gives a short whistle and hisses.

"Hurste, over here!"

Hurste looks at him quizzically, and then hurriedly jumps over to the bench next to Veela and Ikka. He pulls some thumbnail sized, circular nuts of a straw coloured hue out of a hidden pocket and holds them out to them. His expression is innocent.

"Nuts?"

Veela grins. "Yes, please."

He grabs them and offers some to Ikka, but she is already standing, walking away from the two. Veela shrugs and consumes them all. He sits merrily with Hurste as the younger man offers up a steady stream of nuts, but his attention is focused on Ikka as she approaches Delu and Daracha. She is bound to do something he does not want to miss.

• • •

Delu and Daracha are still discussing possible break out scenarios when Ikka sidles in next to them. She doesn't directly join their conversation; she merely nods to show she is now listening and then goes about inspecting the wooden patchwork door. She feels the girth of the pieces making its composition, the grain flow of each post and their densities. She peers out between the pieces at the dark corridor beyond. There appears to be no movement, no eyes or ears within reach. She turns back to their conversation, interrupting in a low voice.

"Do you have a plan? For once we're outside this cell?"

Daracha says, "We reclaim our weapons, grab minimal supplies, head east through the tunnels, and surface before any notice we're gone."

"Do you think it's possible?"

"Yes. We can escape without the Settlement noticing.

Whether or not the airships do…"

Delu agrees. "Once we're out of this, the only difficult part will be finding our weapons. They're bound to be in a guarded place, probably under lock and key as well."

"For such a peaceful colony, this Settlement sure has a lot of locks and keys."

"It's from the old days when the Settlement was just beginning."

Even in the darkness, Ikka can see the sadness flit through Delu's eyes as he remembers.

He says, "They would put people in these places while they detoxed. Until they calmed down and were ready to integrate into the Settlement." Delu recollects himself. "So our possessions are likely to be along this tunnel or one of the ones connecting. But first, we have to break out."

"Well, that I can help with." Ikka gestures to two of the horizontal beams on the door. "These two are quite weak. By slicing at the right angle, I should be able to hack our way out."

Daracha says, "But they took all our blades."

Ikka shrugs. "I always carry a spare. Do you have any better ideas or shall I start?"

Ikka peels off her racing jacket and hands it Delu to hold. She untucks her racing blouse and fiddles with something beneath it for some moments before retrieving an eight-inch long sheath with strings attached to its top, base, and middle. From it, she withdraws a blade. It is half an inch thick at its base, two inches in width, and hewn from rock.

She tests the lower piece of timber first, confirming with herself the best place to strike, and then draws the blade with immense power into the beam. It travels three inches deep with this first blow. Chiyo whistles in appreciation. His hair is sandy coloured like Madoc's, but his face more expressive.

He turns to Callyr and says, "What a blow! Did you see that?"

Callyr responds solemnly, "We all saw that."

"Yeah, well, it was great."

They all watch with interest as Ikka exacts a second strike, shearing the blade straight through. She takes a moment to find another weak spot two feet across the beam and launches a new attack on the wood. This only requires one blow, and then the piece between the two strike points falls clean off the beam and onto the dirt floor on the other side of the door.

Into the corridor.

Onto someone's foot.

• • •

"Ouch." That someone turns out to be Aldric. "What are you lunatics doing now?" His eyes scoot between the fallen timber, the hole in the door, and the cell full of guilty faces. He shakes his head and holds up an old, iron key. He says, "I was coming here to help to you escape, but it seems that's not necessary anymore. Shall I leave you to it?"

Delu says, "Your assistance will always be greatly appreciated. You are a constant help in our cause."

Aldric smiles and walks to the locking mechanism. He talks as he moves, enjoying a captive audience for his voice.

"The Mother has sent everyone except the watchmen to sleep early this night. She says we need our rest to deal with the stresses your 'insane faction' has caused this day. The oldest inhabitants agree with her—they've been doing it for so long now they wouldn't possibly know how to start contradicting her views. It's complete faith or nothing for them. But there are others who support you, though they wouldn't say it out loud. I've been sent to help orchestrate your exit to the surface. So if you'll follow me, your possessions and provisions are this way."

He swings the cell door open and offers them a smug smile. It diminishes in strength when he notices the sharp blade still resting in Ikka's hand and the look of calculative attention in her eyes, but she smiles reassuringly at him and he regathers himself, gesturing for the troop to follow him down the east corridor.

• • •

They stay close to each other as they walk, shooting furtive glances down the corridor behind them and ahead. Aldric is oblivious to their unease, chatting happily as he leads them through the darkened bends.

"Of course everyone was relieved when you didn't resist The Mother's arrest. Not that we thought you would, Delu, but there was no telling if Ikka would convince you lot to act a bit more like a resistance in that moment. No disrespect meant, Ikka, but it's quite clear you don't suffer fools and you were eyeing The Mother like you considered her one, so we were all very grateful when we didn't have to fight you. Not that I would have. But you know, it would have created a fair amount of stress for everyone involved." He gives a little chuckle, but stifles it when he peers over his shoulder and sees rows of blank faces behind him. "Well, you're all rather excitable aren't you? Don't worry, we're nearly there. Just around this next corner."

The corner is sharp, and when they turn it, they come face to face with Azzam. He offers a tight-lipped smile as the group stands still, unsure how to react.

"We don't have much time if you are to reach the outer tunnels before your presence is discovered missing in the morning. I have collected all of your possessions that were seized, and have packed what I hope are enough supplies to last you a few weeks." Azzam looks to Delu. "You know how to live off the land, yes? That will help."

He gestures to Aldric to go collect something, and then directs Delu's faction to the row of supply packs lined against the corridor wall past him. He stops Delu and Daracha from walking by him, and Ikka stops uninvited to watch the exchange. Azzam reaches into his jacket and removes a piece of paper, unfolding it several times before handing it to Delu.

"I have written down here which tunnel links to take to exit. This is one of the least-used passages, but one that I have personally kept maintained over the years. When you exit to the surface, you will be in the base of a ravine. Stay close to the left wall as you travel in an easterly direction. After seven miles, a cave will appear on the right hand side of the giant metea tree. It is unoccupied, and you can take shelter there for one night. To the rear of the cave is a tunnel that stretches for nine miles, from which you will exit at the edge of the forest, where it meets the open desert. It will be much quicker than the route you've usually used, and should help keep the location of The Settlement hidden.

"Most importantly, there is a device I believe may be of some help to you on this path. As you enter the tunnel from the cave, approximately twelve feet in on the left wall, count the eighth stone up from the ground. It can be removed, and behind it in a sack is a navigation system from an X-Runner. It's currently switched off, but Esej will understand how to power it on. He's good with mechanics. You can use the nav system to help find the facilitators."

Delu inspects the paper as Daracha runs his scarred hand down it.

Daracha says, "You kept an old nav system? Why?"

Azzam says, "I suspected it might come of use one day. It is foolish to disregard things which you do not understand."

He holds his hand up for silence, and they hear footsteps approach. Daracha's eyes scan the darkness. "It's Aldric."

Aldric approaches with several decommissioned drinking canisters in his arms. Azzam takes one and unscrews the lid. He reaches three fingers in, and, when he removes them, they are covered in a dark green putty.

"This is a mixture I have devised myself. Crushed paili leaves ground with mael nut oil and sparing amounts of water. If you coat your skin with this, it will conceal your body heat and keep you hidden from the airships."

They stare at the goop with interest. It is thick, a dark velvety green that sits in a contained puddle on Azzam's fingers. It doesn't drip, but seems held together by the glue-like oil.

Daracha says, "Paili leaves are poisonous."

"To consume. The chemicals stored in their leaves drop human body temperature and cause instant hypothermia and organ failure. However, harnessed as a surface paste, the mael nut oil provides a base that prevents the poisons from soaking into the skin, while the chemicals in the crushed leaves still believe they are being consumed and launch into action, significantly dropping the external body temperature and creating a wall between your body temperature and the outside air. Once exposed to the air, the leaves have a limited lifespan. They'll provide you cover for four hours, maximum. There's a secondary jar in each of the supply packs so you can re-apply before the four-hour mark. Eight hours should be enough for you to reach the cave and be shielded from the airships. From there, you're on your own."

Here Azzam very carefully removes a handkerchief from his jacket and wipes the paili mixture from his fingers. He refolds the square of fabric so none of the goop can leak before returning it to his jacket. When this is done, he looks back up to Delu, Daracha, and Ikka, and seems surprised that they are still standing in front of him. His shrewd green eyes peer out at them in a manner Ikka finds both comical and endearing.

He speaks, his tone irritable. "Is there something else you'd like to hear me say?"

Delu says, "Yes. Why are you helping us?"

"That?" Azzam turns and reaches for the unclaimed supply packs against the wall, shoving them in Delu, Daracha, and Ikka's chests as he speaks. "I'm not a fool. You were going to find a way to leave whether or not The Mother gave permission. This way, I can help ensure the Settlement remains protected from the Facilitators and you have the most possible chance of success—which I still calculate is slim, I may add. Now, if you wouldn't mind, I'm growing old and I would like to get some sleep before I have to tear the Settlement upside down in the morning looking for you. Follow the S1 to T4 to U5 tunnels to get to the outer post. That's where you should apply the paili salve before the tunnels start to thin and rise. Try not to miss any spots larger than a few inches because that's as large as the insects get in that section."

They shoulder the packs and watch as Azzam starts to walk away from them, back towards the heart of the Settlement. After nine paces, he adds an afterthought over his shoulder. "Oh, and Aldric will be joining you. He's too young to never see the sun again, and his absence will account for why you were able to escape, as well as mask my involvement."

Aldric's face is of complete surprise, immediately overcome with joy. He shouts after Azzam, "Thank you!" but the council elder merely waves his hand over his shoulder as he continues on into the darkness. Delu contemplates his vanishing figure and speaks to no one in particular as he begins to lead the troop down the S1.

"I always thought he was too intelligent to not care."

# CHAPTER TWENTY-TWO

K'VINNA is observing Chloe's brain functions when U'ngdom drifts in. The younger Gu'ten is insolent, entering without knocking or requesting an invitation. As ne enters, K'vinna has nir grey labour tentacles wrapped around Chloe's form, instructing her through the consciousness to move this way, move that way, walk backwards, sit down, stand up, turn her upper body from one side to another. Ne is monitoring the effect following directions has on her thought process, how much brain function she does or doesn't have to apply to complete these tasks. K'vinna wants to know if she is still aware of nir emotions in the periphery of her mind's sight, or if it is the instructions that are in the periphery, mere factoids unworthy of her full attention.

It is the minuscule hairs on K'vinna's tentacles that first alert nem to U'ngdom's brazen entrance. Ne turns nir bl'omsterlok towards U'ngdom, nir tentacles still engaged to Chloe's limbs. The movement is slow, an authoritative speed designed to showcase nir displeasure with the unannounced arrival. Nir dark, saucer-like eyes regard the subordinate Gu'ten with irritation tinged dismay.

U'ngdom speaks first, nir vocal tones oscillating from underneath nir tentacle roots.

"I was summoned."

K'vinna doesn't immediately respond, nir mind turning back to Chloe in the consciousness.

*This one, never communicate with. You have no thoughts, other than the basic functions of your bowels and your need to eat and sleep. Do you understand? Do not show you can hear me.*

K'vinna's eyes are still fixed on U'ngdom when ne hears her answer.

*Yes.*

K'vinna's black tentacle around her arm releases, and the grey conglomeration dance as a singular entity, releasing the specific limbs they were investigating to act as a swarm, tossing Chloe back into the realms of the tank and re-initializing its glass walls. Once this is done, K'vinna turns nir back to U'ngdom, floating to rest on the chair behind nir desk. Ne sets about attending to the research teams' daily progress reports awaiting nem in the research division's consciousness loop. As two of nir black tentacles plug in to the information stream, U'ngdom tries again.

"K'vinna..."

K'vinna waves a huddle of nir grey tentacles in the air, a gesture to be silent. U'ngdom ignores it.

"Please, K'vinna. You summoned me here. Before you punish me, I wish to speak in my defence. I only did what was necessary. I've studied all of the research of all the researchers who have come before. There are flaws inherent within the system. The fo'ster-vi'kle isn't a viable—"

K'vinna cuts nem off before ne can finish, a swarm of nir clear grabbing tentacles shooting across the table and seizing U'ngdom where ne stands, dragging nem forward, so nir bl'omsterlok slams onto the desk. K'vinna towers over nem from nir seat, nir voice echoing harshly through U'ngdom's f'et layers.

"Do not presume to speak first in my presence. What you have done is treason. And why? Because the ignorance of youth makes you presume your mind can decipher a blatant flaw skimmed over by the brightest minds of our predecessors? I could have you executed for what you've done. No trial. No chance for defence. Murdering a Gu'ten is treason. Infecting your own offspring with the be'lysning is inexcusable."

K'vinna's breath, rumbling from underneath nir bl'omsterlok, sends eerie ripples across U'ngdom's face.

"I will let you live, though, and take on the burden of your treason. From now on, you do not work amongst the division as G'nist's assistant. Instead, you shall work here, in my chamber, under my constant supervision. You will do nothing without my permission. You will not think without my permission. You will not speak to anyone outside of these walls without my permission. Do you understand?"

When ne speaks, U'ngdom's voice is without defiance. There is a weakness tracing it.

"Yes, K'vinna."

"Very good. Now tell me of your research. Try to defend it."

U'ngdom clears nir throat, a sound akin to a small rock falling through different layers of water.

"I believe we are wasting—"

K'vinna glowers down at U'ngdom.

"What was that? I cannot hear you."

U'ngdom re-attempts speaking, adding more deep tones to nir speech.

"We're wasting our resources trying to improve upon a research method that is inherently flawed."

K'vinna intones, "Is that so?"

"It… it would have been perfected decades ago if it were possible to find a cure this way. But it isn't."

K'vinna leans closer, the vibrations of nir words causing ripples across U'ngdom's bl'omsterlok.

"And you think you know better?"

U'ngdom's eyes blink under K'vinna's stare.

"Yes. K'vinna, the technologies have changed and our methods still aren't working. There is a very basic reason for that. It's our use of the humans."

It is K'vinna's turn to stiffen. Ne says, "Go on."

"They're nothing like us. They have none of the brain function, no similar anatomy or genetics. Our species are both born from organic matter, from a single cell, but from that moment of inception on, our biological evolutions have been completely separate. The fluid percentage of their bodies is obscenely high, incomparable to our gaseous-based compositions. And their brains… only two barely functioning spheres, one tiny, dormant cerebellum… the exact arguments that have been utilized over generations to justify our experimentations on and enslavement of their species is the exact reason why we haven't found a cure to the be'lysning. They are not like us."

U'ngdom pauses to gauge K'vinna's reaction. K'vinna's mind is impenetrable and nir body language hostile. U'ngdom swallows and continues.

"We will only find a cure when we test on ourselves. An infant Gu'ten, before reaching the consciousness, has no knowledge of life or of death. They can feel pain, but it is nothing compared to the pain of generations of Gu'ten dying slow, knowledgeable deaths from the be'lysning. If my methods can save lives—save our species—I say they are worthy, acceptable losses. The survival of our species is what is important here."

K'vinna's grip on U'ngdom feels ready to relax, but then the senior Gu'ten speaks and nir tentacles push harder on U'ngdom's bl'omsterlok.

K'vinna says, "How many?"

"How many?"

"How many offspring have you killed?"

"Three, but each time I get closer. I'm making significant progress."

K'vinna sighs, nir giant bl'omsterlok shuddering with the motion. Ne removes nir vice-like grip on U'ngdom and reclines back on nir floating chair. U'ngdom remains still on the tabletop, unsure if ne is allowed to move. K'vinna offers no verbal guidance, waiting in silence until U'ngdom retracts nir mass from the desk. Ne floats in front of it.

"K'vinna, please let me prove that there is a cure to the

be'lysning. I know I can find it."

• • •

K'vinna outlines to U'ngdom the conditions of which ne shall work in nir chambers. At first with synthetic substances, simulating Gu'ten genocode, infecting it and using nir work-in-progress methodologies to cure it. Ne is welcome to extract from Chloe's body anything necessary to assist—although K'vinna assumes from nir speech ne will want none of her—as long as ne leaves her brain intact. Once ne has a 99% success rate with the simulated Gu'ten tissue, ne is allowed to spawn one offspring, deny it contact with the consciousness, infect it, and then cure it. If the cure is a failure, there will be dire consequences.

No one else is allowed to know what is transpiring inside K'vinna's chamber, only that it is secret research and the reason why the breeder is in the quarters. She will be the cover for U'ngdom's actual research. Any violation of any of these terms will result in U'ngdom's death, and U'ngdom is not to think K'vinna will negate on this threat, as ne has no particular regard for the younger Gu'ten and will act mercilessly if necessary, as U'ngdom has done to nir own offspring. Once the terms have been discussed, U'ngdom sets to work, and K'vinna returns to absorbing the transcripts of G'nist's and K'nurre's research teams. Ne knows to expect a visit from them both—especially G'nist— once they learn of this secret project taking place outside of their labs. They have worked their whole lives to attain the position of research team leaders. They will not be pleased.

• • •

U'ngdom hums to nemself while ne works. It is low, discreet enough that a Gu'ten's aural receptors would normally not notice it, but K'vinna is now always listening for sounds from Chloe and picks up on the noise. The frequencies are low, like echoes in a resonant chamber. They remind K'vinna of another's memory in the consciousness, of murmurs in a large, naturally occurring cavern on S'vekke. U'ngdom's soft chorus intrigues K'vinna enough for nem to leave nir desk and hover over to the partition between their workspaces. Ne opens the curtain, gesturing to U'ngdom to continue as if unwatched. The younger Gu'ten is not perturbed by nir audience.

U'ngdom is working with a cluster of synthetic Gu'ten cells, which have been infiltrated with a strand of the be'lysning. The blue sheen of the Gu'ten cells has been stained milky white, highlighting the presence of the be'lysning in a large quantity. U'ngdom is now endeavouring to poison the disease. This is where nir research differs from the standard practice. G'nist and K'nurre's teams are focusing on methods that shield the Gu'ten cells' penetrability with a protective barrier of fo'ster-vi'kle. U'ngdom is not employing the fo'ster-vi'kle whatsoever, but instead attempting to modify the Gu'ten cells' molecular code to produce a synthetic gas into their incubation. It is an interesting approach. U'ngdom described it as creating an environment that was inhospitable to the be'lysning. Unfortunately, all of nir attempts thus far have also been inhospitable for the Gu'ten cells. At least the fo'ster-vi'kle treatment does not hasten the host Gu'ten's demise.

As U'ngdom works, K'vinna becomes inspired and steps forward into the younger Gu'ten's domain. K'vinna helps nemself to a selection of the youth's tools, accessing a different passage of synthetic cells and be'lysning in the work pod. K'vinna examines their compositions, remembering an observation ne made when ne was more researcher than supervisor. Perhaps eradicating the be'lysning is too ambitious, but immobilizing it is an option. Not with the fo'ster-vi'kle, or by changing the Gu'ten gas composition, but by inserting genetically engineered vesicles that will act as solvent cages—little prisons around each of the be'lysning cells. If successful, the only issue will be creating such vesicles that are immortal, as previous Gu'ten scientists have only been able to create solvent cages with a lifespan of twenty seconds. Not enough to be even a short-term solution.

It is U'ngdom's turn to watch K'vinna with interest, surprised to see the older Gu'ten at work. Ne takes notes of each step K'vinna takes, handing nem implements before they are even asked for. The two work like this for some time, mute masses in conference.

# CHAPTER TWENTY-THREE

THE FINAL cavern at the end of the U5 tunnel is small, a tiny outpost that can barely contain the small reconnaissance troop. The air is spread thin, and already they have become measured in their breaths.

They undress with efficient speed, applying the paili goop to their flesh, meticulous to not miss any large sections of skin or get it too close to their eyes or mouths. They even rub it through the roots of their hair to mask their scalps. It feels cold to touch, stinging like many needle points lightly pricking into their skin, but it is bearable and so they carry on. Ikka changes and applies the salve in the same area as the men. They are all focused on their tasks, and she doesn't feel threatened by her naked body or theirs. At present, they are canvasses for the paili mixture, a means of escape, and nothing more.

They re-dress as soon as they are covered, and Daracha arranges them in order for the journey. Delu and Gaarwine will take lead, followed by Hurste and Madoc, then Aldric, Ikka, and

Veela, Esej then Chiyo, Callyr then Daracha follows behind. In the small space, eleven feels like too many people to sneak out of the Settlement, but they know that when they reach the facilitators it will feel like far too few.

Without any words of encouragement or final speech, Delu plunges into the tunnel. Gaarwine follows, and the others wordlessly file in. As Ikka waits, she notices Aldric's lack of chatter. She gives his arm a gentle squeeze above his elbow. He nods, offering a meek smile, a movement that pulls at the fast drying green second skin on his face. It pinches the flesh glued to it, causing him to wince before taking a deep breath and stepping into the tunnel. Ikka tosses Veela a grin.

"Are you ready?"

"I'd follow that charming slime covered face anywhere, buddy."

"Uh huh."

Ikka turns away from him and steps up onto the small ledge under the tunnel, lifting her body onto the tunnel floor. She picks herself up onto her hands and knees and begins the crawl to the surface.

· · ·

The tunnel is dark. Once Ikka's eyes adjust, she notes that the tunnel is in poor condition compared to the tunnels that she and Delu had followed into the Settlement. The earth in the floor, walls, and ceiling has not been smoothed down. Instead, small rocks poke up from the ground and the sharp edges of larger rocks in the walls protrude into the crawl space, making the journey hazardous for both the travellers' hands and heads. Ikka has to curve her torso low to the ground, to prevent her pack getting caught or ripped on a protruding rock as she crawls.

This tunnel also smells different. Danker, muskier. The air vents are more sporadic, and the scent of the paili salve tampers with what fresh air remains. Paili smells both sweet and acrid, like a fruit half dissolved in stomach bile and then thrown back up. It is overwhelming, but with time the smell deadens, as the subconscious has no choice but to numb the nostrils' senses. The troop moves forward in silence—the only noises are those of scraping knees and the displacement of pebbles under hands, occasionally accentuated by a grunt of pain. Time moves without note in this fashion, seconds undergoing seamless transitions into minutes and hours.

The procession halts as they reach a wider berth in the earth where the tunnel becomes high enough to sit comfortably. With minimal words, each crawler shows their secondary supply of paili mix to the person behind them, and then begins applying a fresh layer of the tonic to their skin. It's more difficult this time as there's no space to easily remove their clothes, so instead they have to reach into them like they're deranged with an itch, arms forcing their way down the tops of pants and angling for the knees.

The second half of the crawl feels longer. Hands and knees become weary. With each new lift, arms feel heavier and legs seem filled with lead. Packs force shoulders closer to the ground and eyelids yearn to close. Ikka is fighting micro-sleeps when an insane cackle rips through the oppressive silence. It's Madoc.

Ikka can see his short sandy hair shaking up past Aldric. She tugs on Aldric's ankle and hisses at him, "What's he laughing at?"

Aldric peers forward and then turns back to her, trembling, his face white beneath the paili.

"There's a monster. He's laughing at a monster." His eyes widen. "You don't think it's one of them, do you? Not one of the facilitators?"

"No. They're too large to fit in this tunnel. Press your body against the wall so I can see."

Aldric nods, his lips quivering as he moves to the side. Past him, Ikka can see Madoc, his entire body shaking with laughter. His eyes are wide and he makes sharp inhales between each spurt of noise. His left hand is hovering above a strange creature, seven inches in length. Its torso comprises of three connecting ovals of a faded grey with thin stripes of black circling their orbs, like cracks and age lines in old stones. Six legs jut out from each oval, slight but stony, one and a half inches in height. At first glance, the creature doesn't have an obvious head, it appears to be a collection of rocks ambling on stilts, but there is a small growth on the underside of the front orb. From this bank of flesh protrude three eyes, one to the front and one on each side. They are the size of the tip of Ikka's pinky finger and consist of many tiny scales of luminescent purple. There is no visible mouth. Madoc is captivated by this creature, his hand hovering over it in anticipation of reaching down to stroke its back.

Ikka says to Aldric, "It's okay, it's not one of the facilitators. It's just a bug." And then she speaks louder, attempting to capture Madoc's attention.

"Madoc, I wouldn't touch that if I were you. Most

creatures down here aren't used to human interference. Best to just keep moving forward. Okay?"

Madoc doesn't respond, his eyes transfixed on the bug. He snaps his hand back and forth in the air above the insect's back and giggles when it freezes in defence. He holds his hand still, and the creature cautiously scuttles a few inches. He waves his hand again, and it halts. He giggles once more.

"Stupid creature, scared of a moving hand."

Up ahead, Hurste has realized that Madoc is no longer behind him and is tugging on the ankles of Delu and Gaarwine for their attention. Behind Ikka and Veela—who is garnering some information from Ikka's communication—Esej, Chiyo, Callyr, and Daracha also grow concerned.

Ikka tries again. She speaks slower.

"Madoc. Leave. It. Alone."

Madoc doesn't register her voice, his mind altered by the paili. Next to him, Aldric breaks into cold sweats. He talks even faster than normal.

"I don't like being here anymore. The monster scares me. And the air's too cold. I don't think the air's meant to be this cold. Is it meant to be this cold, Ikka?"

"Ikka?" Hurste's voice calls down from in front. "What's going on? Madoc's not responding and Delu wants to know why you've all stopped."

Ikka yawns. "Well, Madoc is infatuated with an insect, Aldric has the chills, and I think it's time I had a sleep. That's a good idea. We should all have a nap." She yawns again. "Goodnight."

Hurste and Veela watch in surprise from either end as

Ikka rests her head on her forearms and settles down to sleep. Madoc keeps taunting the insect, whose fiery purple eyes are dilating in individual bursts as his hand flies around it. Hurste's eyes widen when he notices the insect for the first time. The expression on his face is a clearly painted portrait of *oh dear* as he reaches into his chest pocket and retrieves a flat oval nut. His fingers run over it for a few seconds, tracing its contours to identify it without looking, and, with precision, he aims it on the ground in front of the bug.

As the insect scurries to inspect the nut, Hurste hooks his feet under Madoc's armpits and drags his face farther up the tunnel to place the creature out of Madoc's line of sight.

"Hey, you took me away from my pal."

"There's more up ahead."

"Really?"

"Yes, just pass me, catch up to Gaarwine and Delu, and they'll help you find them."

Still giggling, Madoc crawls off in search of the forward troops. Hurste turns back to Aldric, who is frozen in terror watching the insect prepare its meal. It stabs the middle legs from its front oval into each side of the nut and then lifts it over its topside to the middle oval, where the centre ring expands into a pit of gnashing teeth. The insect drops the nut inside, where it is ground to a pulp in seconds. As its front legs return to the dirt ground, the mouth closes up, and the insect scuttles towards Aldric's knees. Aldric doesn't know what to do, but whimpers until at the last moment the insect burrows into a small crevice in the ground. Aldric clutches at his chest trying to slow down his breaths, but he is in too much of a panic.

Hurste crawls closer to him, twisting in the tunnel so that his face can face Aldric's.

"I—can't—breathe—it's—too—cold—I—can't—breath—"

Thwack.

Hurste slaps Aldric, then grabs him by his shoulders and stares deep into his eyes.

"You're breathing fine. Now come on. We've got to keep moving up the tunnel. You've stayed still for too long and your body temperature's dropped, but all we have to do is move and you'll start to feel better, okay? So what we're going to do is, I'm going to go first, and you grab hold of my ankle and move forward as I move. If you get scared again, just yank on them and I'll come back and help you through it, okay?"

Aldric nods, and Hurste offers him a reassuring smile.

"Great. Just grab my ankle and you'll be fine."

He navigates turning around in the tight space one more time and waits until he feels Aldric's hand grab on his ankles. He doesn't grimace, but reaches into his chest pocket and extracts three more nuts. He thoughtfully tosses them into his mouth and starts crawling forward, Aldric in tow. Further back, Veela attempts to wake Ikka, but she doesn't stir when he shakes her. He frowns and holds his hand against her neck. Her pulse is so faint he has to push hard to find it, and her skin is freezing to touch. He turns her face towards him, peeling back her eyelids to look at her eyes. Her pupils are microscopic and don't even flicker when he exposes them to the tunnel light.

"Shit."

Veela's eyes to travel to Ikka's mouth and see the dried

trickle of dark green on her brown lips. Some of the paili mixture has ingested directly into her system. He tries not to panic. He reaches into her pack and wrenches out the water canister. He parts her mouth and guides some water droplets inside, hoping they will help.

He shouts behind him.

"Esej, Chiyo. Do either of you know an antidote to the paili?"

"What?"

"Why?"

"It's Ikka. I think she's sick from the paili. She has a pulse, but I can't wake her up."

There is muttering in the gloom, and then Chiyo's hand passes forward a different, spikier type of leaf held between two sheets of paper.

"Don't touch it with your skin. Just put it in her mouth. It's not an antidote per say… but it burns. It might wake her up."

Veela brings the leaf up to Ikka's lips with care, as though it may disintegrate at any moment, and as he places it in her mouth he hears Esej hiss at Chiyo, "What on Earth are you carrying *varme* for?"

As soon as the leaf touches Ikka's tongue and Veela closes her mouth around it, her eyes shoot open in pain. Her pupils expand until the warm brown of her irises are completely unseen and she tries to cough the leaf out. Veela holds her mouth shut, his eyes holding hers in an apologetic gaze.

"I'm sorry, buddy, but I've got to keep you alive and letting you sleep ain't going to do that. You ingested some of the paili. We can't let you fall asleep again, all right? You've got to work with me and keep crawling out of this tunnel."

Ikka's jaw tightens as she works to clamp it shut on the burning flame, and her eyes narrow at Veela to let him know she understands.

"Yes. I know, you can tell me how much you hate me once we reach the surface. For now just keep pushing forward. Okay, buddy?"

Ikka steels herself and moves her arms and knees forward. It isn't easy; her entire body is covered in pins and needles, and her hands feel fat and swollen as she tries to pull herself forward. Veela crawls close behind her, trying to help by pushing her forward with her pack. He suspects she will punch him for it afterwards, but he needs to know that there will be an afterwards. Even with the varme in her mouth, her body is dangerously cold. There is no knowing if she'll collapse at any moment or will even make it to the surface. But he has to hope, and tune out the constant loop playing in his head of Esej's disbelief it was *varme* Chiyo gave to him.

# CHAPTER TWENTY-FOUR

IT IS THE NIGHTS that Chloe finds strangest in her little cell. K'vinna and the other alien who now works in K'vinna's chambers leave, the lights are switched off, and Chloe is left to her own devices in her tank. At first K'vinna would ensure no gaps were in the heavy maroon curtain covering the cage's walls before ne left, but with time ne has left her little peaking holes. Once the chamber is vacated by both of the aliens, the space descends into silence, no more muffled traces of their strange bubbling speech or purposeful movements drift into her cell. Without their bizarre floating torsos to distract her, she stares in wonder at the relics in the room.

K'vinna's desk—if that is what it can be called—is the largest item in the space. A glistening pod composed of translucent materials similar in appearance to the aliens' bodies, resting very lightly upon one central glass post. There are no objects on the desk's surface. K'vinna does not use it as a desk, but instead plunges nir tentacles inside the pod and is able to do

nir work this way. From her view in the tank, she can see no
objects, lights, or images within the incandescent sack, but
imagines it is through this bulb that K'vinna can connect nir
mind to the data system of the building. It is as though ne is
plugging nemself into a computer to access all the other
networks. At the desk K'vinna also has a chair, a floating flat
circle of glass on which ne will sometimes rest nir upper torso—
nir bl'omsterlok—on, nir hundreds of tentacles cascading over its
edges.

Other than these two objects, the main chamber is
mostly empty. There are no windows, no shelves or storage units,
no obvious light fittings, even though during the designated
working hours the space is always lit a glowing white. Since the
advent of the smaller alien also working in this chamber, a
curtained partition has been placed to one side of the room.
Behind it, Chloe has glimpsed flashes of metal and the glimmer
of an object similar to K'vinna's desk but smaller. Whenever the
curtain on Chloe's tank is removed, the partition is closed, so she
cannot see what work the other alien is undertaking, nor has
K'vinna even told her nir name.

There is a point every night when other, smaller
creatures enter the chamber. At first, Chloe could never see them,
only hear their strange sucking sounds from inside her darkened
tank. Now that K'vinna leaves small gaps in the fabric, she is able
to witness the night creatures in their disgusting yet cute glory.

In The Race when she would camp with her father,
Chloe would sometimes find snails, small animals that would
carry their houses on their backs and leave a trail of slime
wherever they crawled. These night creatures have a similar

design, but, instead of being an inch or two in length, they are one or two foot long. The circle houses they carry on their backs are iridescent with intricate patterns wrapping the curves of their shells. Their actual bodies are soft and unsegmented with colouring homogeneous to their houses, but lined with fuzzy, soft white hairs on the topside and an oozing stream of clear mucus on their undersides. In place of inset eyes, they have two white whisker-like hairs protruding from the front of their bodies, little pinpoint eyes of light blue or purple resting on the ends. These eyes bounce as the creatures move, dancing above their bodies and surveying the rooms. Chloe has never seen their mouths, but hears them whistle to each other as they work.

They crawl over everything in the chamber. A flock of five or six of them appear each night to clean. Chloe suspects that this is their purpose, as before they leave they make sure to crawl over every inch in the space, and once they leave everything shines new, no trace of dust or grime visible. Chloe likes to imagine they enjoy their work, their fuzzy bodies grooving to the melody of their whistles as they pass through. She tried to ask K'vinna about them once, but they didn't register as being of interest to nem.

This night, Chloe taps on the wall of her tank as one of the furry creatures passes by the gap in the curtain. The creature takes a moment to identify the noise source, its light purple eyes bouncing on its whiskers until it notices her in the tank. She tries to talk to it through the glass, mimicking one of the tunes she hears from them often. It doesn't respond to the music, but charges forward, inching up the glass in front of Chloe's face, a trail of the clear slime in its wake. As it moves higher, it causes the curtain the budge, and the other furry creatures see the dirty surface of the tank. Within minutes, the whole team is crawling over her glass tank, the fabric curtain in a heap on the ground. When they are satisfied, they slither off the tank and exit from the chamber, the presence of the human inside the tank of no concern to them.

When the lights re-ignite and K'vinna returns in the morning, ne pauses to observe the mess of fabric on the ground, nir saucer-like eyes unreadable as a flurry of nir grey tentacles throw the curtain back on the tank. Lying on the base of the cell and staring at the dark cloth above her, Chloe accepts K'vinna's neglect with resignation, knowing another long day of being ignored lies ahead.

• • •

K'vinna has to be careful when ne interacts with the human in front of U'ngdom. Even with the threat of treason, ne knows ne can't risk the younger Gu'ten's suspicion. K'vinna begins each working day tending to the running of the research division, monitoring and placating G'nist and K'nurre's teams. In the afternoons, once the immediate needs of the division have been met, K'vinna allows nemself time to study the breeder. Ne leaves the o'rdne in her tank between interactions so that now she is prepared when ne signals the tank walls are about to disappear. K'vinna tells nemself it is to save nem the effort of delivering it to her in time—not for her comfort.

Today, when ne lifts the heavy fabric off the glass cage, she is sitting cross-legged in one corner of her cell, a pile of her faecal matter in the diagonally opposing corner. She has her small five-digit limb covering her nose and mouth, and has an expression K'vinna can only identify as dullness of the mind etched across her face. Ne raps against the glass with a column of eight tentacles to draw her attention before using a separate column to activate the water flush functions of the cell.

She is drenched by a brief onslaught of water that douses her and the cell. Her waste secretions are suctioned out of the tank down a grate in its centre, and a gale of cool air looses any liquid from the girl's skin. She doesn't flinch in this process, her face unresponsive, dawdling to even lift the o'rdne to her mouth when K'vinna drops the tanks walls and it becomes difficult for her to breathe. K'vinna has to rush the device the final few inches to her face sucker. Nir voice is reprimanding as ne connects to her with the consciousness.

*What are you trying to achieve, little human, in drawing out your actions so?*

Her mind is displeasingly guarded from nirs, an advent that is occurring with increasing frequency in their iterations. K'vinna is about to berate her further, before realizing that this time the guarding is unintentional. It seems Chloe is merely not thinking of anything, conjuring no images in her mind. K'vinna can see the files in her head, stored information of her lifetime, but it is as though she is hiding amongst the boxes, unable to open any of them or bring them into focus. K'vinna lifts her off the floor of the tank, raising her to rest on top of nir desk. As ne sits her down, ne feels the cool caresses of wind streaming past nir bl'omsterlok, the jolting of a racing vehicle bouncing over rugged terrain under nir body. The jolting turns into vibrations up the length of nir tentacles, and then a sharp stabbing pain somewhere at their base. The girl is having a kinetic memory, reliving the trauma of what her mind deems the b'leie's first attack. Her eyes are still vacant but she is whimpering. K'vinna tightens nir labour tentacles around her arm.

*It's not happening now, Chloe. You are in a safe place.*

Nir words seem to resonate; Chloe's green eyes gaze up at the large pools of darkness that denote K'vinna's own visual sensory receptors.

*Am I?*

K'vinna's mind smiles and offers a dry response.

*Safer than before.*

*I don't know if I should believe you.*

*Do you have a choice?*

The girl is bothered by this response.

*What? It is a statement of fact. You will feel better if you accept the information I offer you, as when the alternative is unproductive worry there is no sense in choosing it.*

*Stop thinking of me as* the girl. *My name is Chloe.*

K'vinna is surprised by her filtering of nir unspecified thought process.

*I'd be more comfortable if you stopped thinking of me as a thing.*

*Very well, Chloe. I want to test some of your neural responses. Nothing that will hurt. More to assess how you think. Are you up for it?*

*What happens if I'm not? Will you put me back in the tank?*

*Yes.*

*Well, I'm up for it then, but I want to stretch my legs first. I'm not sure when I last walked.*

K'vinna gives nir permission, amused by Chloe's ability

to bargain even when feeling void of hope. She hops down from the table, gingerly stretching each of her legs out before her. The stark white floor is cool under her feet, hard like tiles but without gridlines. She takes a few steps forward, unsure which direction to walk. First she heads to the far left corner, next to where her tank usually stands, and then pivots, moving to trace the fabricated divider that obstructs from view where the other alien works. The material looks like it should be soft, but is rough underneath her hand. She contemplates it for some moments, before she remembers the wall that connects this chamber to the rest of the building. Chloe stares at the innocuous wall, her brain struggling to place where the door's exact position would be amongst it or how to summon it to open. As she gazes at the wall, K'vinna sends a flurry of tentacles to draw her back closer to the table.

*That is enough walking for today. Now, we will do our tests.*

K'vinna instructs Chloe to clear her thoughts and to focus on keeping them blank. Ne says ne is going to insert an image into her mind, and ne wants her to push it out so that her mind can return to a blank slate. Chloe nods her understanding, even though it is a pointless gesture while they are connected in the consciousness.

She closes her eyes and attempts to see nothing in her mind's eye. She sees blackness and lines of grey static from where the light of K'vinna's office pierces her eyelids. But overall it is black and silent. A pale tangerine shade appears in the darkness. It doesn't have a specific form, but oozes like wet paint unconstrained by gravity. It drips out of the nothingness, pooling into a spherical waterfall, overflowing further into the blank space. Her inner child wants to imagine a scrubbing brush wiping the ooze out of existence. Or to reach out to it, see how it feels to touch it as it wraps around her fingers. It looks as though it might feel warm—

Chloe stops her thoughts from continuing further. K'vinna's mind is waiting with impatience in the consciousness. She breathes in, and when she exhales the tangerine mess vanishes from being. She waits, eyes still shut, for K'vinna to make nir next move. The next image ne projects is of the sun. It blinds her visual sight, and she physically recoils from the apparition. She cannot flee it though, and her instinctual response to escape the immediate pain delays her ability to squash the image from her sight. When she regains control, she snaps her eyes open, surprised to find they are not stinging. Her gaze narrows at K'vinna's form, animosity leeching from her to nem in the consciousness.

Over the next several days, K'vinna requests to do more tests along this vein, proffering simple images for Chloe to disassemble and sneaking in potentially harmful items like the sun or the b'leie to catch her out. To what end, Chloe does not understand, but the mental frights begin to place her further on edge.

• • •

Chloe's insecurities build as her time outside of the small tank becomes limited to these tests, and she is left to extended periods in the curtained darkness with no reprieve. Her thoughts flit between fragmented memories of The Race, shards of her conversations with Sam, the tormented rants of Hannah in the birthing cell, and of the desolate loneliness that engulfs her in this new tank. K'vinna is busy with nir work. In brief moments during the tests, she can slip into unguarded places in nir mind and procure morsels of nir concerns. K'vinna is consumed with monitoring the other alien that resides in nir office. It is younger and dangerous, although Chloe cannot understand how. There are never-ending queries that K'vinna has to field from other sections, all kinds of concepts that Chloe cannot decode in her partial seconds inside. Overall, she understands that K'vinna does not have time for her, that ne views her as some sort of liability, and that ne suspects she is dangerous at her core. She does not feel dangerous. She is not dangerous, but endangered. She feels her time is running out.

# CHAPTER TWENTY-FIVE

DELU AND GAARWINE sit anxiously at the mouth of the tunnel
waiting for the remainder of their companions to surface. They
keep the paili salve on their skin, as it may come of use on their
surface trek to the cave. Madoc emerges next, still giggling
quietly to himself. When his face is hit with the full sun, his eyes
pop open in wonder and he cackles loudly.

Delu says to Gaarwine, "The paili."

Gaarwine nods, and then he lifts Madoc from the tunnel
opening and places him to the side.

He says, "Ye'll be all right. Just sit here quietly and we'll
see to yer in a bit."

Madoc's response is only to laugh harder and point in
glee as Hurste's face appears next from the underground.

Delu says, "Are you well?"

Hurste nods. "Yes. Ikka was in bad shape though."

Delu's face tenses. It doesn't relax when Aldric surfaces,
helped out by Hurste. He stares with foreboding at the

blackened tunnel.

He says, "Perhaps I should go back down."

Gaarwine shakes his head. "No, lad, it's too crowded. Her buddy'll be helping her out."

"Veela?"

There is a trace of skepticism in Delu's voice, which Gaarwine halts with a tone of reproach.

"He's a good lad. A bit foolish to be sure, but they all are." Gaarwine tilts his head towards Madoc and Aldric to emphasize this point. "And there's no denying he's got her best interests at heart."

Delu says, "That may not be enough."

His face wraps in gloom as he stares at the tunnel mouth. With every shadow or rearrangement of dust, he imagines Ikka's form emerging and is doused in brutal disappointment when it is not. When Veela's face appears, he hopes it is not true. He knows Ikka was to travel before him down the tunnel, so she should be appearing first. But then Veela reaches behind himself, using both arms to yank something up.

It is Ikka, pale underneath her brown skin and green paint, eyes rolled into the back of her head.

Delu and Gaarwine spring into action, helping Veela extract Ikka from the tunnel. She is freezing to the touch and clammy, sweat covering every inch of her paili-lined skin. They try splashing her face with water and gently slapping each side of her face. She doesn't react. Gaarwine pulls out the durable racing blankets from their two packs and they wrap her. Delu uses the sleeve of his jacket to scrub the paili mixture from her face and opens her mouth to pour some fresh water inside. That's when he sees the varme leaf, still resting on top of her tongue. He turns to Veela.

"A varme leaf? Where on Earth did you find this?"

Esej pops his knotted head of hair out of the tunnel.

He says, "You'll probably want to talk to Chiyo about that."

"Hey."

Chiyo follows closely behind him, and scowls at him for the betrayal.

Delu says, "You brought this?"

Chiyo is apprehensive, stepping awkwardly to the side and fidgeting with his sandy hair as he talks. "Well, I guess you could say that... I know it's not allowed, but you never know when these things can come in handy..."

Delu says, "Do you have more?"

"What?"

"I need to give her some water and this leaf already looks depleted. Do you have another I can give her?"

"Yeah. I do."

Chiyo's hands fumbles at the satchel strapped to his chest and he extracts another varme leaf wrapped in paper. He extends it to Delu who expertly places the leaf in Ikka's mouth after pouring some water down her throat. Her whole face seems to wince when the new leaf touches her tongue, though her eyes remain pointed to the back of her skull. In this time, Callyr and Daracha emerge from the tunnel, weary but concerned for the others in their troop. Delu and Daracha talk in hushed tones, and then Delu briefs the others.

"There is nothing else we can do for Ikka here, and it is

too dangerous to stay exposed in this spot. We need to continue onwards to the cave. Azzam's instructions mention to avoid the fiery earth to the right of the cave entrance, perhaps it is something we can harness to fight the chill that holds her. For now, all we can do is walk. Veela, are you right to carry her?"

Veela nods.

"Let's go then."

Veela bends to lift Ikka up, the solemn expression on his face reflected by all the others in the troop. With glum movements, they all collect their packs and begin the journey to the cave.

• • •

The seven miles to the cave are tedious. Not because of the terrain—there are no major ascents or descents, only occasional rocks to be over-stepped. It's because each foot travelled doesn't seem far enough, doesn't feel any closer to finding a cure for Ikka's condition. It weighs heavily on them all, and adds desperation to each step. Two hours pass, and the paili salve still left on their skin begins to dry and flake. Their eight hours are nearly up, the cave must soon be in sight. They spot the metea tree first. The brilliant reddish hue of its enormous trunk tinges the colouring of the path and smaller trees nearby. Its base must be twenty-six feet in diameter, and it has grooves at each third of a foot across its circumference, travelling way up to its peak ninety feet above. Branches as thick as the tunnel they just crawled through extend like intimidating arms covered in thick, viridian green leaves the shape of giant teardrops.

As promised, the cave entrance is sheltered under the metea tree's right boughs, covered by drooping branches and parasitic tree vines. They head inside; Veela places Ikka with care on the floor, others extracting and piling their blankets on her form. She is hidden under a mountain of blankets as Delu exits the cave, trailed by Hurste and Esej. He navigates with vigilance the rocky ground to the right of the cave entrance, stopping every now and then to place his hand on the rocks. Each time, his brows furrow in disappointment when his hand does not flinch in pain. Hurste and Esej watch with curiosity, before embarking on a path of their own. They walk back to the metea tree, and then scurry across the grass in the middle of the ravine to reach the mountain overhang on the other side. They manoeuvre the chaotic medley of ground, shrubs, and rocks lining the mountain wall, not entirely sure what they are seeking.

Then they see it. A collection of darker rocks, black as ash, with steam rising from within them. Esej steps eagerly towards them, tripping over a fallen branch hidden beneath the tall grass. His hands reach forwards to break his fall, but before he impacts, Hurste catches him by the back of his jacket and points eagerly past his face.

"See that mud? It's bubbling."

Past the rocks where Esej was about to land is a small pond filled with muddy water interrupted by sporadic, but definite, bubbles. Hurste picks up a stick and dips it in the mud. When he removes it, a faint hiss of steam exudes the droplets clinging to the wood. He touches it and residual heat floods his finger. He grins, the dimples in his face welling up to the size of the mael nuts his loves so dearly, and he calls out to Delu.

"Delu, over here. We can give her a mud bath."

• • •

Within minutes, Ikka's body has been carried to the muddy pond's edge, a procession of solemn but hopeful faces by her side. Veela stares at the bubbling pond with an air of extreme distrust in his eyes. He approaches it and dips his whole hand in without hesitation, keeping it in there for a minute. As he holds it down, quiet Callyr watches with interest.

He says, "What are you doing?"

"Making sure it won't do any permanent damage to her."

Veela looks away, waiting for the minute to pass in his head, ignoring the overwhelming heat ensconcing his hand. When the time draws to a close, he lifts it dubiously, not allowing himself any extra hope. His hand is bright red, fluorescent in its hue, but he can move it, bend his fingers and clench his fist—his skin is not blistering from the heat exposure, so he grants the others permission to place Ikka in the brown sludge. Gaarwine positions himself at the edge of the pond, and from this spot slides Ikka's body into the mud. As the others monitor her condition, Veela removes his racing jacket, shirt, and shoes and slides into the mud beside her.

In answer to the intrigued looks the others offer him, he says, "I'm not letting her stay in this cauldron a second longer than I find it unbearable."

He moves to sit beside her and works the hot mud over her arms and stomach, and hikes up her pant legs to rub the hot liquid over them as well. While he does this, Gaarwine keeps Ikka's head upright and Delu turns to Chiyo.

He says, "What other plant cuttings to do you have in that magic satchel of yours?"

Chiyo lists what he considers the more notable items in

the satchel's contents. The more he lists, the more proud he sounds of his collection.

"Metea, gumpe, mer, paili, varme, brukt, lakriste, blomstre… Not all are leaves, some are root cuttings."

Delu nods. "That's good. Can you simmer one varme leaf with two shoots of lakriste? I think it will help her to ingest some fire, too. Do it in the cave so we don't send a smoke signal into the ravine."

Chiyo is happy to be made use of, and springs with optimism back to the cave. With Esej and Madoc's help, he builds a small fire and stews the plants with some water. Back in the pond, Ikka is unresponsive, though her shivering has stopped. Veela keeps splashing her limbs with fresh burning mud, and even pats some on her forehead and cheeks. Chiyo returns with a canister of the varme and lakriste water, and with great care Delu spoons the liquid into her mouth. At first it gains no reaction, but, with determination, he keeps spooning it in as the others watch in silence.

And then she coughs.

The motion causes her eyes to roll back forward, though they still do not seem to register the outside world. Delu spoons more liquid in. She splutters, but then swallows it.

Delu gently touches a finger to her cheek and with an even tone says, "It's not quite so freezing."

A ripple of relief passes through the troop, though both Veela and Delu continue their duties with diligent concentration. Daracha leads the other men back to the cave to set up camp for the night—the sun's position in the sky is beginning to wane, and they are all in need of food. As the air begins to darken around them, Delu speaks to Veela in quiet tones.

"I think we should head back to the cave now, dry her up and let her sleep. Hopefully her body will recover by morning."

Agreeing without wanting to, Veela helps Delu remove Ikka's body from the muddy pond, and they carry her back to the cave. They dry her with soft balls of grass and cover her in all their blankets. Veela declines to eat with the others, and instead lies next to Ikka, his arms wrapped around her mountainous coverings.

• • •

Veela's sleep is fragmented. He is haunted by the sensation of drowning, thick black goop forcing its way down his throat and suffocating him, so real in its kinetics that he continually wakes gulping for air. He then feels the thick bundle of blankets wrapped in his arms and remembers the tumultuous state of Ikka's condition. He leans in close, straining his ears to listen to her staggered, shallow breaths—in, out, in, out—until he eventually falls asleep again only to restart the process.

"You're holding on a bit tight, *buddy.*"

Veela is ejected from slumber once more when he imagines Ikka's sardonic tone. He peers down at her face, but her eyes are still seared shut. He searches for any new signs of life, but her breaths are just as ragged, her cheeks still chill to touch. His voice faint, he speaks mostly to himself.

"You can't do this to me, buddy. We've got to fight some monsters. I can't do it by myself. I need you to lead me."

He closes his eyes, fighting back a persistent jerk of a tear sneaking its way out.

"Well you're going to have to loosen your grip a little…"

Ikka's voice is croaky and feeble, and trailed by a pathetic attempt to open her eyes. Eventually, she forces them open, and is unfazed by Veela's dumfounded face.

She whispers, "What? You won't be able to follow me anywhere if I can't breathe."

Veela releases a burst of short, sharp laughter, relief flooding his body. He relaxes his grip around her blanket cocoon, wonder painted across his face. Ikka eyes it suspiciously, but tires under the weight of her eyelids.

"I'm going to go back to sleep now. Try to not look like that next time I wake up."

• • •

By the time of Ikka's second awakening, the rest of the troop are prepared for the next leg of the journey. Supply packs have been refilled, and everyone has cleaned themselves using a small freshwater stream trickling down the left side of the ravine. Now they sit, with hushed whispers, waiting for the day to begin. When Ikka does open her eyes, Veela is no longer at his post beside her, and the others are all on the other side of the cave to allow her quiet. She lies there listening to the sounds in the cavern; the men's whispers bounce off the hard rock walls. They boomerang around the space, muddling in the air, so it seems as though the rocks themselves are whispering, hissing at the occupants inside to move on.

Left to her own devices, Ikka pushes herself upright, so she is sitting in her blanket nest. The effort temporarily winds her, her vision speckling for a few seconds with black dots before clearing and allowing her view of the cave. No one notices her except Callyr, who registers the movement and watches her with silent interest from a few feet away. When their eyes meet, she gestures that she needs water, and he picks his way across the space to sit beside her. Without speaking, he unscrews his water canister and holds it to her lips. She takes a small gulp, and is made aware of the swollen numbness inside her mouth. Her surprise is readable on her face. Callyr perceives her query and speaks in a logical and unfeeling manner.

"All the nerves in your mouth have most likely been destroyed by the tonic they gave you. They used varme, a fire plant that is quite dangerous to touch, let alone swallow. Your senses will return with time. Hopefully."

Ikka says, "Great."

The effort of speaking sends her into a small coughing fit, alerting the others to her awakened state. Delu rushes over, patting his hand on her back to help her break the fit.

"Are you okay, Ikka?"

Ikka nods while coughing, holding up her hand to stop further questions until the internal thwacking subsides.

"I can't feel anything in my mouth, but when I cough it is as though eight tiny blades are cutting up my throat."

Delu smiles, "Sorry about that. It was the only way to keep you alive."

"Yes, Callyr explained."

"Callyr?" Delu looks, and for the first times notices Callyr poised beside Ikka, water canister in his hands. "Yes, it would make sense he saw you first, he is perhaps more observant than even you."

Callyr does not smile at this compliment, but instead nods before rising and walking away. Delu offers Ikka his signature, all-knowing smile.

"He is also not the best at communicating. But come, it gladdens my heart to see you awake. You gave us a big scare. Veela especially, he hardly left your side. I forced him to go outside for fresh air just before, he will be upset his missed your awakening. Now, how do you feel? Strong enough to stand?"

"I can't speak for my limbs, but my mind is ready."

"Here, take my hand. Let us try together."

Holding at first quite softly to Delu's arm, Ikka begins to bend her knees and push her torso up. As her legs disobey her and wobble under her weight, she has to grip tighter and use all her upper arm strength to pull herself to her feet. The motion flips her stomach up and down, and sends a small rush of heat to her head before dropping all warmth to her feet and leaving her upper body unprotected. Delu watches her progression with great concern, so in return she offers him a tight-lipped smile.

"It's colder up here."

He laughs a little, "Perhaps Chiyo will be able to help with that. Chiyo!"

Chiyo approaches, glad to see Ikka awake.

"Do you have the oil, Chiyo? Ikka needs some help staying warm at this height."

Chiyo pulls out a small vial from his jacket, and passes it to Ikka. The liquid inside is thick and translucent with a pale green hue.

He says, "It took me most of the night. Hurste had to give me some nuts and I singed the tips of my fingers, but it should do the trick."

"The trick?"

"Oh, right! Dab a little bit on your finger and place it against your temples and under your neck. It'll deliver a catastrophic amount of heat to your skull that'll fight off any lingering clouds of paili, though make sure you clean your finger before you touch anything else. I made that mistake last night, and can I tell you, it was *not* fun."

Ikka mouths the word *catastrophic* with raised eyebrows back to Delu and Chiyo, but then follow's Chiyo's instructions. Within microseconds, pinpoints of heat plunge deep into her flesh, biting through the fog and clearing up her senses. At once, remaining upright feels easier, and she is able to moderately relax her grip on Delu's arms.

She says, "Thank you, Chiyo. Truly."

He grins and says, "Just don't forget to wash that finger!" before returning to the others in the group.

• • •

When Veela returns, Ikka is pacing on her own, occasionally stopping to dab more fire oil on her skin. He laughs as soon as he sees her, and she scowls at his mirth.

"What?"

"You have four pink dots where you've clearly been applying Chiyo's solution. It's cute."

Her scowl narrows further with menace.

"I'm going to ignore that in reverence for your apparently fighting so hard to save my life."

Veela endeavours not to laugh again at Ikka's stubbornness, as she goes on to offer a stoic, "Thank you." He mimics her standard head tilt, but says no more. They hold this bizarre equilibrium for a moment, until Daracha rallies the troops to continue their journey.

# CHAPTER TWENTY-SIX

FOR CHLOE, all of the days begin to morph into one. Even with the light changes for night and day, she has no grip on how long she has been under K'vinna's watch, no concept of anything other than trepidation for the next onslaught of K'vinna's tests. She still wants to trust K'vinna—needs to if she is to maintain any of her sanity—but she grows increasingly wary and unhinged. This day—whichever day it is—K'vinna has been called away from the chambers, but ne left Chloe's tank uncovered. She sits, her face pressed up against the glass, staring without seeing into the brightly lit room.

The younger alien withdraws the divider that usually hides nir workspace. Ne moves forward, extending nir many tentacles in a manner that is reminiscent of a human stretching. The section of the chamber that is nirs is much smaller than K'vinna's, and much more cluttered. The walls are lined with shelving units. All kinds of instruments that Chloe cannot identify jostle for space on the shelves, jutting out over the narrow ledges. In the centre of the alien's section is a small bench, sitting at Gu'ten bl'omsterlok height above the floor. There are enclosure rails on the bench to stop its contents tipping over, and what appear to be harness ends latched on at three points on each side.

Chloe's throat tightens as the possibilities of the bench's purpose sink in. In all likelihood, it is another human who is to be strapped to the work surface. She saw something like it when she first escaped from the birthing cells; live humans with their torsos cut open, organs on display. Perhaps that will be her fate when K'vinna has gleaned what ne desires from their visualising sessions. Before she can continue this train of thought, the alien obstructs her view of the table. Ne hovers with nir back to her, a team of nir reaching tentacles extending to one of the cabinets underneath a side bench. They weave about each other with both individual and complex hive-mind purpose, one unlatching the cabinet door, two others poised to prise it open, and seven more moving in unison to extract a two foot long object from the pristine shelf within, retracting quickly to then drop it into a bevy of waiting tentacles. Chloe watches in disbelief as the object is dropped from the sack onto the bench—it is a miniature Gu'ten, tossed dispassionately onto the hard gurney and strapped down without consideration.

Though her tank walls mute most outside sounds, Chloe still hears the small alien wail in fear and then screech out in pain as the older alien stabs it with a needle. Ne hooks its bl'omsterlok to two different tube apparatus, beginning a bizarre process of distillation, extracting a pallid white liquid from the infant and filtering it through an ink-like substance before returning it to the bl'omsterlok. The able-bodied alien pays no heed as the youth's warbled cries continue. Chloe wishes she could also ignore them, but is so starved for stimulation that she can't avert her eyes. She keeps her face pressed up against the tank wall, the cries vibrating through the glass and, in a perverse manner, massaging her skull. She stares at the trail of liquid entering and exiting the creature's body and the small spasms of the tiny tentacles peeking over the bench edge, and tears begin to form in her eyes. The salty fluid binds her cheeks to the glass, and she stays there watching until the chamber divider is reinstated. Shortly after, K'vinna returns and Chloe barely registers nir presence. Her mind is somewhere else; it is unclear if it will ever return.

• • •

The human's behaviour is starting to concern K'vinna. Ne is no expert in their idiosyncrasies, or even certain that they possess any, but ne can tell that Chloe is becoming mentally absent. Ne has ceased feeling her extraneous thoughts and reactions when ne offers new images in their intelligence tests. Instead, there is only dulled compliance. Today, as K'vinna left the curtain off the tank as ne works, and ne has been surprised that the breeder has done nothing but sit still all morning. She is crouched in the back left corner of her tank, head resting against the glass, eyes facing the chamber ceiling with listless vacancy. At one point, K'vinna rapped against the glass and her only response was a slight movement of her pupils. Nir tests will not yield accurate results if the girl's brain enters an unending slumber.

An idea occurs to K'vinna and ne plunges an entwined bar of three consciousness tentacles into nir liquid-filled desk.

They penetrate deep into the heart of the device, connecting with the building's internal consciousness loop. K'vinna's mind becomes a chasm overflowing with the information stored by every mind that has ever worked in The Facility. Ne glides through the ocean of information, seeking out that of one particular division. When ne arrives at it, the fat folds on nir bl'omsterlok crinkle in a manner reminiscent of a human smile.

The access portal for the breeding division is simple to navigate. Within moments, K'vinna finds nir mind roaming through the genetic histories of every human the division has produced. It does not take long for nem to locate the information for this most unique human, C-H-L-O-3. Flipping through her lineage yields no interesting results. All of the breeding females before her performed adequately, with C-H-12 not requiring termination until after her fifteenth gestation. There are currently four other C-H-L-Os active in the division and three more still maturing in The Race circuit. None of these humans have shown any signs of abnormality or of the vivacious nature required by C-H-L-O-3 to escape the birthing division.

Ne searches back through the security footage, wondering for the first time how the girl staged her escape. Watching through the vision, the girl's behaviour in captivity matched that of the other breeders in the tanks close to hers. Skipping through to the day of the escape, K'vinna is bemused at how easily the girl is able to exploit the weakness of the b'leie. It is astonishing that more of the breeders aren't attempting it. Or it would be astonishing, if they were not heavily sedated so often. It is highly unlikely that any of the breeders would be able to recall the events of this day.

K'vinna searches for any other anomalies from within the breeding division. Any peculiarity in the humans birthed or those then farmed for fo'ster-vi'kle harvesting. At first, no flaws are conspicuous. As per U'mulig's many gloating sessions at Facility meetings, their productivity numbers are without fault. K'vinna searches deeper, mining for hidden information ne technically shouldn't have access too, and, with great persistence, ne finds something. The memories of a now deceased breeding division worker hidden away behind many safeguards. Ne pries them out.

The dead Gu'ten's entire existence absorbs into K'vinna in an instant. Ne sees everything ne had seen, feels everything ne had felt, thinks everything ne had thought. The overwhelming emotion ne is ensconced by is guilt. Guilt of deception of the company, dread of being found out. The promises of nir superiors that no one will find out is not assuring. Guilt followed this Gu'ten to the grave. Such unnecessary guilt too, K'vinna muses. When a breeder was deemed inept but too young to be terminated without damaging the division's statistics, they would be smuggled back into The Race circuit, snuck into X-Runners newly vacated by an ovulating breeder, and then the circuitry of the racing vehicle would be rewired to state it was being occupied by a human male.

K'vinna is tempted to connect to K'lappstol's channel in the building's loop to alert nem of this fraud, but ne knows it is unwise to upset U'mulig while the problem of the human Chloe remains unsolved. Ne withdraws nir tentacles from nir desk and exits the consciousness loop.

• • •

K'vinna hovers in the centre of nir office while the girl, Chloe, paces a large circle around nem. Every step she takes awakens a muscle, ligament, or tendon that has been dormant in her many hours in the tank. Her mind is still dozing, apprehensive of waking for more of the brutal mind tests. In her peripheries, she can see the large alien watching her, the dark shadows under the fat layers on nir bl'omsterlok drifting to follow her movements. Three of nir black tentacles extend and glide over to her. She watches as though her body is not her own, as the clammy thin strings approach her and wrap around her right arm. Immediately, her whole body flushes with the warmth of K'vinna's presence within her mind.

*You seem distressed, human Chloe.*

She doesn't look nir way, but keeps pacing, her wide circle of the room causing K'vinna to have to rotate with her to keep nir grip on her arm. She grits her teeth a little, breathing out a small fraction of her frustration. She shoots K'vinna an image of the young alien strapped to U'ngdom's work table and an echo of the infant's cries.

*Is that what's going to happen to me?*

K'vinna doesn't respond immediately, nir reaction distinctively guarded.

*It is, then. When you're done spooking me with these little tests.*

*Spooking you?*

Amusement seeps into her mind, then is brushed aside by a sterner countenance.

*The intention is not to spook you, but to understand the extent of your cognitive function. U'ngdom's experiments are inconsequential to your existence.*

Chloe is not calmed by this response. K'vinna feels it and decides to try a new line of reasoning. Chloe feels this intention and interjects before ne can commence.

*Why do you care if I'm upset? You can't really care, not the way you keep me locked up all day long, only to come out for your stupid tests and then be shoved back inside again.*

There is a terse edge to her mental voice, quavering with all the rage of betrayed adolescence. She bites the back of her lip as she turns to glare at K'vinna, tears stinging as they scrape their way past her eyes. How foolish she looks from nir viewpoint, completely exposed in her spongy flesh, red hair matted against her face and neck, puerile liquid excreting from her eyes. There will be no sympathies from the foreign creature before her, she knows the depths of its feelings towards her are a curiosity, scientific, and analytical. She cannot pout and manipulate it to her will, or smile to endear it to her goals.

*Goals? There cannot be achievable goals in your life.*

Chloe juts her chin out at nem defiantly.

*There can. I'm going to get out of here. I'm going to find my father. And we're going to go a long way from here.*

*To where? You are in the domain of the Gu'ten. This whole planet is under the rule of the Gu'ten. There are multiple Gu'ten facilities spread across the surface of this planet. There will be nowhere for you to go.*

Her inner strength falters at this statement, but Chloe responds with what she hopes is not naivety.

*I'll find a way.*

More tears bite at her eyes, and then she feels a physical

disgust emanate from the alien. K'vinna attempts to block out nir view of her, but she glimpses it before ne drops the connection and uses nir labour tentacles to push her back to the tank. Down her legs drips the blood of her session, no mechanical diaper or fabric to cover it. She expects K'vinna to shut her into the tank without a second thought, but instead ne turns nir back to her, reaching into the desk to connect with the building's loop for a few moments. When ne is done, K'vinna turns to face her, extending a posse of nir black tentacles once more.

*For now, it is best if you stay above the tank floor. It will be more sanitary since you refuse to wear the b'leie. And perhaps I will indulge you a little and tell you the story of U'ngdom's experiments. You will see that you have nothing to fear from nem.*

• • •

As K'vinna begins to explain the methods behind U'ngdom's science, a small troop of the furry, white, slime-producing creatures arrive in the chambers. They produce a few harmonic notes when they enter, to which K'vinna responds with a few of nir own gurgling sounds. The petite creatures seem to understand and begin a meticulous crawl over the floor, suctioning up Chloe's bloodstains with their clear slime excretions. They do not limit themselves to the stained stretches of floor, but cover the entire span of the room—other than Chloe's tank base. They are not perturbed by her presence, cleaning up until the very edges of the tiles. One is barely two feet away from where she stands, its bouncing eyes inviting and pastel. She reaches down, her hands yearning to touch its soft fur. As her hand descends, the next series of movements are so sudden they seem to happen in slow motion.

The soft blue eyes swivel to examine her. A thunderous
*NO!* hits her consciousness. The creature's round gooey mouth
opens and pivots in her direction, two rows of seven sharp edged,
decayed brown teeth searching out her descending arm. A pack
of K'vinna's clear reaching tentacles swoop in and yank her arm
back, moving her into the centre of the tank floor. The furry
creature closes its mouth, returning to an image of utter cuteness,
continuing its cleaning mission across the floor.

*The D'ekercee are carnivorous, Chloe. It is best to leave them
be.*

Chloe nods, her heart still pounding against her chest.
*They look so cute though.*
*To your mind, perhaps. I do not see them so.*
*But you can speak to them?*
*Yes. The D'ekercee and the Gu'ten have had a reciprocal
relationship over the last millennium. Their unique body chemistry
disinfects our environments in a satisfactory manner, and in return
we protect them from the elements, their predators, and provide them
with adequate food sources.*
*And what do they think about us humans?*
*I believe they do not think about you. There is no benefit you
could provide them, other than as a food source yourselves, which we
do not allow them. It was initially a cause of discord with them. They
saw no reason why they could not at least sample live human flesh.
There is something in your odour that appeals to them.*

There is a trace of disgust lingering in their joint mind
as K'vinna considers the prospect of anything enjoying a human's
aroma. It is hard for Chloe to take offence to this, she can smell
herself as K'vinna smells her, and it is repugnant. She watches as

the squad of D'ekercee exit the room, their eerie whistles lingering in the air between her and K'vinna.

*Why don't you let them eat us?*

*You think we should?*

*Why not? You have so little concern for us otherwise.*

*That is untrue. As per company policy, the utmost care is taken in the harvesting of the fo'ster-vi'kle, including adequate care of the human breeders and test products. None die unnecessarily.*

As K'vinna thinks, Chloe tries to skim through nir mind for other information pertaining to these thoughts. Any unrequested images that accompany the statements from this section of nir mind, any further clues as to the extent of the prison Chloe is locked in. She strives to bait more out from nem.

*You can't really believe that.*

*Which part?*

*That this is adequate care.*

*You are fed, housed, cleaned. The human males we allow to roam free, to live their lives to the fullest in The Race. And those of you we require close access to in this building—we do not allow the D'ekercee to tear your flesh from your limbs, piece by piece, having you bleed to death as they chew as slow as only they can. Yes, I believe that this is adequate care.*

Chloe pouts in frustration, but she can tell there will be no convincing K'vinna that humans are worthy of better treatment than this horror. Nir mind is resolved on the matter, and now Chloe's is as well. She will accept this treatment no longer.

# CHAPTER TWENTY-SEVEN

IT IS STILL daylight when Delu's contingent of explorers emerge on the other side of the mountain, careful to remain in the tunnel's mouth as they scour the land outside. As Azzam stated, the edge of the mountain skirts the line where the forest ends and the desert begins. The early afternoon sun pounds with unflinching moxie against the burnt orange sand, creating a haze of heat that is painful to view. The cliff lip they are positioned behind is fifty feet above ground level and allows them to survey the land for some distance. The line of trees to their left appears too straight to be a natural phenomenon; from above they seem ordered, of a planned genesis. Chiyo looks on them with interest.

"It's a plantation. Do you recall the liquid meals from The Race? I'd bet anything the main ingredient is harvested from those trees."

His comment is acknowledged, but then quickly forgotten as Daracha removes the X-Runner navigation box from his pack and Delu requests Esej turn it on. The troop stands in pensive silence as Esej unscrews the back lid and adjusts some of the cabling. The computer hums to life, a high-pitched whistle remaining once the motor cogs quiet down. Esej flips it over and the screen shows them the best route to take to cover the most ground in The Race that day. There are a couple of scoffs, and Esej quickly retunes some controls at the back of the computer so the screen zooms out and they can scout for other X-Runners in the area. There are three within a twenty-mile radius of them, two to the east and one to the south—too far to walk to unless they can estimate where they will be docking for the night. They begin debating which X-Runner will be the best target.

Ikka interrupts, "I'm sorry, is the plan to steal an X-Runner and travel to the facility in it?"

Delu says, "That has been our initial thought, yes."

"Won't that be too obvious? They'll definitely be able to tell the X-Runner is filled with more people than its quota and be able to track our every movement. No element of surprise, which, as far as I can tell, is the only advantage we might possibly have."

Daracha says, "We can cover more ground in an X-Runner. Travel farther, faster."

Delu says, "We're hoping Esej can disable the X-Runner's functions that send information to the facilitators."

Ikka says, "And what makes you think you'll be immune to the vehicle's brainwashing?"

"Limited exposure," Daracha says. "Look, Ikka, you've been instrumental in rallying the troops, but this is something we've been planning for a long time. Let us handle this part. You just focus on remembering anything that may be helpful once we're there."

"Yes," Delu says with a gentle smile. "Thank you, Ikka."

Ikka bites her tongue, stepping away from the group to converse with Veela in hushed tones. "I don't trust this. Using an X-Runner is like delivering ourselves to the facilitators on their terms."

"Yeah, but how else are we going to find them?"

"There's got to be other ways. You can't say an X-Runner ever took you to them before. You might as well just stand in the middle of the desert waving your arms until an airship came to pick you up."

"Think that'd work?"

"Don't be an ass, Veela. Those things clearly shoot on sight."

Veela grins, "Yeah, well maybe we could trick one into landing."

"With?"

"Our collective charm?"

Ikka blanks him, continuing a new train of thought, "Would you come with me if I deem it necessary to branch off on our own?"

Veela doesn't hesitate. "Of course."

Ikka inclines her head and then disappears into her thoughts, following the rest of the procession down the cliff in silence.

• • •

The afternoon has the troop scaling down the mountain and beginning to cross the hot desert sand. They tie spare shirts around their heads to block the sun from their eyes, but they still squint and stumble. They tramp towards the northeast to a small rise located on the navigation system's topographic display—a likely docking position for at least one of the X-Runners tonight. As for their own protection, the general theory is that they are far enough from the airships' previous sightings of Settlement occupants that they will not be searched for out here, and that the haze of the desert heat will provide cover for their body heat signals if a routine scan does occur. Ikka still needs to re-apply the varme oil at regular intervals, but she now walks without assistance. Veela watches her closely, and Delu often looks to check Veela is by her side. When they reach the small hill, they position themselves amongst the boulders at its base, and wait for night to fall.

• • •

Not long after dark, an X-Runner arrives at their position. They wait in silence for its racer to exit, but after half an hour it is apparent this will not occur. Gaarwine suggests a method that was employed when the Settlement was first forming—to intrigue the racer out of the vehicle. They build a campfire nine feet away from the X-Runner door and sit around it talking loudly and eating their dinner as they wait for the racer to become so curious they must exit. It doesn't take long—within ten minutes, the X-Runner door opens and a well-groomed man with neatly cropped hair and a spotless racing uniform stands in a defensive posture in the doorway.

He says, "Who are you?"

"My name is Delu Dhara. Would you like to join us?"

The man glances around the circle.

"You're not wearing standard issue racing clothes. Where are your vehicles?"

Delu says, "We do not travel in X-Runners. We left them behind some time ago."

"Left them behind? Were you disqualified or something?"

Delu smiles graciously. "Something like that. Would you like to join us for a drink?"

The racer considers them before drawing a breath and saying, "Just one minute."

He disappears back into the racing vehicle and returns a few moments later carrying a small bottle of the X-Runner liquid meal. He carries it with care over to the fire and sits in the only available space, between Delu and Daracha. He doesn't seem at ease, but offers them all a tight smile.

"I'm Kueni. You said your name was Delu?"

"That is correct. This is my companion Daracha. We travel together with the rest our party. We thought the boulders at this hill would provide us sufficient shelter for this night."

Kueni glances at the different faces round the fire. His eyes rest on Ikka for a second longer, surprised when his brain confirms that he is seeing a female, and he quickly brushes that surprise away as the chemical controlled portion of his brain tells him it's rare to see a large group of humans. They're always spread out, it's not of particular note that one is female—females exist, after all.

Kueni says, "If you're no longer in The Race, why are you travelling through the racing route? Where are you travelling to?"

He takes a swig of his liquid meal while he waits for his answer. Ikka, Veela, and the others of Delu's faction are also eating their dinner, crunching down on pale root vegetables, eating them raw. Each time one of them bites, Kueni reacts, his spine stiffening with unease. He doesn't know it, but he hasn't heard a human bite or chew his entire life. The sounds are penetrating deep in his subconscious, unhinging the sense of order that controls his acceptance of The Race.

Delu answers him, "We are trying to reach the facilitators. We have questions we'd like to ask of them."

"You don't think it's dangerous walking to them this way? X-Runners must be hurtling across the desert at all hours of the day. They might not see you and run you over."

"That had in fact occurred to us. We were wondering if you might offer us safety in your vehicle."

"In my vehicle? I'm in this race to win. I don't have time to make detours."

Delu nods, his gaze not penetrating Kueni's but instead directed at the fire.

"Can you tell me, Kueni, how long have you been racing?"

"Just the past couple of months."

"And what were you doing before that?"

"I was… What kind of question is that?"

Delu turns to smile at him.

"I am trying to help you understand that you actually have all the time in the world."

Kueni's forehead furrows, frown lines materialising on his tightly wound face.

"I don't know what you're getting at."

"Can you remember a time before The Race, Kueni? If you think hard enough, I believe you'll find there never was one."

The frown lines crease deeper.

"It's been a long day…" He stands. "I think I need to retire for the night. It was a… pleasure meeting you."

Daracha grins up at him, the firelight on the back of his head causing menacing pockets of shadows under his eyes and cheeks.

"The pleasure was all ours, Kueni."

His arms flash forward and ensnare Kueni's ankles, yanking hard and dropping him to the ground. As soon as Kueni's upper body hits the dirt, Daracha pounces forward and holds a blade to his throat.

Delu says, "Sorry, Kueni, but we will be needing your X-Runner whether you are willing to share it with us or not. Gaarwine—"

Gaarwine is already by Kueni's side, rolling him over and binding his hands behind his back.

"Sorry, matey, but it has to be done."

Delu turns away from Kueni and looks back to the rest of the faces round the fire.

"Esej, Callyr, Madoc, can you look at X-Runner? We need to stop it from sending information, but it must still be able to receive it."

They nod and stand with haste, Esej particularly excited to play with a new toy. As their figures hurry across to the runner, Delu, Daracha, and Gaarwine's attention is fixed on Kueni. Ikka nods to Veela to hand over the nav system from the ground. It is switched off, but having watched Esej's earlier use, Ikka is able to switch it on at the back. There are four dials underneath the monitor screen that turn to the left and right in increments and also push down on themselves. Ikka manoeuvres them to zoom out wide on the map and scan for the nearest refuelling stations.

Watching over her shoulder, Veela whispers, "You still thinking of splitting?"

Ikka nods. "Yes, once the others sleep. I do not trust their plan to travel in that *thing*."

She returns her attention to the computer system and notes that the closest refuelling station is nineteen miles to their northwest, back near the forest's edge. She switches the machine off and tucks it behind her back. In the darkness and shadow play of the fire, none of the others note this sleight of hand.

Delu's attention leaves their hostage and returns to the rest of the group.

"We should sleep. Esej, Callyr, and Madoc will probably have to work through the night, but the rest of us must recoup for the morning. It will be a big day."

They nod in agreement, gathering their blankets from their packs and spreading out around the fire. Delu walks over to Ikka, kneeling down to speak to her as Veela pretends to not listen from beside her.

He says, "I fear you do not agree with our methods, Ikka."

She says, "No."

Delu smiles at her bluntness.

"I appreciate that you always speak your truth."

Ikka does not respond, other than to tilt her head a little.

"We will take care of Kueni as best we can."

Ikka still doesn't answer.

"This is the quickest way to take us to the facilitators."

Ikka says, "And you think speed is the most important factor in reaching them?"

Delu says, "We will be less worn down if we travel this way. We need our energy for when we find them."

"And what do you plan to do once you find them? Drive into a loading bay and storm the building?"

"You know I would not be so unconsidered."

"Do I? You're taking the easy option without really thinking it through. These are the vehicles that are single-handedly controlling and monitoring the entire human population, and your first thought upon returning to the surface is to commandeer one and steer it to your will? It's ludicrous."

"I am sorry you see it that way."

There is pain in Delu's eyes, but Ikka cannot offer him a comforting smile. Her face remains piercing, questioning his choices.

"Me too. We should sleep. As you said, it will be a big day."

Delu nods, and Ikka sees he wants to say more but cannot. He moves away, finding his own place in the darkness, and Ikka scowls up at the stars in the sky. Despite not having seen them for weeks, their presence agitates her. She has reclaimed so many memories since last witnessing their speckled beauty, but to her they represent thousands of unanswered questions. As she drifts off gazing at them, she wonders if any of them are on her side.

# CHAPTER TWENTY-EIGHT

AFTER THE incident with the D'ekercee, K'vinna needs some time away from Chloe. Ne was genuinely worried for her safety when the incident transpired, and ne knows ne needs to reclaim a scientific distance from her. K'vinna drifts into the communal research chamber, hoping to distract nemself with the others' work. Ne hovers past different work pods, watching Gu'ten researchers attempting to improve the fo'ster-vi'kle. How futile their methods seem in light of U'ngdom's research. As K'vinna watches them, ne is aware of G'nist heading directly for nem. K'vinna wonders how to avoid the forthcoming discussion, as ne has grown weary of the old crone's dialogue. G'nist is joined on nir journey by K'nurre, and when T'vil notices the passage, ne also joins in. It is a matter of moments before all three Gu'ten crowd around K'vinna, cajoling nem into a small meeting chamber.

Once they are all positioned, K'vinna appraises them, a bemused tone to nir voice when ne speaks.

"So? What matter would you three like to discuss?"

G'nist seems too enraged to speak, K'nurre too careful. T'vil speaks for them.

"Forgive us, K'vinna, but we believe we deserve answers. We trust in your leadership, but work has not been carried out in secrecy in this division for an age."

G'nist blurts, "We have a right to know what is going on."

K'vinna vibrates at a higher frequency—a Gu'ten sign of mirth.

"A *right*, G'nist? How is that?"

"I have dedicated my life to finding a cure to the be'lysning. Forty-three years! I have contributed more to our species' salvation that any Gu'ten alive. And now you have risen a young research assistant up through the ranks to work for you in secret? I deserve more respect than this!"

"I am protecting your mind from being distracted by U'ngdom's methodology, G'nist. You should be grateful. I am ensuring the research division's attention does not become sullied until we know it is a viable research path."

K'nurre speaks quietly. "And what about the breeder?"

"What about the breeder?"

"The one in your chambers. There have been rumours you engage with it, interacting in non-scientific ways."

K'vinna's eye shadows glare at K'nurre. Nir vocal gurgling takes on a malicious tone.

"Non-scientific ways? We are researchers, not gossips. I expected more from you, K'nurre."

"And I expected more from you." This time it is T'vil

speaking, nir voice pained. "Whatever is transpiring in your chambers, you are distracted, neglecting some of the basic functions of your role. You need to spend less time in there and more time out here on the floor. How will you represent the division well at the next facility meeting if you do not know what we have been undertaking?"

"Because I know what I have been undertaking. I work later than all of you, reviewing all of your daily logs. I know everything that happens in this section. The ignorance does not go two ways."

A thud echoes through the chamber, and then a young research assistant appears in the doorway.

"Pardon the interruption. K'vinna, T'arahn has asked for you. Ne is nearing death."

The youth exits and K'vinna glares at the senior staff.

"I will inform you of U'ngdom's research when the time is right. *Not* before then. Do not presume to demand answers from me again. Your disrespect will not be received as tolerably."

K'vinna floats upright, swooping out of the chamber into the greater division floor. Ne does not have the time to deal with the insecurities of nir staff, and ne is not ready for T'arahn to die.

• • •

K'vinna enters T'arahn's chamber at speed, frantic to speak with the elder Gu'ten before nir passing. T'arahn feels the air displacement caused by nir arrival.

"K'vinna, is that you? No one else would come to visit me. Thank you."

K'vinna is at a loss for words. T'arahn has been there from the very inception of K'vinna's life. The same body that lies before nem dying is the one that birthed nem.

K'vinna says, "I am not ready for you to go."

"No, but you'll be okay."

K'vinna cannot understand T'arahn's cavalier attitude. Ne longs to reach out and touch nem, connecting with nir mentor in the consciousness one last time.

"We're so close to finding a cure, T'arahn. Can't you hold out a little longer?"

"I don't think so, K'vinna. Even as we talk I can feel the rest of my life leaving me. Promise me you'll look after yourself? Don't risk getting caught communicating with the breeder."

K'vinna nods and, knowing T'arahn cannot see nem, says, "As you wish."

K'vinna stays, hovering by T'arahn's side for many hours whilst the elder Gu'ten approaches nir death. No others come to say farewell, paranoid of infection or too busy with their own work. When the end does arrive for T'arahn, nir entire bl'omsterlok is frozen a murky white. It is only then that K'vinna feels safe to touch nem, whispering to nir departed friend.

"I will miss you."

• • •

Chloe is left in her tank with the curtain unslung once more. She has spent more minutes staring at the oppressive white walls surrounding this room than she can count. Her mind still hopes to see something new, to feel some new sense of mental stimulation. Today, she is lucky. The other Gu'ten is bustling in and out of nir section, a methodical shamble of tentacles that move with a purpose Chloe can't comprehend. She can hear the echo of K'vinna's mind, this alien is called U'ngdom.

The thick sack that encapsulates the non-tentacled portion of U'ngdom's form is smaller than K'vinna's. Nir movements, less practiced. Chloe can spy the small, infant Gu'ten strapped to the bench in the middle of U'ngdom's workspace. The odd assortment of pipes and fluids are rigged once more to its body, and Chloe can hear it whimper through the glass walls of her tank. U'ngdom hovers above the bench, nir movements agitated, and then ne turns, nir ominous eye shadows regarding Chloe in her cage.

U'ngdom drifts in Chloe's direction, nir torso sack floating at level with the ceiling to Chloe's tank. As ne moves towards her, Chloe can see a smaller sack between the dancing tentacles to the base of U'ngdom's bl'omsterlok that is puffing in and out as the Gu'ten moves. It is translucent, clear in an unguarded way. There is nothing inside it or, at least, nothing visible to the human eye. U'ngdom halts in front of Chloe's tank, looking down at her body in a posture she cannot decode. Ne floats there, unmoving other than the subtle drifting of nir tentacle tips, as Chloe gawks up at nem. Chloe can hear K'vinna's warning, *Don't trust this one, don't let it know that you can understand.*

The tank dissolves around Chloe and with dread she inserts the o'rdne into her mouth. The Gu'ten peers at her as she does this, a movement suggesting curiosity at her awareness of this procedure. Two of what Chloe thinks of as a Gu'ten's grabbing tentacles shoot out and wrap around Chloe's wrists. She is then dragged to the other section of the chamber, small friction burns marking her limbs as they scrape across the floor. She is dumped onto a secondary bench, which is lined up next to the one containing the infant Gu'ten. Even as her body impacts on the metal surface, restraints are applied to her arms, neck, and legs.

At first it doesn't occur to her to be scared, she is too grateful for the mental distraction. As the Gu'ten has nir back turned to her, rummaging through items she cannot view, she manages to turn her head to her left, so that she can see the infant Gu'ten. A loose sack of swirling gas, nir eyes are more defined than any of the adult Gu'ten she has seen. There are five deep blue pupils residing in each of the dark eddies of liquid that Chloe associates with adult Gu'ten's eyes. Three of the pupils in each pond are staring in wonder at Chloe, and the remaining two are trained on U'ngdom's movements. Nir tentacles are only fifteen inches in length, and are yet to display the different colourations adorned by adult Gu'ten. They are bunched under a thick restraint, as is the base and top of the infant's bl'omsterlok. It is hard for Chloe to tell if ne is trembling, but as U'ngdom begins to turn around, all of the infant's ten pupils gather to watch nem in fear, and a small puffing sack at the base of nir bl'omsterlok goes into overdrive.

The infant Gu'ten begins to wail, an eerie cry expressed as high-pitched gurgling. Chloe pities nem, that ne can still feel fear after all ne has already gone through. She no longer feels fear, but detached curiosity as U'ngdom fixes nir attention to her. She wonders to herself if what is to come will be worth the break in the daily monotony. It is a foolish, conceited thought, and one that is ripped from her immediately.

A cluster of U'ngdom's grey tentacles start prodding at Chloe's body, feeling the veins and arteries in her arm. A glass cylinder, five millimetres in width, four inches in length, is inserted with swift precision into her wrist. She doesn't yelp, but is taken by surprise as three of the four inches disappear under the skin and into her ulnar artery. It causes a ridge in her forearm, one that she can't see from her strapped position, but can feel against the slender bones in her wrist as she moves her fingers. Small waves of nausea begin to drift up her arm, crossing her chest, and travelling down her stomach, past her groin and covering all the distance to her toes. The waves roll up and down, causing her muscles to twitch in discomfort as they are passed.

The bench beneath her begins to dissolve. What she thought was metal becomes a thick, luminous sludge. It engulfs her body in a suffocating embrace. She can still breathe thanks to the o'rdne in her mouth, but she can only see a hazy outline of U'ngdom through the silver grime. It simultaneously feels like she is floating and pinned down. The waves of nausea continue as U'ngdom's figure drifts in and out of focus above her. Two tentacles plunge into the ooze near her hips, followed in quick succession by five more, each plummeting with a thunderous echo into the goop. Each new movement displaces the dense slime so that it pushes uncomfortably against her ear canals. Yet, this pain is the least of her concerns.

One of the tentacles is wielding a blade. It is minuscule. Chloe can't see it in the haze, but she is acutely aware of its bite against her flesh. She is not sure of the incision's depth, only the searing burn of its cut. She is not allowed time to absorb the extent of the agony before two tentacles propel into the cut, pushing their way inside the wound. She imagines she can see at least eight inches of them disappear beneath her skin. They weave amongst her organs until they find their target. She has no idea what it is, but is floored by excruciating pain as the object is twisted, pulling at all the sinews and arteries holding it in place. The tentacles are unforgiving. They keep yanking, pivoting the object until Chloe is screaming into the o'rdne. No sound emits into the sludge, but the tears that eject from her eyes float in self-contained bubbles to the surface of the slime.

As she screams and the tentacles corkscrew the unknown organ to the point of no return, Chloe is aware of a new figure hovering in the outside of her peripheries. It is K'vinna, and she hopes for salvation like she has never hoped for anything before. It does not come, and instead rage wraps around her brain as ne drifts away from view and U'ngdom's tentacles rip the organ from her body. The pain is so acute that it pushes her to the edge of consciousness. As she teeters in and out of consciousness, she gazes at the object now floating beside her in the goop. Barely half an inch in length, it is a puckered grey oval. Specks of blood waft around it and near the incision in her flesh. Black speckles also fill her view, though she cannot see where they are from. Her fingers lazily extend towards the grey oval, even though they have no chance of reaching it. The black speckles become larger and larger until her entire view is skewed and she passes out.

• • •

K'vinna is morose when ne returns to nir chambers. Ne is so distraught from T'arahn's passing that ne doesn't notice Chloe's tank is empty. When ne does, K'vinna pays attention to nir aural receptors, registering unusual noises from U'ngdom's section of the chamber. When K'vinna enters the section, ne is numb to the sight before nem, nir mind unable to act.

U'ngdom has Chloe inside one of the liquid work pods, clearly un-anaesthetised. She is screaming through her o'rdne as U'ngdom's tentacles penetrate her abdomen and are attempting to remove an organ. K'vinna wonders whether or not ne had approved this. U'ngdom turns to nem, and, without ceasing nir work, extends a consciousness tentacle to connect with K'vinna.

*One of the research assistants told me of your meeting with T'vil and the others. I thought if I were to show them a memory of my dissecting the human, they may leave you along. Better, now that you are here, you can show them a memory of you watching me do it. Shall I continue?*

K'vinna can see that Chloe has spotted nem through the pod's gel. Her eyes are hopeful, imploring nem to save her from this place. Ne cannot.

*Yes, U'ngdom. Continue.*

K'vinna stays and watches as U'ngdom continues with nir wrenching and removes one of Chloe's ovaries. What possible use U'ngdom will claim for this organ, K'vinna cannot imagine, but ne doesn't need to. Once the deed is done, K'vinna exits through the divider, unwilling to look back. Ne knows Chloe will not forgive nem.

• • •

Chloe wakes up sobbing. It is uncontrollable, her pathetic sobs fighting against the o'rdne and shaking her body against the cold bench she is still strapped to. When she opens her eyes, she cannot see U'ngdom, but is face-to-face with the infant Gu'ten on the bench beside her. All ten of nir little pupils are watching her, and she is sure she can see concern in all of those eyes. Two of nir tentacles disengage from the pack and extend towards her across the small gap between them. They hover with uncertainty above her arm. She rotates her hand beneath the strap pinning her arm down so that her palm faces up in an offering. The two tentacles hesitate for a moment longer, and then lower down onto her hand, wrapping around her palm with gentle deliberation. The infant looks at her in confusion, unsure as to the next step, following instincts that have not yet been fulfilled. Chloe offers a weak smile, though she is sure ne won't understand what the movements in her face mean. She folds her fingers over the tentacles and invites the infant to enter the consciousness with her.

When their minds connect, it feels as though a cool towel has been placed over Chloe's forehead. Her sobbing ceases, and she allows her eyes to shut as she focuses on the serene innocence of the infant Gu'ten's mind. She can feel nir joy at connecting with another being for the first time. Ne has been yearning for this since nir creation, without ever knowing what ne had been denied. Ne is concerned for her, disturbed by her tears and treatment by the cruel one. Ne does not know the word cruel, but when the infant considers the ominous floating mass that is U'ngdom, ne is filled with pure fear and concern. Ne wants to know if Chloe is okay, and the questioning feeling tips Chloe over the edge again. Tears spill out of Chloe's eyes, and she squeezes the infant's tentacles in as reassuring a manner as she can. They lie like this, hand and tentacles entwined, for many hours. There are no words, thoughts, or feelings they can offer each other to feel better, only the helpless camaraderie of both having no hope in sight.

# CHAPTER TWENTY-NINE

HANDS SHAKE Veela's shoulders, and his eyes open to Ikka's face peering down at him, a finger held against her lips. Her brown hair and skin disappear into the night sky, but her eyes twinkle, reflecting the moonlight. He smiles at her, and in silence they pack their sleeping blankets, moving as faint outlines against the night sky. They head northwest, eyes and minds not turning back to the companions they have left behind, yet as their feet patter across the dirt, the hairs on Ikka's arms stand erect under her jacket, sure they are being watched. Without falling out of pace Ikka gently touches the back of Veela's right hand with her left, the out of character gesture alerting him to danger. In controlled movements they unsheathe their weapons and stand back to back, eyes scanning the dark horizon.

Ikka projects her voice, "Reveal yourself."

She hears a faint rustle, the sound of fabric rubbing on fabric, and advances towards the sound's source. Before she reaches it, a small round object catapults forward and impacts on her shoulder. It does not hurt, but leaves a slight grease stain on her jacket and rebounds onto her left hand, exposing itself to be a nut. She looks from it to the darkness ahead.

"Hurste?"

"And Chiyo."

The two young men step into Ikka and Veela's line of sight, packs on their backs and sheepish expressions on their faces.

Hurste says, "We hope you don't mind, but we saw you two leave. We want to come with you."

"Oh?"

Chiyo says, "We don't trust travelling in an X-Runner either."

Ikka doesn't speak, instead scrutinizing Hurste and Chiyo's faces for some time. Veela doesn't say anything—he likes both men and would appreciate their company, but understands Ikka must make the choice. She will be the unanimous leader of this troop, if she decides to let it become one.

Ikka says, "Are you sure this is what you want? To leave your friends behind?"

Both men nod, their expressions solemn.

Hurste says, "This isn't about friends. We're no use to anyone if we're caught, and travelling in an X-Runner is the same as walking into a trap."

Ikka smiles at them, though her eyes don't commit.

"Well, we have many more miles to walk before daybreak. Let us not waste more time."

• • •

The sun rises after a six or seven hours, peeking over the

horizon. They have travelled thirteen miles, and they have six
more to go before they will reach the forest edge. They stop for a
brief break to chew some of Hurste's never ending nut supply
and simmer some of Chiyo's leaves into a tonic he says will give
them strength. Then they continue, hopeful to reach the trees'
shade before the sun climbs higher and begins to burn their
flesh. They do not talk as they walk, careful to conserve their
breaths. It is very different from the last time Ikka crossed the
desert with Veela, the flashbacks now solid memories that
motivate her towards retribution. Chiyo and Hurste seem
unlikely additions to their party, both weedy looking with long
limbs and narrow faces, and a knowledge base restricted to plants
and nuts. At least there will be no starving in their company.

Two hours later they see the forest edge in the distance,
and Ikka stops to review the readings on the nav system. There
are no X-Runners or other ship signals on the map. She chooses
a point half a mile south of the refuelling station, where the
brush is thick, for them to travel and set up camp for the day.
She powers the nav back down, and they reach their destination
three quarters of an hour later, hiding themselves under a thicket
in the bush. Then they lie down to rest, their bodies weary from
the night and previous day's journey. Sleep comes fast, and they
do not wake until the sun begins to sink.

• • •

As dusk approaches, Ikka departs the thicket, leaving her
companions to their rhythmic, snoring-articulated dreams. She
steps with care through the scrub, her tough fabric-soled racing
boots making only gentle indentations on the forest floor. She
walks with one of her blades extended, prepared for hostile attack

at any moment. None come, and fifteen minutes later she catches sight of the refuelling station. Its exterior is made from the same materials as an X-Runner's body, strong metals welded together at abstract angles. Instead of a simple square, the building is made of twelve connecting surfaces, positioned so that each faces the sun, lined with modules of polycrystalline. The electrical docks for refuelling the X-Runners are mounted from the ground in front of the structure, accompanied by two pipes that refill the liquid meals and withdraw the vehicles' waste. There are no visible entry points to the structure, but Ikka is not looking for any. She scours the grooves and imperfections in the ground around the building's base. When she has lapped the building twice, she nods to herself and returns to the thicket and her friends.

• • •

Veela and Hurste are munching on mael nuts when Ikka returns.

She says, "Do you two think of anything other than eating?"

Hurste blushes, and Veela shrugs.

Ikka says, "I think I've found us a way to the facilitators. Where's Chiyo?"

Veela says, "We thought he was with you."

Hurste quickly follows with, "He's probably searching for more edible plants."

"Perhaps." Ikka sits down beside them. "Hopefully he will return soon."

• • •

All traces of the sun have vanished when Chiyo returns.

He has three stalks of a plant fifteen inches in length, one and a half inches in diameter, and the satchel strapped to his chest is bursting with fat dark green leaves shaped like four inch spades. He is whistling as he returns, and offers a broad smile to the group.

"I've found us more food. If it's okay, I'd like to prepare it before we head out."

Ikka nods her assent and Chiyo gets to work. He retrieves three different shaped knives from his satchel and begins peeling the long stalks. On the outside they are a pale green, but, as he carves out the root, the shading intensifies to a bright green with underlying hues of blue. He slices it lengthways four times, and then turns it across and slices those pieces four times lengthways also. As he cuts, a watery liquid an opaque shade of green yields from it, staining his fingers. Veela looks at it in skepticism.

He says, "Are you sure this stuff is edible, buddy?"

"Ha. Yes, I took it from the plantation. I think it's what the X-Runner liquid meals are gleaned from."

"The plantation?" Ikka looks up from the nav system, "You went there just now?"

"Yeah, it's about twenty minutes south, the one we saw from the cave. I just had to know… if it was what I thought it was."

Veela and Hurste stare at Chiyo in amazement. Ikka studies him.

She says, "You felt safe there? Did you see anything? Did anything see you?"

"No. The plantation was deserted. Just me and the trees.

But there were tracks. Vehicles, I think. Ones used to harvest the leaves. Oh and giant metal machines cutting the leaves, but I kept my distance from them and they definitely didn't notice me."

Veela says, "Giant metal machines are your afterthought to that answer? Geez, buddy."

"And you're sure they didn't notice you?" Ikka says.

"I'm sure," he says with confidence.

He begins to wrap parcels of three long pieces of stalk in one spade shaped leaf each. He hands them to Veela, Hurste, and Ikka and keeps one for himself.

"It might not look like much, but I think it'll taste good. They smell like the core ingredients to the liquid meals to me."

He offers an optimistic smile and then takes a swift bite of his spade wrap. He chews thoughtfully, his eyes half-closing as his mind registers the flavours. Once he swallows, his eyes snap open and he looks at the others with a sense of pride.

"I knew it. If you ignore the fact that you're not drinking it, the flavours are so familiar it's eerie."

The self-satisfaction vacates his face when he realizes the others haven't taken a bite yet.

"It tastes good, I promise..."

Ikka says, "You're as peculiar as Hurste and his nut addiction. No wonder you two left the Settlement."

Veela—who has just taken a bite from his spade wrap— has to fight a choke of laughter at Ikka's words. Ikka notices and bangs hard on his back, saying, "Here, let me help you."

He swats her hand away and says to Chiyo and Hurste, "Don't take her personally. She doesn't know how to be polite.

This tastes good."

After completing the meal, Chiyo uses meticulous care to clean his small blades.

Ikka says, "We better get moving. I scouted the refuelling station while Chiyo was finding his plants. The power it generates is self-contained, but the feed and wastage pipes are not. You can see them just under the earth's surface, snaking away from the building. I say we follow them back to their point of origin, and when we get there we assess the best possible method to infiltrate the facilitators' establishment, whatever that may be.

"Okay." Chiyo nods.

Veela says, "Let's do this."

Hurste plops another nut into his mouth.

"I'll take that as all in favour, then," Ikka says.

• • •

For the most part, the four companions trek without conversing. Ikka leads them to the refuelling station, its panelled roof shimmering in the moonlight. She shows the men where the pipes exit the structure, and they follow them along the border between the forest and desert. Ikka's attention is focused on tracking the pipes, Veela on observing Ikka, while Hurste and Chiyo on absorbing all the new visual stimuli. Dirt passes under their feet accompanied by vines of sallow yellow and green. With distance they morph into erratic shrubbery with small white flowers on spiked stems, and then the pipes lead the quartet into denser forest. It is not composed of the same bush trees located in the land over the Settlement, nor of the barely matured deep green trees of the plantation. These trees have broader trunks of a wood so dark they dissolve into the night sky.

They have been following the pipes for three hours when Ikka stops without warning, causing Veela to stumble into her. He begins to apologize, but realizes she is paying him no heed. Her focus is on the ground. She kneels down, hands reaching in the darkness, moist chunks of dirt collecting between her fingers. She scoops at the earth, digging with her hands to decipher which direction the pipes have gone under the soil. She follows her excavation to a thorny bracket's edge and, without missing a beat, slips out her knife and hacks it apart. Under the scattered remains of the bracket the pipes join up with two larger pipelines. It is difficult to deduce which direction on the new pipeline is toward the source of origin. Hurste places his hands on one of the pipes as if to feel which way the liquid is flowing through it; as he does, Ikka removes her pack and recovers the nav system, stepping aside as she powers it on. She only keeps it on for a few seconds—long enough to widen its radius and scour for the closest refuelling station. She returns it to her pack and eyes off Hurste's soothsaying of the pipe.

"Has it told you which way to go yet?"

Hurste's dimples widen in embarrassment and he shakes his head.

"That's okay. There's another refuelling station southwest of here, so I'm guessing that means we should keep following the pipes to the north. Unless any of you have other suggestions?"

They don't, so the four of them continue to the north late into the night.

• • •

The hour before dawn finds Ikka's party of four still following the pipelines with no indication in the darkness as to whether or not they are heading the right way. Tall black tree trunks tower over them, boughs of leaves whispering in the night breeze above their heads. The whispers aren't the only sounds though—there is a low humming in the distance, the faint whirring of something not born from nature. Ikka raises her hand to slow the three behind her, cautious of what to expect. She takes her steps with care, not timid but determined in their stealth. The pipeline reaches a point where thick bush blocks any of the dawn light from seeping through, and Ikka has to cut into it, pushing her torso through the hedging. One of the others— she isn't sure which, her attention is too captivated by what lies before her to notice—whispers asking what she can see. She does not respond, but pushes at the plants beside her head to make space for the others to also witness what lies ahead.

The facility.

Standing tall and ominous in the distance.

A giant sterile structure of white.

# CHAPTER THIRTY

MANY DAYS pass before the incision in Chloe's abdomen heals and she is able to move without being crippled by excruciating pain. The dulled agony of her standing becomes bearable, but is stalked by the anguish of K'vinna's betrayal. Chloe has not responded to K'vinna's efforts to engage with her in the consciousness. Through her sadness she has been able to block nem out, stonewalling nem and refusing to accept the o'rdne until ne is forced to seal the glass tank once more. She lies or sits with her back towards K'vinna's desk, refusing to look in nir direction. K'vinna is not worthy of her consideration, for ne has shown no consideration to her.

Chloe dreams of the open desert plains of The Race. What she would give to feel the fresh air on her face once more, to hear her dad's bashful ramblings, to experience possibility. When Chloe thinks of these things, she weeps, silent tears streaming down her cheeks. Her hands grab at chunks of her hair, pulling just above the roots to alleviate some of the pressure in her head. Sometimes it works, providing her brief moments of sublime release, but more often than not she is haunted by the worn visage of Hannah's face and the forlorn melody of Sam's song. She wonders what they would think if they knew the truth of the situation outside of their birthing cells. Would they believe it? What would Sam do if she understood the reality for all of her children's lives? Would she stop training and allow herself to reach her end?

As Chloe stares at the muted tones of the dark curtain, her rage overtakes her sadness and her blood boils. She pivots her body so she is facing the wall of the tank that looks towards K'vinna's workstation. She seethes and begins to bang her tiny fists against the glass of the tank. She bangs again, and again, her eyes staring daggers at the pompous gatekeeper of her existence as the curtain is unveiled. K'vinna peers down at her, surprised at the call for attention from the small human who has been so adamant in ignoring nem. Chloe keeps banging against the glass even as K'vinna dissolves it and there is nothing left for her to bang against. She begins banging against the floor, her wrists bouncing off the hard tiles. K'vinna is at a loss, unsure how to react to Chloe's tantrum. Chloe fumes, banging harder and harder against the floor until the pain cuts through her rage and she gives up, hopeless.

• • •

Once Chloe's wrists have been strapped and sealed in a beige film, she sits in silence, her legs dangling off K'vinna's desk. The alien stares at her, black tentacles hovering above her good arm, debating whether or not to attempt engaging her. Ne tries and nir first thought is pleading.

*Please do not harm yourself again.*

Chloe keeps her mind vaulted shut, refusing to give the Gu'ten any kind of response.

*I am concerned for you. I do not wish you trauma, Chloe.*

Chloe grunts in derision. She debates internally whether or not to engage. She settles for projecting her skepticism, and then cannot help it. She launches into a tirade.

*How can you say that and mean it? I can feel that you mean it, but it's not possible that you wish me no harm. Everything that has happened to me, you think is justified. I can feel it in your indifference. I am worth nothing to you. You let that monster cut me open and pull that thing out of me and you did nothing.*

*There was nothing I could do.*

*You could have stopped nem. You could have saved me.*

*I told you from the very beginning that I could not save you, Chloe.*

*Not like that.*

K'vinna's mind dips into silence, and Chloe follows nem there. There is a loss between them both, an implicit understanding that K'vinna will not regain Chloe's trust. K'vinna knows ne should not be bothered, that Chloe is merely a breeder, but ne doesn't believe that to be the truth anymore. K'vinna tries a different approach.

*I would like to address what you have thought, that I believe everything that has happened to you to be justified. How much have you absorbed from our time together? How much do you understand of what has transpired to my species, the impetus that led us to your own?*

Chloe stares up at K'vinna, a hurt deeper than irritation

in her eyes.

*You don't get to ask me that. You don't get to ask me anything anymore.*

*No?*

*No.*

*Then what would you prefer we discuss, Chloe?*

Chloe purses her lips, her fingers fiddling with the wrapping on her arm.

*Nothing. I never want to hear your mind inside my head again.*

*Pardon?*

*I said, I never want to hear your mind inside my head again.*

*That is unfair, Chloe. And untrue. I have come to understand that you require more stimulation than to wish for a life without communication, even if that source of communication is me.*

Chloe glowers at K'vinna.

*Fine. Tell me your excuses. But don't expect me to understand.*

• • •

K'vinna doesn't believe ne needs to justify nemself to this human, but ne wants to justify nemself to her. It is the most peculiar event in nir life to date. Yet, ne has to be careful, even as ne thinks, ne can feel Chloe reading nir feelings.

*Chloe. I have heard you think of your time in the b'leie tank as a "birthing farm." Do you know why that* farm *exists?*

K'vinna can sense a ripple of discomfort travel through her mind at the mention of the b'leie. She is still haunted by its attacks.

*For babies?*

*Incorrect. Human offspring are a by-product of that which
we need. It is the fo'ster-vi'kle, the nutrient-dense foetus sack, that is
of value to the Gu'ten.*

K'vinna can feel Chloe's confusion, so ne projects to her
the image of a placenta ejected from a woman's body post-birth.
Chloe screws up her face at the sight of the bloody red and
purple mass. K'vinna empathises, not because it is an obscene
sight to nem, but because most objects of human anatomy are as
repulsive. This one at least holds a use for the Gu'ten.

*A use for the Gu'ten?*

*How did you... You grow more adept at accessing my mind
every day, even when your own is so feeble. Do not take that as an
affront. You yourself must have noticed your body weaken these past
days. It is of great concern to me.*

*Because you won't be able to perform more tests on me?*

*Chloe...*

*Don't. Tell me why the gross thing is of use for you.*

K'vinna sighs, a little ripple crossing through nir
bl'omsterlok.

*My species is dying, Chloe. Our home planet is diseased. The
fo'ster-vi'kle is the only treatment we have been able to source. We
need it to stave off the effects of the disease.*

*You keep us chained up for that? That's madness.*

Chloe shows K'vinna the torment of Sam, the insanity of
Hannah.

*It's efficiency, Chloe. Left to their own devices, distracted
with child-rearing, the human species do not reproduce at a sufficient
rate for the treatment of all the Gu'ten on S'vekke. We have to ensure
that production yields are consistent or more will suffer from the*

*be'lysning.*

Chloe is quiet. Her mind adds up pieces of fragmented thoughts previously snatched from K'vinna.

*What does this disease do to your kind?*

K'vinna steels nemself, reaching back into nir mind to some of the first memories ne was ever given. The memories of a great plague and those first to die.

*We Gu'ten will live over two hundred years when left to our own devices. We are peaceful by nature, and much more advanced than your human race. Over a century ago, a disease ravaged our home planet. We call it the be'lysning. It acts slowly at first, revealing itself in small physical manifestations, as murky dots in our bl'omsterloks. With time, the dots expand, interweaving and dirtying all of the systems that compose our forms. By the second year of infection, we are in near constant pain. By the fifth year of infection, we cannot move, we cannot see, we cannot feel. We are left with no form of connection to the outside world other than through the consciousness—and none will connect with us then, as the disease can pass through it.*

*We do not die until seven to ten years after infection. They say the agony of silence is the worst of all. Our first scientists found no cure on S'vekke, so they travelled to other star systems. It was then that we found Earth and, through it, discovered the fo'ster-vi'kle. It does not stop the disease, but it slows the brutality of losing our senses. We can stay lucid into the eighth and ninth years of infection. This is why we farm your race, Chloe. We need to save ourselves.*

Small tears glide down Chloe's cheeks. She closes her eyes, willing herself the strength to retort.

*You can't think that that's enough.*

*Enough what?*

*Enough reason to do all this. To torture us in this way. You're exchanging your agony for ours. What gives you the right to do that?*

Chloe can sense a temporary flash of confusion from K'vinna before another long dormant memory sifts to the top of nir consciousness. It does not feel like it appeases nem.

*It was decided long ago, Chloe, that our need to survive as a species was more vital than yours to roam freely. Humankind was self-destructing. Fo'ster-vi'kle farming enabled both humankind to flourish and the Gu'ten to prolong our extinction while searching for a more substantial cure.*

*Flourish? Do we look like we are flourishing to you?*

*Since the breeding farm has been in effect, your numbers have increased one thousand per cent.*

*One thousand per cent?* Chloe shudders.

*This does not please you?*

*How many of us? How many have gone through what I've been through? How many have been chained, tortured, left to rot in those cells?*

K'vinna pauses, debating the merit of telling Chloe the truthful answer.

*Don't even think about lying to me.* Chloe stares deep into K'vinna's saucer like eyes. *I can pry it from you if I want to, but you owe me more than that.*

K'vinna is shocked by Chloe's threat. The small human has grown more masterful of the consciousness than ne thought possible.

*There are upwards of sixty thousand breeders in the dominion of this Facility.*

Chloe breaks her lock on K'vinna form. She gazes down at her hands, eyeing off the frail state of her arm. Her mind's voice becomes weaker, forlorn.

*Sixty thousand.*

She doesn't bother to project to K'vinna, floored by the number swirling around in her head. It is so large, too abstract. She has no way to comprehend it, other than as an amplified scream shaking her brain so much that it hurts to think any longer. She begins to slump on the table, and K'vinna sees no choice but to return her to her tank to sleep.

• • •

Chloe wakes shaking, but not on the cold tiles of her tank. She is drifting on layers of squirming rubber, little hairs prickling against her skin. Her eyes open to the reality of being arranged on K'vinna's many tentacles, the alien resting on the floor of her tank, having watched her as she slept. The moment her eyes open, she feels K'vinna's mind knocking on hers in the consciousness. She resists, holding the warmth of connection at bay. They have never been so physically entwined, and she considers the moment with curiosity before her rage returns. She snaps into the consciousness with vehemence.

*What is it?*

K'vinna reels from the onslaught of aggression. It is strong for a creature so small. Ne projects with careful consideration.

*I wish to apologize. I tried earlier, but I believe I chose the wrong approach. I suspect what you require of me is an explanation, of not intervening in the actions of U'ngdom. I am in a precarious situation, human Chloe. It is my responsibility to my species to lead the search for the cure to the be'lysning. It is a duty I am bound to, and one which I can be punished for failing.*

*I have taken great personal risk to keep you separate from the birthing division, as I feel there is something unique in your mind, something from which we can learn. What, I am unsure. I am able to keep you here under the pretence of researching the be'lysning cure, but if any were to find out the truth, it would be my undoing, and yours. It is for this reason I could not intervene when U'ngdom operated on you. I assure you, I have reprimanded nem, but there is only so much I can do without arousing suspicion. Do you understand?*

As K'vinna's speech ends, K'vinna notices an eerie look in Chloe's eyes, a certain polemic edge that fills nem with unease for her next thoughts. But they do not come. Chloe does not sever the consciousness connection, but is quiet within it. She removes her body from the soft padding of K'vinna's tentacles so that she is standing, her head a foot higher than the top of K'vinna's gaseous bl'omsterlok. She reaches out and places her good arm on the silky surface of nir bl'omsterlok. Her gaze is not imploring, but stoic, as small tears line the rims of her eyelids, flushing her pupils so they shine a more vivid green. What she says next is meek, but unyielding.

*I understand, but I do not forgive you.*

She breaks the consciousness link and steps to the far corner of her tank, squatting down and wrapping her arms around her knees. She looks to the ground, keeping her gaze out of reach of K'vinna. They sit this way for some time, disconnected. K'vinna sends out a tentative tentacle that nudges against Chloe's knee with a gentle rapping. She does not react, so it settles down upon her knee, and she feels the warmth of the consciousness tapping on her mind once more. She lets it in, but only so far as to listen, not to let any of her feelings out.

*I am sorry, Chloe. I do what I think is best.*

Chloe doesn't respond to K'vinna. Nir words drift around her head, insulting her further. *I do what I think is best.* Torturing an entire species cannot be what is best. It is selfish, despicable. Chloe keeps her arms wrapped around her knees, her eyes cast down and refusing to engage with the alien. She can feel K'vinna thinking, attempting to find a new explanation to get her on side, but ne is prevented. An alarm begins screeching through the chamber. It is louder than anything Chloe has heard before and it pierces her skull like the shrillest of screams. K'vinna is immediately distracted by it, leaping into the air and breaking their connection. Ne floats at speed out of the chambers, not taking the time to seal Chloe in her tank, instead only closing the chamber doors. For the first time, Chloe is free to wander round the chamber unwatched. Or would be, if the piercing alarm was not so brutal on her mind. Instead, she stays huddled on the corner of her tank floor, too scared to move.

# CHAPTER THIRTY-ONE

SHARDS OF morning light reflect off the facility's bizarre white walls causing it to shimmer like an apparition in the distance. It is gargantuan in height, over nine stories high and equally wide. There is no movement outside of the building, and no way from this vantage point to discern if there are any obvious routes inside. Ikka turns away from the building and steps back inside the thicket to the flora's protection from sight. Veela follows her as she sits down on the forest floor, extracting her sleeping blanket from her pack. He gives her a querying look.

"We need rest. We are protected here for the moment. When our brains have re-energized, they'll be better at conducting the next stage of the plan."

"Uh huh."

She narrows her eyes at him. "Don't look at me like that. I'm not giving up. I'm recuperating."

Veela's eyes smile in amusement at her. She scowls.

"Fine, you can take the first guard shift since you're so

full of energy. Make sure those two head to sleep soon, too."

"Yes, boss."

Her scowl deepens but Veela remains unaffected. He tosses a twig at her as she lies down, her head nestled between two tree trunks. No sooner has her head touched the ground than her mind is swamped in darkness. And screams.

• • •

She realizes the screaming is hers. Her throat is sore from the effort, her vocal chords brutalized by the evocations. Nothing good comes from the cries, only more pain. The tentacled beasts have stopped drilling at the crevices below her waist, ceased the excavations nearly a day ago. But now they have returned with more instruments of destruction, this time positioned around her head.

A small pack of tentacles emerge forward from the swarm above her, five swooping in to pry her mouth open, and a sixth dropping some liquid onto her tongue. It stings. It spreads first down her throat, and then across her shoulders and down to her hands. A warm numbness that accumulates like the taste of lead in her mouth. And then the heat travels south, and a sensation of wetness overcomes her pubic region. She is sure she hasn't urinated herself, that those muscles haven't lost control, but it feels identical to the sensation of peeing. This wetness and the taste of lead continue as the numbness claims her legs and feet.

She tries to swallow, but her jaw will not move at her command. She attempts to look to the left, to comprehend the blur at the edge of her peripheries being wielded towards her, but her eyes will not budge. She is trapped inside her numb body, unable to do anything but see, and that fragile capacity is fading as she even thinks that thought.

Her vision fades. Not to darkness. But into a bright unknown.

• • •

Shouts evict Ikka from her dream. It is Chiyo, panicked, his arms tugging at her shoulders.

"I think it's them, I think they have them!"

Ikka is up in an instant, sprinting to the opening in the treeline. The large white building looms in the distance. It is positioned inside a natural basin, void of boulders or trees, but lined with three-foot tall grass in an insipid yellow hue. On the east end of the basin a great plume of dust rises and meets with the air. It is caused by the eight wheels of a racing vehicle dragging across the earth, stirred up by three airships flanking its rear. There is no way to externally identify if it is the racer driven by Delu and his team, but the likelihood of another X-Runner travelling in search of facilitators is very slim. Veela and Hurste peer over Ikka and Chiyo's shoulders. Hurste's face drops by two or three shades.

"That's Delu, isn't it?"

No one responds, their focus all locked on the scene before them. The racer and airships are approaching the building at breakneck speed. There is nothing friendly about their shared trajectory. One of the airships gains distance, lowering down to hold position directly above the X-Runner. Even at this distance, the shift in air pressure under the ship is distinct. It looks like a sheet of glass has descended above the X-Runner and is vibrating maniacally. The X-Runner begins to drift above the ground, caught in the airship's pull. As it rises closer to the airship, the roof of the runner begins to warp, folding backwards and disintegrating in places.

The other two airships swoop in, flanking each side of the captive runner. They extend mechanical arms that siphon in large chunks of air, swelling in size, before shooting powerful blasts at the X-Runner. The rear left and right quadrants of the runner explode under the pressure, and the vehicle is careened out of the first airship's control. It limps forward on its remaining five wheels, the entire back portion of the racer now missing, scattered across the desert floor in flames. The airships gain on it steadily, but before they do—a small figure leaps out of the vehicle, tumbling onto the grassy ground below, and then running at speed away from the airships and the facility building.

Ikka's throat clenches tighter, scared for the fate of the stick figure below. Even at this distance, she recognizes the body language. It is Aldric. One of the airships peels off to chase him as the other two regain their control over the errant X-Runner. Aldric makes it twenty feet before the airship extends its cannon and pulverizes his form. Tears lash at Ikka's eyes as she watches the murdering airship rejoin the others, and use their combined forces to drag the disabled X-Runner towards the stern facade of the facility.

She loses all sense of hearing while watching the beginning of the end for their old companions. Her vision blurs as she stumbles back through the thicket to where she was just resting. Time doesn't move, and gravity slows her limbs as her mind attempts to reject what she witnessed. She is vaguely aware of Veela following her, his voice only present in the outskirts of her mind. But then she sits, her legs giving way beneath her and her faculties crashing back to her as her knees and ass crash to the ground. Veela crouches in front of her, peering with concern into her eyes.

He says, "Are you okay, buddy?"

Chiyo and Hurste hover to the side, watching. Ikka surveys them all, cautious to frame her thoughts.

"No." A half sob escapes Ikka before she can continue. "Well, yes, I'm fine. I'm always okay, cutting my losses and walking away as soon as someone disagrees with me. But they're all probably dead—Aldric definitely is—because I was too arrogant to stay and try to reason with them."

"What?" Veela says, "No, this isn't your fault."

Chiyo and Hurste shake their heads behind Veela to agree.

Ikka bares her teeth at Veela in frustration. She snaps, "Yes it is. I'm a selfish, self-righteous asshole and I'm a coward on top of that, too."

Veela grits his own teeth, his jaw clenching. "Right, and what does that make us? We're the ones who followed you, selfishness and cowardliness and all."

Ikka shakes her head. "That's not what I meant. You're just..."

"What? Followers with no ability to make choices of our own?" Veela's voice begins to rise, hard and strong for the first time. "Listen to me, Ikka. We *all* chose to leave them. We *all* felt unsafe following their lead and stealing a X-Runner. We were *all* petrified of their choice and thought there had to be a better way. You don't get to take that away from us." Veela takes a breath, calming himself down, taking Ikka's hands in his. "Look, maybe we all made a colossal mistake abandoning our companions, but that is not your sole responsibility, and it is not going to define us. What matters is what we do now. If we sit here crying or if we do something to save our friends."

Ikka sits in silence for some moments, her eyes still red from crying. She looks at her hands in Veela's, and then at the waiting faces of Chiyo and Hurste. Her lips curl into a faint smile as she finally locks eyes with Veela.

She says, "Well, obviously we're going to do something to save our friends."

# CHAPTER THIRTY-TWO

THE ALARM is a discordant twang, reiterating its presence over and over as K'vinna hurries through the corridors of The Facility. K'vinna understands its meaning, but is surprised by its occurrence. This frequency of alarm denotes an outside attack on The Facility. Normally an attack wouldn't require the skills of a research division member, but it was accompanied by K'vinna's personal frequency, amongst others.

The chamber K'vinna is called to is on the mid-level of the building where the docking stations for patrol vehicles are located. When K'vinna arrives, there is already a caucus of high-ranking Gu'ten from various divisions, noisily debating who is responsible for the current situation. K'vinna doesn't listen to their warbling, ne looks past them out the clear side wall of the chamber to where three of the Gu'ten fu'gler are chasing down an errant X-Runner that is approaching The Facility at speed. The fu'gler are semi-autonomous flying machines, operating via heat sensor and echo frequency parameters; they auto-relay all

information gathered via echo vibrations to The Facility and are
remotely controlled via the same method by three fighter Gu'ten.

The fu'gler chase the X-Runner with a relentless fervour,
firing low frequency pulses in its direction. Patches of earth and
dust erupt around the X-Runner as the pulses miss their
trajectory, until one strikes true. The rear left corner of the racing
vehicle crumples under the pressure. Smoke plumes from the X-
Runner's wound and the vehicle begins to jolt off course. The
fu'glers seize their chance and fire off two more pulses at the X-
Runner. The rear and right walls crumple, and the vehicle skids
to a halt. A tiny humanoid figure flings itself from the rear left
quadrant and begins running for shelter in the tall grass
surrounding The Facility. The fu'gler circle it without mercy
before firing off three sequential pulses. There is no more
movement in the grass, only smoke. The three Gu'ten remotely
operating the fu'gler are instructed to tow the crippled X-Runner
and its contents back to the loading dock. The caucus of Gu'ten
become silent, all curious as to what they will find inside—and,
more importantly, who they will be able to blame.

• • •

There are two sets of doors separating the outside of The
Facility from the chamber the senior Gu'ten are gathered in.
Once the fu'gler drags the crippled X-Runner through the first,
the doors seal behind it and the chamber is decompressed. Once
the docking station is ready, the second set of doors open and the
Gu'ten move forward to inspect the X-Runner wreckage.

The X-Runner is scanned for signs of life with thermal
sensors, and seven readings are found. Four lower level Gu'ten
are sent inside to drag the humans out; they reappear moments

later with six barely conscious and one recently deceased human males. No sooner are they lined up for inspection than the political one-upping begins. K'vinna loiters to the back, waiting for the reason for nir personal invitation to be revealed. For the moment, ne is ignored as K'lappstol begins berating the others.

"Eight humans travelling in the one vehicle? How has this occurred? K'raste? U'mulig?"

K'raste is the head of race operations. Ne frantically plugs into the building consciousness loop to scan through nir records for possible explanations. U'mulig is defiant.

"I would wonder, how long this has occurred, undiscovered by race operations?"

K'lappstol looks to K'raste. "Well?"

K'raste is saved by a younger technician appearing from within the wrecked vehicle.

"Excuse me, K'lappstol. The vehicle records show change in occupancy numbers occurred two days ago."

K'vinna doesn't have to look to U'mulig to feel nir smugness. K'lappstol is unsatisfied.

"But why? What could possess these dull-thinking creatures to abandon their own vehicles and lump into this one? Are any of these the one originally assigned to this X-Runner?"

The technician answers before any of the seniors can respond.

"Yes, sir. The deceased one on the ground. These others have no identification numbers."

"No identification numbers?"

K'lappstol and the other senior Gu'ten all peer at the six humans in front of them. They are gasping, their clothes smoke-stained and lungs unable to cope with the building's manipulated atmosphere. There are no identification chains around their necks. K'lappstol scowls, an expression that is visualized by folds appearing in the skin of nir bl'omsterlok.

"For S'vekke's sake, give them o'rdnes. We may need them alive yet."

O'rdnes are applied to the humans' mouths, and K'raste raises nir voice again.

"Uh, K'lappstol. I am unable to locate any unoccupied X-Runner's on our system, or unaccounted for humans. I do not believe these humans are from within the race complex."

"Then where are they from? U'mulig? Did they originate from the breeding division?"

U'mulig motions to one of nir underlings who drifts forward and extracts blood from each of the humans. Ne drops the blood into a small liquid scanner and places one of nir tentacles inside the ooze as well. After a few seconds, ne nods to U'mulig, who in turn speaks to the vice chair.

"Yes, they are ours."

U'mulig's assistant places one of nir other tentacles in the building consciousness loop, so ne is connected between the small gel scanner and the wall mounted consciousness. A few more moments pass before the assistant reaches to U'mulig with another one of nir black consciousness tentacles, and the two communicate in silence. U'mulig addresses K'lappstol once more.

"All six of their racing vehicles, and I suspect also the one belonging to their charred companion out there, were reported vacant and seized many years ago. They have not been accounted for by the race operations division for over two decades."

K'lappstol's attention swoops in on K'raste.

"Is this true?"

K'raste analyzes the new information entered into the building consciousness by U'mulig's assistant. K'vinna can see the tension creasing K'raste's bl'omsterlok.

"Yes."

K'vinna watches as there is more conjecture as to how and why these humans were able to disappear within the race system and then reappear in the one X-Runner speeding towards The Facility. K'vinna is able to remain unquestioned long enough to feel confident ne will be safe from the K'lappstol's gaze, until nir continual opponent smirks in nir direction.

"K'lappstol, perhaps a scientist from the research division may be able to explain this unexpected anomaly to us."

All eyes in the room turn to K'vinna, floating conspicuously at the back of the group. K'vinna knows not to keep K'lappstol waiting.

"Well, whilst the research division does not interfere in the operations of The Race system, I would be happy to inspect the humans present for any anomalies."

"Very well." K'lappstol dips three of nir labour tentacles, a permissive action. "You may proceed."

K'vinna is taken aback.

"Here?"

K'lappstol responds, "Is there a problem with that?"

K'vinna replies, "Of course not." And drifts towards the humans, dreading what ne must do next.

• • •

Upon closer inspection, the six humans show different physical characteristics. K'vinna wonders if ne can determine which one possesses the most intelligence from their physical attributes. It would save time to inspect the smartest of the group, if one such specimen exists. Aware of the many Gu'ten watching nem, K'vinna knows ne must choose quickly. Ne suspects the disquiet within the research division has reached the other departments, and that nir continued leadership is at jeopardy in this moment.

All six of the humans are similar in height, though the first is the tallest by a few inches. The human to the far right is the roundest, and K'vinna surmises this may be an indication of its capacity as a leader, delegating tasks to the other humans. As K'vinna ponders, a young technician brings forward a tray of implements that may be of use to K'vinna's inspection. Items designed for slicing, sawing, and peeling.

An internal shudder ripples through K'vinna's bl'omsterlok. As a cluster of nir tentacles reach for the sawing tool, an image of Chloe's appears in nir mind. She is huddled on the floor of her tank, the b'leie round her waist. The anguish in her eyes shames nem.

"Is there a problem, K'vinna?"

K'lappstol's gurgles encroach on K'vinna's thoughts. K'vinna refocuses, nir many tentacles holding the rotund human in place, wrapping around its skull and upper torso. *His*, not *its*. K'vinna hears Chloe's voice reprimanding nem and wants to stop nir next actions. But ne can see U'mulig in nir peripheries, waiting for a moment to strike. K'vinna's tentacles wrap tighter around the saw, while those on the human's head reposition. For

the first time, ne looks into its eyes. One of the eyes is defunct, a
scar and dead flesh marring its surface. The other is brown, and it
gazes at K'vinna, scared yet defiant. K'vinna issues a silent
apology to it through the consciousness, and then raises the saw.

• • •

Chloe is still huddled in the foetal position, memories of
the building alarm still screaming inside her head. It has left her
with a violent headache, but after it ceases she becomes more
aware of her current situation—her moderate freedom. Never
before has she been able to move through K'vinna's chamber
unwatched. Her hands glide over the walls as she walks the
entire perimeter. They are smooth, unmarked by any faults.
There is no residue on them from the creatures that clean them
nightly. There is also no crease at any point to reveal the invisible
door that opens upon K'vinna's summoning. Chloe steps over to
K'vinna's desk, the strange glowing tabletop. There is nothing
upon it, but Chloe has seen K'vinna place nir black tentacles—
the one ne uses to touch her when entering the consciousness—
inside it. She stands in front of the desk, staring into the vast
nothingness of its glaze. And then, without any hesitation, only
longing for something else, she reaches her right arm inside it.

The tabletop swarms around her arm, dragging her
whole body down towards it. Her eyes grow wider than she has
ever felt them feel, and she is stuck in the moment, unable to
even blink. She doesn't see what's in front of her, but is instead
transported in sight to a directory of bright lights. As she
switches her attention from each light to the next, she can feel
their contents. K'vinna's notes on her. Reports from different
Gu'ten under K'vinna's supervision. Division targets and budgets.

She sees a darkness beyond the lights, and by concentrating on it, she selects it. She is overwhelmed by three times the number of lights in a myriad of colours. Each one has a different focus, separate to that of K'vinna's division. She flips through them, scanning a millennia of information that barely registers to her. She pauses at the inventory of active race participants, her eyes frantically search for her father's code.

Thousands upon thousands of racer codes flit by her, but she is unable to find him. His code is missing in the system. Chloe wants to cry, but she has no control over her physical body at present. While she is connected to this directory, she is unable to exist outside of it. She keeps searching and finds a light housing visual surveillance of various sections in The Facility. She sees the breeding division first, a literal sea of cells, all filled with pregnant women. She is sickened at the sight, but she keeps scanning. She sees the laboratories where humans lie cut open. She sees pens filled with human infants connected to tubes. And she sees K'vinna cutting a man's head open.

• • •

Chloe does a double take when she sees K'vinna and stops her scanning immediately. She watches in horror as K'vinna saws open the top of a man's skull, a crowd of Gu'ten watching on. K'vinna peels back the skin lining the man's head, so that his facial details are obscured by a waterfall of blood. Once K'vinna has finished removing the man's skin, ne saws through the bone protecting the brain. There are five other human men next to K'vinna, their reactions varied states of terror. One drops to his knees, passing out. Another vomits where he stands. Chloe wants to gag as she watches K'vinna reach two of nir smallest tentacles inside the human's brain, rifling through the complex layers of muscle. Ne pulls the entire brain out of the skull to inspect it more closely, and lets the body of its owner drop to the ground. Chloe cannot watch any more. She disengages from the tabletop consciousness, and an onslaught of tears force her to the chamber floor.

• • •

In The Race, Chloe had always felt a distinct sense of possibility. The possibility of gaining miles, of overtaking the other racers, and of putting more land between them and their competitors. She can remember her longing, so strong, to win. She doesn't even know what they thought they would win. Her fragmented memories of her time in The Race now seem so pointless. Void of all hope or possibility. They never had a chance.

Tears burn her eyes as they stream down her cheeks, and her chest thumps as her breaths become shorter and sharper. She hears Sam's worn voice in her head—*Just breathe, girl*—but it only angers her further. She scratches at her arm, her blunt fingernails raising heat to the surface of her skin. It's a short relief—the searing pain in her head is temporarily redirected to her arm, but as fast as the red lines fade on her arm, the pain returns to her mind. She scratches at her legs, and snot begins to trickle out her nose. She reaches to the roots of her hair and yanks, trying to relieve the pressure at its source. It doesn't work. With each short breath, she feels more pain. It is so unnecessary, so cruel.

And then, her mind pauses. It latches onto that thought. *Unnecessary.*

As sudden as they started, her tears stop. She wipes her
snot away with the back of her hand and stands. It leaves a sticky
trail on her skin, but she doesn't notice. She stares around
K'vinna's office once more, with new purpose. There are a
displeasing lack of objects in it. She moves to the curtained
segment, and walks into the other alien, U'ngdom's, domain. The
infant Gu'ten is still strapped to the bench, murky white puddles
now present in the inky contents of its bl'omsterlok. Only two of
nir pupils manage to move to watch her, the other six are
crystallized in place, unseeing. She doesn't pause to comfort nem,
but surveys the rest of the benches and shelves. Everything has
been packed away. Like the doors to exit K'vinna's chambers, her
human eyes can't locate the doors to the cabinets. But it's okay.

Chloe starts undoing the infant Gu'ten's restraints. What
tentacles ne can still move caress at her arm as she works. Once
all three restraints are undone, she gently lifts nem up, holding
nem close to her chest. Ne clings to her like a human baby
carried on its mother's hips, and they walk this way back to
K'vinna's desk. Chloe plunges her arm into the tabletop and once
more her body becomes paralyzed, and her vision is filled with
bright lights. She scans through them, searching with more
energy than she can recall ever feeling, and she finds it. The call
system for the D'ekercee.

She calls.

• • •

Chloe delicately places the infant on the floor in the
centre of the chamber and lies down beside nem. Ne is nervous
as ne clings to her, attempting to summon the consciousness but
unable to establish the connection. Chloe lets nem in, and is

bombarded by a wave of confusion and intense physical pain. She projects to the infant the feeling of air streaming in through an X-Runner window, the gentle rocking of the massive vehicle racing beneath them. The infant calms a little, unsure what these sensations are, but enjoying them.

*I'm sorry you've had to experience so much pain.*

The infant's two pupils watch Chloe in confusion, understanding her thoughts but not how ne is receiving them. Ne has not yet been trained how to think.

*It's going to be over soon. We're going to experience a little more pain, but then I promise it will be over. You won't have to hurt ever again. Neither of us will.*

The infant raises some of nir tentacles to Chloe's face, tracing over her skin. She reaches up with her hand and touches them lightly. She hears the doors to the chamber open, and the eerie whistling of the D'ekercee follow. She smiles at the infant Gu'ten and sends nem one last thought.

*Everything is going to be fine.*

# CHAPTER THIRTY-THREE

THE WALK TO the plantation is short. Chiyo leads the way, and the others follow in swift succession. Silence and grim determination adorn their steps until they are greeted at the plantation by an array of automated machinery. Taller than the height of three humans combined, the machines are vertical columns of organization—tending, caring for, and clipping the plantation's trees. The plant cuttings are then transferred to shorter sorting machines that place the chosen leaves into trough shaped vehicles that move autonomously back to the facility. It is in one of these vehicles that Ikka, Veela, Hurste, and Chiyo intend to commence their infiltration of the building.

Ikka and Hurste move first, cutting through the maze of trees, ducking under the swooping arms of organizational machines, and running to the nearest trough vehicle. They climb up over the vehicle's port side, Hurste boosting Ikka up, and then Ikka leaning back to pull Hurste over. They land on the same leaves that Chiyo presented them with earlier, broad, dark green fonds that are cool to touch. They nestle deep in the back corners of the trough, keeping their distance from the sorting machine's arms as it dumps more leaves atop of them. There is no way for them to see if Veela and Chiyo have been successful in stowing into another vehicle, so they listen for telltale sounds of capture or injury. None come, and when the sorting machine is content with the number of leaves in their trough, it pushes a button, and a lid snaps shut over the vehicle's tray, trapping Ikka and Hurste inside.

The ride is bumpy and stuffy. Even with the cushioning of the leaves, their ankles, knees, and shoulders are shoved up and down against the walls of the trough. They brace themselves against each other and the walls, but they can feel multiple bruises forming with each corner or dip in the path. The vehicle engine is discreet, near silent compared to the mechanical roars of the X-Runners. There are no noises on the horizon, only the bumps and bangs from inside the trough. Soon, even these quiet. The vehicle reaches a flat stretch of land, slowing its advance. They must be entering the valley basin and, when that is passed, they will enter the facility.

• • •

As the vehicle rolls to a stop, Ikka's stomach muscles tighten. She sits still, rigid as she listens to a door opening, and feels the vehicle begin to drive inside. Hurste sits beside her, his fear distracting him from even consuming nuts. Ikka offers him a grim smile of encouragement, but it does not reach her eyes. She is focused on the indentations of the knife handle in her right hand, and the shorter stabbing blade nestled in her left. The second largest blade in her collection now resides with Hurste—

hopefully adrenaline will show him how to use it. There is a click from outside, and then the roof above them slides open. A powerful shaft of clinical, bright light floods the trough, but then a figure crosses in front of it. Not human, not machine. It is one of the monsters from Ikka's dreams.

It doesn't notice them at first. The bulbous sack that makes up its form is not concerned with looking inside the vehicle, only in sweeping it out. Tentacle after tentacle rises into the trough, scraping plant fonds down to an unseen destination. With each new load, the tentacles reach closer to where Ikka and Hurste are hiding. Ikka is unflinching, consumed only with determination. Hurste is overwhelmed, but fighting to remain still. It is at this point that the air starts to become potent in their lungs.

With the first haggard breath, the tentacle closest to them freezes, feeling the change in air movement. With the second haggard breath, the tentacle lunges towards them and is met with both of Ikka's blades. With the third haggard breath, a swarm of fourteen tentacles descend, yanking and throwing Ikka and Hurste from the back of the truck to a hard, unyielding ground. It hovers above them, a floating monster with hundreds of grey, black, and clear tentacles, and then, as quick as it had thrown them to the ground, it exits the room, a door appearing and disappearing as it leaves. They have a few moments to take in their surroundings—a large, stark white room with multiple harvesting vehicles parked with plants and bizarre machinery stacked at their bases—before a different, larger door materializes and a new vehicle arrives from outside. They run over to it, shouting to Veela and Chiyo, and are relieved to hear responses from inside. Ikka pries open the roof and, with Hurste's help, makes a gap large enough for the others to climb through. They pause to catch their breaths, and then a sound rings out.

Shriller and louder than any sound these humans have ever heard before, they know it must be an alarm. A signal alerting the entire building that there are renegade humans inside.

# CHAPTER THIRTY-FOUR

THE D'EKERCEE enter K'vinna's chamber accompanied by a symphony of haunting whistles, their luminescent purple eyes bobbing along to the rhythm of their eerie song. There is no apparent leader to their pack, but with uniform coordination their song changes pitch, a shrill higher note urging them towards the bodies in the centre of the chamber. The bodies of Chloe and the infant Gu'ten.

The infant stirs in Chloe's arms, nir tentacles and bl'omsterlok quivering with fear. Chloe issues nem calming thoughts in the consciousness. She fights to soothe nem, but her own mind falters as the D'ekercee approach them, opening up their mouths to reveal their vicious decayed teeth. Even with their mouths open, the whistling continues, the notes accelerating with excitement as they reach the base of Chloe's feet. They fan out, gliding along a trail of slime to encircle Chloe and the infant Gu'ten. As they fall into formation, their whistles shriek even louder, piercing Chloe's ears. And then they pounce.

The first bite sends a ripple of shock up Chloe's spine. Her body jolts as rows of razor sharp teeth sink into her right calf, tearing a chuck of flesh from her leg. Chloe screams through her o'rdne, her teeth biting hard on the metal to brace against the pain, but it offers no relief. There is only agony, nerve endings screaming as more D'ekercee and more sets of gnashing teeth attack Chloe's legs, her torso, her arms. The infant Gu'ten is wailing in pain beside her as ne is devoured, nir tiny form no match for a legion of D'ekercee. Ne is shred into pieces, the gaseous composition of nir bl'omsterlok leaking out and nir outer skin deflating. The goop that remains of nir innards is lapped up within seconds by a cluster of D'ekercee, while the rest continue to gnaw on Chloe's extremities. She doesn't fight back, but her body recoils from every attack until it has no strength to do even that. Chloe's mind becomes disconnected from the pain, and she can no longer even hear her own screams. Her thoughts wander, and the bright white of the chamber ceiling morphs into the burning desert sun. She can feel the crisp desert air streaming past her, and the cavernous engine of an X-Runner growling underneath her. She is finally going home.

• • •

When K'vinna finishes nir inspection of the human leader, ne is dismissed to continue nir examination in the research division with nir full array of tools. Ne is accompanied by an array of assistants from nir department and from several others. U'ngdom had been the one to suggest the interdepartmental assistants, but K'vinna knows it was so ne could keep a closer watch on nem. K'vinna had tried to rebuff the proposal, but was overruled by the caucus. Every division head present wanted to be able to monitor the situation, lest blame should fall on nemselves. The hoards of assistants drift close behind K'vinna as ne enters the research division and instructs T'vil, G'nist, and K'nurre on further examination of the human. It is only once G'nist and K'nurre are bickering over how to delegate the testing that K'vinna is able to slip away to nir chambers.

As K'vinna approaches the opening to nir chambers, ne can tell that something is amiss. The hairs on nir tentacles flair up, the vibrations of whistling reaching nem. And as ne opens the chamber door, the visual imagery assaults nem. The floor is a moving tapestry of white fur and red blood as over twenty D'ekercee glide around each other and over a mangled human body—Chloe's mangled human body.

K'vinna swoops in, dread, rage, and fear encompassing nir consciousness, as nir tentacles move in a frenzy, flinging D'ekercee this way and that, anywhere but near Chloe. The small creatures shriek in outrage as they are flung across the chamber, impacting so hard against the walls and floor that their fuzzy exoskeletons snap and their inner muscles are left to drag their useless shells from the room. All this happens in moments, and then K'vinna is at Chloe's side. She is in terrible shape, covered in a garish mix of her own blood and the D'ekercee's slime.

K'vinna carries her over to U'ngdom's work station and nir many tentacles go into overdrive, hooking her up to oxygen, synthetic human blood sacks, and cleaning and sealing her many wounds. When K'vinna finishes nir hurried work, Chloe's appearance is even more alarming. Chunks of flesh the size of a human palm are missing from all over her body, her face included, and so much bone is missing from her right leg that K'vinna had to slice it off completely under the knee. She is as pale as the white walls of the chamber, and her breaths so microscopic that K'vinna is not optimistic she will survive. K'vinna slumps onto the floor beside the workstation, one consciousness tentacle left behind to monitor her unconscious thoughts. Ne taps deep into her mind, witnessing the minutes and the feelings and the thoughts that led to her decision to call the D'ekercee. K'vinna replays them over and over, absorbing every iota of her rationale. As it sinks in, ne quivers with sadness. Chloe had told nem over and over again, and ne hadn't understood; so, the first time ne had left her unattended, she had seized her chance. She had chosen to end her own existence rather than be used by the Gu'ten any longer.

• • •

K'vinna lies in silence on the chamber floor for some time, nir mind totally uninterested in the goings on of the research division outside nir chamber walls. When a young assistant comes to deliver news to K'vinna of progress in the examination, ne orders nem away. Ne doesn't even register the content of nir speech, the division nir belongs to, or nir reaction to the sight of a division leader crumpled on the floor. None of this information seems relevant to K'vinna anymore. Ne has failed Chloe. Ne has failed nemself. Ne has no purpose anymore—other than to wait, and to hope, and to protect what is left of Chloe's life. But then a new alarm rings out. There are intruders in The Facility.

# CHAPTER THIRTY-FIVE

IKKA, VEELA, Hurste, and Chiyo crouch behind one of the harvesting vehicles, their eyes glued to the wall where the first monster exited. Their breaths are raspy, but manageable. They don't have a plan, only survival instincts and adrenaline.

The shrieking alarm ceases, and then the door reappears. As it opens, a whoosh of new air enters the room, the composition of which is foreign to their bodies. Their ears block in response, and they become hyper-aware of the movements in their jaws. Their already laboured breaths are assaulted, and the bizarre air from before the invasion becomes a precious commodity in their lungs. They have no time to consider this atmospheric predicament. Two tentacles sweep into the room. They are grey—delicate, but menacing looking—and moving with an inquisitive grace. At first they only peek three feet around the corner, but in swift succession they are accompanied by an entire hoard of tentacles, swooping around the door as one great entity. Chiyo inches around the side of the vehicle in wonder, and Hurste moves forward to pull him back. He stops, transfixed as the body of the entity reveals itself from beyond the corner.

The creature hovers in the doorway, sizing up the four quivering humans poorly camouflaged behind the harvesting truck. The moment seems to stretch out, their already slow pulses forgetting to continue as their minds comprehend what is before them. There is a queer beauty to the floating dance of the tentacles, a flowing pattern of black, clear, and grey. It is almost seductive in its balance, immobilizing the humans' minds from action.

Then a single tentacle rises, a clear one, poised one foot in front of the creature's floating sack. It seems to point between Chiyo and Hurste, and then adjusts its aim to rest solely on Hurste. Before any of them can question the intended purpose of the limb, an extension from within the tentacle shoots forward all twelve feet to Hurste, seizing hold of his torso. Two more clear tentacles quickly take aim, wrapping around him further, and the combined strength of the three tentacles drag him back towards the creature. Hurste lets out a boyish shout of protest, and begins beating against the tentacles with his blade. His cutting has no traction, and a bevy of grey tentacles wrap around his arms and wrists, the knife dropping to the ground.

Chiyo, Veela, and Ikka watch on in shock until Veela leads a charge. He pulls his blade from his pack and runs forward, attempting to slice at the tentacles holding Hurste. Chiyo and Ikka follow, each with their own blades hacking, but the creature tosses them aside with ease. It has the advantages of easy breathing and over seventy disposable limbs. As it fends them off, eight of its grey tentacles combine to form two mega-limbs that take hold on opposing sides around Hurste's head. Ikka is the first to realize what is going to happen next, and calls to Veela and Chiyo to leave this room for the one beyond. They don't want to abandon Hurste, but they have no hope of saving him. All three swallow down their guilt, the motion causing their ears to pop, and run past the creature into the room beyond. As they plunge into the denser atmosphere of the new space, they hear Hurste's last scream followed by a sickening crack.

• • •

They try to put as much ground as possible between them and the floating monster. The room they sprint into is filled with industrial machinery, pipes, complex filtration devices, and rows upon rows of cone shaped mounds. As the three companions stumble farther into the room, their breaths become more and more laboured. The air in this new section hurts their lungs, and Ikka begins to notice black dots in the peripheries of her vision.

Only necessity enables their legs to carry them farther into this new space and away from the monster behind them. Tears glisten in the corners of Chiyo's eyes for their fallen friend, but he says nothing as they move forward. He is the first to see the tentacles begin to back into this wider chamber, and he pushes at Ikka and Veela to move faster forward. Two more of the creatures appear from the opposing end of the space, and Veela and Ikka attempt to backpedal. The three of them stare at each other in terror, unsure of their next move, and then Ikka pulls the two men down to the ground with her, and they begin to crawl behind one of the large cone shaped devices. They stay low to the ground, listening with strained ears to hear which way the new monsters move.

They are not the only ones listening. The two Gu'ten near the chamber entrance pause where they float, spreading their tentacles out in a wide fan. The minute hairs lining their tentacles stand on end, feeling for foreign movements in the air. At first they sense nothing, so the Gu'ten drift slowly forward on the cleared path towards the harvesting chamber where the third Gu'ten hovers. As they pass between two rows of cones one pauses, its hairs picking up the smallest of movements—there are laboured breaths at the other end of this row disturbing the layers of air and rippling back towards the Gu'ten.

Ikka's vision is nearly half-black, deteriorating from lack of fresh oxygen. She holds a hand over her own mouth, attempting to soften her struggling breaths. Chiyo is silently applying a toxic combination of paili and varme to her temples and throat to help as Veela peers around the edge of the cones. He pulls his head back in with haste, his eyes wide. He gestures that the aliens are drifting their way and that they need to move, fast. Chiyo nods, but Ikka barely has it in her to understand. Chiyo and Veela each shoulder one of Ikka's arms, and the two of them scuttle across two more rows of cones out of the aliens' sight. They both then try to peer back and keep track of the third creature, and as they do Ikka silently drags her body away from them between some other cones. She lies down low, determined not to be an obstacle in her companions' survival. When Chiyo and Veela turn back, she is nowhere in sight.

• • •

As K'vinna lies crumpled on nir chamber floor, ne

watches the chaos of this new human attack through the building consciousness. K'vinna is surprised when one of the humans—the one most affected by the building's atmosphere— hides from the other two, self-sacrificing to increase its companions' chances of survival.

A new ripple of sadness crosses over K'vinna's being. Ne knows this valiant gesture will be in vain. Even unburdened, the other two humans are no match for three Gu'ten. They will perish. K'vinna withdraws nir tentacle from the consciousness and returns nir attention to Chloe's broken form. She will also perish, ne is certain.

K'vinna calms nir guilt, and hardens nir resolve. There is at least one human life ne can save today.

• • •

On the lowest level of the facility, Chiyo and Veela are crawling between different cones attempting to remain un- captured. They have not seen Ikka since she removed herself from their company. The Gu'ten are still split into a pair and a single, trailing them from either side. It is becoming increasingly difficult to move between the cones unmasked. They are now close to the centre of the room, constantly peering this way and that. They see a clear path between themselves and the room exit, and begin a hurried crawl for it. They are three rows from the exit when Veela spots Ikka at a diagonal three rows behind them, passed out on the ground. He tugs at Chiyo's shoulder to gesture he'll go back for her, but as he does one of the prowling Gu'ten appears at the other end of the diagonal and locks in on Ikka as well. It is impossible for Veela to make it to her first; Chiyo pulls him back towards the exit, away from certain death, but then a new set of tentacles appear in the doorway.

Veela and Chiyo freeze as a new alien fills their view and they pull backwards, splitting to cones at either side of its gaze. The hairs on their necks begin to stand on end as they feel it approach, and they watch the distant aliens close in on Ikka. Veela cannot pull his eyes away from the sight, tortured by the thought of her end more than of his own. Yet, they have still not been seized. The newest addition to the room should have reached them by now. Veela peers back around the cone and comes face to face with the creature. Its body sack is mere inches from his face. He can feel little ripples of air bounce off its fleshy, near translucent skin as it peers at him. Before he can think to act, one of its grey tentacles shoots forward and places a small contraption in his mouth. It feels strange at first, but then his breaths become fluid, less strained and laboured. Before he registers that this creature has helped him, the alien shoves a similar device in Chiyo's mouth and then begins stalking, very low to ground, towards Ikka and the other aliens.

The movements of this new alien are stealthy. It weaves in and out of the cones so as to avoid the other aliens' view, reaching Ikka moments before they do. One of its tentacles shoves a breathing contraption into Ikka's mouth, while twelve others grab at different parts of her body, yanking her behind its form. As they release her, another ten of its tentacles get to work on the cone nearest to the oncoming alien, levering part of it open and excreting from within a high concentration of a powdery blue gas. As soon as the gas seeps into the air, the creature flings Ikka towards Veela, and half its mass becomes grounded to the floor. Likewise, the chasing Gu'ten becomes grounded and the creature's tentacles combine in thick columns to create great arms that pull it forward. The other two Gu'ten in the chamber appear from between the cones, floating forward to the source of commotion. They are similarly sucked to the ground as they near the gas's toxic limits, and have to drag their torso sacks along on the ground.

Veela and Chiyo make a sprint for the door, carrying Ikka between them while their assailants are slowed behind them. The next room they enter has a bizarrely similar layout, but the cones within it are covered in panels of a charcoal grey. They carry Ikka forward four rows, and then pause between two cones to attempt to revive her. Veela begins pumping against her chest, hoping to kick-start her heart. Ikka shows no sign of taking breaths. Veela can only hope the contraption in her mouth is helping, not hindering. Chiyo stands guard, his eyes alternating between the room behind and the field of cones ahead.

• • •

Inside, K'vinna barely has four feet on the Gu'ten behind nem. Ne is conscious of every inch they gain as ne drags nemself forward, aiming for the room's exit. The other two Gu'ten are worker level, and have no doubt recognised K'vinna as a division leader. Despite this, they are still pursuing nem; they know K'vinna has acted contrary to Facility protocol. K'vinna has no doubts that they will subdue nem by whatever means necessary. As K'vinna moves farther away from the leaking gas, nir tentacles and bl'omsterlok begin to lift away from the ground again. As ne pushes through the doorway, ne registers the three humans clustered between the cones. K'vinna has no time to help them where they rest. It is more important that ne reach the control panel in this room to permanently disable the other Gu'ten and provide these humans with a significant advantage.

K'vinna moves forward at speed, charging towards the control panel in the far right corner of the room. Ne quickly navigates through the cones, and nir tentacle hairs alert nem that two of the other Gu'ten are close behind. They begin reaching for K'vinna, their tentacles pulling back on some of nir tentacles. K'vinna is unable to shake them, but doesn't let their attachment slow nem down. The worker attached to K'vinna tries to connect to nem in the consciousness, but K'vinna doesn't let it in. The worker resorts to warbling out loud.

"Halt! In the name of the K'lappstol, I demand you to stop!"

K'vinna doesn't react, still charging forward. When ne is ten feet away from the control panel, the second worker Gu'ten catches up, joining with the first to pull on K'vinna's tentacles and prevent nem from moving forward. K'vinna is at an impasse, nir reacher tentacles only extend eight feet. Ne will need to shake off at least one of the worker Gu'ten in order to move forward and save the humans.

• • •

Veela continues pumping Ikka's chest, frantic to revive her. Chiyo watches with morbid fascination as, at the far end of the room, two of the alien creatures attack one of their own—the one that provided them with the breathing contraptions. He cannot determine which alien each mass of tentacles belongs to, nor can he understand their intentions. His focus is drawn back by muted spluttering—Ikka coughing through the breathing device. Her eyes are still not open, but the noise is enough to draw the focus of the third enemy alien who is just entering their current chamber. Instead of joining the alien tussle, this one's shadow eyes seem to pivot towards them and it starts drifting their way without hesitation. Ikka's eyes are still moments away from opening, but Chiyo grabs both Veela and Ikka by their shoulders and leads them away from this threat. The yanking motion wakes Ikka, and she is catapulted into consciousness how she left it—being pursued by alien monsters through cones. Veela and Chiyo are both glad she is awake, but unable to move her at the speed they need to in order to avoid this new threat.

In nir corner, K'vinna is still struggling against the two worker Gu'ten. Ne poises six of nir labour tentacles around the two nearest cones, acting as a brace between nemself and the worker Gu'ten. Ne then inhales nir compromised tentacles. That is, through autonomy ne drops them, disengaging from them like a lizard from its tail. It is a painful procedure—excruciating as the nerves sever—but K'vinna has no other option. As the weight of the dependent worker Gu'ten also drops off with them, K'vinna's bl'omsterlok and remaining tentacles rebound forward towards the control panel. Without pause, K'vinna opens the panel and rewires the interface. Within seconds, the heavier density grey gas the Gu'ten rely upon to lift them upwards and float floods out of the building. Every Gu'ten in the entire facility will now be grounded.

Veela, Chiyo, and the now conscious Ikka look on as the alien pursuing them crashes to the floor and is once again a limp sack barely two feet off the ground. Its many tentacles combine into stronger limbs, pulling itself the final few feet towards them. This time they are ready. Their breaths are steady and their weapons are in hand. They begin hacking at the tentacled limbs, sawing into them and spreading them out into useless three-foot stumps, unable to support the wait of the torso sack. The creature begins gurgling a strange sound as they approach closer to its centre, tones they cannot hear so much as they can feel. Distress. Chiyo steps in amongst the wriggling stumps and brings his blade down into the centre of the liquid sack. As he tears outwards with his blade, a thick, shimmering blue goop pours out from the gash, and the creature wilts in front of their eyes. The three companions watch with disbelief, not fully confident of what has just transpired. They don't have time to comprehend the ramifications of this moment. From the other end of the room, the clamour of the other three aliens is reaching peak violence.

Veela, Chiyo, and Ikka sprint over to the commotion, wary of the three writhing masses of aliens fighting. There are some tentacles lying abandoned on the ground, and two of the aliens are clearly ganging up on the third—the one that helped them. They are tearing at it from either side, pulling viciously at its remaining tentacles. Veela and Chiyo charge in, blades cutting at the alien closest to them. Ikka skips around to other side, running and jumping off the nearest cone to land square in the middle of the other enemy alien, blade pointed down. As she lands, her body weight pushes the knife in so far her arm is engulfed in the alien's bodily fluids, the strange shimmering blue goop staining her skin before flooding out of the creature and pouring across the floor. Veela and Chiyo are still hacking at the first Gu'ten, but Ikka doesn't join them. Making sure the friendly alien's eye shadows are on her, she drops her blade at her feet and walks towards it, her arms outstretched. Her hands reach to touch the front base of its body sack, resting lightly on the deceptively translucent skin masking its blue insides. She isn't sure how to talk to the creature as she stands there, least of all because of the breathing contraption in her mouth. She tries instead to communicate with her eyes, conveying that she means the beast no harm. As she is thinking, this one of its black tentacles slides around her arm and a warmth travels up her arm to her head.

*Beast? I suppose that is an appropriate term.*

Ikka baulks, the voice in her head is most certainly not her own.

*No, it is mine. The* beast *before you. Thank you for your assistance just now.*

Ikka glances at Veela and Chiyo behind her, to see if they are also hearing this creature speak. They are not. They are standing dumbfounded, watching as Ikka and the alien stand entranced with each other. The alien they were just fighting has also been reduced to a wilted mass.

*No, it is only you and I connected at present. Now, focus. There is not much time before others will come for us. I am going to tell you how to find the ones you came for.*

# CHAPTER THIRTY-SIX

IKKA, VEELA, and Chiyo run through different corridors, a map firmly etched into Ikka's mind from her interaction with the alien, K'vinna. Veela and Chiyo do not know where Ikka is guiding them, as they have not yet figured out how to talk through the breathing devices. Instead, they trust that Ikka knows what she is doing. K'vinna informed Ikka that they were on the utility level of the building. Their friends are in a holding pen the level above. Ikka was unable to discern from K'vinna which of their friends are still alive, and she is not naive enough to suspect they all are.

The building is not designed for creatures with legs, so to ascend a level they have to climb up the light panels illuminating the ascension shaft. At the next level, they have to fling themselves from the panels they are clinging to across a three-foot gap to the next floor. Ikka is light enough to make it, but Veela and Chiyo both land on their chests, legs dangling and wind knocked out of their lungs. Once they recover, the trio continues down the hall, eyes scouting for any villainous movements. After passing a distance that could have housed four different chambers, Ikka stops outside a blank stretch of wall. She traces her hand across the smooth, white facade until she finds a groove. When she does, she raises her blade and juts it into the imperfection. She steps back as a small hum begins and a faint light illuminates the crease in the wall. Ikka grabs the hilt of her blade as the doorway opens, preventing it from clanging to the ground. She steps in without hesitation, and Veela and Chiyo follow with caution.

The room is dark, but new sections of the room become illuminated as they step forward. Ikka moves right to the back of the room where five figures are huddled in a cage. As the light turns them from silhouettes into individuals, Ikka gasps through her breathing device at the sodden states of Delu, Daracha, Callyr, Madoc, and Esej. The men all look in deep shock, void of any will to live. Ikka opens the tank that holds them. Veela and Chiyo help them all up to their feet, and then they carry who they can to the exit. Ikka supports Delu on her shoulder as she walks, peering back out into the hallway for their escape. They need to travel halfway down this corridor then through two rooms to its left, to reach the ground level access ramp Delu's group had originally entered through. At the opposing end of this corridor, Ikka can see two aliens approaching them, dragging their bodies across the floor. She signals to Veela and Chiyo that they need to hurry, and they scurry as fast as they can to the exit before the enemy aliens arrive.

They make it into the left hand chamber before the aliens reach them, although Ikka is unsure how to make the door close behind them. So it remains open, a deadly invitation for the following creatures to strike. This room is empty, void bar hanging chains connected to unknown devices. Ikka opens the door to the next chamber, and they come face-to-face with the last door to their freedom—and the last obstacle between them and it.

There are two aliens guarding this chamber, and the contents that Ikka recognizes as the kind of ship that shot Delu's racer down. Despite being stuck to the ground, these two aliens are poised for attack. Their thick, combined tentacles are coiled, ready to pounce. They circle in on the humans as Ikka, Veela, and Chiyo rest their wards down. They each raise their blades and step forward, searching for an obvious method to gain the upper hand. Even contained to the ground, the aliens are larger than them and have the advantage of many more limbs.

Veela steps forward first, drawing the attention of the aliens as Chiyo and Ikka charge individually to the backsides of the creatures. They begin slicing from the back, hoping to reach the more precious central organ. One of the limb columns picks Chiyo up and slams him against the ground. Not once, but twice. The thuds are deafening, though his scream is muted through the breathing device. Veela charges forward at the offending alien, slicing forward as he moves. Ikka is dancing over and under the different columns attacking her, nicking some but making no deep cuts. Chiyo doesn't stand back up, he lies moaning on the ground. A column connects with the back of Ikka's shoulder, flattening her to the ground. It goes in for a killing blast, but is intercepted by a broken pillar of rock. It is wielded by Daracha, who offers Ikka a hand up with a new respect in his eyes. She inclines her head at him before running back into the foray. Daracha follows her in, and the two alternate slicing with beating, unrelenting until the alien is completely subdued.

Veela is not fairing as well. He is getting cornered at the other side of the room, the other men too weak or shell-shocked to help. He has suffered major blows to his arms and legs, but is still fighting, hoping to slice the creature down. Ikka and Daracha run to his aid, attacking from the creature's backside, drawing its attention away from their friend so he can deliver the killing blow. The resulting goop wave is wretched, staining all their clothes. As Veela and Daracha return to help their other companions, Ikka walks to the control table K'vinna envisioned in her mind.

It is similar to the complex navigation consoles of the X-Runners, but cleaner and twice the size. Ikka follows K'vinna's instructions, keying in a sequence of buttons that cause the large inner door to open. Once the grate has completely risen, there is a small chamber before a secondary, clear door sits shut. Ikka keys the next sequence, and this door also opens. There is a whoosh as the outside air slams into the inside atmospheric conditions, and an unstable composition sits in the centre. Ikka joins her human companions, this time acting as a crutch for Veela, as they walk down the ramp and exit the building.

It is startling to feel the fresh air slap their faces and they are able to drop the breathing devices from their mouths. They walk warily down the ramp, not looking back until they are several hundred feet from the building. As they rest their injured friends to the ground, there is a collective sigh amongst the group.

Ikka kneels in front of where Delu sits, crumpled in defeat. She clicks her fingers in front of his eyes to check his pupil reactions. He seems to snap out of his state and stares at her in wonder.

"Dear, Ikka. You saved us. Thank you."

Ikka shakes her head. "Not me, us. Chiyo. Veela. Daracha. Even Hurste before he fell."

"Hurste? Gaarwine, Aldric, and Kueni also passed. There have been too many losses..."

Delu trails off, his head looking downwards in shame. Beside them, Veela and Esej are collapsed on the ground. Chiyo and Madoc are nearby, eyes watering. Callyr sits, stoic, watching and waiting for Ikka to make her next move. She grabs Chiyo's satchel and tosses it to him.

She says, "There has to be something in here that will help them. Ask Chiyo. I need you to look after them for me."

Callyr nods, beginning to rifle through the satchel and examine its contents.

Delu peers over at Ikka, his eyes glimpsing out through his tears. "Where are you going, Ikka?"

Ikka says, "With the facilitators stuck crawling on the ground, now's the perfect time to save those women. I'm not going to miss this chance for anything."

Daracha nods from his place on the ground. "I'll be joining you then."

Ikka raises her eyebrows into an *oh?* and Daracha says, "Those monsters killed my friends. I'm not going to let you do this alone."

# CHAPTER THIRTY-SEVEN

DARACHA AND IKKA walk in a stoic silence back towards the facility. There is a quiet respect between them and a healthy reverence for the challenges they are yet to face. As they near the building ramp, they both reinsert their breathing devices and walk forward, weapons raised. After they enter the first, clear door, they see the secondary door is closed ahead of them. They approach it cautiously and jump a little as the outside door closes behind them. They wait, blades at the ready, as the secondary door opens before them, to reveal a solitary, waiting alien slumped on the floor. Daracha moves to charge at it, but Ikka holds him back. She recognizes it as the friendly one, K'vinna. Ikka places one her blades in the belt of her pants and steps forward, her empty hand outstretched. She tries to focus her mind as the creature sends a black tentacle forward, and gently wraps it around her arm.

She thinks, *You were waiting for me?*

*I knew you would come back. You are here for the breeders.*

*The breeders?*

*The human females. I could feel your pain.*

*Are you going to help me find them?*

*In a manner of speaking, yes. I will show you how to find them. I can be of no physical assistance in this state. The breeders are three levels above this one. There are hundreds of Gu'ten—my species—between you and them. Even limited to the floor, you and your companion are no match for them. You will need to access the main ventilation system for the building and kill our atmospheric controls. That is the only way you can destroy us and save your kin.*

K'vinna's instructions continue, in specific detail, as to how Ikka and Daracha are to move throughout the building, find the ventilation and atmospheric systems, and destroy the atmospheric balance that the Gu'ten require to breathe, and live. Ikka pays close attention as K'vinna implants this information in her mind, and Daracha watches on, curious. When everything has sunk in and K'vinna has wished Ikka the best on her journey, Ikka realizes that the alien has signed its own death warrant.

*What about you?*

The creature seems to smile at her in her mind, touched by her concern.

*I fear the time of the Gu'ten is over. Now it is your turn.*

*Thank you.*

Ikka offers a sad smile as the alien removes its mind from hers, and she gestures to Daracha for them to keep moving. As they exit the room, she looks back, feeling the alien's sadness linger in her mind, and she grabs a coil of rope harvested from the captured X-Runner. After that, she only looks forward.

• • •

Ikka and Daracha move down the second level corridor with as much stealth as they can muster, weapons at the ready. They see movements in the shadows and hear noises in the air. Yet, they see no Gu'ten. They should be relieved, but they are filled with a constant dread. Following K'vinna's instructions, Ikka guides them down a service corridor, one less travelled by the Gu'ten. K'vinna warned that some other flesh-eating creatures use this path, but that they are unlikely to be out during a hostile period. Unable to communicate this with Daracha, Ikka is forced to gesture that something low to the ground is violent in this section. The claw gestures and wild eyes she uses to express this are peculiar, and she can only hope Daracha understands her meaning. They walk farther down the service corridor, which is still constructed in white but very poorly lit. There is only a faint glow of light at intervals and large pools of shadows between. And then there is an eerie whistle.

A pod of furry white creatures come streaming at them, sharp teeth glinting in the faint light. Even Ikka is caught off guard by the small creatures' tenacity, but after the day's events, she has no hesitation in machete chopping them. Chunks of white fluff go flying, and eerie whistles turn into eerie screams. After the first eight have been dismembered, the others disappear as quickly as they had arrived, unwilling to meet a similar fate. Daracha mimics to Ikka her earlier pantomime of a small creature with claws, followed by an exaggerated motion she can only decode as *what on Earth?* Her response is a stony glare, and she continues on their path.

The service corridor ends up leading them to a ramp, obviously intended for the small fluffy creatures, connecting to the floor above. They continue up that path and then weave down three other service corridors to a conspicuously blank door. Ikka strokes it open, and they marvel at what they see inside. It is a room similar in size to the harvest vehicle chamber, but clean, lined with glowing surfaces and large viewing screens of the entire building. They stare in amazement at the array of images—of the depth of the Gu'ten menace. There is footage of the breeding chambers where cells and cells of women are chained naked to the ground. Ikka's stomach tightens at the sight as she remembers her own horrors in this place. Daracha paces, glaring at the screens, unsure of Ikka's next plans. Ikka is not unsure. She is the surest she has felt her whole life.

Ikka paces forward, standing in front of the central console. She eyes the floating liquid table, pursing her lips tight before plunging her arm deep inside it. The cold goop envelopes her arm. It feels like the blue goop that spilled from the dead Gu'ten, but she can feel it tingle, alive in its containment. Her mind feels the warmth that it felt when K'vinna spoke to her, but more powerful. She remembers the alien's instructions and replays in her mind the visual sequence it had shown to her. It is a succession of commands that the console picks up on through her mind and follows. Once the sequence is over, she hastily withdraws her arm. No goop remains on her skin. Daracha throws her another *what on Earth just happened?* look and she can only shrug in response. The mouth breathing devices are a hindrance to explanations, and there is no chance pantomiming a legible response. Instead, she gestures for them to move on, only one more complicated step left in sabotaging the building.

• • •

K'vinna is in substantial amounts of pain. It is not the continuous dull ache and loss of senses ne has felt others suffer from the be'lysning through the consciousness. It is a sharp throbbing, the screaming of severed nerves from nir dropped tentacles. Sixty-seven remain unscathed, struggling to drag K'vinna's full body weight across The Facility to nir chambers. Ne has never had to move this way before. It is only from instinct and others' memories in the consciousness that ne knows how. Ne crawls past chambers filled with other struggling Gu'ten and can hear them gurgling in panic and confusion. This is not a situation they have ever prepared for—humans with the talent to compromise the building. Not that they would have been successful without K'vinna's interference.

K'vinna reaches the ascension shaft that connects this level to that of the research division and faces a new obstacle. Ne has never had to travel through it without floating. Nir remaining tentacles split from five thick columns into twenty-one columns of three and one column of four. They spread out into the shaft, cliques of reaching tentacles shooting upwards to hook onto light fixtures and other grooves. K'vinna's bl'omsterlok hangs downwards from its base, hoisted without ceremony up the shaft and onto the next level. The resultant bouncing leaves K'vinna feeling like nir mind is swirling around and around inside nir bl'omsterlok. The tentacles recompose themselves back into five thick columns, pulling K'vinna forward to nir chamber. But there is one last challenge ne must face—the writhing mass that is U'mulig, waiting outside nir chamber door.

• • •

As K'vinna nears U'mulig, the other Gu'ten gurgles

antagonistically nir way.

"I knew you could not be trusted, K'vinna. This is your work."

K'vinna does not respond, nir ten pupils searching for a weapon to use against U'mulig.

"What have you been creating, K'vinna, in that lab of yours? You have made the humans more powerful, smarter or stronger than evolution would have allowed them."

K'vinna gurgles in derision, staying a safe thirteen feet away from U'mulig.

"I have done no such thing, U'mulig. I have observed, whilst you have tortured and killed and fiddled with their genetics. And put the barren ones back into the system. I know you've been hiding your accidents, U'mulig."

The other Gu'ten is taken aback for a moment, but then charges forward, nir reaching tentacles shooting out and trying to pin K'vinna's down. As U'mulig lunges for K'vinna's bl'omsterlok, K'vinna counters by employing two of nir thick columns from behind nem to swing over and then down onto U'mulig's bl'omsterlok. U'mulig is temporarily stunned, and K'vinna tries to drag nemself away, knowing ne is handicapped in this battle. But U'mulig catches up, nir reaching tentacles once more engulfing K'vinna's circumference. U'mulig tries to strangle K'vinna's bl'omsterlok, squeezing tighter and tighter, causing K'vinna's insides to bulge against nir f'et. The translucent layer of K'vinna's f'et stretches out so much that the blue shine of nir innards becomes visible. U'mulig's black consciousness tentacles wrap against the stems of K'vinna's ones, and U'mulig shouts into K'vinna's mind.

*You are a traitor.*

K'vinna glares back into nir mind.

*No, I am a monster. We all are.*

U'mulig begins to object, but K'vinna shuts nir thoughts out, focusing on nir survival. U'mulig's tentacles are applying so much pressure to K'vinna's bl'omsterlok that K'vinna's vision is dying, so K'vinna uses the consciousness to share the view from U'mulig's eyes. K'vinna is floundering, and nir tentacles are no match for U'mulig's vice-like grip on nir bl'omsterlok. There are no counter points in the hallway K'vinna can lever nemself with, or objects to crash down on U'mulig. There are no weak points in U'mulig's entity, other than nir filtration sack.

All of U'mulig's tentacles are at task seizing K'vinna's bl'omsterlok and at the base of K'vinna's consciousness tentacles, leaving U'mulig's filtration sack exposed. K'vinna's reaching tentacles shoot out to it, wrapping around it, yanking and twisting with more strength than K'vinna knew ne had left in nem. U'mulig is taken off guard, and on instinct releases nir grasp on K'vinna and uses nir tentacles to pulling nemself farther away. K'vinna doesn't release nir hold, pulling against U'mulig's body weight and tearing the filtration sack clear of U'mulig's bl'omsterlok. The other Gu'ten gurgles in protest, nir innards seeping out the opening onto the corridor floor. The blue liquid pools around U'mulig's stranded frame, deflating nem gradually, the goop preventing the last movements of U'mulig's tentacles from grabbing on anything tangible. K'vinna turns away, not disgusted, but also not pleased. What K'vinna feels is an absence of feeling, a lack of caring anymore what happens to any of the Gu'ten.

• • •

Ikka and Daracha leave the control room. They scale
back through the service corridors, turning into a chamber right
near the ramp between the levels. When Ikka traces the door
open to this chamber, it is immediately clear that the commands
in the control room were successful. It is a ventilation chamber,
and the flaps to all of the pipes have mechanically opened, their
contents spilling into the room, overpowering Ikka and Daracha
so much that they are lifted off the ground as they enter. Ikka
attempts to sign to Daracha that he should stay outside the
chamber, but he is determined to follow her through. She
anchors the X-Runner rope she grabbed outside the door, and
they propel their bodies forward through the air with wide
strokes, moving to an unopened pipeline in the back of the room.

It is the building's main water pump. The Gu'ten do not
require water to survive, the only purpose for them is providing
hydration to the humans. The pipe has no opening in this room,
but travels through it from the pump in the lower utility level of
the building, to the breeding division, one level up from this one.
The gas Ikka flooded into the room via the opened pipes, while
vital to the Gu'ten's survival, is composed of chemical
compounds that react in a detrimental manner when exposed to
water. The gas will combust and explode. Once Ikka and
Daracha have opened the water pipe, they will have roughly five
seconds to evacuate the room before the outside wall is blown
away and the entire building becomes compromised.

Ikka removes Chiyo's remaining canister of paili paste
from her jacket, and they both cover their faces and any exposed
skin. Daracha is surprised that Ikka would place paili on herself

again, but accepts that it must be a necessity. Ikka then removes a different paste she recovered from Chiyo, a brown clay that is secured inside a binding of leaves. As she unwraps it, Daracha's eyes widen, and he seems to understand her intention. She points at the rope end looped over her arm, and gestures that he should leave the room. He considers for a moment, nodding and using it to pull himself to the doorway. He stays just outside of the door, ready to pull her out. Ikka begins tentatively placing the clay on the water pipe, careful to only touch the leaves holding it. As the clay settles on to the metal pipe, it begins to hiss and a faint smoke rising from its surface. Ikka waits until she has spread the clay over one foot of the pipe, and then she tugs on the rope. She kicks as Daracha pulls, hearing the hissing from the pipe rise into a crackle as the metal begins to dissolve. It takes only moments, and she is three feet away from the exit when she hears the first gurgle of water. She is one foot away from the exit when she hears the first mini-explosion, and only just safe around the corner, slammed onto the ground by Daracha, when the mini explosion transforms into a mega-explosion.

Fireballs rip out the doorway after her, compounding over her and Daracha's heads, reacting again and again with all the diluted gas spread throughout the corridor. K'vinna said it would happen like this—the diluted gas still reacting with the already formed water-fire ball, potent enough to cause a chain reaction of mini-explosions across the building to deplete this vital gas, suffocating the Gu'ten within their own safe haven. The initial large explosion was substantial enough to gut the building wall, allowing an influx of outside air into the facility, further hastening the atmospheric cleansing. Ikka and Daracha are singed from the fireball, their clothes burnt in places and the hair on their heads wilted at the ends. For the most part, the paili has protected their skin from burning, although Ikka can feel patches of skin on her back where her clothes have melted onto them. She steels herself for the pain when she stands, determined to not let it interfere with her goal. Daracha is in worse shape than she is, having partially shielded her body with his own. His eyes are not open—he seems to be unconscious—but she can feel a heartbeat on his neck. She looks around for any of the fluffy atrocities and, when she sees none, she decides to leave him behind to collect on her way back out.

# CHAPTER THIRTY-EIGHT

K'VINNA is inside nir chamber when ne hears the explosion. Ne is slumped on the floor next to Chloe's body, listening to her faint heartbeat. Ne has hope now that she might be able to survive. Ne has given instructions for the human woman, Ikka, to find her once all has passed. K'vinna keeps nir tentacles wrapped around Chloe's arms and upper torso, nursing her form as ne reaches into the building's consciousness loop to survey the damage to the building. The atmospheric changes are already at a detrimental level on the second floor of the building, and the ripple of disturbance is hastily dancing throughout the rest of the building. Within four minutes, K'vinna's own level will be compromised, the entire building in ten. K'vinna looks around nir office, reflecting on all that has passed inside its walls. Nir entire life, K'vinna has never left this building. Ne was born and raised inside The Facility, destined for a life of saving nir species. K'vinna is amazed it has taken nem all this time to realize nir purpose was not to save the Gu'ten from the be'lysning, but from nemselves.

K'vinna burrows through the consciousness, sifting and searching through the old archives. Memories of memories of memories, the visions of the last Gu'ten on S'vekke before the disease took hold. The planet is beautiful, not composed of synthetically created gases, but an atmosphere of thriving interchanges, gases of all different colours, rainbows that gave life flowing freely through rock formations of silver, and native Gu'ten homes, hanging caverns of tall stalactite caves. K'vinna can feel the long dead Gu'tens' joy in this place, pure contentment in its home. K'vinna skips through the memories and sees the be'lysning ravage S'vekke. It acts like a harmless moss at first, staining the silver rocks brown and causing no other change. And then those Gu'ten that come into contact with the moss begin to weaken, losing their senses and their bl'omsterloks turning an unhealthy white as their bodies rot from the inside. The Gu'ten contained it at first, quarantining those infected and exterminated the deadly moss. Yet, as they evolved, the moss did too, overcoming their evasion and morphing into an airborne disease. They eventually had to abandon their home planet, travel as far across the galaxy as they could. And it still found them. Ate away at them one by one. K'vinna turns away from this thought. Ne can feel the air starting to separate around nem. The compromised atmosphere has reached nem.

K'vinna searches for happier memories. Ne scans through the consciousness with fervour, seeking solace in nir final moments. There is none within the collective Gu'ten memory. K'vinna disengages from the consciousness, no warmth of others' minds to provide nem comfort. Instead, ne thinks of

Chloe. K'vinna thinks of her first impression of nem. A floating sack of liquid with shadows for eyes. It brings K'vinna a comfort, similar to the warmth of the consciousness in nir mind. Ne thinks back over their conversations, of her continual determination to survive, her demands in exchange for cooperation. And ne thinks of the glow, the strange way her face contorted and her face sucker rounded when she was pleased with something. It was always such an amusing sight. K'vinna keeps flitting through these memories, thinking of nir friend, until the correct atmospheric conditions expire and nir bl'omsterlok ceases to function.

• • •

Ikka returns to the main control room, steeling herself and reinserting her arm in the strange, luminescent table. Once inside, she recalls the next series of instructions the alien had placed in her mind. It doesn't work at first, as her mind is too distracted by the pain of the melted skin on her back. She tries again, focusing on each image K'vinna showed her for some time before moving on. When the sequence finishes, she watches the screens to see if it worked. She can see in the birthing cells, the cages holding the women begin to dissipate and, one by one, the mechanical diapers drop from their groins. The women look confused, unsure what to do next. Some mill about to each other, arms outstretched, touching another's skin for the first time in years. Confident the device has understood all the instructions, Ikka removes her arm from it once more. Ikka casts her mind over the second map the alien gave her and runs.

When Ikka reaches the first level the women are kept on, they are all utterly perplexed, stumped by their apparent freedom. They talk anxiously amongst themselves, huddling in groups of four or five. Ikka's arrival startles them even further—a woman in clothes. Seeing them breathe reminds Ikka that the air is safe for humans now, and she flings the breathing device from her mouth. She looks from one worn face to the next, also stumped on what to do. A waifish looking woman with delirious blue eyes breaks from the crowd, stepping forward to her, arms outstretched.

She asks, "Have you seen my children?"

Ikka doesn't know how to respond. The woman takes a step closer.

"Do you know where they took them? There was a boy, and a girl, and another girl, and then a boy, and then a girl, and then another girl, and another girl, and another girl, and then a boy."

Another woman steps forwards, with stringy brown hair and a swollen belly. She places her arms around the first woman's shoulders.

"Sssh, Hannah. They're not here anymore. This woman is someone else." She looks over at Ikka, exhaustion staining her entire face but a glint of hope in her eyes. She gestures to the fallen diapers, and the missing walls. "Was this your doing?"

Ikka nods, still lost for words. All of the women watch, waiting to see what she does next. Ikka offers them a weary smile.

"If you follow me, I'll show you the way out."

• • •

Ikka sends some of the strongest women to the upper levels to collect the women contained in those cells, and leads the rest to where Daracha waits, concussed but conscious. He is lifted up by two of the able-bodied women, and Ikka leads them all to the loading ramp that exits the facility. She slips away as the horde begins walking out. She has one last mission inside.

When Ikka arrives at her destination the alien, K'vinna, is already dead, nir body a limp mess on the floor. Yet, some of nir tentacles are still extended up, wrapped around a human girl propped on a bench, attached to medical apparatus. She is awake, but crying. She seems unaware of the condition of her own body or even Ikka's presence in the room. She is focused only on the inanimate Gu'ten.

Ikka steps forward cautiously and clears her throat. The young girl looks up to her with swollen eyes, and Ikka takes in the full scale of damage to the girl's body. She tries not to stare.

She says, "I'm Ikka."

The girls sniffs and nods, not really hearing Ikka's words. Her eyes turn back down to K'vinna's body, her voice cracking as she speaks.

"I don't understand. Ne's not responding anymore. Why isn't ne responding?"

Ikka takes another step closer, a hand reaching out to touch the girl's left shoulder.

She says in a quiet voice, "Ne's dead, Chloe."

Chloe snaps her attention to Ikka, her eyes widening and tears spilling down her disfigured face.

"Why?"

Ikka falters as Chloe's body shakes under the weight of her grief.

"Ne died to save you, Chloe. So that I could save you."

"Save me?" Chloe stares around her prison, bewildered. At her tank, at the lifeless Gu'ten at her feet, tentacles still wrapped around her good arm. She begins shaking again, her whole body trembling with sadness. "I didn't think I'd ever get saved."

She begins crying all over again, but this time Ikka doesn't falter. She lunges forward, catching the girl's frail body in her arms, wrapping her up in a hug. She whispers into Chloe's ear.

"Hush now, it's all right. I'm going to look after you. I'm not going to let anything bad happen to either one of us again, okay?"

Chloe nods, her good arm clinging onto Ikka's back.

Ikka says, "Okay. I'm going to let you go now, but only so I can pick you up. I'm going to carry you out of here."

"Okay."

Ikka steps forward and detaches the medical apparatus connected to Chloe with great care, and then lifts her. Ikka is meticulous with every movement, and slowly carries Chloe through the facility. As they reach the lower level and begin to join up with the legions of women still streaming out the building, the sunlight touches Chloe's face for the first time. She breaks down and sobs in Ikka's arms one more. Ikka doesn't feel any of her normal confusion or discomfort from the physical contact. She hugs the girl tighter as she carries her and whispers into her ear.

"Everything is going to be fine."

• • •

Outside of the building, a procession of some seventy

thousand full-bellied and naked women mill about. Some of them break down and cry, overwhelmed by the sight of the outside world, the touch of fresh air on their skin. They step cautiously on the earth, delighted at the sensation of grass on their toes. Others walk hand in hand, relishing the opportunity for human contact. Some others walk by themselves, soaking in their new reality in quiet awe.

Ikka navigates through them, searching out her friends. When she reaches them, they stare at her in reverence, silent as they register that state of the girl resting in her arms. Half of one of her legs is missing, and there are chunks of flesh missing from all over her body, covered with a strange type of synthetic second skin. The girl's chest is heaving with sobs, and Ikka's face is grim. Veela stands up to greet her but fumbles, his body still weary. Callyr helps him rise as Ikka reaches them, and Chiyo and Madoc help Ikka place Chloe gently on the ground. Delu wakes from where he was resting and stands to join them as well.

Veela looks to Ikka with pride and amazement.

"I can't believe you did it. I mean, I can, you're incredible, but all of these women are free thanks to you."

Ikka shakes her head, grimacing when the motion stretches the burnt flesh on her neck.

"We all did it, and we have much work to do. All these women will need clothes, for a start."

Delu says, "And we'll need to tell the Settlement. And free the racers from their vehicles."

Chiyo says, "They'll free themselves when the refuelling stations stop feeding them."

"It's not that simple, though." Ikka pauses, unsure how to

continue. The men—and many of the nearby women—all look to her, curious. She tosses up in her mind how to phrase the information to come next and decides there is no delicate way to say such a thing. "This isn't the only facility, and we're not on Earth."

There is a beat of prolonged silence where those around her decide whether or not to believe her before nervous chatter breaks out. Her words seem to have echoed out from her central group and passed on to all those around them. There are fearful whispers amongst the crowd.

Ikka is aware of all the whispers, of all the faces staring to her for hope. She cannot be the one to give it to them. Her whole life has been void of hope, filled with only suspicion. But then she looks down at Chloe's face and is reminded of her promise to K'vinna. She will protect this girl against this world and the menace of the Gu'ten, no matter what the requirements of herself. If she has to lead thousands of others to reach this end, so what of it? She will not back away from this task. She will save them all if she has to.

Ikka clears her throat and looks resolute to all those around her.

"It's true, we are not on Earth. This is not our home planet, but neither is it the aliens'. We are all descendants of prisoners of war, birthed in *that* building. But we are not the only ones. There are more buildings like this one scattered all over this planet, run by more aliens who will see us as a greater threat now than ever before. We need to recoup and build our numbers from those in The Race, so that when they come for us, we can fight back. And we will fight. We will *never* be theirs again."

. . .

As the sun sets that night, it is seen by nearly seventy thousand new sets of eyes, marching along behind their new leader, this strange, stern woman named Ikka. There is one set of eyes, though, that are not concerned with the sunset. Chloe is totally absorbed by her saviour, this wonderful, strong woman named Ikka, who once more is carrying her in her arms. As Chloe gazes up at her dark, soft face and sharp, intelligent eyes, she finally feels peace inside.

Everything is going to be fine.

# ACKNOWLEDGMENTS

I SPENT THREE years writing, and then another three years drafting and revising this novel, so as you can imagine, there are a lot of people I need to thank.

Firstly, Vincent Geronimo, who charmingly answered my questions about whether or not eating honey was vegan, by saying it was 'stealing, which was mean'. I later verified his statements, and became vegan. Jasreet Badyal introduced me to feminist thinking, and discussions with her helped reframe my understanding of the world. The culmination of both Jasreet and Vincents' influence manifested into an adrenaline pumping dream of a race, which Sho Ya Voorthuyzen was so kind as to wake me from, when he had a nightmare. I thank all three of them from the bottom of my heart.

Over time I discovered I was a terrible self-motivator, and that I needed people beside me at cafes and libraries in order to focus on my work. Tim Marshall, Tarah Carey, Luke Tierney, Rei Tamori, Polly Pierce and Sheri Lucas, thank you for sharing your focus with me. Early conversations that were also influential to this process took place with Jamie Chong, Latifa Karmay, Khada Kuraki, Alison Finch, Aaron McCann and Leigh Richards. Some scientific clarity was provided by Sundara DeSilva, Jesse Fryk, and my brother, Alan Burt.

My test readers Roy Sasano, Tim Marshall, Polly Pierce, Tom D Wright and Valerie Burt are all superstars. Roy and Tim were both generous enough to read two different versions of this novel, taking painstaking notes each time, and tolerating many conversations with me where I asked them how they felt about different aspects of the story. (If you think there are too many commas in this story, it's Roy's fault. He was constantly telling me I didn't use enough).

My editor Ellen Michelle cured this novel of its grammatical ailments, and Alan Chen created a cover design more wonderful than I could have imagined. I thank them both, profusely.

I would also like to thank my best friend, Linda Smith, who has always treated my wild brain with kindness, and encouraged me in all my creative pursuits for the past eighteen years.

Finally, I would like to thank my partner Michael Niemi, who keeps me sane, emotionally supports me, encourages me, and always offers up suggestions when I ask for them, even though he knows I'm going to ignore nearly all of them. He always inspires me to do better, and helps me in that pursuit. Thank you, baby. I love you

# ABOUT THE AUTHOR

**PARADOX DELILAH** lives in Vancouver, British Columbia with her partner and their feline overlords.

She is a professional stick holder—of microphones, above actors' heads—and spends a lot of her daily life imagining different worlds.

She has also been a vegan for over eight years, and highly recommends you consider becoming vegan, too. After all—

Every meal is a choice.

Choose kindness.

CPSIA information can be obtained
at www.ICGtesting.com
Printed in the USA
LVHW092301081119
636856LV00001B/77/P

9 781999 271602